**Turn to the back of this book for a sneak preview
of Elizabeth Bevarly's next novel,**

The Ghost and Mrs. Magill

FAST

&

LOOSE

• Elizabeth Bevarly •

BERKLEY SENSATION, NEW YORK

THE BERKLEY PUBLISHING GROUP
Published by the Penguin Group
Penguin Group (USA) Inc.
375 Hudson Street, New York, New York 10014, USA

Penguin Group (Canada), 90 Eglinton Avenue East, Suite 700, Toronto, Ontario M4P 2Y3, Canada
(a division of Pearson Penguin Canada Inc.)
Penguin Books Ltd., 80 Strand, London WC2R 0RL, England
Penguin Group Ireland, 25 St. Stephen's Green, Dublin 2, Ireland (a division of Penguin Books Ltd.)
Penguin Group (Australia), 250 Camberwell Road, Camberwell, Victoria 3124, Australia
(a division of Pearson Australia Group Pty. Ltd.)
Penguin Books India Pvt. Ltd., 11 Community Centre, Panchsheel Park, New Delhi—110 017, India
Penguin Group (NZ), 67 Apollo Drive, Rosedale, North Shore 0632, New Zealand
(a division of Pearson New Zealand Ltd.)
Penguin Books (South Africa) (Pty.) Ltd., 24 Sturdee Avenue, Rosebank, Johannesburg 2196,
South Africa

Penguin Books Ltd., Registered Offices: 80 Strand, London WC2R 0RL, England

This is a work of fiction. Names, characters, places, and incidents either are the product of the author's imagination or are used fictitiously, and any resemblance to actual persons, living or dead, business establishments, events, or locales is entirely coincidental. The publisher does not have any control over and does not assume any responsibility for author or third-party websites or their content.

FAST & LOOSE

A Berkley Sensation Book / published by arrangement with the author

PRINTING HISTORY
Berkley Sensation mass-market edition / April 2008

Copyright © 2008 by Elizabeth Bevarly.
Excerpt from *The Ghost and Mrs. Magill* copyright © 2008 by Elizabeth Bevarly.
Cover design by Annette Fiore.
Stepback art by Don Sipley.
Interior text design by Kristin del Rosario.

ISBN: 978-0-425-22085-6

BERKLEY® SENSATION
Berkley Sensation Books are published by The Berkley Publishing Group,
a division of Penguin Group (USA) Inc.,
375 Hudson Street, New York, New York 10014.
BERKLEY SENSATION and the "B" design are trademarks belonging to Penguin Group (USA) Inc.

PRINTED IN THE UNITED STATES OF AMERICA

10 9 8 7 6 5 4 3 2 1

*For Beverly and Bruce Cote,
and Katie, Griffin, and Graham.*

*Thank you all for including us in so
many lovely events and adventures when
we are so woefully hosting-challenged ourselves.*

·One·

NOTHING BROUGHT MORE JOY TO COLE EARLY'S heart than watching the day dawn from the railing of a racetrack. As he sipped strong black coffee from the cardboard cup in his hand, it occurred to him that Santa Anita was one of the most glorious tracks for doing just that. At barely six A.M., the crisp yellow sun was cresting the Saint Gabriel Mountains in the east, spilling over the shallow green peaks to limn them with gold. A trio of tall date palms stretched high over the grounds of the track between Cole and the foothills, black silhouettes against the young sunlight, their broad fronds fluttering in the cool, early April breeze.

It was that magical moment between darkness and light, nighttime and day, when anything—*anything*—seemed possible. Closing his eyes, he inhaled the mixed aromas of damp dirt and expensive equine, a fragrance found nowhere else in the world but at the track. His chest filled with something big and indefinable, a sensation he'd never quite been able to identify, but one that made him feel as if nothing in his life would ever go wrong again. Only at the track did

Cole feel it. There was just something about the confidence of the owners, the arrogance of the trainers, and the dominance of the Thoroughbreds all meeting and commingling that spawned a force of energy that was almost a living, breathing thing.

He opened his eyes again and let that energy wash over him, bathing in it as if it were the fountain of youth—which, quite honestly, he couldn't say it wasn't. Thoroughbred racing was ageless, the sport of kings for centuries, a place where any Average Joe could, with one lucky bet, become a king himself. And Cole should know, since it hadn't been that long ago that he was an Average Joe. Now he was one of the top Thoroughbred trainers in the country, dubbed nothing less than "King Cole" by the racing media.

These days, he could afford to look the part, too. His dark hair was expertly and expensively cut to seem carefree and cavalier, and his suits were tailored by one of LA's finest couturiers. Today's was a dark olive that matched his eyes, paired with a dress shirt and necktie, both silk, that were the color of Fort Knox gold. His Bulgari sunglasses were tucked into his breast pocket beside another scrap of gold silk, this one perfectly folded with three points showing, just as his tailor had shown him to fold it. His shoes were Gucci, his wristwatch was Movado, his underwear was Parah. Hell, even his grooming products bore a European name whose pronunciation he'd had to look up on the Internet.

Cole really didn't give a damn about his physical appearance, but having been thrust into the media spotlight two years ago with a sensational win at the Pacific Classic, he'd consciously begun to cultivate an image as a player. It wasn't an image anymore, though. Cole Early was a player. A major player. And his status was only going to explode in . . . He glanced at his watch, also gold—real gold—turning it a little to catch a shaft of gilded sunlight. In roughly ten hours and fifty-two minutes.

Any day at the track was a good one, as far as he was concerned. But this day was going to be his best yet. Because this was the day that Silk Purse, the filly Cole had trained from infancy to age three, was going to win the Santa Anita Derby.

He was as certain of that as he was his own name. He didn't care what the handicappers were saying. The thirty-eight-to-one odds on the horse right now only meant Cole would be that much richer at day's end after plunking down the cool ten grand on the animal he always slid through the pari-mutuel window, figuratively speaking, whenever he had a horse running. Of course, all his bets were handled by electronic transaction now, so large had they become, something that took a lot of the tradition and fun out of the racing experience. But the end result would still be the same. Three hundred and eighty grand if the odds didn't change by race time. Not to mention a nice share of the winning purse, worth three-quarters of a million dollars itself.

Even better than the money, however, was the fact that when Silk Purse crossed the finish line ahead of all the other horses, she'd qualify for the Kentucky Derby, four weeks from today. And that race, more than any other right now, was the one Cole wanted to win. Because it was the first jewel in the Triple Crown, a lovely little tiara that was going to sparkle nicely once it was sitting on Silk's head. That would put the horse in an elite group of only eleven other Thoroughbreds—and put Cole in an even more elite group of only nine other trainers—to win the distinction. And it had been three decades since the last ones, Affirmed and Lazara Berrera, had managed it.

As recently as a week ago, Cole hadn't been confident of today's win. But something had happened to the horse over the last six or seven days, and the new kid exercising her had a way with animals that had made Silk Purse seem happier somehow. Cole could just feel victory in his gut, and his gut had never steered him wrong. The filly might not be as experienced as some of the other horses running today, and she faced a gender bias the other entrants didn't. But she hadn't lost a race yet. She wasn't a favorite among the bettors and bookies, but by God, she had more heart than any horse Cole had ever encountered. And he'd met more than a few animals with potential, because he'd been training Thoroughbreds since he was a teenager. Silk Purse was going to go all the way to the Belmont finish line, or his name wasn't—

"Cole Early!"

He turned at the summons to see Susannah Pennington, Silk's owner, emerging from the paddock with her hand lifted in the air. She was dressed for Derby Day in a short, clingy red skirt and white frilly blouse, an enormous red straw hat encircling her platinum hair like a halo. It was a mystery how she navigated the damp earth on spike heels, also red, but damned if she didn't manage it with grace and style, picking her way carefully over the uneven sod.

Cole returned her wave as he watched her approach, appreciating, as he always did, the length of bare leg extending from Susannah's short skirt. At fifty-two, she was ten years his senior, a dynamo in the field of high finance and a self-made millionaire many times over, just as he was himself. She owned three other horses in addition to Silk Purse, all of them fillies, all of them sharing her initials, and all of them stabled and trained by Cole at Early Farms in Temecula. Silk Purse showed by far the most promise, though a one-year-old, Sinful Pleasures, would perform very nicely when she started racing in another year or two.

"How does our girl look this morning?" Susannah asked as she came to a halt beside Cole and assumed the position: weight shifted to one foot, arms resting on the track rail, fingers loosely clasped, her gaze focused on the gray filly who was now running on the far side of the track.

"Poetry in motion," Cole told her. "She's really taken to the new kid exercising her. What's his name again?"

"Jason."

Cole nodded. "You should pay him more, make sure you keep him around."

"Done," Susannah immediately agreed, just as she always immediately agreed to Cole's suggestions.

"She and Esteban have clicked extremely well, too," he added, giving well-deserved props to the horse's jockey, Esteban Santos. "I like him. He's been good for her."

"I thought you said he was too inexperienced," Susannah reminded him, smiling, since she'd been the one who'd had to convince Cole to give the young jockey a chance. Susannah had a thing for young jockeys, though, and Cole had been afraid she only wanted Esteban to ride Silk Purse because he was her current lover.

"I stand corrected," he told her. "The kid's got talent. And heart. Just like the horse, come to think of it."

"I told you they were a good match."

Cole grinned. "You and he are a good match, too. And he's lasted a lot longer than the others. Is there something I should know, Susannah?"

She arched a pale blond eyebrow. "Maybe. We'll see how he does today."

"With the horse, or with you?"

Her grin went supernova at that. "Oh, he's already done *fine* with me today."

Cole chuckled. "The day's barely started, Susannah."

Her answering smile was dazzling. "I *know*," she said, punctuating the words with a wistful, hopeful sigh. "There are still so many hours of it left to fill."

"Don't exhaust the poor guy," Cole warned her. "He's got a big race today."

Susannah waved a careless hand. "And he'll be in *ex*cellent spirits for it, I assure you."

They watched Silk Purse make another circuit of the track, her glossy gray coat turning first silver, then gold, as the early morning sun washed over her. It was a Very Good Sign, another indication that the fates were smiling down on them. Cole just had a good feeling about the day. And the horse. And the race. And about every damned thing else in the universe. As the sun rose higher in the sky, so did his spirits, and when another of his and Susannah's horses placed in the fourth race, he began to feel almost invincible.

As the time drew closer for the horses in the Derby to receive the call to the gate, Cole and Susannah made their way to the Director's Room to watch it. The elegant—and very exclusive—restaurant was open only to the wealthiest and best connected track patrons. It was a thing to behold, with its finely carved pine walls designed in the 1700s and its crystal chandeliers dating to Regency England. Must have cost a fortune to import it all, Cole thought as he entered the richly appointed room. But then, richness was evident all around him here, in the patrons as well as the decor. It wasn't unusual to find movie stars, pro athletes, and business tycoons milling about with the owners and trainers, especially on Derby Day.

Had someone told him twenty years ago—hell, five years ago—that he would someday feel right at home hobnobbing with the Thoroughbred elite, Cole would have laughed in that person's face. Not because he hadn't thought he had what it took to be a power player, but because he'd had no desire to join such ranks. He'd spent his life scoffing at the rich and famous, thinking them shallow and superficial and undeserving. Now he was one of them. And truth be told . . .

Well, hell, Cole thought as he and Susannah shouldered their way toward a window. It was a damned nice place to be.

The moment before the start of a race was even more magical a moment than the one before dawn. It was almost as if the world came to a stop in those immeasurable, cumbrous seconds. As if sounds, smells, and sights all smudged into a blur, bulging with fear and hope, expectation and anticipation. As Cole watched Silk Purse make her way toward the starting gate, he could feel all of those things humming just beneath his skin, accelerating his senses to the point where everything around him seemed almost surreal. Something exultant and potent vibrated in his chest, pressing harder as his horse entered the gate. In his mind, he could hear the metallic click of the latch closing behind her, then the muffled, anxious murmuring of the horses as they readied themselves for flight. And then, then—

"They're off!" cried the announcer through the speakers, and Cole felt the air *whoosh* from his lungs, as if he were the one pummeling the dirt beneath his feet while he ran with all his might.

"Go, baby, go," he murmured under his breath, voicing what had become the official slogan of the Thoroughbred industry, so often had the words been muttered over the years.

Without even realizing he was doing it, he began to bounce on the balls of his feet, his eyes never leaving Silk Purse. She left the gate strong but was quickly squeezed out when the horses on each side of her pulled ahead. She dropped to fourth, then fifth, then sixth. But Cole wasn't worried. Her favorite part of a race was the final length, the straightaway after the last turn when she just seemed to be overcome with a burst of energy that sent her down the stretch like a cannon shot. Esteban knew that, too, so the jockey bided his time with the animal, steering her into an opening whenever he saw a break. Gradually, she moved ahead, into fifth, then fourth, then third place. Cole held his breath as horse and rider rounded the final curve, and then—

"Oh, yeah," he breathed solemnly. "That's what I'm talkin' about. You go, girl. You go."

Silk Purse exploded at that point, Esteban pulling her to the outside so she could run at will. This was what Cole had recognized in the animal that no one else had seemed to see yet. Her unmitigated love of running, the sheer joy the animal seemed to feel when she had the room and opportunity to just *run*.

And, man, did that horse run.

By the time she reached the finish line, Silk Purse was a full two lengths ahead of the second-place horse and the crowd around Cole was screaming in surprise. He, too, let out a cry that came from the very deepest part of his soul, the place where he stored all his hopes, desires, and dreams. He turned to Susannah and kissed her full on the lips, a gesture born of nothing more than pure euphoria. Then the two of them erupted in boisterous laughter, clinging to each other's shoulders as photographers, sportswriters, and news crews pressed around them, shouting questions, snapping pictures, and thrusting microphones between the pair.

For the moment, Cole ignored them all, looking at Susannah instead. "We're going to the Kentucky Derby," he told her with a huge grin. "And then to the Triple Crown. There's nothing—nothing—that can stop us now."

OKAY, SO THERE WAS ONE THING THAT MIGHT STOP them, Cole was forced to acknowledge later that night. Or, at the very least, stop him.

"What do you mean there are no rooms left in Louisville?" he cried into the telephone as he poured himself a second celebratory brandy. "It's a big city. There must be a lot of hotels."

He heard his travel agent, Melissa, sigh on the other end of the line. Although her agency had closed two hours ago, he'd called her on her cell phone and dragged her out of a wedding reception to make his travel arrangements for his trip to Louisville at the end of the month. Hey, he threw a lot of business Melissa's way, and she'd told him herself to call her anytime he needed her services. And hell, she had two other sisters who'd be getting married someday. It wasn't like this was her only chance to be a maid of honor.

"There are indeed a lot of hotels in Louisville, Cole," she told him, the statement punctuated by what sounded like the ruffle of some stiff fabric. "Hang on a minute," she added. "I have to shift the phone to my other ear on account of there's this big-ass bow on my shoulder that's about to put my eye out. Yeah, sure I can wear this piece of crap dress again someday. Hah." He smiled as he waited for Melissa's voice again. "There, that's better. But there are also a lot of out-of-town visitors in Louisville. Derby is the biggest time of the year for travel to that city. I'm telling you, there are no rooms left. Nothing. Nada. Nil. El Zippo."

"What's Susannah doing for lodging?" he asked, knowing Melissa handled her travel account, too.

"She's staying with some friends of hers in Shelbyville. And their son in Lexington is going to share his apartment with Silk Purse's exercise boy. But Susannah had to call in a couple of favors even for that."

Cole blew out an exasperated breath. "Can't you find a hotel for me in Lexington?" he asked. "That wouldn't be so bad. It's only what? An hour or so away?"

"Lexington is also full up."

"Frankfort?"

"Full."

"Southern Indiana?"

"Full."

"How about—"

"Cole," Melissa interrupted, "there are no rooms within two hours of Louisville. You should know better than anyone how important the Kentucky Derby is to the Thoroughbred industry. People make hotel reservations a year in advance for that. I even tried the fleabag motels. I'm telling you, there is nothing left, hotel-wise."

Something in her voice made it sound as if all were not lost. "Hotel-wise," Cole repeated, hopefully. "You say that as if there are alternatives to hotels. What? Like could I get a condo or something? That'd be fine."

"There are no condos to be had, either," Melissa told him. "But," she added, just as he was opening his mouth to say more, "I can get you a house."

"A house?" he repeated, having never considered such a possibility. Now that he did, however, he kind of liked the idea. There would be more privacy in a house. More freedom. More room to stretch out. Of course, most furnished rental houses sucked when it came to decor, but, hell, he wouldn't be there all that often. And it wasn't like he hadn't lived in dumps before. Years ago, granted, but he didn't mind slumming for a couple of weeks.

"Yeah, a house," Melissa said. "Evidently a lot of the locals who don't care about the Kentucky Derby—"

Don't care about the Kentucky Derby? Cole thought incredulously. How could a person *not care* about the Kentucky Derby? Especially someone who lived in the same city where it took place every year? That was just . . . wrong.

"—will clear out of their houses," Melissa continued, "and rent them out to people who can't find hotel rooms or who just want the comfort of a house instead. A few of the houses that go up for grabs are pretty nice, too. Six and seven bedrooms, some of them. Stately old manors. Or new McMansions in gated communities. With country club memberships. Access to pools and golf courses. We're talking massive luxury for some of these places."

Cole perked up considerably. Now *that* was the way to spend time at the Derby.

"Unfortunately, those are all gone," Melissa said.

Of course.

"Besides," she continued, "the houses that go up for grabs are only available for the two or three days surrounding the race, and I know you and Susannah are planning to be in Louisville for a couple of weeks. So I did some calling around after you called me, and I found a guy who specializes in Derby rentals. He said he could guarantee me a house for the two weeks preceding the race in an area called the Highlands, which, according to him, is a very nice neighborhood, parts of which are very upscale. And lucky for you, Mr. Real-Men-Don't-Cook, he said there are lots of restaurants within walking distance of just about every street."

"Walking distance," Cole repeated distastefully. She called that lucky? Nobody in southern California ever *walked* anywhere. That was even more wrong than not wanting to be in Louisville during the Kentucky Derby.

"Anyway, I've got the house on hold if you want it," Melissa said, "and I think you should grab it. I sincerely doubt you're going to find anything else. Certainly not for two weeks. You really came down to the wire on this, Cole."

"Very funny," he replied, though he had to admit that the racing metaphor was apt. He really should have booked a hotel the minute he realized Silk Purse had even a tiny chance of winning Santa Anita. He just hadn't wanted to jinx it, that was all. Booking a room before having the win in their pocket had just seemed like the perfect way to ensure Silk *didn't* win.

"I'll take it," he said.

"Don't you want to know how much it's going to cost or hear about the amenities?" Melissa asked.

"It doesn't matter," he told her. "I need a place to stay. Whatever you have to do to get this house for me, do it. At this point, I'll take what I can get."

· Two ·

LULU FLANNERY SCRIBBLED ANOTHER INSTRUCTION ON a hot pink Post-it note and slapped it onto her cable remote control, trying again to recall the precise moment when she'd lost her mind. Oh, right. Now she remembered. It had been the second her friend Eddie told her she could get five thousand dollars for renting out her house the two weeks before Derby. It had been bad enough that she'd succumbed so quickly—and easily—a few months ago when he told her she could get fifteen hundred renting her place out for three days. Now she was agreeing to do it for two weeks.

Greed. It was a heinous little bugger.

However, at some point during the frenzy of housecleaning she'd performed over the last two days to leave the place spotless for whoever would be staying here for the next two weeks, she'd begun to have second thoughts. And then third thoughts. And then tenth thoughts. And then one hundred and fifty-seventh thoughts.

Everything she owned was in her little Highlands bungalow. All her personal, intimate . . . stuff. Sure, she'd locked up what few valuable items she had—*valuable* being a relative term, anyway, since they were mostly relative to the term *worthless*. The actual cash value of Lulu's valuable possessions probably only totaled around four hundred dollars. But the sentimental value she carried for things like her grandmother's pearl choker and earrings and her mother's autographed photo of Dean Martin—even though, alas, it was autographed to someone named Buddy—far outweighed any monetary value that might be assigned such things.

That was beside the point.

The point was that Lulu was about to rent out her home to a total stranger who had no vested interest—financial or emotional—in it. Hence the flurry of note-writing she'd undertaken since waking that morning. She'd wanted to make sure her unknown guest or guests didn't abuse or misuse—or, okay, *use*—the things she didn't want them using. But she'd done her best to be polite when saying "Mitts off," and had taken great care in just how she phrased her instructions.

The note on the cable remote, for instance, said, *"Remember, there are no more late fees at Blockbuster, and it's only four blocks away. Walking is so good for your heart!"* The last thing she needed was to be billed for a bunch of pay-per-view movies she didn't even get to watch herself.

"It'll be fine, Lulu," Bree Calhoun said as she tugged closed the zipper on the bag Lulu had packed for the two weeks she'd be spending with her best friend. "Remember, Eddie said there's a thorough screening process that all his clients have to go through. He's not going to let some jerk rent your house. He'll only rent it to the finest of families."

Lulu threw her a disbelieving look. "Please, Bree. If it meant collecting a commission, Eddie would rent my house to the Manson family."

Bree made one of those okay-you-got-me shrugs. "Five thousand bucks is five thousand bucks," she said. "Even after Eddie's commission, that's like six months' worth of mortgage payments in two weeks' time."

Good point, Lulu thought.

"Plus," Bree added brightly, "you get to enjoy the pleasure of *my* company for two weeks. Not to mention all the
luxuries of Casa Calhoun, including, but not limited to, my
vast collection of Orlando Bloom DVDs and all the Skinny
Cow ice cream sandwiches you can eat. Life just doesn't get
any better than that."

Lulu smiled. It would be fun bunking with Bree at her
apartment, she had to admit. It would be like when they were
kids having sleepovers. Except this time they could stay up
past midnight watching TV without their parents yelling at
them to go to bed, and they wouldn't have to sneak sips of
Cella Lambrusco from the bottle in the refrigerator door. After all, it would be so much more mature and tasteful for the
two of them to watch *Pirates of the Caribbean* in their
underwear while drinking Bellinis.

"Just let me leave a few more notes for my prospective
renter," she said, "and then we can drop off the keys with
Eddie."

Bree shook her head with enough emphasis to send her
long black hair flying. "Lulu, you've already left about five
hundred notes. Your prospective renter is going to have trouble finding the coffeemaker as it is."

"Oh, the coffeemaker is off-limits," Lulu said as she
nudged an errant russet curl from her cheek and tucked it behind her ear. Unfortunately, it fell forward again, refusing to
be contained with the rest of the dark auburn mass she'd tied
back with a scrap of black fabric. Her T-shirt, too, was
black, and short enough to keep coming untucked from the
waistband of the faded jeans that rode loosely on her hips. "I
stuck a note on it saying it was off-limits, too."

Bree rolled her Caribbean blue eyes. Like Lulu, she wore
jeans and a T-shirt, though hers was dark red and sported the
logo of her favorite brand of beer. "You can't have the coffeemaker be off-limits," she said. "That's inhuman. We the people are entitled to the pursuit of life, liberty, and a cuppa
morning Joe."

"I don't think that's in the Bill of Rights, Bree."

"Well, it sure as hell should be."

Lulu sighed. She supposed her friend was right. Which probably meant . . . She screwed up her features a little as she said, "So then I guess I should take the Post-it note off the fridge, too, huh?"

Bree gazed at her blandly for a minute. "I think you're missing the point here, Lulu. When people rent a house, they kind of expect to have use of certain amenities. Like, say . . . oh, I don't know . . . the appliances. I mean, it's one thing to lock up your jewelry and bankbook. But whoever's renting the place, to the tune of *twenty-five hundred dollars a week*," she added meaningfully, "is going to expect the use of the kitchen from time to time. And the bathroom," she added when Lulu opened her mouth to speak again, obviously anticipating what would come next.

With another sigh, Lulu spun on her heels and made her way across the hall to her only bathroom, tugging off the note she'd stuck on the door there. Bree, who'd followed her, shook her head again, more slowly this time, but smiled. "Maybe we should do a final walk-through, just to be sure there's nothing you forgot."

Reluctantly, Lulu nodded. And she did her best to keep her mouth shut as Bree removed the sticky notes she had placed prominently on not just the remote, but the television, the CD player, the cabinet holding her dishes, the pantry, and the back door.

"I just painted the deck," she said by way of an explanation for that last.

"And you have a beautiful backyard that whoever's staying here will doubtless want to enjoy," Bree told her. "Especially in the evenings. Our evenings are lovely this time of year."

"Whoever's staying here will probably be going to parties in the evenings," Lulu pointed out. Parties were, after all, one of the main reasons people visited Louisville during Derby.

"Then you won't have to worry about them using your deck," her friend replied. "And you can wash the dishes when you come home," she added, "and the sheets and towels and anything else that might get cooties on it while someone else is staying here. It'll be fine, Lulu," Bree said again. "Anyone who can afford to drop that much money for two weeks' lodging will behave responsibly and take care of your things."

Lulu told herself to listen to her friend. It wasn't like she had a lot of priceless antiques or anything. Her house was a two-bedroom, one-bath bungalow from which she had managed to squeeze out a third bedroom in the attic, and it still had some scarring on the hardwood floors and plaster that was chipped in places. But she'd been refurbishing it by herself for almost a year now, and she felt responsible for the place in a way that was almost maternal. She just couldn't tolerate the thought of some stranger inhabiting it who didn't care for the house the way she did.

"But what if the renter is someone who has bad karma?" she asked her friend now.

Bree patted her hand. "Your fierce dogma will protect the place."

"What if the renter is full of negative energy?" Lulu asked.

"Your positive attitude will overwhelm it."

"What if they do something to mess up all my *ex*cellent feng shui?"

"You can ask your chi about that if it happens."

"What if they break my glass?"

That, finally, seemed to stump Bree. Because it was an important consideration. Lulu made her living—barely—by designing and creating art glass. Her home was full of her work. The more exquisite—and expensive—pieces, she'd carefully packed away and taken to her Main Street studio. But there were too many for her to remove them all.

"If they break it, they bought it," Bree finally said. She handed what was left of the Post-it notes back to Lulu.

"Make a note of that and put it in a prominent place. And then we need to get the keys to Eddie. He said your prospective renter is arriving at five o'clock. And don't worry," she added as Lulu penned the last of her notes for her guest. "Whoever stays here will feel right at home. I'm sure they'll love the place as much as they would their own."

LULU'S FRIEND EDDIE RAFFERTY WORKED FOR HOT Properties, a three-person agency he'd started with his brother and his partner that the trio ran out of Eddie's shotgun house in Phoenix Hill. A big chunk of the company's income was made during the weeks prior to the Kentucky Derby, thanks to their success in renting out private residences, like Lulu's, specifically for that event. When he wasn't renting out houses to out-of-towners for that first Saturday in May or selling real estate to locals, Eddie was dressing like Liza Minnelli in her Sally Bowles persona at the Connection downtown, belting out "Cabaret" and tap-dancing with an elegance and finesse Lulu would have envied, had she had any desire to dance on stage in platform shoes before hundreds of people.

Which, of course, she didn't. Not just because she was more comfortable in her Birkenstock knockoffs, thank you very much, but because the thought of being in the limelight that way frankly made her want to break out in hives. In fact, being in the limelight like that *had* once made her break out in hives. Years ago, when she'd been interviewed at a local craft fair for some puff piece on the news, back before she'd realized how much she didn't like being thrust into the spotlight. Now that she knew she didn't handle attention well, she avoided it. Of course, that resolution had come too late for the tens of thousands of viewers who'd seen her bloated like a rancid pufferfish on live, local, late-breaking news and were probably still plagued by the nightmares.

Anyway, it was just as well Lulu had chosen the career path she had, cloistered away in her studio where she could create beautiful glass and sell it, both there and from her website online. That way, she had minimal contact with the outside world, and there was little chance anyone would take much notice of her. Certainly, hardly anyone ever stopped her in the grocery store anymore and said, "Hey, aren't you that pufferfish girl who was on the news that time?"

Because it was rush hour by the time the two women arrived at Eddie's house, Bree couldn't park on the street, so she offered to circle the block while Lulu ran inside, relinquished her keys, and signed the rental agreement. Unfortunately, Eddie had a client with him when she entered, so she stood just inside the front door and waited for him to finish.

The entire front of the shotgun house was a glassed-in porch that the business partners had done a passably good job of turning into an office. What walls there were had been painted an inoffensive taupe, the wood trim an even more inoffensive white. The concrete floor had been painted with a faux mosaic, and the late afternoon sun spilled boisterously through the wide frosted panes of the jalousie windows. Charcoal sketches of local landmark homes—completed by Eddie's partner Devon—dotted the walls. There was a desk situated at each end of the wide room, both comfortably cluttered with computer paraphernalia and paperwork. Eddie had his blond head bent over his work at the desk nearest Lulu, but the other one was vacant as the workday drew to a close.

While Eddie finished up with his client—a man with pale brown hair and soft brown eyes who had smiled kindly in response to Lulu's own smile when she entered—Lulu did what she always did while waiting for something. She let her gaze rove hungrily over every aspect of the scene, just as any other visual artist would. But since she already knew the details of Eddie by heart, her attention naturally fell on the man who was with him.

An academic, she decided immediately. Probably an English professor. And a poet. He just had that look about him, all rumpled, cerebral, and sweet. He gave her the impression of being the sort of man who would feed stray cats and water his neighbor's plants while they were away. Not especially handsome, but pleasant-looking and tidy, the kind of person you wouldn't mind having sit next to you on a crowded bus.

Lulu brightened. Maybe Eddie really did only rent to people who had good references—and even better auras. In fact, it was entirely possible that this was the very man who would be renting her house for the next two weeks. Eddie had said he needed her keys by five o'clock today, which was only minutes away, because that was when her renter was due to arrive.

To test the theory, Lulu crept forward and, very discreetly, extended her hand past the man to settle her house keys on Eddie's desk. Eddie looked up at her when she did and smiled gratefully, his brown eyes full of obvious relief.

"Your timing could not be better," he told her.

Bingo, Lulu thought. This guy had to be her renter. Suddenly, she felt much better about the weeks ahead. The man just had goodness and decency stamped all over him, and she was confident he'd take good care of her house. Eddie thrust at her the contract that she'd already read but put off signing, and she hastily scrawled her signature across the bottom line, no longer worried about the care and feeding of her home. Then she dropped the contract, too, onto Eddie's desk and turned to make her way out.

But just as she was reaching for the knob to open the front door, it came swinging toward her instead, with enough authority and velocity that it nearly slammed into her. Lulu leapt backward just in time to miss the door, but not quickly enough to avoid the huge, dark-haired man who barreled through it. She ended up flat on her fanny, arms braced behind her, legs akimbo, the breath momentarily knocked out of her. That last wasn't because of her tumble, however. No, her breath didn't leave her until Lulu looked up at the man who had nearly trampled her and found him glowering down at her.

Truly. He had the nerve to glower at her. As if *she* were the one who'd been responsible for their collision. But even that wasn't what made her stop breathing. It was the rest of him that did that.

He was, in a word, incredibly gorgeous. Okay, so that was two words. One word just wasn't enough to describe a man like him, not even a word like gorgeous. His black hair had fallen over his forehead upon impact, above eyes that were a darkish green Lulu couldn't recall ever seeing on another human being. His suit was a color she didn't see often on men, a deep plum that should have looked feminine but instead only enhanced his masculinity. His shirt and tie were both steely gray, and neither was in a state that could be called tidy. His collar was unbuttoned to the third button and the necktie loosened to the same level, revealing a strong throat and scattering of dark hair beneath. He was huge, easily topping six feet, perhaps as much as a foot taller than her own five-four.

But it was his face that commanded her attention and held it, all planes, angles, and edges, from the blunt jaw to the narrow nose to the truly spectacular cheekbones. And those eyes, so focused and intense and so very, very *green* . . .

She realized she was starting to feel dizzy and gulped in a deep breath, then shook her head a little in an effort to clear out the buzzing that seemed to have overtaken it. The big man extended a hand to her, and, automatically, she accepted it. Just as she was noticing how his big paw swallowed her fingers, he was tugging her up from the floor, with enough force that she was literally swept off her feet before coming to an unsteady landing before him.

"Sorry about that, sweetheart," he said in a voice that was deep and booming and bore not a trace of apology. Then he turned his attention to Eddie and opened his mouth to say more—obviously having already forgotten about Lulu. To his credit, when he saw that Eddie was with someone else, he closed his mouth again to wait his turn. He clearly wasn't happy about doing that, however, because he hooked his hands on his hips impatiently and began to fidget.

Lulu reminded herself that she'd completed the task she'd come in to do, and that Bree was circling the block, waiting for her. But the big man was still standing between her and the door, and there was just something about him that prevented her from asking him to move. She told herself that the artist in her simply wanted to take a moment to appreciate physical beauty, since the artist in her did indeed appreciate physical beauty, regardless of how it manifested itself. This guy was beautiful in a way she didn't often see, a beauty that was almost strident thanks to the boldness of his character and his larger-than-life charisma. Just by virtue of entering the room, he'd overpowered it, imbuing it with whatever it was that made him *him*.

He looked at Lulu and found her studying him, but instead of glowering at her this time, he smiled, and—*whoosh*!—there went the air rushing out of her lungs again. Because he had the kind of smile that made a woman want to immediately shimmy out of her underwear. And then hand it to him. On a silver platter. And tell him to just go ahead and keep the platter, too.

"You a visitor here, too, sweetheart?" he asked.

She told herself she should be put off by the way he kept calling her sweetheart. Usually, she wanted to smack guys who called her things like that. But the way he said it was different from the way other men said it. With other men, it came out sounding like an epithet uttered to keep a woman in her place. With this guy, it came out sounding like a luscious temptation to make Lulu do things she normally only wrote about doing in her journal.

She shook her head again to clear it of its odd thoughts, then realized the gesture was also a response to his question. "No, I live here."

"Lucky you," he replied, sounding genuinely envious.

Pleased that he would be impressed by her hometown, she smiled and replied, "I agree. It's a great place to live."

"I bet. Having a legendary track like Churchill Downs to visit whenever you want," he said reverently. "Being able to go to the most famous horse race in the world year after year. That's gotta be great."

She deflated some. There was so much more to Louisville than the track, so many things to see and enjoy that had nothing to do with horse racing. But this guy was obviously one of those people who came to town only this time of year only to watch the horses. They flashed their cash, threw around their weight, and generally ran amok, usually at dozens of parties that had sprung up over the years to preface the Derby. Then they left town hungover and exhausted the morning after the race, never having explored anything else.

"Actually, not that many locals go to the Derby," Lulu told him. "Or, at least, not to the part of the track where you can actually see the race. We're generally relegated to the infield, where it's a zoo, thanks to all the scalpers and corporate ownership of the good seats. It's visitors like you who end up having the real Derby experience. The rest of us mostly watch the race on TV from home."

The look he gave her then was probably the same expression he wore when he found a slug—or, even more appropriately, *half* a slug—on the bottom of his shoe. But all he said was, "Not a race fan, huh?"

Actually, Lulu loved the Derby itself and hadn't missed seeing one that she could remember—on TV, anyway—in all her twenty-six years. Even when she'd had to be in Michigan once on Derby Day, she'd managed to make it to a TV in time to hear the strains of "My Old Kentucky Home" as the horses made their way to the starting gate. It was something that always brought tears to her eyes, which, she supposed, was hokey, but true. Any native Louisvillian worth his or her salt would admit to the same.

She didn't, however, mention any of that to the man before her. Instead, she told him, "I've only been to the Downs a couple of times in my life. And I've never been to the Derby."

Now he looked at her as if the half-slug on his shoe had

developed leprosy. Then he smiled that underwear-divesting smile again and said, "Well, now, sweetheart, that's just crazy talk." He dug into his inside jacket pocket and withdrew a credit card–shaped piece of cardboard. "Here," he said, thrusting it at her. "A clubhouse pass to the Downs. You can thank me later."

Somehow she refrained from rolling her eyes. Big Daddy Race Fan was just so nice to the li'l ol' local girl. She crossed her arms over her midsection. "Thanks, anyway, Big Daddy, but I have plans that day." Mostly, she planned to steer clear of people like Big Daddy Race Fan.

"Oh, come on," he said in that indulgent tone of voice people used with underlings they were trying to humor. And just like that, Lulu's back went up again. "Be the first local to watch the Derby from the clubhouse," he said. "Make your city proud. Don't worry about putting me out. They sent me a dozen of these things."

"I'm not worried about putting you out," she told him. "The pass won't be good for Derby Day. They never are."

His smile fell. "They're not?"

"Read the fine print," she told him. "That's why they sent you a dozen of them."

He flipped the card over and did just that. "Oh."

She almost felt sorry for him. He'd probably been thinking he'd have clubhouse privileges and all kinds of special treatment for Derby—for himself and eleven of his closest friends. Friends he doubtless planned to make while he was buying pitchers at Hooters. Poor guy. It was hard for someone like him to face the fact that he was just an Average Joe, not the big-time player he envisioned himself to be.

"Have fun in the infield, Big Daddy," she told him as she finally found the wherewithal to push past him and make her way to the door. "Don't forget your sunscreen and Mardi Gras beads."

· Three ·

COLE WATCHED THE YOUNG WOMAN WITH THE WILD
red hair and disheveled clothes—and really nice ass—push
through the door to the Realtor's office. Then he continued to
watch her—and her ass—as she strode down the front steps
without a backward glance. Then he watched her—and her
ass—some more as she waited on the sidewalk by the street,
again without turning around once, until another young
woman in a very disreputable-looking car pulled to a stop to
let her in. The redhead did look back at him then, lifting a
hand in farewell and smiling in a way that said, "I got the
last word, sucker. *Nyah, nyah, nyah, nyah, nyah.*" Usually,
Cole hated it when people looked at him that way. With her,
though . . .

He still hated it.

Man, what an unpleasant, unhappy, unaccommodating
harpy. So much for southern hospitality and southern belles.
With that riot of unruly red hair, those icy blue eyes, and the
battered clothes, she'd looked more like Raggedy Ann's evil
twin. Craggedy Ann. And she'd been about as personable, too.

Though she smelled kind of nice, he thought further, something spicy and exotic that reminded him of horse liniment—which was actually a compliment, because horses smelled damned nice when they were cleaned up and shiny. Patchouli, he realized, recalling the scent from the brand name of a soap they used at one of the stables where he'd trained horses. Except it smelled way nicer on Craggedy than it had on the horses. And that was *really* a compliment.

Not that Cole cared. About her smell or her eyes or her personality or any of it. The joke was on Craggedy. He didn't *need* a pass to get into the clubhouse at Churchill Downs. Hell, he could watch the race from Millionaire's Row if he wanted. And he would, too, dammit, just to show Craggedy Ann.

He shoved a hand through his dark hair and expelled a cragged . . . uh, he meant ragged . . . sigh. His flight from LA had been brutal, and he hadn't had a decent bite to eat since yesterday. His stomach was churning on black coffee and a couple of breath mints, and he wanted nothing more in the world than a thick steak and pile of steaming potatoes, bookended by a good single-malt Scotch and a snifter of premium brandy. The only thing that stood between him and that at the moment was claiming the house that would be his for the next two weeks.

He thought again about Craggedy Ann. Could be worse, he told himself. He could have to share a house with the likes of her. Turning to the Realtor who had finally greeted him, Cole silently vowed that his last thought about Craggedy Ann would be just that—his *last* thought about her.

IT COULD BE WORSE, COLE TOLD HIMSELF AGAIN A half hour later as he cut the engine of his rental car and studied the house that would be his home for the next two weeks. Really. It could. The place could be, um . . . Well, okay, it *was* pretty small, a squat brick bungalow that didn't look as if it could possibly contain the three bedrooms the Realtor had assured Cole it did. But the house could be, uh . . . Well, yeah, it was pretty old, too, he thought, probably dating back to just after the First World War. But at least it wasn't . . . Well, actually, it was kind of ramshackle, as well, with paint chipping off the front shutters and concrete steps whose edges were chunky with wear.

Beggars can't be choosers, he reminded himself. And God knew he'd stayed in worse places in the past.

At least Melissa had been right about the house being located in a good area. Even though Cole wasn't much for historic neighborhoods and preferred the shininess and cleanliness of freshly built areas, the surrounding houses were all well kept and upscale, many of them large and elegant. And he'd been gratified to see, as Melissa had promised, the wealth of restaurants on Bardstown Road as he'd followed the Realtor's directions. Not that he intended to *walk* to any of them. But the drive would be minimal, and there had seemed no end to the variety of selections. Of course, he'd be spending the bulk of his time at the Shelbyville Farm where Susannah was stabling Silk Purse for now, and later at Churchill Downs, but it was nice to know he could pick up something when he did venture home at the end of the day.

Home, he thought again as he pushed open the door of the big Town Car and stepped onto the driveway . . . immediately noting the crunch and crumble of dissolving concrete beneath his foot. He glanced down with a look of disgust and sent a silent plea skyward that the interior of the house was in better shape than the outside. Because the outside, he noted again, could definitely use some work.

He collected his carry-on and garment bag from the trunk and made his way up the front walk, taking care to sidestep a couple of places where the cobblestones buckled into a tripping hazard. There were two keys on the ring the Realtor had given him, and it went without saying that the first one Cole chose was the wrong one. Balancing his luggage precariously, he finally managed to get the door unlocked, then he kicked it open with his foot—a little harder than was necessary, thanks to his irritation. It bounced against the inside wall, then rebounded with enough force to smack him in the face as he crossed the threshold and stepped inside.

Okay, he supposed he'd asked for that, he thought as his carry-on slipped from his hand on impact and landed on his toe. And maybe that, too, he thought further, automatically lifting his foot from the floor to rub his injured toe against his calf. When he did, his carry-on tipped over and hit a small table beside the door just hard enough to knock something off of it that shattered upon impact with the floor.

Cole closed his eyes at hearing the crash. One foot in the door, and already he'd broken something that didn't belong to him. When he opened his eyes and looked down, he saw that whatever it was had been made out of brightly colored glass. Probably a vase, he thought. Hopefully nothing expensive that any person with half a mind would know not to put near a front door, since anyone and his carry-on might break something expensive were it situated in such a place. Then Cole peered around the front door and saw an ugly notch in the plaster where the door had slammed into it. So much for the damage deposit. For some reason, though, he couldn't quite shake the feeling, however bizarre, that the house had kind of enjoyed seeing him get battered.

Jet lag, he told himself. He ignored the fact that, having flown east, he was still on Pacific Time and should be three hours fresher than anyone in Louisville. Flying always made him irritable, no matter where he was going or when he arrived. And sometimes it made his brain a little weird. Nevertheless, when Cole closed the door behind himself, he did it with infinitely more care, making a mental note to clean up the glass once he got settled. Then he turned to survey his surroundings.

The house was much nicer inside than out. Whoever lived here was obviously more concerned with interiors than she was with exteriors. He felt confident using the feminine pronoun because there was no question that at least one person who lived here was a woman. Although the furnishings weren't overly girly or anything, there was just too much . . . stuff . . . for this to be an exclusively masculine domain. Too much color. Too much comfort. Too much care.

The living room spanned the entire front of the house, but had been fairly well separated into two distinct areas by the careful placement of furniture. To his right was a love seat and chair angled toward an intricately tiled fireplace, giving the feel of a living room, and to his left was a makeshift library of two chairs and a table near floor-to-ceiling shelves crammed with books. The walls were painted a rich dark yellow, a color that complemented both the warm berry and blue of the floral pattern on the fireplace grouping and the cool sage of the library chairs. Two different but complementary jewel-toned Oriental rugs spanned the hardwood floors on each side of the room, and the floors fed nicely into the natural woodwork of the doors and windows. What looked to be original oils of pastoral landscapes and sketches of European cafés hung on the walls, and gauzy curtains the color of the chairs framed the windows.

The overall feeling was . . . happy, Cole decided. And . . . pleasant. Even though *pleasant* wasn't a word that turned up in his vocabulary often. Calm, too, he thought further. Which was a word he used even less frequently. It was the kind of room that just made a person feel better for having entered it.

Immediately across from the front door was a hallway that led into the rest of the house, and to the right of that, near the fireplace, were French doors opening into another room. Shunning the traditional entry of the hall for the wider one offered by the doors—there was no need to risk breaking anything else—Cole made his way into a dining room with a broad bay window. A massive buffet littered with whimsical, brightly painted wood-carved animals and flamboyant pottery took up virtually the entire wall across from it, dwarfing the small table and two chairs by the window.

The colors on the walls in here were a tranquil turquoise blue, offset by countless paintings of lush gardens that hung on the walls.

Clearly, his hostess was a collector of art who had very eclectic tastes. Cole wasn't much of a connoisseur himself, but from what he could tell, the house's owner had good taste. Certainly, she liked things that were colorful.

Through a door on the other side of this room, Cole found the kitchen, its red walls, retro coffee advertisements, and old-fashioned appliances pulling more reluctant smiles from him. A breakfast nook in the corner was encased on two sides with wide windows that looked out onto a backyard that was surprisingly private, thanks to a veritable jungle of foliage along the outer rim. Through a second kitchen entry, he found himself in a hallway painted yet another bright color—this time something reminiscent of a tropical sunset—looking down into the living room again. There were two more doors on his right, and another on his left, between him and the front door. The room on the left was a bathroom, he discovered as he passed it, while the first room on the right was a home office. The third room was filled with boxes and odd bits of furniture and miscellany that made him think whoever lived here had moved in fairly recently and hadn't yet decided what the purpose of this room was to be.

So where was the bedroom? he wondered.

Turning around, he noticed a door at the other end of the hall that he'd overlooked before. Opening it, he saw stairs and understood there was more to the house than he'd initially realized. Although he'd noted a window above the wide front porch when he was outside, he'd thought it was for decoration or to offer some sparse illumination to the attic. As he climbed the stairs, twisted around a cramped landing, then climbed some more, he discovered that what was once an attic had been turned into a master bedroom. Well, okay, maybe it wasn't so masterful, since, like the house, it was small and a little crowded, its ceiling low in the center and slanted on both sides. However, like the rest of the house, it made Cole feel comfortable and at ease.

Until he topped the final step and banged his head on the ceiling. Wow, it was even lower than he'd thought.

He blew out an exasperated breath as he hunched down enough to keep it from happening again. Another indication that the owner of the house was a woman. Or a jockey. Or a troll. Or all of the above. At six feet three, Cole knew he was taller than the average man. He'd always kind of liked the fact, had even taken advantage of his size from time to time to intimidate some unfortunate slob who tried to challenge him. It had never occurred to him that his size could be a detriment. But the ceiling in this room clearly wasn't six-three. More like six-two. Which meant he was going to have to remember to duck every time he stood up here. Or else be beaten senseless by the end of his first week in residence. The house would probably enjoy that immensely.

Carefully crouching, he made his way to the bed and tossed his garment bag atop it, settling his carry-on beside that. As he unpacked, he took in his surroundings, noting how this room was darker than the rest of the house, due to its lack of windows, but how the owner had managed to brighten it up by painting it a sandy color and eschewing curtains on the one small window. The rugs, too, were lighter than in the rest of the house, wool dhurries with buff pastel geometrics. The bed was an antique white wrought-iron number of a size Cole had never seen before, not quite single, but not quite double, with a dresser and writing desk of mottled bird's-eye maple.

He switched on a lamp to combat the dusky darkness, sending a rush of pale pink light into the room. Everything was tidy and well-maintained, right down to the computer on the desk that bore only one small Post-it note. Cole was impressed. His computer at home was covered with reminders to himself, and his desk was constantly obscured by dozens of documents and letters that needed attention.

It wasn't until he opened his suitcase and began to unpack

that he realized the note on the computer wasn't the only one in the room. Moving toward the closet—and taking care not to straighten up as he did so—he saw one there, as well, on the right side of the set of double doors. In sturdy block letters that were in no way feminine, someone, presumably the owner, had written, "*Left is traditionally the route of nonconformists. Right is the route of the traditional. Enjoy the right side of the closet.*"

He grinned. So his hostess was a nonconformist, was she? Opening the right-hand door, he found the inside cleared for his belongings, including the shelf above the hangers and the floor below. The narrow space offered just enough room for the suits, shirts, and shoes he'd brought with him, and the shelf offered space for his carry-on. A perfect fit. It was nice when things worked out that way. Maybe this wouldn't be such a bad little house after all.

He started to turn away from the closet, then, for some reason, opened the left-hand door, too. It wasn't an invasion of privacy, he told himself. The door wasn't locked, and there was no note saying he couldn't. He was just curious to see what the clothing of a nonconformist looked like.

Vivid, he immediately saw. Literally every color of the rainbow, and then some, met his eyes as he scanned the interior of the closet, which was crowded to capacity, doubtless because his hostess had condensed two closets into one to make room for her guest. But where he had anticipated suits and business wear—since what else would anyone have in their closet?—what he found instead were garments that were gauzy, sparkly, and velvety, and in no way suitable for business attire. The floor below them was completely obscured by shoes—all of which, he noted right away, fell into three categories: functional, quirky, and comfortable. The shelf above was filled with hatboxes in a million colors and textures. The interior of the closet was such a stark contrast to the pale furnishings of the room, as if someone had exploded a color bomb inside it whose power they had greatly underestimated.

There was no telling what was in those boxes, Cole thought as he pushed the door closed again. What was strange was that he actually felt a twinge of curiosity about what their contents might be. What difference did that make? he asked himself. Who cared? The only thing he should be curious about at the moment was where he was going to stow his underwear.

As he clicked the closet door shut, his gaze lit on the dresser, and he was surprised to realize he was looking for another note. He smiled when he saw it, on the bottom right-hand drawer, and immediately went to see what it said.

"*Right makes might,*" it read in the same angular lettering as the one on the closet. Then, in parentheses below, "*It also makes room.*"

Pulling the drawer open, Cole found it empty—and perfectly sized for the rest of his belongings, including his underwear. Naturally, that made him think that at least one of the other drawers contained *her* underwear. But that, he thought, *would* be a violation of privacy. So he refrained from prying. Nevertheless, he felt another surprising flutter of curiosity about what her underwear might look like. Probably like the things in her closet, full of rich color and lush textures. He was already forming an impression of his hostess as something of a hedonist.

As he stood again—forgetting about the ceiling and bonking his head again—he noted a framed photograph on the dresser. Five women stood ankle-deep in water a fair distance from the camera, water that was clear enough and calm enough that Cole was reasonably certain it was the Caribbean. One of them, he wagered, was his hostess, and he studied each in turn. Four of the five wore swimsuits revealing enough to make him like what he saw. The fifth wore a T-shirt that fell down over her thighs, but it was wet enough to mold some truly luscious curves. All of the women seemed attractive, though the one in the T-shirt was squinting into the sunlight, her face obscured even more than the others' by the shadow of the baseball cap she wore.

The blonde in the white string bikini, he would wager, was breathtaking. Cole wondered if she was the owner of the house. Then he wondered why he was wondering that. He *should* be wondering if Silk Purse had been settled at Susannah's friends' farm by now.

Collecting his toiletry kit, he made his way back downstairs and unpacked his things in the bathroom. A note affixed to the mirror informed him that the hot water sometimes took time to actually *be* hot water and that *cold* was sometimes a relative term. It ended with the philosophical observation that "*Patience is a virtue—not to mention very cool.*"

Cole smiled as he tugged the Post-it note from the glass and started to wad it up. But he stopped before completing the action and smoothed the scrap of paper out again. Then he stuck it back on the mirror. Hey, he might need to be reminded of the water's idiosyncrasies later.

It had nothing to do with the idiosyncrasies of the note writer.

HE SPENT THE REST OF THE DAY EXPLORING HIS surroundings, trying to get acclimated to his new digs and figure out where everything was. But as familiar as he became with the house during that foray, he got to know his hostess even better. In her linen closet, he found an assortment of lotions with exotic fragrances like Tahitian Gardenia and Moroccan Mint. There were a half-dozen bottles of nail polish with colors like Basque in the Sun and Days of Wine and Roses. A little basket held what looked like hundreds of eye shadows and lip glosses with glitter and sparkles and God knew what else.

The wine rack in her kitchen held only two bottles of wine—one red, one white—both excellent, inexpensive vintages that told Cole she knew her wine, even if she didn't drink it much. Her pantry didn't hold a lot, but what was there told him she didn't shop at the grocery store, but at boutique delis and health food stores. On one shelf, neatly aligned, was a row of cooking spices like cumin, turmeric, and paprika, the sort of spices used in international cuisine. He knew that, because he liked to eat international cuisine. Her bookcases held a variety of literature, everything from paperback romances to gritty thrillers to historical maritime novels to biographies of world leaders. Her CD collection, too, was varied and extensive, the majority of artists people Cole had never heard of before. As he pulled one CD after another from the shelf, he realized a good many of them were imports from places like India, Algeria, Portugal, and Saudi Arabia.

And then there was the glass.

It was in every room in some form or another. The panes of the window over the kitchen sink were each a different color, each poured by hand complete with tiny bubbles. The big bay window in the living room boasted a wide border of stained glass over each section that was decorated with some kind of fat yellow flower. There were coiled plates, braided bowls, and twisted vases. There were abstract pieces he couldn't begin to identify. All of it wrought from the richest colors he'd ever seen, colors that seemed to transform, shift, and come alive as the sunlight tumbling through the windows changed and stretched. Clearly the house's owner was not just an art collector, but someone who liked to enjoy on a daily basis the art she amassed.

Whoever his hostess was, she wasn't like any other woman Cole knew. The brightly colored clothes and shoes in the closet suggested someone of a Bohemian nature. The cosmetics in the closet were more suited to a girly-girl fashionista. The health foods made him think more of an organic type. The good wine was characteristic of a sophisticate. The world beat music, an aesthete. The literary selections— many of them, anyway—an academic.

Just who was the owner of this house?

He remembered the photograph in the bedroom of the five women on the beach. He'd seen the same five women in other photographs around the house, too, in different poses, clearly still on vacation. One magnetted to the refrigerator had them all sitting on the deck of an open-air bar with a different beach behind them, all of them laughing and wearing sunglasses and/or floppy hats. The white string bikini had been wearing shorts and a different bikini top in that photo, the other women shorts and T-shirts.

The picture on the mantelpiece in the living room showed all five women standing in front of Tiffany's on Fifth Avenue in New York. Each of them wore a rhinestone tiara and long black gloves, and each struck a Holly Golightly pose. It was that photo that Cole looked at now, studying each of the women in turn as he tried again to guess which was the owner of the house. This photograph, too, had been taken from a distance, so it was hard to make out each of the women's features. The white string bikini he knew right away, because the long blond hair cascaded over one shoulder. He thought he could make out the baggy T-shirt one, as well, because, as in all the other pictures, she looked slightly uncomfortable. Her hair was pulled severely back in this picture, and she was squinting into the camera again, two facts that only added to her appearance of discontent.

There was no way she could be the house's owner, he decided. No way had glitter eye shadow or ruby red nail polish ever touched that woman's person. His money was still on the string bikini.

Strangely, though, it was the uncomfortable one to which his gaze kept straying. Why, he couldn't imagine. But there was something about her . . . maybe even something kind of familiar. . . .

His cell phone rang then, scattering his thoughts. He pulled it from his pocket and saw Susannah's number, so he flipped it open.

"Hey, Suz," he said as he settled the photograph back on the mantel.

"All settled in?" she asked without preamble.

"As settled as I can be."

"You don't sound very settled. Is the house awful?"

"No," he replied quickly. "It's actually kind of nice. In a Bohemian, girly-girl, organic, sophisticated, aesthete, academic kind of way."

There was a slight pause at the other end, then, "Yeah, okay, whatever. Look, I just wanted to let you know that Silk Purse is loving the bluegrass here at the farm and cavorting about with glee. Jason's already got her back in her routine, so all is well there. Denny and Faye told me to invite you to dinner tonight, so come whenever you're ready and you can check everything out."

"Sounds good."

She started to give him directions, but he told her to stop until he could locate a pencil and paper. He moved to a credenza in the corner of the room and opened drawers until he found both in one, alongside an address book, a roll of stamps, and a sketchpad upon which someone had sketched a design of overlapping, amorphous shapes.

Quickly, he jotted down Susannah's instructions and folded his phone closed. Then, unable to help himself, he withdrew the sketchpad and flipped through it. There were other designs on other pages, some of them similar to the glass pieces in the house. So his hostess wasn't just a collector of art, he thought. She was also a creator. These were doubtless her own pieces decorating the place.

Although he would have thought he'd have pretty conventional taste when it came to art—not that he ever gave that any thought—he liked his hostess's work. He liked the way the colors blended and melded, and he liked how something as fragile as glass could look so powerful and audacious.

She was definitely an interesting person, his hostess. It was too bad he'd have to return to California without ever making her acquaintance.

· Four ·

BREE'S APARTMENT WAS BARELY A MILE AWAY FROM
Lulu's house, but where Lulu lived on a quiet, tree-lined,
seldom-traveled little byway, Bree lived right on Bardstown
Road, at the very hub of Highlands action, above a bar—
nightclub was just too uppity a term for Deke's—whose
claim to fame was launching local bands. As a result, rarely
did an evening at Bree's pass without the steady accompani-
ment of *thumpa-thumpa-thumpa* from the drums of whoever
was the featured act below. By Monday night, Lulu had been
slammed by the all-girl punk ensemble WMD (Women of
Mass Destruction), twanged by the southern fried rock band
Finger Pickin' Good, and rapped by the hip-hop group Da
Streetz. Never let it be said that Deke's taste in music was
anything but eclectic. Needless to say, her sleep every night
had been cluttered by raucous dreams, everything from the
banjo-picking mutant in *Deliverance* to overweening low-
riders to marauding giant tampons.

But Monday night, thankfully, Lulu lucked out, because
the band shooting into orbit that night was a jazzy combo

called Smuuth, which, Bree told her, was supposed to be
pronounced "smooth," but no one got that and used the short
u sound instead, making them, well, Smuth.

Smuth, however, was indeed a very smooth band, so there
was hope for pleasant dreams this evening. In fact, Smuth
was so smooth that the two women decided to brush their
hair, tuck their T-shirts into their jeans—Lulu's was white,
Bree's was yellow—slip their bare feet into their sandals and
go down to enjoy them live. They took their usual seats at
the bar and ordered their usual beer, greeting and/or waving
at all the regulars. As always, the television above the bar
was turned on with the volume lowered, tuned to a local
channel that was, at the moment, airing a network cop show.
So Lulu and Bree did what they usually did on such nights
out—those when Bree wasn't pulling a bartending shift at
the bar in the Ambassador Hotel—and enjoyed the music,
chatted with friends, and danced on the few occasions when
the mood took them.

Until the local news came on as Lulu took the first sip of
her recently refreshed beer, and her attention was suddenly
snagged by a face that flashed by on the screen above the
bar.

"Hey!" she exclaimed before she could stop herself,
pointing up at the television set.

"What?" Bree replied, surprise mingling with alarm on
her face at Lulu's tone. "What's wrong?" She turned to look
at the TV, too, but by then the image had switched over to
one of the news anchors, so she turned to look at Lulu again,
her expression now puzzled.

"That guy," Lulu said, pointing more adamantly at the TV
screen.

"Who? Scott Reynolds? What about him? Besides the
fact that his hair, as always, looks fabulous?"

"No, not him. The other guy that was up there a second
ago."

"Sorry, Lu. Missed him. Who was it?"

Lulu shook her head slowly, as if that might negate what she'd just seen. Impossible, she thought. There was no way she could have seen the guy from the realty office Friday afternoon on the local news. He'd just made such a big impression on her subconscious that she was seeing him in places he couldn't possibly be. After all, hadn't he crept into her thoughts more than once over the weekend? And not just because she'd been reflecting on what a big jerk he was, either. In fact, that hadn't been one of her reflections about him at all, since most of her reflections about him had had him dressed in a Speedo and passing a piña colada to her from the neighboring beach towel. And the rest of her reflections about him had sort of been lacking the Speedo altogether.

But she wasn't concerned about the errancy . . . errantness . . . errantularity . . . waywardness of her thoughts tonight. She wasn't. Really. Honest. She *wasn't*. Thinking about the guy from the realty office in a Speedo just meant she'd gone way too long without a beach vacation, that was all. And "beach vacation" wasn't any kind of metaphor for anything sexual in nature. It wasn't. Really. Honest. It *wasn't*.

Um, where was she?

Oh, right. The man at the realty place in a Speedo. No! The man at the realty place on TV. Which he wasn't. Was he?

But no sooner did that question erupt in her head again than his face did indeed flash on the screen. She knew it was him, because there wasn't a man alive who had a smile that oozed sex and charm and made women's thoughts go all errantular the way his did.

"That guy," Lulu said again, wagging her finger at the TV once more. Before Bree had a chance to respond, Lulu grabbed Doug the bartender by the sleeve and said, "Turn up the TV, quick."

Doug arched an elegant dark brow at her, doing his best to

ooze the kind of sex appeal that Realty Office Guy came by naturally . . . and coming in way under par. In fact, Doug's rating on the sexy odometer hovered somewhere between Dwight Schrute and Larry the Cable Guy. Except he didn't dress as well as either of them.

"Say please," he purred to Lulu like a rusty jackhammer.

Instead, Lulu rolled her eyes and reached across the bar for the remote control herself, pointing it at the TV, and pushing the volume button. Hard. Fortunately, the band was taking a break, but there were still a few disgruntled grumbles from other bar patrons when the man on the screen's voice usurped the canned music. Without hesitation, Lulu shushed all of them with a wave of her free hand and a hasty, "C'mon—it's only for a second."

The minute she heard the man's voice, though, she knew without question it was him—not that she comprehended a word of what he said, because her thoughts were zinging in a million different directions by then. And not that she'd even needed to hear his voice to cement his identity to begin with. Or even the reminder of the curious green hue of his eyes. All she'd needed to confirm her suspicions was the zinginess of her thoughts and the warmth spreading throughout her midsection. That warmth turned to an explosion of embarrassment, however, when she saw letters scroll beneath his name, letters that her muzzy brain was just coherent enough to understand spelled out: *COLE EARLY, TRAINER OF DERBY ENTRY SILK PURSE.*

Then the remote control slipped from her numb fingers, and she muttered, "Oh. Hell."

"What?" Bree said again, her gaze ricocheting from Lulu's face to the TV screen.

Lulu held up a finger in the internationally recognized body language for "Hang on a sec." Although Bree clearly wanted to ask more, she closed her mouth and, along with Lulu, watched and listened to the man on TV.

"Of course I'm confident," he was saying in response to whatever question he'd been asked, sounding vaguely insulted by whatever it had been. "Silk Purse is not only going to win the Kentucky Derby, she's going to win the Preakness and the Belmont Stakes, too. That filly's taking home the Triple Crown, or my name isn't Cole Early."

Well, so much for that last futile hope that WAVE had scrolled the wrong letters under the man's name. Or the more likely hope that Lulu was too addlebrained to have read them correctly. Well, okay, so the addlebrained part *wasn't* in question, since she was clearly that, and had been since running into Cole Early, Trainer of Derby Entry Silk Purse.

The camera cut back to the interviewer, a young perky blonde Lulu recognized as a newly minted correspondent for the station, since the newscast was the one she watched nightly. For some reason, though, tonight the woman looked even younger, perkier, and blonder than usual. And although Lulu was by no means an expert on the subject, the correspondent also looked vaguely orgasmic at the moment. Then again, Lulu remembered well that shimmying-out-of-your-underwear effect that Realty Office Guy—no, Cole Early, she corrected herself—had on a woman.

"There you have it, Scott and Dawne," she cooed into the camera, licking her lips as if trying to savor some leftover bit of cotton candy. Or, more likely, Lulu thought, she was picturing Cole Early in a Speedo, too. "The first trainer to officially arrive in Louisville for the Derby, even though his horse was the last entry for the race." Something must have caught her eye over the camera operator's shoulder, because she smiled and said, "Ronnie, can you get a shot of that?" after which the camera swung wildly in a one-eighty to reveal Cole Early standing at what looked like a very crowded bar, surrounded by young women thrusting pieces of paper at him.

Then the correspondent's voiceover said, "And just like he is when he's at home in southern California, he's already surrounded by fans. All of whom, not too surprisingly, are female." The camera swung back to her again, but instead of looking into it, the way any self-respecting, self-absorbed TV personality should, she was still gazing over the camera operator's shoulder at Cole Early. She identified herself for the viewers, said she was reporting from Fourth Street Live, and, almost as an afterthought, concluded, "Back to you, Scott and Dawne." She was already tossing someone her microphone and walking away before the camera shot cut back to the studio.

Then the news anchor was back on the screen, smiling his news anchor smile, which was pleasant, sunny, and safe, and nothing at all like Cole Early's.

And Lulu repeated, "Oh. Hell."

She turned to Bree, who was looking at her with no small amount of concern.

"Lu?" her friend said in a voice Lulu remembered well from their childhood. It was the one Bree had always used in Brownies or art class when they were doing a craft and Lulu glued something to her forehead without realizing it. She hadn't heard her friend use it since the pufferfish girl incident. "What's wrong?" Bree asked. "Why do I get the feeling you're about to tell me something that's going to make me say, 'Oh, Lulu, what have you done?' Again."

Pointing at the television again, Lulu told her friend, "I met him the other day."

"Scott Reynolds?" Bree asked, brightening. "Did his hair look as fabulous in person as it does on TV?"

Lulu shook her head. "No, not him. Cole Early. The guy they just interviewed."

Bree's dark eyebrows arched so high, they disappeared under her bangs. "You met Cole Early? Are you serious? Why didn't you tell me? You know the entire goal of my life is to be the kept woman of a guy like that. If you've met him, it puts me within one degree of separation."

It wasn't hyperbole on Bree's part. Her life's goal really was to be the kept woman of some rich guy. Ever since kindergarten, where she and Lulu first met, she'd said she was going to grow up to marry one of the richest men in the world. By sixth grade, she had begun doing research and making graphs. By high school, she'd narrowed it down to where her ambition in the senior yearbook said: "To become Mrs. Bill Gates. Or Sra. Carlos Salinas. Or Sig.ra Silvio Berlusconi. Or Fr. Ingvar Kamprad. Or Princess Sabrina bin Talal bin Abdul Aziz Al Saud." Bree had always been an equal opportunity gold digger.

With the harsh reality that set in with college, however— the realization that there were very few billionaires walking down the streets of Louisville on any given day—Bree had become less adamant about the *Forbes* and *People* magazine lists, not to mention necessarily wanting to marry the guys. These days, all Bree wanted—and Lulu did mean *all* she wanted—was to find a guy who raked in at least a high seven figures a year and drove (choose as many as applied) a Ferrari, Maserati, Porsche, Lamborghini, Mercedes, Jaguar, or at least a really nice Lexus. During Derby time in Louisville when most people were trying to decide which horses had the most potential to win the race, Bree was trying to decide which out-of-towners had the most potential to array her in Prada.

It wasn't because she was shallow that she'd developed such an ambition at such an early age, however. It was because she never knew her father and grew up watching her mother struggle for meager amounts of money, security, and self-confidence. Although Lulu didn't necessarily agree with her friend's certainty that money could not only buy happiness, but also security and some righteous self-esteem, she didn't begrudge Bree her quest. Lulu's own home life growing up hadn't been the most stable in the world, and Bree had expenses these days that Lulu sure wouldn't want to shoulder.

But neither did she have any desire to put her happiness and her future in someone else's hands. Bree, however, couldn't wait to unburden her burden onto someone else. Preferably someone with open table reservations at Spago and an account at Tiffany's.

Lulu met her friend's accusatory gaze sheepishly. "I didn't tell you I met Cole Early because I didn't know the guy I met was Cole Early. I thought he was just some jerk guy."

Now Bree looked at Lulu as if she wanted to smack her forehead. Hard. And not Bree's forehead, either. No, Bree looked like she wanted to smack *Lulu's* forehead. Hard. "Okay, number one," she began, "how could you *not* know Cole Early when he's been in the paper like every day for the past two weeks?"

"Oh, the sports section," Lulu said. "Who reads the sports section?"

Bree gaped at her. "In April? In Louisville? Oh, I don't know, Lulu. Maybe *everybody?* 'Cause how else are you going to know which horse to pick for the Derby?"

Lulu shrugged. "I usually just pick the jockey silks I like best."

Bree closed her eyes, and judging by the almost imperceptible movement of her lips, Lulu was pretty sure she was counting slowly to ten.

"Or sometimes," she added, "if the horse has a name I like, I go for that."

Make that twenty Bree was counting to.

Finally, she opened her eyes. But she continued as if the break in conversation had never happened, "And number two, even if you didn't know Cole Early, how could you possibly mistake that . . . that paragon of perfection, that ideal of impressiveness, that gem of juiciness, that nonpareil of numminess, that—"

"Bree?"

"What?"

"You're starting to drool."

Without missing a beat, Bree swiped the back of her hand across her lips, lifted her beer to enjoy a healthy swig, then concluded, "How could you mistake that . . . that hard copy of hunka hunka burnin' love . . ."

"Oh, now, you're reaching for that one."

". . . that masterpiece of manhood and monument for moolah . . . How could you mistake that for *some jerk guy*?"

Lulu fidgeted on her seat a little. Bree did sort of have a point. "Well, he acted like kind of a jerk guy when I talked to him."

"You *talked* to him?" Bree squealed.

"And he did knock me down," Lulu told her. "And he barely apologized when he helped me back up."

"You *touched* him?"

"He knocked me down!"

"You *touched* him?"

"Bree!"

Bree expelled a sound that was a mix of impatience and intrigue. And then she said, "Oh, Lulu. What have you done?"

"I didn't do anything," Lulu protested. "Except maybe, you know, talk to him like I thought he was, um, an idiot."

The sound Bree expelled then wasn't a mix of anything. It was totally, crystal clear in its meaning. That meaning being, *Oh, dammit*. But all she said was, "Tell me what happened."

Lulu replayed the incident at Eddie's office for her friend as quickly as possible, leaving out the panties-shimmying part and focusing instead on Cole Early's obnoxious arrogance. But somehow, through the telling, Cole Early's obnoxious arrogance came out sounding really suave and charming. She had no idea how that happened. Lost in translation and all that. Anyway, Lulu concluded the story with, "Probably, he won't have to watch the race from the infield after all. Probably, he'll be standing in Millionaire's Row." She shrugged a little and did her best to smile. "My bad."

Bree shook her head slowly. "This close," she said, holding up her thumb and index finger about two nano-millimeters apart. "I was *this* close to finally meeting my meal ticket. I could have been on Millionaire's Row right beside Cole Early, watching the race with him."

Not that Bree would have been watching the race, Lulu knew. Or even Cole Early, for that matter. No, Bree would have been too busy waving down the vendor selling those thousand-dollar mint juleps with the ice imported from Antarctica and the sugar flown in from Aruba. And flaunting her Derby hat by Gabriel Amar for Frank Olive, since she did have a soft spot for the designer who donated the proceeds of his hat sales to local charities.

Lulu patted her friend's shoulder with almost genuine sympathy. "I'm sorry I couldn't be Pandarus to your Cressida and Cole Early's Troilus. But, hey, look how that turned out. I mean, Troilus and Cressida lived, but they didn't get catharsis. What's up with that?"

Bree brightened, but Lulu doubted it was because she was up for a rousing discussion of the Bard. "Wait a minute," she said. "If you ran into Cole Early at Eddie's office, then he must be renting a house from Eddie, right? Eddie can tell me where he's staying."

"Well, except for that pesky confidentiality of clients thing that Eddie embraces," Lulu reminded her. "He won't even tell me for sure who's renting my house."

Bree waved a breezy hand. "A small matter. Eddie will divulge anything for the right price."

"Which you can't afford."

"I'll figure something out. Maybe I can blackmail him."

"Gee, Bree, I'm thinkin' that a man who dances in public dressed as Liza Minnelli probably doesn't have a lot of dirty little secrets he fears someone might expose."

Bree looked unconcerned. In fact, Bree looked like she was making plans. Plans that might even include Cole Early in a Speedo. She grinned slyly as she said, "That reporter on TV just now said she was reporting from Fourth Street Live, right?"

Lulu nodded, not sure she liked the look on Bree's face.

"Could you tell which bar they were in?"

Lulu shook her head. She'd been to Fourth Street Live exactly two times. And both times, she'd been visiting the bookstore, not one of the numerous bars the entertainment complex boasted.

Bree deflated some. "Me, neither." Then she brightened

again. "But how many bars could there be at Fourth Street Live?"

Lulu shrugged. "Just a shot in the dark, but I'd say about twelve hundred."

Bree waved a negligent hand. "No way. There couldn't be more than ten or fifteen."

Which was about ten or fifteen more than Lulu wanted to visit, if she was reading Bree's expression right—and she was reasonably sure she was.

Bree eyed the last few swallows of her beer, as if trying to decide whether or not it was worth spending the extra couple of minutes necessary to finish it. Then she pushed the glass away and stood.

"C'mon, Lulu," she said as she grabbed her purse from the barstool beside her. "We're going downtown. And when we find your good buddy Cole Early, you're going to introduce us."

Interfering with her friend's life quest wouldn't cost Lulu her friendship with Bree, she knew. But it might cost her a limb. So Lulu swept up her own purse and followed Bree to the exit. She told herself to tell Bree she was going back up to the apartment, that her friend was on her own when it came to hunting down Cole Early, because tycoon trapping expeditions weren't Lulu's thing at all. But Bree had a bad habit of biting off more than she could chew when it came to achieving her life's ambition—never mind the fact that Cole Early was an infinitely tastier morsel than some of the other "bites" Bree had hooked up with for brief spells in the past. Someone had to keep an eye on her and keep her out of trouble.

Which was the *only* reason Lulu was going along with her now. It had nothing to do with the memory of Cole Early's smile or the way he called her "sweetheart." Or the thrill of heat that had shot up her arm when he'd taken her hand at Eddie's office. Or the stupid, unfounded fear that Bree might just wind up on Cole's arm at the Derby, leaving Lulu to watch the race on TV alone.

It was because she wanted to make sure Bree stayed out of trouble.

Nevertheless, she had to battle a ripple of apprehension as the door to Deke's swung closed behind them, and Bree said, "You know, Lulu, this just may be our best Derby yet."

· Five ·

COLE WAS HAVING TROUBLE REMEMBERING THE
name of the nightclub—or was it a restaurant?—into which
he had wandered. Even after three full days in Louisville, he
hadn't yet acclimated himself to the Eastern time zone and
kept getting ravenous around ten o'clock, which was dinnertime in his part of the world. Tonight was no different, and,
finding nothing to eat in his rented house—mostly because
he hadn't bothered to stock it with anything other than es-
sentials like brandy and Scotch—he'd called a cab and asked
the driver to take him someplace where he could get a decent meal, a decent drink, and some decent music.

Of course, he'd done that his other nights here, as well,
only to have the driver drop him a few blocks from the house
and charge him outrageously for the trip. So tonight, Cole
had specifically said he wanted to go somewhere *besides*
Bardstown Road, and the driver had dropped him here, in a
monstrous entertainment complex filled with nightspots,
only one of which—the Hard Rock Café—he recognized.
He'd chosen the nearest door and walked through it, barely

noticing the name of the establishment. The place was nice—if a little more into Bourbon than he was himself—but it wasn't exactly what he'd had in mind.

In spite of being three hours ahead of everyone here, he was sure he felt three times as exhausted, and he just hadn't had it in him to look around for something else. Besides, the music playing *was* decent, and, even more important, there had been plenty of seats at the bar when he entered. So he'd loosened his necktie spattered like a Jackson Pollock painting and unbuttoned both the amber suit jacket and top two buttons of the plum-colored dress shirt he'd had on since before dawn, and he'd claimed one of the empty seats for his own.

They hadn't stayed empty for long, however, because within minutes of sitting down, the seats on each side of Cole had been occupied, by women whose names, like the nightclub/restaurant/bar's, he could also no longer remember. Nor could he recall the name of the woman standing behind him who had crossed the room immediately behind the other two to press her spectacular breasts into his back—*those* Cole did remember. And probably would for some time. They'd chatted him up while he ate his dinner—making the enjoyment of it pretty much impossible—and consumed three drinks for his every one. Although he'd made numerous—polite—attempts to make clear his desire to be left alone, they were either too inebriated or clueless to take the hints. The same way the women just like them at a restaurant the night before had been. And the same way the women just like them at yet another bar the night before *that* had been.

What a jerk he'd become, he thought. He was a disgrace to his gender. Whining about an overabundance of beautiful women who wouldn't leave him alone. At this rate, he was going to have to trade in his membership card to Studs Unlimited for one from Sissies Anonymous instead.

Within hours of his arrival in Louisville, though, the vultures had begun circling. And not just the fans, like the trio of beauties smothering him now, but the press, too. Not a single night had passed since he'd come to town that he hadn't been spotted by someone from the local news and pressed for an interview—TV, newspapers, periodicals, websites, it didn't matter. All of them wanted to talk to Cole. And Cole, mindful that publicity was always—*always*—a good thing, had happily talked to all of them. Or, at least, he had pretended it was happily. He just hoped he could keep it up. If the next two weeks were like the last three or four days had been, however, he was going to be stretched too thin to be good to anyone. Including Susannah and Silk Purse.

Not that he wasn't used to being recognized and courted by the press. No matter where he found himself, Cole was always surrounded by admirers. But he'd hoped his reputation hadn't preceded him to Louisville yet. He had wanted his time here to be fairly anonymous for a while, so that he might enjoy a gradual immersion into the adventure that would become the Kentucky Derby Experience. Simply put, he'd wanted to be himself for a little while before shouldering the mantle of King Cole.

He should have known better. Rock 'n' roll had groupies for its bands. Major League had Baseball Annies for its players. NASCAR had Track Bunnies for its drivers. Thoroughbred racing had something similar for its trainers that no one had yet formally christened. So for lack of a better phrase, Cole had always dubbed such women—because they were overwhelmingly female—Trainer Hangers. Of course, his profession wasn't the only one in the industry that had its overly enthusiastic fans. He'd also found names for Owner Followers, Horse Nuts, and Jockey Junkies. But, all modesty aside, the trainers were the elite members of Thoroughbred society, often better known and more recognizable even than the owners. Certainly they were the most flamboyant members of the horse world. And just like rock stars and pro athletes, many of them commanded, whether actively or not, *a lot* of attention from—mostly female—admirers.

Cole was one of those many. And, truth be told—at least

early on in his career—he had actively courted the limelight. But now that the limelight dogged him wherever he went, he was starting to wish for a little more shadow time. During racing's off-season, he had more success deflecting the unwanted attention—not that it was *always* unwanted, mind you, even now—but it never went away entirely. And during race time, in racing cities like Louisville or Mar or Saratoga or Baltimore, trainers were treated like royalty. Usually, that didn't bother Cole at all. Usually, he welcomed the attention. Usually, he reveled in the way women pursued him. Usually, he let the women catch him.

But there were times, infrequent though they may be, when he just wanted to be left alone, to enjoy himself without the added distraction of being King Cole. Especially when he was facing the biggest race of his career.

He glanced down at his watch for perhaps the tenth time in as many minutes and sighed loudly enough that he hoped the blonde on his left—Randi? Rhonda? Renee?—would get the hint. Naturally, she didn't. Instead, she wrapped her perfectly manicured fingers around the premium Bourbon Cole had just ordered and hadn't yet had a chance to taste and lifted it to her own mouth for a sip.

She grimaced after sampling it. "Even though I grew up in Kentucky," she purred in a voice he was reasonably certain she had altered for effect, "I absolutely loathe Bourbon."

Cole was about to ask her why she'd felt compelled to drink his then, but refrained. "Let me order you something else," he offered magnanimously. To himself, he added, *And then go away.*

Before Randi/Rhonda/Renee had a chance to reply, the brunette on his right piped up, "I'll have a screwdriver."

Cole shuddered. How could anyone do something as heinous as adding juice to a perfectly good spirit like vodka? In spite of his revulsion, he started to lift a finger to signal the—female—bartender. But she was there before his hand was even fully in the air, ignoring the people who had clearly summoned her before he had, slapping a cocktail napkin down on the bar in front of him.

"What can I get you, Mr. Early?" she asked.

He turned to look at the brunette, wishing like hell that he could remember her name. Susie? Cindy? Sally? "Sarah," he finally said out loud when he recalled it, relief washing over him, "would like a screwdriver."

"Vicky," she corrected him. "Vicky would like a screwdriver."

Damn. He hadn't even been close.

"But I can be Sarah if you want," she offered, leaning in even closer to curl her own perfectly manicured fingers over his thigh and give it a gentle squeeze. "In fact, for you, Cole, I can be anybody—or anything—you want."

"So can I," Randi/Rhonda/Renee said from his left.

The redhead behind him—Barbie? Bobbie? Belinda?— pressed more intimately against him. "Me, too," she joined in, her voice sultry in his ear, her breath hot on his neck.

Randi/Rhonda/Renee slipped her arm over his shoulders, threw a very suggestive look at the other two women, leaned in very, *very* close to his other ear and added, "If you'd like, we can *all* be anyone and anything you want . . . together."

Hello. A part of Cole's anatomy that didn't normally misbehave in public suddenly jumped to attention with a rousing chorus of *Hoo-ah!* What Randi/Rhonda/Renee, Barbie/Bobbie/Belinda and Whatshername were offering was an opportunity the average man only dreamed about, then lied about in a letter to *Penthouse*. He didn't kid himself that if he'd been any regular working stiff—if one could pardon the crassness of the pun—the three women wouldn't have given him the time of day. It was only because he was Cole Early that such offers ever came his way. Not that he'd ever been offered a four-way before—just how did that work, anyway?—so this was a bit of a treat, even for Cole.

Which was why he was so surprised when he heard himself say, "I appreciate the offer, ladies, but I'm kind of waiting for someone."

Their disbelief was almost palpable. As was their disappointment. As was the seemingly fifty-degree drop in temperature as they removed their hands from his various body parts, collected their drinks, and walked away. Cole was about to breathe a sigh of relief and reach for his own drink, but he was immediately surrounded by a new batch of women, each of whom draped herself over him in much the same way as the ones who had just left.

It was going to be a *looooooong* two weeks, he thought morosely. How was he supposed to guide Silk Purse to the finish line when his attention span was being hindered at the starting gate?

The thought had just wrapped itself around his brain when, in an effort to deflect one of the new women's sultry, hot, lascivious, yada-yada-yada looks, he shot his gaze across the crowded bar and saw a familiar face. It took a moment for him to recognize it as belonging to the woman he'd met Friday afternoon at the realty office, the one whose laughing eyes and smug grin had stayed with him long after she'd gone—mostly as an irritant in his belly. Something erupted in his belly again at seeing her now, but, surprisingly, it wasn't irritation this time. In fact, it was kind of . . . sort of . . .

Nah. It couldn't be happiness. That would be nuts. But he was . . . relieved—yeah, that was it—to see Craggedy Ann standing on the other side of the room. Because now he had a legitimate someone to be waiting for/know/halfway-recognize that would fend off any future groups of luscious women who might want to press their bodies into Cole's and offer to, um, do the, ah, remarkable thing that Rosina, Betina, and Samantha had just offered to do.

Craggedy was wearing pretty much the same thing she'd worn on Friday, and her plain jeans and white T-shirt looked completely out of place amid the colorful cocktail and dance club attire of the other patrons. Out of place, too, was her obvious lack of makeup and the fact that she didn't seem to have even run a brush through her unruly mop of russet curls since he'd last seen her. But what was most out of place was his reaction to her. Because as he observed Craggedy Ann looking so uncomfortable and alien in her festive surroundings, Cole found himself sympathizing with her. Maybe because he'd been feeling so uncomfortable and alien in his festive surroundings, too.

Without even thinking about what he was doing, he stood and began to make his way across the room. But it was so crowded—and so many people wanted to greet him, or congratulate him, or ask him who he liked for the Derby, as if that wasn't the dumbest question in the world—that his progress was constantly impeded. He started to feel like he was in one of those dreams where the thing he was struggling hardest to get to kept getting farther and farther away, and the faster he tried to run, the more unattainable it became. Then he realized Craggedy Ann was craning her neck and looking around the room, as if she were searching for something—someone—too. And then his anxiety rose, because what if she found that person before he had a chance to get to her? He might never see her again.

Then he realized how foolish he was being. He didn't even know the woman's name, had exchanged maybe two dozen words with her, none of which had been especially warm. Hell, he didn't even *like* her, weird sympathizing notwithstanding, which was probably only a result of indigestion, anyway. What did he care if he never saw her again?

Nevertheless, for whatever reason—probably the aforementioned indigestion, or maybe jet lag, or, hell, it was probably from the damned concussion he got every night banging his damned head on the damned ceiling in the damned bedroom—seeing Craggedy again felt a little bit like good luck. And like everyone else in the Thoroughbred business, Cole was just superstitious enough to believe he needed all that he could get.

He inched forward again, smiling and shaking hands and replying as quickly and politely as he could to everyone who wanted a piece of him. Just when he was within inches of being able to call out—or better yet, *reach* out—to her, Craggedy turned away and melted into the crowd. He lunged forward in the direction into which she'd disappeared, pushing aside a man who stepped in front of him without even caring how rude the action may have been interpreted. But he was immediately encircled by throngs of people again. He pushed himself up on tiptoe, and since he was already taller than the majority of people there, was able to see a good many of the heads surrounding him. But none sported a crop of ragged red curls that invited a man's finger to loop itself inside one.

As quickly as she had appeared, Craggedy Ann was gone. And so, Cole realized, was the last of anything that might have resembled a good mood.

"HE'S NOT HERE, EITHER, BREE," LULU SAID AS SHE curled a finger through a belt loop of her friend's jeans so she wouldn't get separated from her amid the crowd at the Maker's Mark Lounge. Heavens, if this was what Fourth Street Live was like on a Monday night, Lulu would continue to confine her visits to Borders. The only thing that made her more anxious than being the center of attention was being in a huge crowd. What kind of person actually *enjoyed* this kind of lifestyle?

"He has to be here," Bree replied, surging forward through a trio of men who were nearly twice her size, and who each gave her a thorough once-over as she passed. She was completely oblivious to their once-overs, since they didn't look like their net worth collectively was more than a buck-and-a-half. "He wasn't in Felt or Sully's or the Hard Rock. This is the only place we haven't checked yet. He's *here,* I tell you." She swiveled her head first right, then left, then right again. "Somewhere."

"We missed him," Lulu assured her friend. "He was probably getting into his car just as we were getting out of yours." She looked at her watch, then thrust her arm forward, in front of Bree's face. "It's almost one o'clock. Who in their right mind stays out this late at night?"

Bree glanced over her shoulder at Lulu and made a big production of looking at the scores of people thrashing around the place.

"Okay, okay," Lulu conceded as the music pumped louder and the pulsating of the crowd notched upward. She raised her voice accordingly, fairly shouting as she added, "Lots of people stay out this late. I bet Cole Early's the early-to-bed, early-to-rise type. Don't those horse people get up at the crack of dawn to exercise their pets?"

"Thoroughbreds aren't pets," Bree yelled back. "They're worth millions of dollars, a lot of them."

"They still get their owners up early to take them out-side."

This time when Bree looked over her shoulder, she was gritting her teeth. "Not their owners. And not their trainers, either, necessarily. They get their exercisers up early."

"Maybe Cole Early likes to—"

"Cole Early is not an early-to-bed type," Bree interrupted her. "Trust me. He may not be on the short list of Rich Guys I Want to Bag, but I've read enough about him since he won Santa Anita a couple weeks ago to know he's as sure a thing as I can get right now. So I'm not gonna hedge my bets."

Honestly, sometimes Lulu just wanted to smack her best friend. Bree talked about men as if they were . . . Well, in this case, racehorses. But she also talked about men as if they were commodities. Or investments. Or possessions. Or careers. Or prey. She almost never talked about men as if they were human beings.

If she were anyone but Sabrina Calhoun, Lulu wouldn't tolerate it. But she knew Bree well enough to understand her friend's shortsightedness in this, even if she didn't condone it. Bree had even better reasons as an adult to want to marry well than she'd had as a kid. And anyway, deep down, Bree was capable of deep and abiding loyalty and affection—just look at her friendship with Lulu. The whole man-woman thing, though . . . Bree just hadn't ever had the opportunity to witness what a healthy adult relationship was like. Someday she'd meet a man who dropped her in her tracks, a man she'd fall for heart and soul, and then she wouldn't care what he did for a living, or what kind of car he drove, or how fat his investment portfolio was, or if he even *had* an investment portfolio.

"Man, I hate it when they slip the snare this way," Bree grumbled. "It takes forever to set up a trap the right way."

Okay, *probably* she would meet a guy like that someday, Lulu reluctantly amended.

"Oh, no," Bree muttered then, barely loud enough for Lulu to hear.

"What?"

"Rufus is here."

Lulu smiled. Speak of the devilishly handsome. Or, at least, think of the devilishly handsome. Because even if she hadn't been thinking about Rufus Detweiler by name, she'd certainly been thinking about him in spirit. As far as she was concerned, Rufus was exactly the man Bree should be looking at for potential happiness. And not just because the guy was already head over heels in love with her, either.

Lulu followed Bree's gaze to the bar on the other side of the room and, within seconds, she had identified him. It was strange to see him sitting on the patron side of the bar, when he was usually behind one working alongside Bree. But he seemed perfectly at home with all the people surrounding him, even if he stood a good two or three inches taller than even the tallest guy. He was leaning back against the bar, one elbow propped nonchalantly on its surface, the other tipping a longneck bottle of beer into what Lulu had remarked on many occasions was a thoroughly sexy mouth. The tiny halogen light fixed in the ceiling above him sent a wash of light cascading down over him like an inverted V, lighting dark amber highlights in his near-black hair and chiseling even finer what were already *very* well-honed cheekbones.

His white pin-striped oxford shirt was untucked over faded jeans that hugged his lean legs, enhancing the innate grace of his spare frame.

He looked like a poem, Lulu thought wistfully. A tragic sonnet of unrequited love written from the deepest recesses of the heart. He was just a gorgeous, gorgeous man, and totally not her type. Which was just as well since, in case she hadn't mentioned it, the guy was totally sprung on Bree.

"Rufus!" Lulu called out, jumping up and down and waving her hand to get his attention.

Immediately, Bree spun on her and clamped a hand over her mouth. "Are you *crazy*?" she hissed. "The last thing I want when I'm looking for Cole Early is a guy like Rufus anywhere in my personal space."

Lulu yanked Bree's hand from her mouth. "Oh, who cares what you want?" she said. "I like Rufus. He's a good guy. Rufus!" she called out again, doing the jumping and waving thing even more adamantly.

Amazingly, he heard her over the din of the bar, turning his head in her direction, smiling and lifting a hand in greeting when he saw her. Then, when he looked to her right and saw Bree with her, his eyes went brighter, his smile turned incandescent, and everything about the guy seemed to absolutely glow.

What the hell was the matter with Bree, that she couldn't see Mr. Right-Under-Her-Nose?

As if wanting to make that painfully evident, Bree quickly turned her back on both Lulu and Rufus and started scanning the other side of the bar for whatever she thought it was she wanted. Rufus did a good job of pretending not to notice, but Lulu saw how his features dimmed a little at her friend's behavior.

Nevertheless, he had perked up by the time he approached, beer bottle still in hand. "Hey, Lulu," he greeted her warmly. As he always did, he leaned forward and brushed her cheek lightly with his lips, taking her hand and giving her fingers a gentle squeeze as he did. When he drew back, he looked at Bree—who still had her back to him—and said a little more coolly, "Bree. Good to see you, too."

"Hey, Rufus," she replied without turning around.

Lulu had known Rufus roughly eight hours less than Bree, who had worked her first shift with him two years ago at the Ambassador Bar before Lulu came in to meet her friend for drinks afterward. As she'd waited for Bree to finish up, Lulu had chatted with Rufus, and it had taken approximately three minutes for her to realize the guy was already hung up on Bree. It had taken her three-and-a-half minutes to realize Bree would never give him the time of day, because it took Rufus only thirty seconds to give Lulu an answer to her question about what he wanted to be when he grew up. That answer being a momentary blank stare followed by, "A bartender. I love this job."

To Lulu, the answer told her everything she needed to know about Rufus—and made her like him even more than she already did. Job-loving was a major, major factor in essential human happiness. Anyone who loved his or her job, regardless of what it was, was someone to be admired, because it meant they went their own way, did their own thing, and didn't care what society thought about them. Bree, however, equated Rufus's professional contentment with a profound lack of ambition. Because there was no way his work would lead to reeking piles of filthy lucre, and how could you not want reeking piles of filthy lucre? So that was the end of any chance Rufus might have with Bree on the romantic front.

"What are you guys doing here?" he asked Lulu. But he was looking at Bree when he asked it—or, at least, at Bree's back. "I don't think I've ever seen you out and about down here. Bad band at Deke's tonight?"

"Great band at Deke's tonight," Lulu told him. "But—"

"But I'm here looking for someone," Bree said, finally spinning around. "Someone, ah, special."

Oh, sure, *now* she looked right at Rufus, Lulu thought. To

hammer home that he wasn't anything special. Funny, though, how she seemed to stumble a little over the words when she looked at Rufus. And her voice, too, seemed a little more shallow and a little less certain. Funny, too, how she didn't seem able to hold his gaze for more than a second or two before it went skittering over his shoulder.

"Oh, yeah?" Rufus asked with seeming unconcern. "Who?"

"Just some guy," Lulu said.

"Cole Early," Bree said at the same time.

Rufus had started to lift his bottle for another sip, but halted it shy of his mouth and smiled. "Cole Early," he repeated dispassionately.

Bree nodded, still looking over Rufus's shoulder, but seemed about one-tenth as certain about that now as she had a few minutes ago.

"The trainer," he said in that same flat tone.

Bree nodded again, a little more slowly this time, looking about one-one-hundredth as certain now. And it wasn't just her gaze that ricocheted this time. She turned her whole head to avoid looking at him.

"The one with a horse in the Derby," Rufus said.

Another nod, even slower. Another substantial drop on the ol' confidence meter.

"The one whose picture is on the cover of the new *Louisville* magazine? The one who they featured in the *Scene* this weekend? The one who's been on the news every night for the past few nights surrounded by incredible-looking women? That Cole Early?"

Bree didn't even manage a nod this time. Though Lulu was pretty sure Rufus's question was rhetorical.

"You think he's potential Sugar Daddy material?" he asked.

Like, oh . . . everyone else on the planet, Rufus knew Bree's big ambition in life was to bag herself a rich caretaker. Which was doubtless why he'd never made known his feelings for her. Well, not to anyone except any person with an IQ higher than zero who looked at him whenever he was somewhere in her zip code.

Bree did nod in response to that one—sort of—and, very softly, said, "Yes."

Rufus grinned again, biting his lip in a way that was truly adorable and would have melted the heart of any self-respecting woman. Lulu was practically swooning, and she loved Rufus like a brother. If Bree wasn't purring at least a little bit inside, then she needed to go see the Great and Powerful Oz for a new heart.

"Bree," he said, "Cole Early was in here a little while ago, and—"

"He's here?" Bree interrupted, looking panicky now.

"He *left*," Rufus told her, the warmth in his voice cooling. "But while he was here, no fewer than ten women came up to him—all of them dressed way better than you, I might add," he dropped in as if he couldn't help himself, "and the guy wasn't interested in any of them. Last time I saw him, he was heading for the door. Alone."

Bree looked a little hurt after the better dressed comment—not that she hadn't asked for it—but recovered admirably. "Of course he left alone," she said. "He didn't meet *me*."

Rufus started to say something else, seemed to think better of it, and turned to Lulu instead. "Wanna dance?" he asked.

Lulu's eyes went wide at the invitation. Not because it surprised her, but because the last thing she wanted to do was go out onto a dance floor and move her body in a way that might draw attention to herself. It wasn't that she was a bad dancer. On the contrary, she loved to dance. At home. Alone. Just her and her iPod. If she went out there with all those people jostling her and looking at her, she'd immediately invent a new dance: the Pufferfish Girl Fandango.

"Uh, that's okay, Rufus," she said. "Thanks anyway." She was about to say more, but something over his shoulder caught her eye, and she was pretty sure it wasn't the same thing that had caught Bree's a moment ago. Because a man was emerging from a poorly lit alcove. A dark-haired man in an amber-colored suit. A man she remembered all too well.

Cole Early was still here.

Something hot detonated in her belly at seeing him again—probably the burger she'd downed at Deke's, since the place was known for its music, not its food. 'Cause it couldn't be excitement at seeing Cole Early again. The guy was a boor, he was arrogant, and he was self-centered. Not to mention he was the kind of tourist she found most annoying, one of the ones who threw their weight around with a lot of flash, dash, and cash. Of course, he did have that smile that made a woman want to . . .

Um, never mind.

Then she realized that if Bree saw him, too, she'd go right over to the guy and introduce herself, and then introduce Lulu, too, and then Lulu would have to talk to him again, and she totally didn't want to do that. Nor did she want to be with Bree when her friend was doing the feminine wiles thing she did so well. When Bree flirted, no matter the circumstances, she was dazzling. Standing beside her in such situations, Lulu invariably ended up feeling like the bedraggled street urchin selling flowers to the theater-going hoi polloi. Dead flowers, at that. From a dirty alleyway. In the rain. On a Monday night, when no one was even going to the theater to begin with.

She quickly grabbed Bree and spun her around so that she was facing Lulu and Rufus, and not Cole Early. And she said something she was certain would make Bree call it a night. "If you want to dance, Rufus, maybe you and Bree could—"

"No, we have to go, Lulu," Bree cut her off.

Perfect, Lulu thought.

"There's no reason to hang around here," she added.

Not so perfect. Poor Rufus. Damn Bree.

Bree circled Lulu's wrist with sure fingers and gave her hand a tug. Unfortunately, the direction she tried to tug her into was the same one that led to Cole Early, which was in the opposite direction of the exit.

Time to get serious about leaving.

"But we just got here," Lulu whined. "Let's have a beer with Rufus."

"Suits me," Rufus said amiably. "I'll even buy."

"Can't," Bree said succinctly, this time really turning for the exit. "We have to go. Like I said, no reason to stay." She lifted her head as if she intended to shake it defiantly at Rufus, but the minute she caught his eye, her dark brows arrowed downward, two bright spots of pink appeared on her cheeks, and she immediately dropped her gaze again, looking embarrassed for saying what she had.

In spite of that, Lulu thought she saw Rufus dip his head forward almost imperceptibly, as if to silently concede the round to Bree. Something about the gesture, though, told her he wasn't giving up on the battle just yet.

After checking to make sure Cole Early was well and truly out of sight—thankfully, he was—Lulu gave Rufus an *Oh, well* kind of smile, lifted one shoulder and let it drop. "See you later, Rufus," she said.

"Next time, I'll collect that dance," he replied with a smile as she let her friend pull her toward the exit.

But Lulu wasn't sure if he was talking to her, or to Bree.

· Six ·

COLE ARRIVED BACK AT HIS RENTED HOUSE A LITTLE
after two, fumbling for a good five minutes with his key
ring because he'd forgotten to leave on any exterior lights, and
because he'd slipped the house key onto his own key ring
and couldn't find it amid the jumble of keys he always carried on his person. Let's see, that first was the key to his
Maserati, the second was the key to the Merc, the third was
the key to the SUV . . . no, that was the fourth key. The third
was to the truck he drove at the stables. Then came the key to
the big house on the farm, then to the main stable, then to
the tack room, then the shed . . . He counted out a few more
and ticked them off mentally as he went. *The penthouse in
LA, the condo in Miami, the cabin on Lake Arrowhead, the
sailboat, the runabout, the Jet Ski, the snowmobile* . . . Ah.
There it was. The key to his rented house in Louisville.

He sighed with much fatigue as he pushed it into the front
door and turned it, fighting with it a little to make it work and
telling himself the house was *not* trying to keep him locked
out. Again. Man, not only did he have a way-too-overactive

imagination—Take *that*, house, he thought as he finally got the key to turn—he had way too many keys. He pushed the door open gently, but only because he didn't want to break anything, not because he feared pissing off the house. Again.

How had he ended up with so many keys? he wondered as he shoved them back into his pocket. And why did he feel like he needed to keep them with him all the time? He remembered when he was hired for his first job, as a junior in high school in Charlottesville, Virginia, at Buck Trenton's stables. He'd only had one key, then—the one Buck had given him for the stables he mucked out every day. Eventually, he started filling feed bins, too, and by the time he graduated from high school, Cole was grooming and exercising some of the younger horses.

During his four years at UVA with a double major in animal husbandry and business, Buck had taken Cole under his wing and showed him the finer points of training. Buck had said Cole had a way with horses—and he'd been right. Cole may not have known his father very well—he and Cole's mother had divorced before Cole even started school and had taken a job in Ocala—but the elder Early had been a fine trainer, too, right up until his death two years ago from cancer. The Earlys had worked with horses in one way or another for generations. It was in their blood. Cole was just the latest branch of the tree to bloom. None of the previous Earlys had seen success like his, though. None had even come close. They sure as hell hadn't carried around as many keys as he did.

Cole pushed the door closed behind him and leaned back against it, taking a moment to acclimate himself to the little house that was so unlike his own. He'd left a light on in the living room, a stained glass number with an overly decorative base that was, like much of the rest of the house, a little too feminine for his tastes. Funny, though, how welcome it made him feel. The bright color palette, too, which should have seemed too manic and chaotic, soothed him more than the dependable browns and benign beiges of his own décor. His house in Temecula was a sprawling ranch of nearly four thousand square feet with broad windows that looked out on green pastures and running horses no matter what room he occupied. It had state-of-the-art everything, a media room he rarely used, a Hollywood perfect pool he used even less, a gourmet kitchen his cook assured him was perfect in every way, and a master bedroom he didn't sleep in nearly enough—and never with guests. Those occupied the numerous spare rooms, some of which, he realized now, he couldn't remember what they looked like.

He closed his eyes as he tried to remember. But the only room that appeared in his head was the tiny bedroom upstairs he kept bumping his head on. And that room, he could see better than he did his own back in Temecula. He opened his eyes again, smiling reluctantly at the living room that was probably a quarter of the size of his back home. Funny, though, how after just a few days, it felt more like home to him than his own house did.

Pushing himself away from the door, he strode to where he'd left his laptop charging earlier, shrugging off his suit jacket as he went. Tired as he was, he was still too wired to sleep, and, having spent much of the day in Shelbyville and the rest of it in meetings at Churchill Downs, he hadn't checked his e-mail for more than twenty-four hours. He unplugged the laptop to take it upstairs, stopping long enough in the kitchen to pour a couple fingers of cognac into the only thing he was able to find that resembled a snifter— something the house's owner probably poured her morning OJ into, because it was short and etched with flowers and was in no way suitable for a Napoleon that would probably suffer a major inferiority complex as a result.

He sipped the cognac slowly as he ascended the stairs to the bedroom, bumped his head—again—before remembering to stoop, then set his laptop on the bed and pushed the On button to power it up while he shed his work clothes and donned a pair of navy silk pajama bottoms. But when he seated himself on the bed and opened his computer, all that greeted him was a blank—and dark—screen.

He pushed the On button on the side of the apparatus again. Nothing happened. He pushed it a third time. Nothing. He checked to make sure the battery was snug in place. It was. Another push of the button. The laptop lay there lifeless.

Dammit.

What the hell was the matter with this piece of crap computer? he wondered. Bad enough this house wasn't equipped with wireless and it had taken Cole fifteen minutes to locate someone in the neighborhood whose service he could pirate. Fat lot of good it did now that the damned machine wasn't even working. He went back downstairs to retrieve the power cord and bumped his head on the ceiling when he returned. He plugged one end of the cord into the laptop and the other into a wall socket, then pushed the On button *again*.

Nothing.

He looked at the big computer on the desk. The one that belonged to the house's owner. The one with one of the ubiquitous pink Post-it notes affixed to it. He'd read this one his first evening here, but now he strode across the room to read it again.

"*Please don't feed the Mac,*" it said. "*She must stay on a strict vegetarian diet to maintain her multitasking capabilities. And please don't ask her for help. She's very shy. If you need a computer, there are several at the library, and being social creatures, they* adore *visitors!*"

In other words, Cole translated, *Mitts off.*

He knew it would be a violation of all that was decent and holy to violate the instructions on that note. It would be the equivalent of opening that drawer in the dresser he was sure housed his hostess's underwear to fondle it, or rifling through her filing cabinets in search of financial information that was none of his business.

Oh, hell, it would just be for a couple of minutes, he told himself, and she would never know, and there might be some really important e-mail that needed his immediate attention, and *blah, blah, blah,* fill in the blank with whatever lame excuse worked, because he *was* going to fire up her computer. He admitted it—he was an e-mail junkie with an e-monkey on his back the size of e-Kong. He needed his e-mail, dammit. He needed that even more than he wanted to fondle women's underwear. That probably said something about his manliness he'd find a little troubling if he took the time to consider it, but, thankfully, he was too busy—manfully busy—to make time for that. So he strode manfully back to his laptop and manfully slammed it shut, manfully clutched his cognac in its glass with the little etched flowers, and made his way manfully back to the desk—first bumping his head manfully on the ceiling again—then reached for the computer with a manful hand . . .

Only to hesitate when he saw the bright pink Post-it note still affixed to the left of the screen.

If she was really that concerned about someone using her computer, he thought, then she would have protected it with a password before she left. Hoping that wasn't the case, he felt around the machine until he found the On button and, with only one more small—but still manful—hesitation, he pushed it.

Oh, yeah, that did it. He could feel his testosterone surging again, having manfully ignored the conventions of courtesy by completely disregarding the wishes of his hostess.

He mentally crossed his fingers as the Mac whirred to life, narrowing his eyes at the screen as he waited for some kind of password prompt to appear. Instead, a background popped right up that was a swirl of bright color. It took him a moment to realize her computer wallpaper was a photograph of some kind of elaborate glass. Or, at least, a detail of something made out of elaborate glass. As he seated himself at the desk, he tilted his head first one way, then the other, to get the full effect. He had no idea what it was. But whatever it was, it was beautiful, like all the other glass pieces he'd seen in the house.

He shook his head to clear it. He had way more important things to do than look at pretty pictures of glass. How did you get the Internet to come up on this thing? He'd never used a Mac before and had no idea what kind of software was on it. The desktop was surprisingly clean, with only a handful of files stacked one atop the other on the far left-hand side. Along the bottom was a row of icons, some of which he recognized by their PC counterparts, the others . . . not so much.

Might as well just start clicking . . .

One by one, Cole moused over the different images, until something called Safari opened up to what was clearly an Internet site. An Internet site about glass—gee, there was a shocker—that he ignored to type in the URL of his ISP. There were dozens of e-mails awaiting him, but nothing too major, and he was able to plow through them fairly quickly—though *all right*, it was more than a couple of minutes. She'd still never know. He had closed the Internet and was about to power down when his eye landed on an icon at the very top of the screen he hadn't noticed before, because it was on the right-hand side and nearly the same color as the bit of glass on the picture behind it. The icon was of a small book. And the words beneath it said, *Daily Journal.*

So his hostess was a diary keeper, was she? Somehow, that didn't surprise him. Considering the belongings he'd found stashed everywhere over the past few days, he knew she was the sort of person who liked to surround herself with things that made her feel good. Things that satisfied her. It made sense that such a person would be introspective enough to want to keep a journal.

Not sure what made him do it, Cole moved the mouse to the little book icon and let it sit there. He wasn't going to open her journal. He wasn't. That would be despicable. Nevertheless, he was intrigued. Intrigued enough, in fact, that he experienced one of those TV moments where he imagined an angel version of himself appearing on one shoulder, and a devil version of himself appearing on the other.

Don't do it, said the angel Cole. *It would be wrong.*

Go ahead, said the devil Cole. And, being a devil, he threw Cole's own words back at him. *She'll never know.*

But the angel Cole hung in there. *How would you like it if someone did the same thing to you?* it asked.

Oh, come on, the devil replied. *Just a peek. You know you want to.*

It's a violation of her privacy, the angel reminded him.

Just read a couple of pages, said the devil. *Hell, it's probably all boring stuff, anyway.*

It's her private thoughts, said the angel. *If she wanted you to read them, she would have written them on the bathroom mirror.*

If you met her in a bar, the devil countered, *by evening's end, she'd probably tell you all the stuff she has written down, anyway.*

Devil Cole had a point, he had to admit. In this age of YouTube and SmokingGun, nobody had secrets anymore, and more often than not, they were the ones to reveal them themselves, often with badly digitized video.

Only the lowest of low and the scummiest of scum would open that journal and read it, angel Cole said. *Only the slimiest of slime and the sleaziest of sleaze and the ickiest of ick and the dirtbaggiest of dirtbags and the—*

Okay, okay, I get it, Cole told his angel. Sheesh.

But his devil cut in again with another *She'll never know,* evidently realizing that was a biggie for Cole.

Back and forth the two aspects of Cole's conscience went, until finally, the devil went over to his opposite shoulder and just shoved the angel off. Then it leaned against his ear and said all kinds of things Cole knew he shouldn't listen to. And then, suddenly, his finger twitched involuntarily, really, and it accidentally, really, clicked on the mouse, which inadvertently, really, opened the file marked *Daily Journal.*

Fine then. Just call me Dirtbag.

He would have immediately clicked the mouse again to close the file, really, but his gaze lit on the words *so wonderfully erotic,* and there was no going back after that.

The file had opened with a word processing program that automatically went to wherever the writer had left off last, so he scrolled to the top of the latest entry and saw that it was dated two nights before his arrival in Louisville. That would have been a Wednesday. Who found something wonderfully erotic on a Wednesday? Okay, yeah, that was also known as hump day, but Cole had never gotten the impression it was that kind of—

Anyway, nobody was erotic on a Wednesday. That was the middle of the week. His hostess, however, evidently spent her Wednesdays a lot differently than most people.

Tonight was incredible, the passage began. *He so surprised me tonight. I showed up needy and demanding, certain I knew exactly what I wanted from him. I'd had a rough day, and I wanted it traditional. I wanted it predictable. I wanted it comfortable. Comfort*ing. *But the way he looked at me when he came to me, I knew he had something else entirely in mind. No, he told me, I wasn't going to get predictable and comfortable tonight. Tonight, I was getting something different. Something dangerous. Something exotic. Something spicy and* hot. *Something he'd discovered in one of the clubs in Bangkok that polite people in the western world never talked about.*

Whoa, this guy got around, Cole thought. Wasn't Thailand supposed to be one of those countries that, when it came to sexual exploration, turned a blind eye to, oh . . . everything? Not that Cole knew, of course. He'd seen something about it on the Discovery Channel.

When he told me what he was going to do, the journal continued, *I really didn't want any part of it. It just didn't seem . . . normal. Or safe. I wasn't even sure if it was legal here.*

Holy crap, what was it? Cole wondered. He read on.

But then he looked at me the way he does when he wants to change my mind—and knows he can. He touched my shoulder in that way of his, then pressed his fingers to his lips in that way that promised untold pleasure. I shiver whenever he does that, because I know what those fingers can do, and how experienced is that mouth. When he does that, I know I have to turn myself over to him completely. To take whatever he gives me and . . . mmmmmm . . . relish it.

Now they were getting somewhere.

Oh, my God, it was so wonderfully erotic. When I opened my mouth and he filled me . . .

Yeah? Cole thought, Go on . . .

The heat of it . . . The texture . . . The taste . . .

What about them . . . ?

It was almost more than I could bear at first, there was just so much. But he kept coming with it, and coming with it, until I couldn't open my mouth fast enough to take it in. I wanted more. And more. And more.

Oh, God . . .

It was the insertion of the cumin, I think, that enraptured me most. Though the way he opened me to the turmeric was spectacular . . .

Wait a minute, Cole thought, his fast-rising, ah, interest suddenly cooling. Cumin? Turmeric? Those weren't sex toys or dirty slang words for body parts. Those were spices. He'd seen them in the pantry downstairs. He backtracked to the first paragraph. Something spicy? Something hot? He read over the entire passage again. She wasn't talking about sex. She was talking about food! She was describing the dinner she had. The *he* she was writing about wasn't a lover, it was a chef. Maybe even her waiter.

Well, hell. He'd gotten all worked up over a Thai dish he couldn't even enjoy now, because she hadn't had the decency to name the restaurant where she'd been eating or even what she'd had. Other than a wonderfully erotic time.

Eating, he thought again. Good God, the woman made eating dinner out sound like forbidden, hedonistic sex. Either she was a woman who had sex *a lot,* or else she was more desperately in need of getting laid than anyone on the planet.

Another piece to the puzzle, he thought as he— reluctantly—closed the journal file. And just like the others he'd found, it was a piece that didn't fit anywhere. Just who was the woman who called this house home?

His gaze strayed to the left of the computer, where he saw a small carved Buddha sitting among his hostess's desk accessories. The figure's hands were lifted high, and he was smiling broadly, clearly enjoying a level of enlightenment that few people knew. Probably, Cole thought, the Buddha never had angels and devils sitting on his shoulders. Probably, the Buddha always knew the right thing to do.

Then again, the Buddha probably never got to read sexy passages about Thai food, either.

Okay, that was enough of that. Cole moused around until he found the prompt for turning off the computer—leave it to Mac users to do everything on the left—and powered down the machine. He looked at the Buddha again, this time seeing the coffee mug full of pencils, pens, and whatnot behind him. It had a quote from Gandhi on it that said, "There is more to life than increasing its speed." A pen jutting out from it bore the words Rainbow Blossom. When he pulled it completely from the container, he saw that Rainbow Blossom was a "Natural Food Market." Another pen was from a place called Carmichael's Bookstore. Others said, "Wild and Woolly Video," "ear X-tacy" and "Lynn's Paradise Café." Cole smiled as he withdrew one pen or pencil after another and found inscriptions for all manner of interesting pastimes. His hostess, it seemed, was a busy woman. But the speed to which she'd increased her life, he bet, was one of which Gandhi would doubtless approve.

Pushing himself away from the desk, Cole rose. As he headed for the bedroom door, his gaze lit on the photograph that sat atop the dresser, the one of five women standing in ankle-deep water somewhere in the Caribbean. He picked it up and eyed each of the women in turn, wondering again which one was the owner of the house, which one was the journal keeper, the one who had possessions and pastimes that so enriched the soul. Although the picture wasn't especially clear, each of the women appeared to be attractive, and they all looked like they were having fun. As much as he tried to focus on the one in the white string bikini, however, his attention kept drifting to the right, to the woman on the end wearing the long T-shirt, whose hair and face were obscured by the ball cap pulled low on her head.

No way, Cole thought. It wasn't possible for her to be the owner of this house, considering all the evidence he'd found inside. It had to be one of the other women, and his bet was still on the white string bikini.

If he wanted, he could find out more about her. He could snoop in her drawers and closets, open some of those boxes in the spare room, plunder her computer files. Hell, he could just go back and fire up the Mac and read more of her journal. She'd doubtless locked up anything that might lend itself to identity theft, but there would probably still be things around the house that would at least tell him her name. A reverse directory computer search on her address would give him that. He could even ask one of her neighbors.

For some reason, though, he didn't want to know her name. And he didn't want to learn anything about her that he couldn't learn by observing the things with which she surrounded herself. He liked the idea of her being a mystery woman, enjoyed the prospect of getting to know her by inhabiting her space. So far, he knew she liked rich, vibrant fabrics, that she created sleek, colorful glass, that she collected fanciful artwork, that she cooked with exotic spices, that her taste in music and literature spanned the globe, that her hangouts all had quirky names, and that she could write really hot passages about dining out. She was fascinating, his mystery woman. And very, very intriguing. And—for now, at least—Cole wanted to keep her that way.

· Seven ·

AS HER TUESDAY NIGHT SHIFT DREW TO AN END,
Bree was doing what she always did about this time: evaluating the guys sitting alone in the bar and trying to figure out which one was worth the most. The main reason she'd sought a job at the Ambassador Bar was because it belonged to the most expensive hotel in town. Anyone who was staying here any time of year had to be banking some serious net worth. During Derby, when hotel prices all over town went through the roof, there was no question anyone staying here was worth buckets of cash.

And finding a man with buckets of cash was the reason Bree was here. Why else would a woman with an advanced degree in English spend the last six years performing manual labor?

Okay, so anyone with an English degree was probably used to doing manual labor. In fact, people with degrees in English were doubtless more employable than anyone else. There were tons of jobs you could get with an English degree, including—it went without saying—bartending. Bree had tried majoring in something that might enable her to make buckets of cash on her own—and meet rich men—but she didn't have a head for business or finance or any of those moneymaking professions. Numbers were just that to Bree's brain—numbers. As in, things to make her brain numb. She'd made straight Cs and Ds until she switched to an English major—a degree she'd earned with highest honors. (Not that that meant higher earning potential, alas.) So she'd had no choice but to conclude that her talents lay not in her mental skills, but in her social skills. In her ability to make friends, to chat amiably, to entertain, and to console. They were all qualities of a good bartender.

They were qualities of a good mistress, too.

Maybe "kept woman" wasn't the loftiest of ambitions, nor was it particularly PC, especially for someone who'd grown up in the post–I-Am-Woman-Hear-Me-Roar era. The women's movement sparked by her mother's generation had been about making sure all future daughters and grand-daughters grew up to have choices, right? About giving women the opportunity to be and do whatever they put their minds to being and doing. And what Bree had always wanted to be was well taken care of. What she'd wanted to do was find security. She'd had precious little of those things when she was a child. And now, with her mother going through what she was going through, care and security was even more important. Not just for Bree Calhoun, but for her mother, Rosie, too.

She pushed the thought away as she collected two martini glasses from the bar, one of which was smudged with dark red lipstick and sticky with the remnants of a Cosmopolitan. The woman drinking from it had left a few minutes ago with the owner of the other glass, a guest of the hotel Bree had spent her last two shifts cultivating for her own. Less than thirty minutes after joining him, the woman had left with him. Two full nights of flirting with the guy, and Bree had bupkus.

Oh, well, she thought. *Easy come, easy go.*

Except that it was never easy to find rich, single guys who were looking for a little arm candy. It was harder still to look like potential arm candy when you were sweating behind a bar in a gin-, Bourbon- and dark-crème-de-cocoa-stained wardrobe of baggy trousers, shirt, and necktie. The men Bree targeted never came, they only went. She was a red-hot mama twenty-six years in the making, and she hadn't even come close to trapping herself a tycoon. Sure, she'd dated some rich guys in the past, but she'd never been able to sustain a relationship with one for more than a couple of months. Certainly none had yet offered to put her up in a Fifth Avenue penthouse with unlimited credit at Tiffany's. Or even in a Cherokee Triangle loft with unlimited credit at Dolfinger's.

So that kind of sucked.

This wasn't how it was supposed to have turned out for her. By now, Bree was supposed to have met at least one of the richest men in the world, preferably two or three, and she was supposed to have dazzled them with her wits, her smile, and her boundless sex appeal. She was supposed to be living in a posh suite and spending her days shopping, brunching, and hobnobbing with other kept women. She was supposed to be like Holly Golightly, running around in opera gloves and tiara, cocktail glass in one hand, cigarette holder in the other, only without the too-pronounced clavicles because she would have actually *caught* some wealthy benefactor and been eating better. She was supposed to be living a life of leisure and being taken care of by a man who indulged her every whim, not struggling to make ends meet and worrying about what new disaster any given week would bring.

Grumble. Grumble. Grumble.

As she washed the lipstick-smudged glass, Bree's gaze drifted to the man sitting at the far end of the bar. He wasn't a bad-looking sort—and would look even better when the lights were out—and he didn't appear to be more than ten or fifteen years her senior, a definite bonus. She'd been reading *GQ* long enough to recognize his suit as a Brioni, one he had to have forked over four figures for, even if he bought off the rack postseason.

Not for the first time, she cursed the bar behind which she made her living, but this time, it was because she couldn't see what the guy had on his feet. Shoes, she had discovered a long time ago, told you everything you needed to know about a person. No matter how well dressed—or how badly dressed, for that matter—a man might be, it was his shoes you really had to pay attention to. Really rich people might scrimp in other areas of their lives, but never on shoes. Really rich men, especially, liked their footwear to be well made, comfortable, and stylish. Forget power suits. Power shoes were what Bree liked to see even more on any prospective Sugar Daddy.

She bet this guy was wearing wingtips of the gods.

He was, after all, sipping a post-dinner snifter of one of the most expensive ports on the menu. And he'd dined on the prime rib. And he'd paid for everything with his platinum American Express Card.

Best of all, he'd done all that *alone*.

What a shame, to be visiting a city like Louisville during Derby, when there was so much going on, and be all by yourself, with no one to enjoy the festivities with. A man in possession of a platinum card ought to be out on the town, having fun with someone, not sitting alone at the bar. Someone like . . . oh, Bree didn't know . . . *her*. She'd spoken with him on and off as she'd worked, had laughed at a joke he told her—even though she'd heard it before—and had responded with just the right amount of interest and perfectly gauged smile to his flirting. She'd made it as clear as she could without donning a hat that said, "*If You Have the Cash, I Have the Inclination.*" All she needed at this point was an invitation. And it didn't even have to be engraved.

Unfortunately, just as Bree was drying her hands on a linen towel, a woman approached her quarry and perched on a stool beside him. Thanks to his broad smile and the way he settled his hand on her shoulder, it was clear the two knew each other and that he'd been waiting for her. With another sigh of resignation, Bree decided to call it a night. Both with her shift—which had actually ended nearly a half hour ago—and her gold digging.

"She's a call girl."

The comment came from behind Bree and, surprisingly, it was in no way surprising. Rufus Detweiler, who had been working behind the bar when Bree started at the Ambassador, was as good at evaluating the customers as she was. But for every step up the social ladder she liked to place someone, Rufus was equally determined to take that person down a peg. She had no idea why he had a chip on his shoulder when it came to the upper class. But that chip was roughly the size of Gibraltar, and it wasn't going anywhere anytime soon.

Bree spun around to face him, thinking, as she always did about Rufus, that it was too bad he wasn't rich. Then again, a rich guy who looked like Rufus—tall, dark, and handsome didn't begin to cover it—wouldn't have to buy the affections of a woman. On the contrary, he could sell himself to the highest bidder, and walk away with even more gold filling his pockets.

"You don't want to mess with a guy who uses a call girl's services," he added. "That's a one-way ticket to blood work you don't want to have."

He'd leaned forward a little as he spoke, so that he could lower his voice. And also send a ripple of warm desire down Bree's spine. A most unwelcome ripple of warm desire, at that. Rufus was the last guy she should be longing for.

Not that she was longing for Rufus, she hastily reminded herself. Any other woman would respond the same way to a guy who towered over her and had rhapsodic brown eyes and silky dark hair that hung nearly to his shoulders and was swept back from a truly beautiful face by a careless hand. And who had shoulders broad enough to effortlessly hoist a keg, and hands skilled enough to perfectly coil a slender length of lemon peel, and forearms sculpted like an Adonis.

And a butt that begged for the cupping of a woman's hands, and legs long enough to cradle a woman's hips, and feet big enough to cause serious speculation about the size of his—

Ahem. Anyway, any other woman would respond the same way to Rufus that Bree did. It had nothing to do with any longings—and, more importantly, any feelings—she might have for the guy. She didn't have *any* feelings for the guy. Which was why she was able to treat him so cavalierly when she saw him at places like Fourth Street Live and he asked her to dance. Just because she still felt guilty about her behavior that night, it wasn't because she cared about Rufus or his feelings. It was just because she cared about, um, looking good. Yeah, that was it.

She crossed her arms over her midsection. "How do you know she's a call girl? Maybe she's his daughter."

Rufus looked past Bree, then met her gaze again and smiled. "Not likely. Not unless he's looking for a visit from social services. Check it out."

She turned again to see that the couple at the end of the bar were . . . *Ew.* It didn't take Emily Post to say that was way too much tongue for public consumption. *Jeez, people, get a room. Even if they do cost seven hundred bucks a night.*

"Okay, so she's not his daughter," Bree conceded, turning back to Rufus. "It still doesn't mean she's a call girl."

He cocked his head to one side. "Maybe. Maybe not. But as long as he's got someone to"—Rufus looked down the bar again, flinched a little at whatever he saw, and looked back at Bree—"do *that* for him, it does make your chances of bagging him pretty slim."

Yeah, yeah, yeah.

"C'mon," he said. "Shift's over. Our relief is here. Tips were substantial for a Tuesday night—gotta love this time of year. Best of all, I invented a new drink."

She grinned. Rufus was notorious for creating new drinks and naming them after great works of literature. "What's this one called?" she asked.

"Tequila Mockingbird."

She chuckled at that. "What's it like?"

He grinned back. "Sin. Because it's a sin—"

"Tequila Mockingbird," she finished with him, paraphrasing a passage from the book.

He listed the ingredients. "A little Cuervo, a little Cointreau, a little passion fruit liqueur. And a little splash of ginger ale to make it sing. Let me whip us up a couple, and we can head for a booth in the back. The band tonight is supposed to be an *ex*cellent jazz combo. Weird name, though. I mean, who'd name a band Smuth?"

She shook her head. "Thanks for the offer," she said. "But the drink sounds like it has too much mocking and too little bird for me."

"Then lemme buy you a beer and we can head for a booth in the back."

She shook her head again. "You're a good guy, Rufus, and truly, thanks, but I think I'm going to head home. I'm beat. And Lulu's staying with me for a couple weeks and has been home alone all night. I'm not being a good hostess."

"Call Lulu and tell her to meet us at Deke's. You'll be almost home, Lulu won't be alone, we'll still hear some great music, the planet will be swiftly tilting on its axis, and all will be right in the universe."

Bree sighed, and patted his arm gently. But that only made her realize that his upper arms were as solid and exquisitely formed as his forearms, something that generated another one of those ripples of warm desire. This one, though, shimmied through her entire body and pooled in her midsection like a puddle of steaming need. Immediately, she dropped her hand back to her side. But her fingertips continued to tingle, as if whatever strange thing was arcing between them couldn't be severed just by physically separating from him.

"Rufus, you're trying too hard," she told him, her voice softer than she had meant it to be, making her sound as if she didn't mean what she was saying. "Like I've said a million times, unless you've got the cash—"

"I'm not interested," he finished for her. He squeezed his eyes shut tight and quickly corrected himself, "I mean, *you're* not interested. Because, me, Bree . . ."

He didn't finish the sentence. He didn't need to. Rufus had made it no secret over the two years they'd been working together that he was *very* interested in Bree, an interest she'd done her best to keep at bay. And not just because Rufus's net worth on any given day could fit into the tip jar, either. But because there were times when Bree found herself not wanting to keep his interest at bay. And, even worse, not caring what his net worth on any given day might be.

It really was as easy to love a rich man as a poor one, she knew. Provided one met a rich man who was a lot like Rufus.

He held her gaze for a moment, his dark eyes earnest. "Maybe the problem isn't that I'm trying too hard," he said quietly. "Maybe it's that I'm not trying hard enough."

Bree ignored the shudder of pleasure that wound through her at the frankly offered declaration. "Rufus . . ." she began, stringing his name out across several time zones. But all she added was, "I gotta go." She scooped up her purse from where she'd stowed it beneath the bar, started to extend a hand to pat his shoulder again, then remembered what had happened the last time she did that and drew her hand back. "You're a good guy, Rufus," she said again. "But I really do have to go."

"You need me to walk you to your car?"

She shook her head. "Not tonight, thanks. I didn't have to park in the garage. I found a place on the street."

"Next time then," he told her.

She nodded. "Next time."

RUFUS DETWEILER WATCHED AS BREE CALHOUN—THE light of his life and the woman he loved, the cream in his coffee and the jam on his bread, the Mc in his McMuffin and the *oo oo* in his Froot Loops, the . . . the . . .

Dang. He was getting hungry.

Anyway, he watched as Bree Calhoun, his reason for living, walked out of the bar without him. Again.

Of course it wasn't that she was always walking out of the bar without him. Again. A couple of nights a week, when she didn't have anyone else to walk out to her car with, she was driving out of the parking garage without him. Again. And there had been a handful of times when he'd walked her as far as the hotel lobby, and then she'd strode out the front entrance without him. Again. And on one especially memorable night, when Lulu was supposed to have picked her up but had to work late, Rufus had driven Bree all the way to the intersection of Bardstown Road where she lived, and she'd exited the car without him.

Ah, good times. Good times.

You're a good guy, Rufus.

How many times had she said that to him over the past twenty-seven months, eight days, nine hours, thirty-seven minutes and—he glanced at his watch—forty-two seconds since he met her? After working together for more than two years, he knew Bree was the woman he wanted to spend the rest of his life with, and she thought he was—he bit back a grimace—*a good guy.*

What the hell was wrong with him that she thought he was a—he swallowed his revulsion—*good guy*?

And it wasn't like Bree was one of those weird women who went for the dark and dangerous type. On the contrary, the woman craved security and stability more than any human being Rufus had ever met. He knew her well enough to realize that was the reason—and not because she was shallow and only craved creature comforts—why she was so dead set on bagging herself a rich guy. Of course, it helped that she had spelled that out to him in no uncertain terms the first time he asked her out. *Bree,* he'd said, *you want to go to a movie sometime? Maybe have dinner and a beer afterward?* To which she had pointedly replied, *Rufus, you're a good guy, so I'll tell you this up front. Unless the reason you're working here is to commune with the common man after a long day of counting your money, I won't go out with you. Any guy I go out with has to have reeking piles of filthy lucre at home. The currency for my affections is currency. The only thing tender I want out of a man is legal tender. Unless you've got the cash, I'm not interested.*

Never in his life had he heard a woman use so many different words for money in one breath. Rich guys, not good guys, that was what Bree Calhoun wanted. Correction: rich guy. She'd settle for one. Provided he had seven figures at his disposal. And although Rufus Detweiler might be many things—a hard worker, a man of his word, a literary mixologist, a reasonably gifted musician, an art lover provided the art in question wasn't too abstract—*rich guy* had never been, nor would ever be, listed on his curriculum vitae.

He swiped a cloth over one last bottle ring on the bar before tossing in the towel—literally, if not figuratively, since he'd never give up on Bree—then called out a halfhearted farewell to the bartender who had relieved him. Then he exited the bar on the side where sat the most recent object of Bree's financial affections. The young woman with him had disappeared, he noticed. Probably needed to do some major lipstick repair after that . . . that . . . gak . . . that exchange of bodily fluids she'd performed with the guy.

The moment Rufus slipped under the bar and appeared on the other side, however, the guy said, "Excuse me. Can I ask you a question?"

Rufus shrugged. "Sure."

"The girl you were working with tonight. Bree?"

Immediately wary, Rufus replied, "Yeah?"

"Is she single?"

Reluctantly, he nodded. "She is."

"Does she have a boyfriend?"

Even more reluctantly, Rufus shook his head. "She does not." He didn't bother to add that the price of her affections was steep, however. He was confident this guy could afford her. He just didn't deserve her.

The guy smiled in a bland, benign, insurance-salesman kind of way. "Just wanted to be sure. I'm going to be in town for another week, and she and I hit it off pretty well, but I wasn't sure if that was because she might be interested or if she was just doing her job, making nice with the customers."

Rufus grinned now and waved a hand airily before himself in a theatrical *pshaw* kind of way. Then he said, "Pshaw. It was definitely because she was interested. Bree's genuinely interested in every customer who sits down at this bar. She's doing so much better since they doubled up on her medication. She's even stopped bringing her gun to work every day."

The guy's smile fell. "She brings a gun to work?"

"Only sometimes."

"Was she, uh . . . packing today?"

"I doubt it. When she's carrying, you can usually see the bulge in her pocket." He looked right and then left, then lowered his voice to a stage whisper. "But, look, don't say anything to the manager, all right? She's in a temporary release program, and I'd hate to see her go back to doing hard time." He pretended to waffle over whether he should say more, then added, "Not to mention, she has a nasty temper when she forgets to take her meds. I mean, if she found out someone had reported her . . ." He did the right-left look again. "Well, let's just say I sure wouldn't want her gunning for me." He smiled. "No pun intended."

The guy nodded enthusiastically. "Uh, right. I won't say a word."

Rufus patted his arm comfortingly. "You're a good guy."

As he made his way to the exit, Rufus wondered how much longer he was going to be able to get away with this . . . this . . . Okay, this deliberate demolition of Bree's efforts to bag herself a rich man. She had to be losing sleep at night, puzzling over why a woman as beautiful, funny, smart, and charming as she was had so much trouble landing what had, over the years, been dozens of potential Sugar Daddies here at the bar. If she ever found out it was because

Rufus had purposely and with malice aforethought sabo-
taged every viable liaison by putting the right—or rather,
wrong—idea into the potential Sugar Daddy's head about
her, she'd kill him. Purposely and with malice aforethought.
Probably with her bare hands. Someday, he thought, that
was going to happen.

But not today.

Today, Rufus had lived to crush Bree's visions of Sugar
Daddy Fairies again. Next time, however . . .

Well. He'd just do like Scarlett and think about that tomorrow.

Oh, man, that gave him an idea for another drink. Gone
with the Seabreeze. He'd make sure to think about that tomorrow, too. In between thoughts about Bree Calhoun. And
thoughts about how he could get her to realize that what a
man carried in his pockets was of no consequence compared
to what a man carried in his heart.

·Eight·

ONE WOULD HAVE THOUGHT THAT BY THE TIME COLE found himself surrounded by a bevy of admirers again on Wednesday night—when all he wanted was to enjoy a meal alone—he would have learned that the only way to do that was to go to the grocery store, buy provisions, and cook something for himself in the privacy of his rented home. But the only thing Cole hated more than not being able to enjoy a meal in peace was having to prepare that meal himself. At home in Temecula, he employed a full-time housekeeper who also cooked his dinner before she left at day's end. On those days he was working at the ranch, she also left something in the fridge for his breakfast and lunch the following day. Whenever he was away from the ranch, he ate out.

He had been delighted to discover that Louisville, when it came to restaurants, was a major buried treasure. Susannah had visited the city on a number of occasions and listed enough recommendations that Cole could eat someplace different every morning, noon, and night and still have places left over for after-hours. What she hadn't warned him about was how crowded many of them would be during the week this time of year. Nor had she cautioned him about the plethora of horse-crazy—and trainer-crazier—fans he would encounter.

He told himself he shouldn't be surprised. He'd also discovered that the two weeks prior to the Derby in Louisville were a veritable mini Mardi Gras of goings-on. But the festivities, as delightful—if sometimes odd—as they were, often hindered Cole's ability to just read the daily racing forms and newspaper, which was what he generally liked to do when he ate alone.

He also liked eating when he ate alone. As in, not being hassled by fans as he shoveled food into his mouth. That was why he'd taken to eating at bars the last couple of nights—literally. At the bar part of the bar, an act of clearly intended I-want-to-be-alone behavior that should have dissuaded anyone from coming up with the request to join him. Especially since he'd been trying for the past couple of nights to wedge himself in on a solitary seat between two men.

And *that* was how he came to find himself seated at the bar in the utterly gorgeous Ambassador Hotel in downtown Louisville—number four on Susannah's "List of Places You Have GOT to Visit While in Town." Granted, Susannah had suggested it as a nightspot. All the more reason, Cole had concluded, to have dinner there. If it was a nightspot, it shouldn't be too busy at the dinner hour, right?

Wrong.

The place had been packed when he entered. But the majority of patrons had been men in business suits, clearly here enjoying an after-work libation before heading home—or out to dinner, or wherever men who had normal nine-to-five jobs went after work. Cole's job was one that had irregular hours that generally ran from sunup to sundown, including weekends. But it had other perks, not the least of which was

working only the hours one wanted to work—provided one
wanted to work from sunup to sundown, including weekends.

Anyway, he'd spied one of those solitary places at the bar
between two men, so he had made his way there and wedged
himself in, trying to be as unobtrusive as possible, and suc-
ceeding for all of three minutes.

That was how long it had taken for a pair of attractive
young women in business suits to move behind him and pretend they were trying to get the bartender's attention, when
really, what they were doing was leaning into Cole and saying, "Oh, excuse me," a lot. He might have given them the
benefit of the doubt if it hadn't been for the fact that every
"Oh, excuse me" had been followed by a sultry giggle and
even sultrier look, coupled with the fact that the first woman
ordered a Sex on the Beach to drink, and the second ordered
a Screaming Orgasm. Cole had been tempted to order a
Could You at Least *Try* to Be Subtle in retaliation, but he was
pretty sure a drink with that name hadn't been invented yet.

He was mentally reviewing Susannah's list of recommendations, trying to recall if there was an establishment on it
called No Dames Allowed when a movement at the other
end of the crowded bar caught his eye. It was the same
movement that had caught his eye two nights before, at a different downtown bar. A movement of russet-colored curls
that drew his eye faster than a yearling with champion
bloodlines.

Damn. It was Craggedy Ann again. Either she was a real
barfly, or Cole Early was the luckiest son of a bitch on the
planet. And considering the way his life had been going the
last several years—Sex on the Beaches and Screaming Orgasms notwithstanding—he was going to have to go for the
latter.

He stood and turned to the two giggling women behind
him. "Ladies," he said, "take my seat, please." Then, without
awaiting a response, he started to make his way toward the
other side of the bar.

Craggedy didn't see him right off. She was too busy talking to the bartender working that stretch of the bar, a woman with long black hair who had her back to Cole. She was dressed in jeans again, coupled with yet another T-shirt, this one a beige V-neck. Since there were no empty seats at this end of the bar, either, she had to lean forward to be heard, between two men who chatted with each other, oblivious to her presence. Probably because her "Excuse me" had been genuine, and she hadn't ordered any drinks with the words *sex* or *orgasm* in them. As Cole drew nearer, he realized Craggedy must know the bartender, because they were talking way longer than it took to simply order a drink, and Craggedy was nodding and smiling at something the woman said in a way that indicated the two were friendly.

And then, suddenly, she laughed at something the woman said, a full-bodied, genuinely delighted laugh that carried all the way across the bar and ended with her smiling in a way that momentarily stopped Cole in his tracks. Because it was the most uninhibited smile—and the most joyful laugh—he'd ever seen or heard from a woman. He remembered a song lyric from a while back about drinking whatever the waitress brought and always feeling full. That was what Craggedy's laughter reminded him of. Of someone who, no matter what life served up, would have a voracious appetite for it and relish the flavor regardless of what it was, because who knew when the feast would come to an end?

He wondered if she was that uninhibited in all her pursuits.

Doubtful, he told himself as he began to inch his way toward her again, remembering the way she'd stiffened up when he touched her at the realty office. He'd named her Craggedy Ann for a reason, he reminded himself. Because she'd been so damned, well, craggedy. Evidently, it was only with her friends she felt so liberated. With him—hell, probably with most men, considering the appalling lack of feminine wiles the woman seemed to have—she'd been as buttoned up, figuratively, anyway, as a Victorian.

Damn. Where was a Sex on the Beach or Screaming Orgasm when you needed one?

As if he'd murmured the question aloud, her head snapped to the right and her gaze met Cole's, her blue eyes flashing when she recognized him, with the same derision she'd shown Friday. Oh, yeah. She was definitely *not* the fun-loving, spontaneous, outgoing type, at least when it came to him. Nevertheless, when her gaze locked with his, for one strange, almost surreal moment, he felt as if everyone and everything else in the room evaporated, shifting into a weird, fuzzy haze that encircled the two of them and arced between them, connecting them in a way that was way too New Agey and chick flicky for his comfort. Then the moment was gone, and the voices of the other bar patrons were filling his ears again, and someone he'd never met before was laying a hand on his forearm and calling him by name and asking him what Silk Purse's current odds were. And Craggedy Ann, he couldn't help noting, was looking at him like an ill-treated foal who wanted to run from its abusive handler.

Oh, hell. She was going to bolt, and then he would have missed another chance to talk to her. Though why he'd want to talk to a woman who had so far looked at him either with dread or fear, he had no idea. All he knew in that moment was that he needed to talk to her.

"Wait!" he called out before he even realized he'd intended to speak.

But Craggedy Ann ducked behind the slender bartender working the bar, who in turn spun around to see what Craggedy was hiding from. When she saw Cole coming toward them, her eyes widened in panic. For all of two seconds. Then she began to look at him with an expression that troubled him even more than the openly sexual looks he'd been fielding from groupies for days. Because the only thing scarier than a sexually predatory woman was a financially predatory one. And this chick, whoever she was, had "Gimme" written all over her.

Not that there weren't a lot of men out there who would have probably been glad to provide for her. She was a beautiful woman, her black hair offset by clear aquamarine eyes and an Angelina Jolie mouth, all of it arranged beautifully atop some more than decent curves that even the mannish white shirt, black trousers, and splashy necktie couldn't diminish. But she wasn't his type. His type was . . .

Well, normally, he would have said his type was any woman whose body had produced estrogen at some point in her life. At the moment, however, he was thinking in more specific terms. Specifically, any woman whose body had produced estrogen at some point in her life and *didn't* look at him as if he were a big ol' ATM. Even if he had, in the past, dated more than one woman he knew was interested in him primarily for one thing, and that was the fact that there were so many numbers before the decimal point in his annual income. That hadn't mattered to him, though, because he'd only been dating those women for one thing, too, and although it had involved numbers—and letters, too—they had nothing to do with the women's earning potential and everything to do with a label inside an article of lingerie they wore.

Craggedy's friend Goldie Digger, he had to admit, would actually fill that requirement—and that article of lingerie—nicely. In spite of that, his gaze was still drawn to her friend. Who, he noted with some regret, wouldn't fill much of anything.

In spite of Craggedy Ann's obvious attempt to hide from him, Cole moved forward again, this time ignoring all the greetings, hands, and questions until he could circle the bar and see her pretending to study a drink menu with the same sort of fascination a high school freshman might show for the periodic table. Smiling, he covered what little distance remained between them until he was standing right behind her.

"Hello, again," he said, ducking his head close to her ear to ensure she heard the words. And also to see if she still smelled like patchouli. Which she did. Which made him feel even luckier for some reason.

She spun around to look at him, her eyes even bigger and more panicked than before, her mouth forming a perfect surprised *O*.

"Hello yourself."

But it wasn't Craggedy Ann who spoke. It was her friend, Goldie Digger.

"Don't I know you from somewhere?" Goldie continued. "Didn't we meet at the Cannes Film Festival last year? Or George Clooney's place in Malibu? Or was it that fundraiser at Bill Gates's compound?"

Wow, Cole thought. If she shoveled it any higher, they were all going to be bagged up as Miracle-Gro.

"Sorry," he said over his shoulder to Goldie. "Never been any of those places." To Craggedy, he quickly added, "We didn't get a chance to introduce ourselves when we bumped into each other Friday. I'm—"

"Cole Early," Goldie said, sounding a little frazzled. "That's the name I was trying to remember."

When Cole didn't acknowledge her remark, she leaned across the bar as far as she could, and damned if she didn't manage to insinuate herself between him and Craggedy. Her feet had to be dangling above the floor on the other side to have managed the feat, but that didn't deter her from wriggling closer still. Even more annoying, Craggedy did nothing to stop her friend from coming between them. In fact, Craggedy inched a few steps to her left, away from him, stopping only when the presence of another body at the bar prevented her from going any farther.

But she didn't stop looking at him, Cole noticed. Unfortunately, she didn't stop looking panicky, either.

"I know we've met somewhere," Goldie hurried on, tossing her hair in a way that probably would have been provocative if she hadn't been hanging over a bar like a limp sausage.

Cole looked at her face long enough to take in the big eyes and full mouth and cheekbones sharp enough to hew logs. Definitely a beautiful woman. And definitely not one he wanted to get to know better. Now the woman *on the other side* of her . . .

Well, it wasn't that he wanted to get to know Craggedy better, either, he hastily amended. It was just that she was a familiar face in unfamiliar surroundings, and Cole was tired of feeling uncomfortable. In situations like this, comfort was found with those who offended you least. Craggedy, by virtue of her appearance at the realty office Friday, was the first friend he'd made in this town. Hell, considering how he'd been juggling his days between the farm in Shelbyville, meetings at Churchill Downs, and a seemingly endless list of Derby-related functions, she was the only friend he'd made in this town.

"I'm Sabrina Calhoun," the woman he wasn't interested in getting to know better went on. "Bree to my friends. So you should definitely call me Bree. In fact, I'm sure you've already called me that. Probably from the other side of the bed." She threw him a dazzling smile that said, "*Just kidding . . . but we could change that right now.*"

"Nice to meet you, Sabrina," he lied, deliberately using the name she'd told him not to. "Who's your friend?"

She seemed stumped for a minute, as if she couldn't believe Cole was expressing an interest in someone other than herself. She was about to speak again, but a customer who'd been trying to flag her down since she'd started talking to Cole called out impatiently and quite adamantly, "Oh, *miss*. I'd like to place an order, please. If you can fit me into your busy social calendar."

For a moment, Cole thought she was going to turn on the guy and tell him that no, as a matter of fact, she didn't have room on her busy social calendar for him. Instead, with a rueful smile for Cole and a surprising amount of grace, she squirmed back down to the floor to perform the job she was hired to do. Something that left Cole free and clear—or, to put it in horseracing terms, fast and loose—to talk to Craggedy.

Funny thing, though. When he turned to look at her again, he couldn't think of a single interesting thing to say.

LULU COULD NOT BELIEVE HER BAD LUCK. BEING IN the same place, at the same time, as Cole Early, not once, not twice, but *three* times in less than a week. Okay, so granted, the first time was a complete accident, and the second time she and Bree had gone out specifically to look for him. And okay, so it was a safe bet that the guy would eventually show up at the Ambassador Bar, since it was the sort of place tourists always flocked to, and Lulu spent almost as many nights here as Bree did when she was waiting for her friend to finish her shift. Still. It showed a remarkable abundance of bad karma on Lulu's part to encounter him again, and she couldn't remember doing anything lately that would warrant that.

On the contrary, she was always careful to do whatever she could to bank up *good* karma. She always held the elevator door for whoever was running to catch it. She always dropped her spare pennies in the leave-a-penny tray at the Circle K. She always tipped 20 percent, even when the service was only worth eight. She always stopped to provide a break in the traffic to let people turn left in front of her. Anything she could do to ward off things like . . . like . . .

Well, like the Cole Earlys of the world.

She reminded herself how arrogant and obnoxious he'd been at Eddie's office on Friday, and was doing a pretty good job of remembering that when he moved in close enough for her to inhale the scent of him. He didn't smell like any man she'd ever met, an eclectic—and not altogether unpleasant—mix of crisp man cologne, sweaty horse, and track dirt. And sunshine, she noted. He had that sort of full-day-outdoors-in-the-sun fragrance about him. The kind that made her reminisce about beaches and tropics and peel-and-eat shrimp with an ice-cold beer. He smelled like both

indoors and out. Like work and play. Like business and pleasure. She liked it.

No! She didn't like it! she immediately contradicted herself. Not only was Cole Early *not* the kind of guy she wanted
to get involved with—flashy and self-important and in town
only temporarily—Bree had dibs.

Not that Lulu thought for a moment that a man—any
man, but especially one like Cole Early—would even give
her the time of day when he could give that, and more, to
Bree. But Bree was on the clock 'til her relief bartender
showed up, and that was still a half-hour away. This was
Bree's chance to finally meet a guy who could give her what
she'd always wanted—the shallow, mind-numbing, thoroughly demoralizing existence of a woman who received
glittering gems and cases of champagne and carte blanche
on Fifth Avenue in exchange for mind-blowing sex with a
guy who smelled of business and pleasure and was probably
hung like the stallions he trained. No way would Lulu ever
trade her safe, quiet, no-glittering-gems-or-stallions-for-me-
thankyouverymuch life for that. Gosh, that would just suck.

Somewhere in the BFF Handbook there had to be a provi-
sion for ensuring that, if a situation arose that offered an opportunity for you to make your Best Friend Forever's dream
come true, then you had a sacred charge to do whatever you
could to make it happen. Which meant chatting up Cole
Early until Bree was free to do that herself, but not being so
interesting that she compromised Bree's chances to catch
him. Lulu was confident that if the situation were reversed,
if it were Bree in the position of making Lulu's dream come
true—whatever that dream was, and someday, Lulu was going to have to figure that out—then Bree would do whatever
she could to ensure it happened.

So Lulu was honor-bound to keep Cole Early here until
Bree finished her shift and could ensnare him with her feminine wiles—which, judging by past experiences, would take
Bree about a minute and a half. And Lulu was also honor-
bound to make sure she didn't do or say anything that would

make her look more attractive than Bree. Hah. Like that would be a problem. Even if Bree didn't have a million times more sex appeal than Lulu, Lulu wasn't interested in doing the feminine wiles thing on Cole Early anyway. Not that she had a feminine wile with her at the moment anyway. Or, you know, ever. She still told herself to watch what she said and how she said it.

Her resolve faltered a little, though, when someone behind Cole jostled him and sent him careening forward, right into Lulu. He didn't bump into her as hard as he had in Eddie's office, just pressed against her in a way that made her aware of him from her breasts to her hips, thanks to the way his body came into contact with hers in both of those places, long enough to make her wonder what it would be like to come into contact with both of those places on him without the burden of . . . oh, she didn't know . . . clothes.

No! She didn't wonder that at all! That was for Bree to wonder about!

"Sorry," he murmured in a voice that was once again bereft of apology. And when her eyes met his . . .

Oh, damn. What had she been thinking about? For some reason, she suddenly couldn't remember . . .

He took a step backward when he could, something that allowed her to think again. Unfortunately, mostly what she was thinking was that she wanted him to bump into her again. Only this time, without the inconvenience of . . . oh, she didn't know . . . being vertical.

No! She didn't want to be horizontal with Cole Early! Bree did! Lulu actually much preferred a different position, one that required the man to be standing behind her while she . . .

Well, this probably wasn't the best place to be thinking about that right now.

"So who *is* the friend?" Cole asked, bringing Lulu back to the matter at hand—and, coincidentally, hands played a big role in her favorite position, which was . . .

Where was she? Oh, right. Remembering that Bree hadn't

had a chance to introduce her and Cole. Which was just as
well, since Bree would have introduced Lulu with her real
name, and something about Cole Early knowing her name
didn't sit well with Lulu just then. Once a person had your
name, they had ways of finding out other things about you,
and she just didn't want a man like Cole having that kind of
access to her. So maybe, since she wasn't going to have anything more to do with him after tonight, she'd just give him a
phony name. An unattractive phony name at that. Anything
to make Bree look better and put her at the center of attention.

Hah. Like Bree wouldn't be the center, right, left, front,
and back of attention the minute she walked into any room.

"I'm, um . . ." She scrambled to think of an unattractive
name, but all she could come up with was her aunt Hortense,
who lived in Waddy and would likely smack Lulu upside the
head if she ever found out Lulu had used her name because
she thought it was, um, unattractive.

"Hortense," she said anyway.

Cole's eyebrows shot up at that. "Hort . . . ah, Horten . . .
uh, Hortense?"

"Hortense," Lulu repeated. "It's an old family name." She
bit back a smile. He was trying so hard to be polite about the
fact that he thought her name was hideous. That was actually
kind of adorable.

No! Not adorable! she told herself. Rude. How rude to not
cover that immediately. Miss Manners would be appalled.

"Hortense Waddy," she said further.

He looked flummoxed for a moment, then stuck out his
hand. "Nice to meet you, Hort . . . ah . . . tense Wad . . . dy.
I'm Cole Early."

Lulu took his hand, thinking she'd give it a good, hard,
unladylike shake. Instead, she melted a little at the way his
fingers closed so confidently over hers and held them. Not
shaking. Not moving at all. Just holding. And feeling really
good.

No, not good! Intrusive. Yeah, that was it.

"It's nice to meet you, too . . . ah . . ." Strangely, Lulu realized she was having trouble saying his name aloud, too. Which was weird. Hey, it wasn't like he had a name like Hortense Waddy or something.

"Cole," he said, helping her.

"Cole," she finally managed to get out.

"Can I get you something to drink?" he asked.

Before Lulu could think about it, she said, "A beer. They have Bass on draft here."

Cole lifted a hand to signal . . . Oh, God, Bree, who looked at Lulu like she'd just betrayed the most sacred trust in the BFF Handbook. In spite of that, she returned to their end of the bar. "A Bass Ale for the lady," he said. "And for me . . ." He hesitated for a moment, then smiled. "I'll have a Bass, too," he finally told Bree.

Lulu did her best to convey through her expression that she was standing at the bar drinking with Cole Early for Bree's benefit. Her friend must have gotten the message, because she smiled in relief and said, "Coming right up, Mr. Early," and turned to pull a couple of drafts. When they were sitting on the bar, tall and frosty, Cole told her to start a tab and then handed one to Lulu.

"What should we drink to?" he asked.

Lulu started to say, *To panties and silver platters,* but stopped herself in time. Instead, she said, "To your horse winning the Derby."

He smiled in response, and she thought it was because he liked the toast. Then he asked, "Do you know the name of the horse I'm running in the Derby?"

Lulu opened her mouth to tell him what it was, then realized she couldn't remember. "Um, no," she said. "I'm afraid I don't." But that was good, right? she asked herself. The fact that she had no idea who his entry in the race was would just make her look like an idiot, something that would only serve to make Bree look better, since Bree had learned everything she could about Cole since his arrival and would surely make that clear once her shift ended and she joined them.

"Do you know anything about me at all?" he asked.

She shook her head. "Not really. I mean, I've seen you on the news and everything, but, uh . . ." Might as well be honest, she told herself. "I haven't really paid attention."

Oh, right. Like that was honest. She'd heard every word he uttered when she'd seen him on the late news nearly every night since his arrival. But only because Bree turned the volume up so loud. And after the news went off, Lulu had replayed every moment of their encounter at Eddie's office. And then she'd been offended all over again by his behavior.

Really. She had. She *had*.

Instead of being put off by her admission, Cole smiled even more broadly. "Silk Purse," he said.

She narrowed her eyes in confusion. "I'm sorry?"

"That's the name of the horse I have running in the Derby. Silk Purse."

"Oooooh," she said. "Gotcha. Well, I promise to bet on him."

"Her."

"What?"

"Her," he repeated. "Silk Purse is a filly."

"Oh, well, I'll definitely bet on her," Lulu said. "I always root for the women."

Although she wouldn't have thought it possible, his smile grew even more, something she found confusing in light of his next question. "You know absolutely nothing about Thoroughbred racing, do you?"

"Um, no. Not really. I love to watch the Derby every year—I keep the TV tuned to local coverage all day, in fact. I like to see the hats and find out which celebrities are in town. And I go to a lot of the Festival events the two weeks before the race. But no, I guess I'm not what you'd call a race fan. I don't really follow the horse statistics or anything like that."

She would have thought that fact would have put him off, but he seemed almost delighted that she had no interest in what had to be more than just a job to him.

He opened his mouth to ask her something else, but a woman suddenly appeared behind him, tapped him on the shoulder, and asked if she could have his autograph. With an apologetic look for Lulu, he turned and greeted the woman, then dashed his name across the cocktail napkin she thrust at him. She tried to engage him in conversation, but he excused himself, politely pointing out to her that he was already having a conversation with someone else. The woman looked past him at Lulu, clearly seeing her for the first time, and frowned. Then she looked puzzled, obviously surprised to find someone of Cole's caliber mingling with someone of Lulu's mediocrity. Lulu lifted a hand and wiggled her fingers in greeting, and somehow refrained from saying, *Nanny-nanny-boo-boo.*

Cole turned back to her with another apologetic smile, reached for the beer he had set on the bar, and opened his mouth to say something . . . only to be prevented by a different woman who suddenly appeared behind him, asking for his autograph again. The look he gave Lulu this time was one of irritation, though the feeling was clearly not meant for her. Again, he spoke warmly to the woman as he scrawled his name on what appeared to be a bank deposit slip, fielded another attempt to compromise his time, and turned to Lulu again. Unfortunately, the two autograph requests triggered a half-dozen more, and for the next five minutes, Lulu watched while Cole interacted with his fan base.

It was a fascinating thing to observe. Lulu had never had a brush with celebrity before. The closest she'd come was having a classmate in third grade named Ronald McDonald. She knew Louisville was overrun by famous people this time of year—at least, when it got closer to Derby Day—but she'd never met any. Friends of hers who worked with the public or who lived close enough to the Barnstable Brown house to ogle the guests at their annual Derby Eve party had caught several glimpses of—or had even talked to—movie stars, athletes, politicians, and such. Bree herself, working at the Ambassador, had waited on dozens of famous people in her day. But Lulu had only heard about such encounters second-hand. She'd never seen the cult of celebrity in action. And now that she did . . .

Well, actually, it looked kind of annoying. It was like all the people coming up to Cole felt perfectly comfortable interrupting a man's evening out just to get him to write something illegible on a piece of paper they'd probably go home and put in a drawer and forget about. Not one of the people who approached him acknowledged Lulu in any way, even though they'd all had to interrupt his attempt at conversation with her and clearly knew he was talking to someone, otherwise they wouldn't have had to preface their demand on his time with "Excuse me, but . . ." When she was halfway finished with her beer, he'd barely had two sips of his. No sooner did he turn around to say something to her than did someone else come up to him and want something.

She was suddenly grateful for the anonymity that art brought with it. Certainly a lot of artists were famous, and many of them actively cultivated their fame. But there were far more—like Lulu—who enjoyed working in their studios, away from the masses, sending their art out for the world to enjoy without having a recognizable face attached to it. Lulu didn't even put her photograph on her website alongside her very brief bio, because she wanted the art, not the artist, to grab the attention.

Yep, there was no chance Pufferfish Girl would ever appear again as long as Lulu performed the job that she performed. And she fully intended to keep it that way.

Cole was still signing autographs—and still hadn't had more than a few sips of his beer—when Bree joined them fifteen minutes later. While Cole was still preoccupied with a particularly insistent young woman, Lulu leaned close and told her friend about the phony name she'd given him, both of them giggling when Bree warned that Aunt Hortense better not get wind of it. Lulu outlined the rest of her plan, too—to make herself look as undesirable as possible in an effort to boost Bree's already abundant charms—so that by the time Cole finally, finally had a long enough break in his renown to catch a breath, the two women were gazing at him innocently, as if neither had been blinded by the sheer wattage of his fame.

He exhaled a long, exhausted sigh, smiled weakly at the two women, then reached for his beer and took a long, leisurely quaff. Then he grimaced. "God, it's warm. I hate warm beer."

"Let me buy you another one," Bree offered magnanimously. Then added, "Somewhere else."

Cole glanced first at Bree, then back at Lulu. And then he grinned. "I have a better idea, Hort . . . ah, Hortense and Bree," he said, only stumbling over her phony name a little bit this time. "Why don't you let *me* buy *you* ladies a drink somewhere else. And then you local girls can tell me all the things I should do while I'm visiting your hometown."

· Nine ·

IF SHE LIVED TO BE A HUNDRED AND FIFTY, LULU would never be able to figure out how she came to be sitting at a table not far from the jellyfish in Felt with her best friend since childhood and the Bad Boy of the Thoroughbred Set.

Just how did one get to be the Bad Boy of the Thoroughbred Set, anyway? she wondered as she reached for the club soda she'd begun drinking when Bree and Cole ordered round number four. Probably, she thought further, she didn't want to know. Because even if she didn't know how a man came by such a distinction, she'd witnessed what it meant to assume it, not the least of which was signing lots of autographs for lots of women, some of whom seemed to lose control of both their spines and their clothing whenever they came within autograph distance of the Bad Boy of the Thoroughbred Set. Lulu knew that because a couple of them had come up to their table at Felt to ask for autographs, and each of them had had to lean forward *waaaaaay* more than was actually necessary when she handed Cole pen and paper, and her dress somehow slipped right off her shoulders. And even though Lulu had never earned less than a B minus in science, she couldn't think of a single law of physics that would explain a phenomenon like that.

"Let's see," Bree was saying now, in response to Cole's question about the must-see Derby events happening while he was in town, "there's the balloon race, the steamboat race, the bed race, the rat race, the wine race—"

"Bed race?" Cole repeated. "Rat race? Wine race?"

Bree nodded. "The Run for the Rosé. I'm doing that one myself. All the local restaurants enter someone from their waitstaff to race with glasses of wine. I'll be representing the Ambassador Bar. The rat race is the Run for the Rodents, and the prize is a loving cup full of Froot Loops. With the Great Bed Race—which used to be called Bedlam in the Streets and was actually *in* the street, but now they're at the fairgrounds—you have teams from local businesses that decorate beds and race them." Bree slung an arm around Lulu's shoulder. "Back in the day, Hortense and I were on the winning team for the copy shop where we worked when we were in high school."

Cole smiled, and just like that, Lulu was ready to skim off her panties and do the whole silver platter thing again.

"And then there's the parties," Bree added. "You've got everything from the Barnstable Brown affair to the Derby Bash, which is great fun and raises money for the Fairness Campaign. Hortense and I go every year. You can come with us." Before he had a chance to decline, she hurried on, "Of course, I'm betting you already have an invite to the Barnstable Brown affair."

He nodded. "Yeah, I do, actually. But I wasn't planning on attending."

"Oh, God, yes, you *have* to attend," Bree exclaimed. "It's *the* party to be seen at. Everyone wants to go to that, but even if you can afford the tickets—and even before the scalpers get a hold of them, they're hundreds of dollars—they're impossible to get. You need a date?" she inserted with what sounded like almost genuine carelessness.

"Wait a minute. I have to *pay* to go to a party I'm *invited* to?"

"All the big Derby parties are fundraisers," Lulu told him.

Bree nodded. "The Barnstable Brown party raises money for diabetes research. The Mint Jubilee raises money for cancer research. The Grand Gala raises money for a bunch of different stuff. It ain't cheap to be a party animal during Derby," she concluded, "but at least you know you're getting shaken down for a good cause."

Cole smiled at that. "Well, that's good to know."

"The Run for the Rosé is Tuesday down on the Belvedere," Bree said. "You should come."

Instead of replying to Bree, Cole looked at Lulu. "Will you be there?" he asked. Then, as if he were fearful the question might be too intrusive, he quickly added, "To cheer your friend on?"

Lulu looked at Bree, who was studying her warily. "I . . ." she began. "I usually do go to cheer Bree on," she said. Somehow, though, she was thinking maybe Bree didn't want her to this year.

"Depends on what's going on at the track that day," Cole said. "But I'll do my best to be there. So I know Bree tends bar, but what do you do, Hort . . . ense?"

Wow, Lulu thought. He almost didn't stumble over her phony name at all that time. Of course, she'd also noticed he'd been going out of his way all night to avoid using it at all. Then she remembered he'd asked her a question about her job that needed an answer. And since most people found the idea of making glass for a living interesting enough to ask a lot of questions about it, she told herself to come up with a fake occupation that wouldn't interest him so that the conversation would stay focused on Bree or, better yet, would be repellent enough to discourage any further conversation about Lulu at all.

Briefly, she thought about saying she styled dead people's hair, but she didn't want to end the conversation *that* completely. So she told him, "I work on the assembly line for a manufacturer of kitchen appliances."

Cole's expression didn't change, so she wasn't sure if he wasn't interested in her alleged job or if she'd already put him to sleep.

So she added, "I'm the one who attaches the little utensil basket to dishwashers."

He nodded at that. "Fascinating." But, like his expression, the word was completely bland, telling her nothing of what he might actually be feeling.

Nevertheless, she managed a smile and tried to warm to the subject. "It is, actually. Not many people realize how much thought and planning goes into where you put the utensil basket on a dishwasher."

"Well, I know I sure don't," Bree said. She punctuated the comment by kicking Lulu under the table, a not-so-subtle reminder to ixnay on the ishwasherday anufacturingmay.

Ightray. Lulu had orgottenfay. This was all about Eebray.

"Anyway," she said, "that's what I ooday. Ah, do. For a living."

She still couldn't tell what Cole was thinking, but at least he wasn't looking at her like she was a few brushstrokes short of a paint-by-numbers horse head.

"Bree's job is much more interesting than mine," she said halfheartedly.

"But *your* job is the most interesting of all," Bree told Cole enthusiastically. "What's it like, living a lifestyle of the rich and famous?"

His expression darkened almost imperceptibly, but Lulu noticed the change and realized this wasn't a line of conversation he wanted to follow. This time she was the one to kick Bree under the table in an effort to warn her away from the champagne wishes and caviar dreams thing.

But Bree either didn't get the hint or chose not to take it, because she leaned in closer to Cole and said, "I mean, I can't begin to imagine what it's like to have everything you ever wanted. Dream job. Oodles of money. California real estate. Oodles of money. Racehorses. Oodles of money. Not to mention good looks and fashion sense." She smiled. "And did I mention oodles of money?"

Lulu winced at her friend's forwardness. Bree was pouring it on even more than usual. Normally, she was a little more tactful. Normally, she only mentioned oodles of money twice.

She waited for Cole to say something snappish, like that it was none of Bree's business. Or maybe he'd be polite and just pretend he hadn't heard her. Or maybe he was just going to stall for a while, she thought further when he only lifted his beer to sip it, and set down the glass without a word. When he finally looked up with an apparent intention to reply, he dragged the tip of his middle finger around the rim of his glass, slowly, carefully, and with great attention. And when he opened his mouth to speak, it was to look not at Bree, but at Lulu.

Then, very softly, he said, "Well, I wouldn't say I have *everything* I've ever wanted."

And suddenly, it was as if the finger making its way leisurely around the rim of the glass was making its way leisurely up her spine instead. Something in his curiously green eyes spoke of barely banked embers and smoldering coals that might burst into flame again any minute if given the slightest little poke. Lulu felt like she was sitting in front of the torch in her studio, the one she had to burn at about eight million degrees to melt the glass to the consistency she wanted before molding it. It was a heat unlike any other in the world, one that surrounded and smothered and entered every pore, settling deep under the skin, scorching down to the bone. A heat that should have been uncomfortable, even unbearable, but was instead oddly pleasurable, because it lent to the creation of something wondrous and beautiful. A heat that would be destructive under other circumstances, but in glassmaking generated something lovely and unique, and fragile enough to need constant care.

She had no idea what to say in response to Cole's remark. She was too busy battling that heat and being swamped by that heat and having that heat seep under her skin. And try as she might, she simply could not tear her gaze from the slow, methodical movement of his fingertip around the rim of the glass . . . and around again . . . and again . . . and again . . . and again . . .

"Wow, is that the time? I had no idea it was so late. We really have to go."

Lulu started at the rush of words, so surprised was she at hearing them. Especially when she realized it was she who had blurted them out. Not only could she not remember having chosen to say such a thing, but she didn't understand why she might have said it, since things were just starting to get interesting with Cole, and even more interesting with his fingers, and—

Oh, right. That was why she'd said it. Because she wasn't supposed to find Cole, or his fingers, interesting. Bree was supposed to be doing that. Even without Bree in the picture, Lulu's getting interested in any part of Cole—or any of Cole's parts, for that matter—would be crazy. Lulu liked men who were slow and steady. Not men who were fast and loose. Not to mention only in town temporarily.

When she looked over at Bree, her friend was gazing at her with both curiosity and suspicion. After a moment, though, she nodded slowly and said, "Um, okay. I guess you do have to get up early to make it to the dishwasher plant on time, don't you, Hortense?"

"First shift," Lulu replied brightly.

She grabbed her purse from the chair where she'd placed it and stood, noting that Bree took a moment longer and was eyeing her now with something akin to wariness. She wondered if her friend had detected the odd sizzle of . . . whatever it was Lulu had felt sizzling when she looked at Cole . . . and wanted it to fizzle out as much as Lulu did. Because Lulu *did* want to fizzle the sizzle. Number one, because Cole Early was supposed to be sizzling with Bree. And number two . . .

Huh. That was funny. She couldn't remember reason number two. Oh, yeah, she recalled suddenly. Because he wasn't her type.

"Thanks for the drinks, Cole," Bree said reluctantly, clearly not wanting to let her catch, however tenuous, get away. As if wanting to ensure that didn't happen, she added, "Are you staying at the Ambassador? Will I see you in the bar again?"

He shook his head, but Lulu wasn't sure if he was answering only one of the questions, or both. "No, I'm not. I've got a—" He halted abruptly, then continued, "I'm staying somewhere else."

"Well, I hope to see you again," she added anyway. "Soon."

Under her breath, for Lulu's ears alone, she added, "Alone. Right, Lulu? Next time we run into Cole, you'll make yourself scarce, right?"

So obviously Bree had detected the weird sizzle. *Damn.* Though why, exactly, Lulu was cursing that development, she couldn't really say. What she did say was, "Yes, Bree." Because there was no way she would ever stand in the way of her friend's lifetime dream.

Even if it was a stupid dream. And even if, suddenly, Lulu was starting to think maybe she had a dream of her own.

COLE WATCHED THE TWO WOMEN AS THEY MADE their way to the exit, wondering when someone had snuck up behind him and hit him with a brick. Because sitting with Bree and Hortense—what *had* her parents been thinking to name her that?—he'd begun to feel and think things he hadn't felt or thought for a very long time.

Like how nice it felt to spend an evening doing nothing but chatting and drinking beer. Cole couldn't remember the last time he'd just kicked back and relaxed for the hell of it.

A beer drinker, he marveled about Hortense—what *had* her parents been thinking? He couldn't remember the last time he'd been out with a woman who'd ordered a beer, either. Hell, he couldn't remember the last time he'd ordered a beer himself. Although he loved an ice-cold longneck at the end of the workday when he was on the ranch, or if he was at a track when he didn't have a horse running and didn't have to be King Cole. He just didn't order it when he was out, because it wasn't the sort of thing major players in the horse-racing industry drank.

And that was another thing. Although Bree had been pretty knowledgeable about the industry he worked in and pretty much lived for, Hortense—what *had* her parents been thinking?—didn't know squat. Cole didn't normally associate with people who knew so little about bloodlines and broodmares and gate assignments and all the things he'd built his career—hell, his very life—upon. Even worse, she knew nothing—and cared less—about "King Cole." How could anyone in this town, at this time of year, after the way he'd been hounded by the local press, not know—or care—about him? She'd talked to him as if he were a regular guy, not the larger-than-life image of a man he'd cultivated for himself in the business.

And that was when another—bigger—brick hit him. Because he realized then how enjoyable it had been to drink beer with Hortense Waddy who knew nothing about horses and cared less about him. And then he was slammed by another projectile, this one about the size of a basement foundation: Drinking beer with Hortense Waddy and her friend had kept the groupies and autograph hounds at bay for a good part of the evening. Once the three of them left the Ambassador and came here to . . . whatever the name of this place was, the celebrity-seekers had dwindled to nearly nothing. Having the women with him had created a nice buffer zone that kept the Trainer Hangers at bay. Of course, that hadn't been the case at the Ambassador. He'd been constantly interrupted in his conversation there. Here, though, it hadn't been a problem at all.

So what was the difference, he wondered? The two bars were both popular, active nightspots. They were both filled with people. The clientele here was a little younger than the other bar, but that should have lent itself to more autograph-seekers, not fewer. The only difference was that, at the Ambassador, Cole had been alone when he entered, something that, he supposed, made him fair game. Here, he'd entered with someone else. Two someone elses, actually, but it would have been safe for any observer to conclude that at least one of the women was a date. People were polite enough to make allowances for a man when he was out socially with a guest, more so than they were when he was out alone.

So it stood to reason that if Cole started going out in public with a guest, people would be more likely to leave him alone. Certainly there wouldn't be any more offers of sexual encounters that might send a lesser man right to the nearest hotel—and, later, to the nearest clinic for a penicillin shot. If Cole could avoid any more of those offers—hell, if he could just avoid more requests for autographs and interviews— he'd be a very happy man. Not only were the sexual overtures even more annoying than the demands for signatures and photographs, but when it came to sexual encounters, *he* wanted to be the one to decide the who, what, when, where, and why. Okay, and also the how. So he was old-fashioned that way. Except for some of the hows, in which case, all modesty aside, he could be pretty damned inventive. So sue him.

He'd also be a more *focused* man if he could avoid those things. He'd be less stressed out about the race. He'd be able to concentrate on what he needed to be doing between now and Derby Day.

Obviously, what he needed to ward off the Trainer Hangers

and preserve his peace of mind for the next week and a half was a buffer zone. To create a buffer zone, he'd need a buffer. Someone of the feminine persuasion who would look to the casual observer like a romantic interest and inhibit the casual observer's approach. Someone who wouldn't compromise Cole's focus on Silk Purse or distract him from his single-minded pursuit of winning the Derby. Someone who wouldn't distract him by being sexually attractive to him, but whose company he would still enjoy. Someone who knew little—and cared less—about King Cole and wouldn't be sexually attracted to him, either.

Someone like Hortense Waddy.

She was pretty enough that no one would question his reason for wanting to be with her. If you went for the wholesome, decent, down-to-Earth-shoes type. Which Cole, of course, did not. And although he could see now why some guys might go for her in a girl-next-door type of way, Cole, of course, never would. And although maybe there was something to be said for a woman who wasn't overly concerned with something like going to great extremes to enhance her physical appearance, no way would Cole be the guy to say it. Simply put, Hortense wasn't his type. So obviously Hortense was the perfect candidate for buffer material. There was just one problem.

He had no idea how to contact her.

But he knew her name, and he knew where her friend worked. There couldn't possibly be more than one Hortense Waddy in the phone book. And if there wasn't one at all, then he'd just make sure he dropped into the Ambassador Bar again when Bree was working. One way or another, he'd see Hortense again. Starting by checking the phone book as soon as he got home.

Home, he repeated to himself, thinking about the little house he'd been trying to escape tonight when he went out in search of dinner, because if he banged his head on the bedroom ceiling one more time, he was going to have to be treated for brain damage. Funny, though, how it wasn't the ceiling he thought about just then. And funny how, in spite of wanting to escape the place, he couldn't wait to get home.

Back, he immediately corrected himself. He couldn't wait to get *back.* Back to the flurry of Post-it notes he was still encountering daily, like the one he'd discovered that afternoon on a big bag of M&M's in the pantry. *"You may eat my M&M's,"* it said. *"But only if you are in the throes of extreme chocolate withdrawal, a condition I fully understand and with which I totally relate. But if you* do *eat my M&M's, you'd better pay me back. Twice the amount. Or else I'll hunt you down like a dog and call you Rover."*

And back, too, he thought fondly, to the daily journal he'd accidentally, really, opened again after inadvertently, really, switching on her computer when he'd unintentionally, really, set his briefcase on the desk too close to the On button. Which, okay, was on the back of the computer, so he'd had to set down his briefcase unintentionally, really, too close to the button four times before it got pushed, but that was beside the point. The point was, he hadn't consciously, really, meant to read the journal again. It had just . . . happened. Once. A day. Maybe twice when he was especially clumsy with his briefcase.

Oh, hell, so he'd kept reading his hostess's journal. It wasn't like she ever wrote about anything of great importance or of an especially personal nature. She wrote about food. Or books. Or movies. Walks through the park. A neighbor's peonies. A particularly beautiful sunset. Somehow, though, she always managed to make every entry sound like some kind of sensual, sexual pleasure that always left Cole feeling like he needed a cigarette. Or a cold shower. Or both.

Now *there* was a woman he could be attracted to. A woman who had color in her house, and sass in her personality, and hedonism in her soul. A woman who clearly enjoyed everything life had to offer. A woman, he thought as he swallowed the last of his beer and rose to make his way out the door, he'd never need a buffer to avoid.

He thought about her all the way home, trying to get a visual on her without the benefit of the photograph to aid him. The long blond hair and lush curves were easy, and, even though all the photos were from a distance, he'd decided at some point that she had brown eyes, because he'd always had a weakness for brown-eyed blondes. She was taller than the other women in the picture, which would probably bring her to about his nose—his forehead, if she was wearing sexy spike heels which, it went without saying, she did. All the time. Even to bed.

What else would she wear to bed? he wondered. Well, hell, that was easy. Nothing. Spike heels and long blond hair. A woman didn't need to wear any more than that to bed.

By the time he got home, Cole's image of the blonde—whom he'd decided was named Delilah—was pretty complete. Delilah was twenty-six years old and worked as a legal secretary. She liked the novels of Thomas Pynchon, the music of Itzhak Perlman, men who wore glasses, snowy mornings in bed, and kittens.

Oh, no, wait. That had been Miss February, he remembered. Delilah liked yachting, single malt Scotch, the music of John Coltrane, and Formula One racing. Yeah, that's it. Okay, and snowy mornings in bed and kittens. Whatever.

After pouring himself a brandy, climbing the stairs to the bedroom, bumping his head on the ceiling—again—and changing into his pajamas, Cole had Delilah completely figured out, right down to the black silk bra and panties that he knew—he just knew—were her favorite choice of underwear. Inescapably, the thought made him drop his gaze to the dresser drawer he was certain contained her lingerie. The small one on top, on the left-hand side. And, just like that, his devil and angel selves appeared on his shoulders again.

This time, though, the angel only muttered a halfhearted, half-heard, *You are such a dirtbag.*

And the devil rubbed his hands together with glee and said, *Let's do it.*

Cole supposed he should credit himself with the fact that

his fingers hovered over the drawer pull for a few seconds before actually grasping it. And, too, he thought it said something in his favor that, even after his fingers curled lightly around the little glass knob, he hesitated. But what truly spoke volumes about his character was that, even after the hesitations, he began to slowly, slowly—oh, so slowly—tug the drawer open.

Just a peek, he told himself. It would only be for a few seconds.

Of course, that was what he'd told himself about the journal, too.

But he'd seen the stuff about *wonderfully erotic* then, he reminded himself. No man could be expected to turn back after reading something like that. Lingerie drawers were way more impersonal than a journal. It was just a lot of fabric without words or thoughts or feelings. He *would* just take a peek with this. It *would* only be for a few seconds.

And it would have been, too. If it hadn't been for the fact that what he saw there on top was *not* black silk. What he saw there on top was instead lavender lace.

Lavender lace. He never would have guessed. Delilah just didn't seem the type. Lavender lace was so . . . demure. So . . . unsullied. So . . . sweet. Lavender lace really was snowy mornings in bed and kittens. And, strangely, he thought, the novels of Thomas Pynchon and the music of Itzhak Perlman. But unlike Miss February, the wearer of lavender lace would actually know who Thomas Pynchon and Itzhak Perlman were.

Before Cole realized what he was doing, he'd dropped his hand into the drawer and carefully lifted the lavender lace from where it lay. Not to fondle it, he immediately told himself, but to see what lay underneath. And what lay underneath the lavender lace was peach lace. And then butter yellow lace. And then pale blue silk. And then pink silk. And then, on the very bottom of the assortment, he hit pay dirt.

Black silk.

Oh, yeah. "Delilah, you little vixen," he said aloud.

Then he chuckled at himself for being so . . . He hastily but carefully arranged all the lingerie back exactly the way he'd found it. Weird, he finally finished his own sentence. That was what he was being. Weird. No way did he normally behave the way he'd been behaving since taking up residence in this house.

He closed the drawer and picked up his brandy, lifting it to his lips for a generous taste. The spirit felt good going down, smooth, warm, and mellow. Unfortunately, the same couldn't be said of himself. As usual, he was too wound up to sleep, and his little foray into Delilah's underthings hadn't helped. He turned and saw her computer sitting on the desk on the other side of the room. He smiled. Maybe a little bedtime reading was in order.

He'd read Delilah's journal often enough by now that the angel didn't even bother to show up anymore. The devil one did from time to time, whenever a passage was particularly steamy. But mostly, Cole was on his own now when it came to the violation of his hostess's privacy.

He rationalized his behavior by reminding himself that she really didn't write about anything all that personal. And she *was* a very good writer. Her descriptive passages on food alone could easily see print in some of the country's leading publications. Like *Playboy* or *Penthouse*. Easily.

He'd gradually been working his way backward through her entries, until he'd read through all of April and March. Now he was into February. The twenty-first, to be exact.

Woke up to snow this morning, the passage began. *Six inches that no one predicted, a total surprise. I'm sitting on the sofa as I write, looking out the window at a winter wonderland. It's gorgeous. Needless to say, I'm blowing off work and giving myself a gift. The gift of a day. To read, or watch a movie, or sketch, or do whatever takes my fancy.*

Cole lifted his brandy for another sip. This was different. All the passages he'd read before this had been about specific experiences or observations. She'd never written about herself in a Dear Diary kind of way. This was nice. A little glimpse into the person herself.

Though it's days like this, she continued, *when I wish I wasn't alone. When I wish there was someone here to turn the cold outside into warmth inside. Someone who would spike his hot chocolate with rum, too. Someone who would sit at the other end of the sofa and play footsie with me under the afghan. Someone who would read aloud to me books filled with grand adventure and epic romance.*

Cole grinned, liking the fact that his hostess had been a single woman as recently as two months ago way more than he probably should.

Someone who would join me in the tub later, for a steaming bath redolent of patchouli, he read on. Then he began to think that maybe he should stop right there. He thought that even more when the next line said, *I can feel him now, in the water behind me, the air around us foggy from the mingling heat of the bath and our glistening bodies.* And then he knew for sure he absolutely had to stop reading when the line after that said, *His hands slide up under the water, over my thighs and hips, along my slick torso, to cover my wet breasts.*

So, of course, he kept on reading.

At first, he only holds my breasts in his hands, gently kneading them, dragging his thumbs over their tops, then tracing the bottom curves. When he rolls my nipples with his fingers, I feel heat explode in my belly. He dips his head to my neck and brushes his lips along my shoulder, then one hand leaves a breast to move between my legs. I open them wider so that he can touch me there, and he strokes my damp flesh with his long middle finger. I spread my legs more, and he covers me with his hand, caressing me, stroking me, fingering me until I shatter inside.

Cole reached blindly for his brandy—for some reason, he *really* needed a drink—and nearly knocked it off the desk before snagging it with shaky fingers. Damn. His hostess sure knew how to warm up a snowy winter day. He told himself he really should stop reading and go to bed. But he knew that wasn't going to happen. Not yet, anyway. He wanted to see how this turned out.

How it turned out was that she spent another page and a half describing how her lover washed every inch of her body, then another page on how he dried her off—and that guy did things with the loofah and towel in the process that Cole was pretty sure loofahs and towels had never been designed to do. Not that he didn't give the invisible lover points for inventiveness. Eventually, though, the action moved into the bedroom, where things really started heating up.

He's standing behind me, she wrote. *I feel his cock long and hard against my back. He guides me to the bed and tells me he wants me on my hands and knees. I do what he says. He tells me to lower my shoulders to the mattress. I obey him. He tells me to spread my legs. I do that, too. He tells me to spread them wider. I spread them as wide as I can. Then he's lying on his back beneath me with his head between my legs. His hands hold my hips in place while he lifts his mouth to lick me. As he tastes me there, slowly, deeply, methodically, his fingers venture into the cleft of my derriere and begin to pull me open and stroke me there. Then one finger pushes inside behind me as his tongue moves deeper into my damp flesh . . .*

On and on, she wrote about her lover's oral and digital skills, until she was coming apart again, and Cole was thinking he was probably going to have to check out his hostess's pay-per-view selections later. That *probably* became a *hell, yes* over the next few pages, because she and her imaginary lover did things for and to each other on that bed that would have them both walking funny for days afterward.

Man, oh, man, he thought when the passage finally—finally—came to an end. Never had she written anything like *that* in her journal before.

Then he remembered that he'd been reading her journal backwards. So it was really that she hadn't written anything like *that* after this particular passage. Meaning she might very well have written something like *that* before. Considering the comfortableness she'd exhibited with the subject matter, chances were good that she'd written something like *that* before. Maybe lots of times before. Just how far back did this journal go, anyway?

He actually moved his hand to the mouse to start scrolling backward and had to stop himself from completing the action. Not tonight, he told himself. No more tonight. No man had that kind of stamina. Except, of course, for Delilah's imaginary lover.

Later, he told himself as he closed the file and powered down the computer. He could read more of Delilah's, ah, exploits another day. Another night. Another day *and* night. What he needed now was sleep. Okay, a cold shower, and then sleep. And then maybe, with luck, a dream or two about a beautiful woman in lavender lace lingerie . . .

· Ten ·

BREE TURNED THE KEY IN HER IGNITION FOR A
fourth time, listened to the engine of the dilapidated Honda
grind ineffectively—for a fourth time—and pressed her
forehead to the steering wheel.

"Dammit," she said eloquently.

"Let me take a look under the hood," Rufus said, striding
to the front of the little red car.

When no one else had been ready to head out to the parking garage that night, Bree had had no choice but to ask Rufus to do the honors, a request she hated to make. Not just
because she didn't want to have to rely on the guy for anything, but she didn't want to encourage him in his romantic
pursuit of her. That sounded so incredibly egotistical, she
knew, but Rufus had made no secret about his feelings for
her, so there was no ego involved—only fact. She just didn't
want to do anything that might give the guy false hope when
she just wasn't interested. So she tried to avoid him whenever she could, even when they had to work shoulder to
shoulder.

Especially when they had to work shoulder to shoulder.

Because, too often, that was a literal state. And whenever Bree's shoulder brushed Rufus's—or whenever her elbow rubbed his, or their hips bumped or any other body parts came into contact, however inadvertently—she was all too aware of him. And aware was a condition she couldn't afford around Rufus. Too often, awareness led to other *-nesses* that Bree didn't want to feel around Rufus. Like attractiveness. And warmness. And keenness. And fondness. She totally couldn't afford any fondness for the guy.

The guy who was bent over her engine right now, trying to fix her car for her. The guy who always walked her out to the parking garage so she wouldn't be accosted by any creeps. The guy who'd given her a ride home one night when Lulu couldn't make it. The guy who, at the last employee Christmas party, put a notice up in the break room saying he'd give twenty bucks to trade with whoever picked Bree's name in the Secret Santa, then, when everyone was supposed to bring a gag gift that cost five dollars, gave her a dozen roses instead.

No way did she want to feel fondness for a guy like that. Because that way lay another *-ness*: madness.

Rufus really was a good guy. But he was a poor guy. And he would always be poor. Not because he couldn't make a decent living if he wanted to, but because he didn't mind not having money. It was almost like he didn't even *want* money. And that, Bree thought, that was just wrong.

"Try it again," he told her.

She turned the key in the ignition a fifth time, but this time, the engine didn't even grind. This time, there was just a disconsolate click.

"Do you have Triple A?" he called from behind the open hood.

"No." For the seventy-five dollar annual fee, she'd figured she could get a week's worth of groceries. At the time, it had been a no-brainer. Now, though . . .

Rufus dropped the hood with a loud clang and came back

to the driver's side window brushing his palms together to get rid of the grime. "I know a guy who's good with cars. He can probably look at it tomorrow and he won't charge you anything."

Probably, Bree couldn't help thinking, because Rufus would tell the guy to send him the bill instead. So she'd have to find some other way to repay him. Some way that didn't involve doing anything personal that might make him think she cared about him. Which she didn't. Maybe she could get him a gift card for someplace. Someplace impersonal. Like Kroger.

Bree eyed him hopefully. "Can't you call the guy now?"

Rufus arched his dark brows in surprise. "At two A.M.?"

She lifted a shoulder and let it drop. "You and I are still awake."

He smiled. "You and I work nights." He leaned toward the window, propping an arm on the roof of the car. "This may come as a shock to you, Bree, but some people don't work nights. Some people use nights for sleeping."

There was something in his eyes that told her he was thinking about something else people used nights for, but he didn't put voice to it. He didn't have to. And, anyway, Rufus didn't do stuff like that. Unlike most guys, he didn't use every opportunity for sexual innuendo to say something suggestive. He was too good a guy for that.

She sighed fitfully. As much as she hated to, she was going to have to ask Rufus for a ride home. She steeled herself for the dizzying sensation that always overcame her whenever she looked him in the eye and met his gaze. Damn. Steeling herself never worked. She still always felt herself drowning in the dark espresso depths of his eyes. There wasn't a man on earth who had more beautiful eyes than Rufus Detweiler. Hell, she doubted there was a woman on earth who had more beautiful eyes than Rufus.

She inhaled a fortifying breath, but all that did was remind her of how good he smelled. How anyone could walk away from working a shift behind a bar and not smell like, at best, rank crème de menthe and, at worst, bar slime, was beyond her. Bree just hoped he wasn't close enough to her to notice the half bottle of Cutty Sark she'd spilled down her front tonight.

"Rufus," she said softly, "I don't suppose I could trouble you for—"

"It would be my pleasure to give you a ride home," he told her before she even had the chance to finish asking.

She smiled, though not too brightly. She didn't want to give him any ideas. "Thanks," she said. She started to say, *I'll make it up to you,* but thought better of it and instead told him, "I appreciate it." She'd tuck a bottle of Grey Goose with a thank-you note into his backpack tomorrow when he wasn't looking. That should take care of the debt.

His old Jeep Wagoneer, complete with fake wood paneling, was parked three spaces away, and he had to unlock the door the old-fashioned way, by inserting the key into the lock, before opening the passenger side door for her.

"Buckle up," he said with a grin as he closed it behind her.

As she watched him stride around the front of the truck to the driver's side, she could have sworn he mouthed the words *precious cargo* to himself as he went. She told herself she should feel indignant at being considered cargo. Instead, the words sent a warm thrill of happiness through her.

Oh, damn. That was one of those *-nesses* she'd been trying to avoid. There would be no thrills of happiness around Rufus.

The two of them chatted amiably on the drive to her apartment about the evening's events, laughing over one especially obnoxious patron. Rufus didn't ask where she lived, obviously remembering from the other time he gave her a lift, but he took a different route from the one she had navigated for him last time. Instead of taking Broadway to Bardstown Road, which would have been the more direct, but less interesting route, he turned down Baxter and drove the more scenic way, making the approach to her intersection via the side street instead of the main thoroughfare. Bree wasn't sure if it was because he was just that familiar with the Highlands and knew to go that way, or if he'd learned more about her neighborhood after finding out where she lived. She decided not to think about it. For all she knew, he lived in the Highlands, too. She'd never asked.

"So where do you live?" she said as he braked for a stop sign a block shy of her building. Damn. That was nosiness. Another -ness she didn't need to be feeling around Rufus.

"Crescent Hill," he told her.

"Oh, I love Crescent Hill," she said anyway. She smiled. "They got some good eatin' there on Frankfort Avenue."

"Oh, yeah, and there's such a dearth of good restaurants in your neighborhood."

"I know," she said with mock disappointment. "You could eat four-star cuisine every night around here. Gets boring after awhile."

He looked over at her, but in the darkness, she couldn't make out his expression. "Some kept woman you're going to be, complaining about four-star cuisine."

Something about the way he said *kept woman* sent another one of those ripples of gladness—damn those -*nesses*, anyway—down her spine. Heat exploded in her belly and seeped outward, pooling in places she'd just as soon not have heat gathering while she was in a darkened car on a deserted side street with a man like Rufus sitting next to her.

"Well, it's just that I'll expect my Sugar Daddy to take me to *five*-star restaurants every night, that's all," she told him. But the words came out a little too cursory, a little too quiet, and a little too uncaring.

Dammit. This was another reason she avoided Rufus. Whenever she tried to emphasize how important it was for her to live the lifestyle of the fabulously rich and unbelievably famous, she never sounded emphatic at all.

"You can just drop me here," she said as he halted the truck for a stop sign, reaching for the seat belt and the door handle at the same time. "This time of night, you won't find anyplace to park. I'll be fine."

"You sure about that?" he asked.

There was something in his voice that made her look up, and she saw a trio of young men standing in a shadow not ten feet from the side entrance of the building she had to use to get to her apartment over Deke's. All of them were holding skateboards, one was smoking, two held bottles obscured by brown paper bags, and all were murmuring low. Bree's neighborhood wasn't a dangerous one, but episodes of mischief and petty crime weren't unheard of. Episodes of worse crimes, though infrequent, weren't unheard of, either. Probably, it was nothing but a few kids taking a break before going back to their shredding. Whatever the hell that was. Probably, they were talking about some new song one of them had downloaded off iTunes by a band Bree had never heard of. Probably, she'd be just fine if Rufus dropped her here at the corner and drove off the way she told him to.

Probably.

"I'll find a place to park and walk you up," he said.

"Rufus, it's not necess—"

"It's no trouble."

"You can just watch from the car to make sure I get in all ri—"

But he'd already turned onto Bardstown Road and was cruising for a parking spot. Just as Bree had predicted, however, between the residences on the side streets and the bars on the main drag that were almost as busy on Thursday nights as they were on Fridays, he had to drive four blocks before finding a space big enough for his Wagoneer. She slung open her door and climbed out before he had a chance to make it around the truck and open it for her—a girl could only take so much courtesy and respect—but as they made their way down the sidewalk, Rufus moved to the outside, putting himself between her and the curb.

Jeez, the guy was too good to be true.

It was a balmy evening, with a breeze playful enough to

dance in Bree's hair, so a handful of revelers had spilled out of the bars and restaurants and coffee shops and onto the street. Music tumbled from nearly every establishment they passed, along with sultry laughter and snippets of incomplete conversation. Countless neon lights and illuminated storefront signs bathed them in first red, blue, then green as they went by, then the rainbow started all over again. Neither said a word as they walked, but somehow, the silence was in no way awkward. She and Rufus might as well have taken this walk every evening, so comfortable was his presence now.

She was even more grateful for it when they rounded the corner of her building and the three boys' heads snapped up almost predatorily. When they saw Rufus, however, they only nodded, greeted him with varying versions of "Dude," and continued with their chat. Bree wasn't offended that the trio summarily ignored her, but something about their lack of acknowledgment also gave her the creeps.

Rufus must have felt a little uneasy himself, because although he nodded in response to the boys, he also opened his palm over the small of her back in a way that was clearly meant to look proprietary. She told herself it should *feel* proprietary, too, but what it actually felt was kind of comforting. And when he said resolutely, "I'll walk you up," instead of telling him it wasn't necessary, she instead nodded and murmured a quiet "Thanks."

He moved between her and the boys as she unlocked the exterior door, then he followed her up the stairs to a landing that opened onto two separate apartments. The one across from Bree's was vacant at the moment, a fact that didn't exactly lend itself to a feeling of safety. So after unlocking and opening her front door, she turned to Rufus and said, "You want to come in for a little while?" Hastily, lest he misunderstand—since why else would she prolong her time with Rufus unless it was because she felt unsafe with restless youth downstairs?—she added, "Just until the guys downstairs take off?"

He grinned, but there was nothing smug or triumphant in it. There was only good guy-ness in it. And suddenly, her stomach was filled with butterflies. And not the pastoral, pastel, prancing-about-the-meadow kind, either. These were the giant, ruthless, predatory kind that lived on the Amazon and carried off Yanomamo children. She'd seen them on the Discovery Channel and knew that was without question what had taken up residence in her midsection.

"Sure," he told her. "No problem."

"Or until Lulu gets home," she said, recalling that her temporary roommate had been dragged to a gallery showing for one of her artsy friends—a showing that would doubtless run 'til dawn, knowing said artsy friend. Not that Lulu would stay for the whole thing. She never did. In fact, it was odd that she'd stayed out this late. "She should be back anytime now," Bree added.

"Why is Lulu staying with you? Is she having problems at home with Mom and Dad?" he asked, his grin broadening. And just like that, the giant butterflies in Bree's belly started doing a raucous mambo.

"No," she said, trying to ignore the flutters. "She rented her house out for Derby and can't go home until next Sunday, so she's bunking here."

"Ah. I've heard about people doing that. I can't imagine letting some stranger live in my place, though."

Not that any Derby visitor would want to rent Rufus's place, Bree thought. Not that she had a clue what his place was like, other than it being in Crescent Hill. But she could imagine. Any guy whose life ambition was to tend bar probably wasn't real big on amenities. Or luxuries. Or furniture. Or ownership, for that matter. Considering he had the same source of income she had, he couldn't afford to own anything. Certainly not in Crescent Hill, unless the place was falling down around him.

She held the door open while Rufus entered, then closed it behind him. Belatedly, she realized she hadn't left on any lights, so she reached for the switch by the front door . . .

only to smack her hand against Rufus's chest. Or rather, the acreage that was Rufus's chest. Good God, she'd never thought he would have such a hard body—he seemed too tall and lanky for that. But what her knuckles grazed was solid rock. Just to be certain, she opened her palm flat over the soft fabric of his white bartender shirt and pushed lightly. Yep. Although his shirt was virtually identical to the one she wore, what was underneath was totally different. He was like Granite Man. Just to be absolutely certain, though, she skimmed her palm downward—*bump, bump, bump*—over abdominal muscles that rippled like the Sahara after a sirocco.

Wow. She never would have thought Rufus would be the gym type. Maybe, just to be absolutely, positively certain, she should—

"Bree?"

"Yeah, Rufus?"

"Either turn on the light you were reaching for, or it's going to stay off for a long, *long* time."

Yikes.

"Uh, sorry," she mumbled as she took a giant step to the right to feel for the switch she'd all but forgotten about.

She flicked it quickly, activating a wall socket into which was plugged an antique standing lamp with an amber glass shade. The room was immediately bathed in soft, ambient gold, giving it a sort of otherworldly aura. The lamp was the very first purchase she'd made for her very first apartment, and when she'd seen the color it cast, she'd bought all her additional furnishings to match it. The overstuffed sofa and club chair were a tawny cognac color, while the pillows tossed onto both and the throw slung over the sofa's back were the color of strong tea. Two prints hanging on one of the creamy walls were of dark yellow flowers framed in gold, while another wall held antique-looking maps of the Aegean and Mediterranean, two of many areas in the world Bree hoped to visit someday—preferably with her Greek tycoon boyfriend Stavros and his fully outfitted yacht. An old steamer trunk covered with the remnants of someone else's travels nearly a century ago served as her coffee table, and two throw rugs that were shaggy with all the colors of the room combined rounded out the decor. Every time she looked at it, she felt like she was watching an old sepia-toned movie.

Usually, coming home and turning on that lamp to reveal her golden room served to calm Bree after a long night's work. Now, though, it allowed her to see the way Rufus's cheeks had darkened in response to her careless touch, the way his pupils had expanded, and the way he'd halfway lifted a hand to touch her. Although his black bartender pants were virtually identical to hers, too, what was under them, it was more than evident, was also way different from what was under hers. Immediately, he dropped his hand to his side and shifted his weight to make his condition a bit less obvious—though, she had to admit, there was no way he could completely hide something like *that*.

"Uh, coffee?" she asked quickly. Even more quickly, she made her way to the tiny galley kitchen to start a pot brewing. Even though the last thing she needed at the moment was any kind of, ah, stimulant. So she added, "Beer? Wine? Scotch? Oh, wait, I don't have any Scotch. Or wine, either." She feared she was also out of beer, but tugged open the fridge door anyway. "Aha!" she said when she saw a solitary bottle of Sam Adams—one of Lulu's—sitting on the shelf. She plucked it out and held it up as if she were a spokesmodel for the brand. "Here ya go. Sam Adams is just waiting to make your night."

The trip across the room had sent the butterflies in her stomach scurrying back to the Amazon, thankfully. But taking their place was an odd knot of tension that clenched tighter with every passing moment. It pulled taut enough to cut off her breath when Rufus began to walk across the apartment toward her. Slowly, deliberately, his eyes never leaving hers, until he stood barely a breath away from her. He extended his hand forward, and she thought he was going to take the beer from her, but instead, he moved his fingers to the dark curtain of hair that had fallen over her shoulder. In one swift, economical move, he brushed it away from her face, dipped his head to hers, and kissed her.

It was totally unexpected. Bree was in no way prepared. Without even thinking—because thought was impossible when a man's lips felt as good as his did—she kissed him back, leaning her entire body forward, as if he were a magnet and she was steel. Hot, molten, malleable steel just waiting to be hammered. When he opened his mouth against hers, she eagerly parted her lips, drawing his tongue inside, tasting him as deeply as she could.

It was all the encouragement he needed. He drove both hands into her hair and turned himself and Bree until her back was against the doorjamb. Then he crowded his body into hers and kissed her more deeply still. She roped her arms around his waist, opening her palms over his back, dragging her fingers down the finely sculpted muscles she felt beneath his shirt. He slanted his head first one way then another, as if he couldn't decide which way he liked kissing her better. She followed every move, giving as good as she got, taking as much as she could. Not that Rufus seemed to mind her demands, since he met them with a fire and passion to equal hers.

Where had this come from? she wondered vaguely. Yes, she'd always found him attractive, but this? This went beyond attraction. This was something she feared she could barely contain. Which was all the more reason, she told herself, why she had to contain it.

Now.

Rufus sucked her lower lip into his mouth and nibbled it gently with the edges of his teeth.

Really, she told herself. Had to contain it *now*.

He traced her upper lip with the tip of his tongue, then rubbed his nose lightly against hers.

Now, Bree. Now.

He threaded his fingers in her hair, gripped a long strand and pulled gently to tip her head back, then rubbed his lips over the sensitive length of throat he exposed.

Now!

She had no idea how she managed it, but somehow, Bree was able to dip her head to the side and halt his progress. He didn't seem to notice she was doing it to stop him, though, and covered her mouth with his again. She kissed him back for a little while longer—since she knew this was never, ever going to happen again . . . dammit—then dragged her mouth from his to pull in a few long gasps of air.

He allowed her that small escape, but pressed his forehead to hers and kept his fingers tangled in her hair. She felt more than saw his smile as he murmured, very, very softly, "So, Bree. It suddenly occurs to me that maybe you might like me a little bit, after all."

She wished she could deny it. But she'd look like an idiot if she tried. She couldn't even deny it to herself anymore. She'd liked Rufus more than she should—more than she'd allowed herself to think about—since her first day on the job. She hadn't wanted to, but there it was all the same. How could a woman not be attracted to him? He was gorgeous, funny, smart, and sweet. He was a good guy. An incredibly hot good guy at that.

"Okay, I admit it," she said softly. "I like you a little bit."

He brushed his lips lightly over her temple, and she couldn't help the purr of contentment that rose inside and rolled out of her. "I think," he said, his breath warm against her face, "that maybe you even like me a lot."

He moved his mouth to skim it over her cheekbone, nuzzle her jaw, and draw his open lips down the sensitive flesh of her neck. The purr of contentment grew to a shudder of delight, and suddenly Bree was curling her fingers in his hair and tilting her head back, to both bring him closer and give him better access. He took full advantage, combing his fingers through her hair and pushing it back, moving his head upward again to rub his nose softly against hers, then skimming his lips across her cheek until he could nibble her ear lobe.

"Admit it," he whispered. "You like me a lot."

"I do," she groaned. "I like you a lot. Too much."

And that was the problem, she told herself. She liked Rufus way more than she should. Enough to risk losing sight of the goal she'd been focused on all her life. The goal that was growing more important every day. Rufus couldn't provide what Bree needed. It was as simple as that. To let this go any further would only hurt them both.

Reluctantly, she pulled her head away from his and stepped back, far enough to move out of the kitchen doorway and, more important, out of his reach. Just to be safe, though, she also turned her back on him before saying what she had to say. If she was looking at him when she said it, she'd lose sight of what she needed to make clear to him. Or she'd lose her nerve. Or she'd lose herself.

"Rufus, I can't do this. Not with you."

He said nothing in response, but she heard him sigh. Loudly. Impatiently. Angrily? Oh, surely not. Rufus was too good a guy to get angry over something like this.

"Because I don't have money," he said.

"Yeah."

"That's the only reason."

"That's the only one."

"It's a stupid reason, Bree."

"To you. Not to me."

"Then maybe you should explain it to me in a way that would make me think it less stupid."

There was no way she could do that. Unless Rufus had grown up the way she had, unless he knew her mother as she was now, Bree couldn't make him understand. In spite of that, she turned around and, still avoiding his gaze, crossed her arms over her midsection in an effort to shore herself up.

"I never knew my dad," she said. "I don't even know how well my mom knew my dad. Hell, I don't know for sure if my mom even knows which guy of a couple she dated *is* my dad. He was a soldier at Fort Knox—that much I do know. My mom could never resist a man in uniform."

Her mother still couldn't resist a man in uniform. There was a new guy at the nursing home who thought he was Douglas MacArthur, and Rosie Calhoun was completely enamored of him. He was crazy about her, too. Of course, he thought Bree's mother was one of the Andrews Sisters and Rosie hadn't exactly tried to dissuade him of the notion. Then again, there were times when Bree wasn't sure her mom didn't think she was one of the Andrews Sisters, too.

"Anyway," she started again, "whoever my father was, he never came around after I was born, and he never sent anything to help out."

Rufus said nothing, but he took a few steps toward her. Bree took a few more in retreat, circling the sofa to put it between the two of them.

"Okay, I get it," he said, stopping. "I promise to stay on my side." He shoved his hands deep into the pockets of his trousers. "Go on."

"My mom was a single mother at a time when it wasn't all that hip to be one, you know? I mean, no one ever gave me a hard time about not having a dad around, and I had friends whose parents had split, but it was tough on my mom. She never got to go to college, and she wasn't trained or qualified to do much of anything." She shrugged. "Except look pretty and be charming. That didn't pay the bills, though, so she worked two jobs. Two crappy jobs. She waited tables at night, and she cleaned people's houses during the day. She'd take me with her on her housekeeping gigs in the summers, when school was out, and I'd help out."

She sighed as she remembered. "Some of those houses she cleaned, Rufus . . . These huge estates in Glenview, and big houses in the east end . . . I couldn't believe how some of these people lived. I couldn't believe they had so much room to move around in, so many things to dust and polish and scrub. Beautiful things," she added. "And the women would be home while we worked sometimes, reading the paper and drinking their coffee. Or they'd come home in their tennis and golf outfits while we were there." She finally met his gaze, levelly and unflinchingly now. "My mom worked *so hard*, Rufus. She was no different from any of them. She deserved to live the same kind of life. But she had *no* life. She had to take care of herself and me instead. I decided a long time ago that I wasn't going to let the same thing happen to me."

"That sucks, Bree," Rufus agreed. "You and your mom should both have had better. But you know what? A lot of people have crappy jobs. A lot of people deserve better than they have. It doesn't make them go out and look for somebody else who has a better life to take care of them. Either they do what they can to improve their own lives, or they make do with what they have. Having money doesn't mean all your problems are magically solved. A lot of times, it just makes more problems."

"I know that," she said. "I know my life won't be charmed and perfect just because there's someone else paying the bills. But it sure as hell would be better than what I have now. I'm not a lot of people, Rufus. I don't want to make do with what I have. I want something better."

"Then make it happen for yourself."

"You don't think I haven't tried?" she said.

He jerked his hands from his pockets and took a step forward. "You majored in English, for God's sake," he reminded her. "That's not exactly a degree that lends itself to moneymaking."

"No, but it's good for making a person smart and articulate and interesting to talk to. Look, Rufus," she hurried on when he started to object, "I tried taking classes in economics and finance and business, and I just don't have a head for it. It's not in my genes. From my dad, whoever he was, I got a strong survival instinct and good strategy skills. From my mother, I got good looks and the ability to be charming when I want to be. Put them all together, and you get someone who knows what needs to be done and can figure out the best way to do it. I knew a long time ago what I needed to do. And I've done my best to do it. Just because it hasn't happened yet doesn't mean it won't. Maybe it's taking longer for me to reach my goal, but I will reach it. I have to."

"You'll hand yourself to some guy—let him take whatever he wants from you—just because he opens his wallet and lets you take whatever you want from it."

She tried to feel militant and defiant when she said, "Damn right." Instead, she only felt tired and defeated.

"It's not a fair trade, Bree. Not even close."

She said nothing to that. Mostly because she couldn't disagree.

When she remained silent, he nodded briskly, then dropped his hands onto his hips in challenge. "Okay. Okay, so let's say you do find a guy rich enough to keep you in the style you imagine you need to make you happy."

Bree thrust her fists onto her hips, too, mimicking his stance, rising to his challenge. "There's no 'imagine' in the equation, Rufus. I know what I need to be—" She couldn't make herself say the word *happy,* since she knew, really, that she would never be that. "To be content," she finally finished. "And it can only be bought with lots and lots of money."

He started ticking things off on his fingers. "Expensive home, expensive car, expensive jewelry, expensive clothes, expensive travel. Did I leave anything out?"

"Maybe one or two things," she told him crisply. "But I think you got the biggies."

He dropped his hands back to his hips. "You think having that will make you happy?"

"Yes," she said. "I do." As happy as she could be, anyway. Because all of those things could be turned into cash if an emergency arose. And cash was what Bree wanted— needed—more than anything. "But it's more than just expensive things, Rufus," she continued. "It's knowing I don't have to worry. It's security. That's even more important to me than the expensive things."

"You think you're going to have *security* in this life you envision for yourself?" he demanded. "Are you serious? Guys who buy women only pay for them for as long as they're interested in them. And they don't stay interested for long, Bree. What happens when your Sugar Daddy finds a new Barbie doll he likes better than you?"

Did he think she hadn't thought about that? Hadn't she just told him she was smart? She sure as hell wasn't that naïve. She knew men didn't marry their mistresses. And she knew they didn't keep them forever. "By the time he gets bored with me," she said, "I'll have moved in his society long enough to have met dozens of men just like him."

Rufus's mouth dropped open at that. "So that's it then?" he asked. "You'll just hire yourself out to the highest bidder? Let yourself be passed around among friends?"

"Oh, don't you dare make it sound tawdry."

"Bree, it *is* tawdry."

"It's not tawdry."

"Then what do you call it?"

"Survival," she said. "I call it survival."

"And what have you been doing all these years?" he asked her. "You seem to have survived just fine on your own." He spread his arms wide. "Look at this place. It's beautiful."

"It's small."

"It's *beautiful*," he repeated. "You have a nice place to live, Bree. You have a decent job. You have friends who care about you. Do you really need more than that?"

"Yes," she told him without hesitation. "I do. Because I'm tired, Rufus. I'm tired of never having anything extra in the bank. I'm tired of dreaming about going places I can't afford to go. Hell, I'm tired of months where I have to decide whether to pay the electric bill or the phone bill or buy groceries. And I'm tired, dammit, of worrying about the future and how I'm going to cope with everything that's sure to come."

She started to tell him about her mother. Wanted to tell him the real reason she was so obsessed with having—and hoarding—money. But maybe it would be better if he didn't know. If he thought she was shallow enough to just want material possessions, then maybe his affection for her would wane. Maybe he'd begin to view her as just some whack chick he didn't want to be around. Maybe he'd stop doing nice things for her, saying nice things to her, being so nice to her. And maybe he'd stop looking at her the way he did sometimes, a way that made her want to fall into his arms and cling to him.

He studied her hard for a moment, his mouth a thin line. "I still don't get it, Bree. I still don't see how you could sacrifice your dignity in exchange for letting someone else, someone who doesn't even care about you on more than a superficial level, hold your future in his hands."

She swallowed hard. "Yeah, well, the way it stands right now, I don't have enough of a future for anyone's hands, do I?"

Rufus shook his head. "You know, for a smart, articulate, interesting woman, you could use some serious education."

She was about to challenge him on that, but the scrape of a key in the front door halted her. Before either she or Rufus could say a word, Lulu came in, chattering enough for both of them.

"I saw the light from the street, so I knew you were still up. Thank God, too, because you won't believe what happened at the gallery tonight. You remember that girl from—" She halted abruptly when she saw Rufus, smiling until she evidently noticed how cool the temperature was in the room. Then, in a cautious voice, she said, "Hi, Rufus." She looked at Bree. "Everything okay?"

Rufus replied before Bree had a chance to, and he spoke as he strode toward the front door that was still open behind Lulu. "Everything's okay with me, Lulu," he said as he brushed past her, giving her a quick buss on the cheek in both greeting and farewell as he went. "Your friend, though . . ." He shook his head again, but never finished his statement. Instead, he looked at Bree and said, "I hope you find what you're looking for. But ya ask me, Bree, you don't even know what the hell that is."

And then he was gone, leaving Lulu to look at Bree, her face a silent question mark. And leaving Bree to look at Lulu without an answer to be had.

·Eleven·

IT WAS A RARE FRIDAY NIGHT WHEN BREE WAS OFF from work and Eddie wasn't performing as Liza Minnelli. So Lulu and her friends took advantage of the anomaly by doing their most favorite thing in the world—congregating at Bree's apartment to watch Orlando Bloom in high def. On this particular Friday night, it was Lulu's turn to choose the movie, and she naturally selected *Elizabethtown*, because she'd seen part of it being filmed while the crew was on location in Louisville. In fact, she'd watched them set up for a scene that included Orlando Bloom. Unfortunately, she'd seen Orlando Bloom's stand-in instead of Orlando himself, but by squinting her eyes just so, she had been able to pretend it was him and so had been content.

"I still think they should have filmed the hotel scenes at the Ambassador instead of the Brown," Bree said as the credits scrolled past at movie's end. But then, she always said that as the credits scrolled past at movie's end. The only difference tonight was that she was wearing jeans and a T-shirt when she said it—much like Lulu and Eddie—instead of her

Nick and Nora pajamas, which was what she and Lulu were usually wearing whenever they watched Orlando in high def.

"Of course you do, darling," Eddie said absently. He had his blond head bent over the DVD case, reading over the liner notes. "The bonus features on this thing are appallingly bad," he said. "There's no photo gallery of Orlando at all. What's up with that?"

"The hotel choice is a tough call if you ask me," Lulu said, scraping the bottom of the popcorn bowl for old maids and coming up empty. So she swiped her finger through an especially buttery spot and licked it clean. "They're both gorgeous and would set off Orlando nicely. He did look awfully dreamy in that Camberley robe, though, I must say."

"Ah, well," Bree said as she reached for the remote control. "Time to go back to the real world." She pushed the button to return to regular TV, just in time for the eleven o'clock news. Inevitably, though, midway through the program there was an interview with Cole Early, and his face was splashed across the screen in all its ruggedly handsome glory. Again.

Lulu's first thought upon seeing him was that he was such a stark contrast to Orlando, brawny where the actor was slender, masculinely striking where the actor was almost androgynously beautiful, his features square and blunt where the actor's were lean and smooth. Her second thought was that she must have done something *really* bad to piss off her karma, because she couldn't seem to escape the man. He was everywhere that she was.

"Not again," she groaned as she grabbed the remote from the sofa where Bree had dropped it. She aimed it at the TV to change the channel, but Eddie snatched it out of her hands.

"Oh, no you don't," he said as he stuffed it down into the cushions on the other side of himself where she couldn't reach it. "With all the bad stuff they've been reporting lately, you are *not* going to change the channels when there's finally something worth watching on the news."

Lulu gaped at him. "You can't be serious. You think Cole

Early on TV—again—is good? He's all they show anymore. I'm getting sick of him."

Eddie made a rude sound of disbelief. "If seeing Cole Early on TV every night is being sick, then take me to the terminal ward now, because I don't ever want to get better."

Lulu shook her head. "You can't possibly think that guy is attractive."

Now Eddie was the one to gape. "Darling, I know you have rather, ah . . . unconventional taste in men, but have you gone *blind*?"

Lulu decided to ignore the last part of Eddie's question and focus on the first comment instead. "What do you mean unconventional? I don't have unconventional taste in men. All I ask is that they be smart, funny, gentle, vegetarian, and that they smell good. And also be good with animals and small children. And bake bread. And grow things. And be handy around the house."

Eddie ticked off a few more requirements on his fingers as he voiced them aloud. "And be boring and dependable and predictable and safe. And also boring. Did I mention they had to be boring?"

Lulu narrowed her eyes at him. "You say 'safe' like it's a bad thing," she said, ignoring the boring part, too. Since—okay, okay—the guys she dated, when she dated, were a little, well, boring. "There's nothing wrong with being safe. A lot of women would be wise to look for safe men."

"Oh, let's leave your more neurotic friends out of this," Eddie said, turning to look pointedly at Bree.

"Hey!" Bree objected. "I'm not—"

"A lot of women *would* be wise to look for safe men," he interjected. "But not you, Lulu. You're the most cautious person I know. You need a little danger to balance out your overabundance of prudence."

"Prudence?" she echoed distastefully. "I'm not prudent."

"Darling, your parents should have *named* you Prudence. Prudence Modesty Flannery. No, Prudence Modesty Chastity Flan—"

"*Chastity*? Now wait just one—"

But Eddie was on a roll. Laughing, he concluded, "Prudence Modesty Chastity Temperance Flannery. That takes care of any amount of fun you might have otherwise."

The barb, even delivered as lightly as Eddie had delivered it, hit home. "I'm fun," Lulu argued. But even she thought the objection sounded halfhearted.

Eddie only sighed. With a gentle, rueful smile, he patted her hand and said softly, "You have your moments, Lulu. And you have the potential for more. But for some reason, you choose to always play it safe."

Lulu knew perfectly what that reason was, even if she'd never voiced it to anyone. She *chose* to always play it safe because she *had* to always play it safe. There was something deep inside her that she had to keep a constant rein on, something she had to make sure never broke loose in polite society. It was something impulsive and impetuous, something untamed and unpredictable, something extreme and exhilarating. Something powerful enough to take her over completely if she wasn't careful to keep it contained. She only allowed herself to tap into it when she was safely cloistered in her studio, creating her art. Because whenever that part of her was unlocked and allowed to roam free, it consumed her entirely.

When Lulu was creating her art, she lost herself to it. Completely and utterly, with a totality that had once scared the hell out of her. These days, she understood it enough to not fear it so much, but she was still plenty wary of it. There were times when she was working that hours passed without her even realizing it. There had been days when she went without eating because she was so deeply immersed in her art, it almost drowned her. Once or twice, she'd spent the night at her studio without intending to, having never even noticed the passage of daylight into darkness into dawn. At times like those, she simply ceased to be herself and became someone—something—else, a creature whose only function, whose only need, was to feel, and to express, and to create. No way was Lulu going to risk that creature coming out for anything other than her glass. God only knew what that part of her might do or say if she didn't lock it back in its cage when she was away from her art.

She told Eddie none of this, however. Hell, she'd never even told Bree. Only other artists could understand that part of Lulu. And a lot of times, she didn't think many of *them* could even relate.

"You never take chances," Eddie continued, bringing her back to the conversation at hand. "And sometimes, to get the really great prizes, Lulu, you have to throw caution to the wind. You have to close your eyes and throw your arms wide, and run blindly forward and trust that what you fall into will be exactly what you need. You're not the sort of person to do that. You could be. But you're not." Before she had a chance to react to what he said—not that she had any idea how to re-act to that—he looked at the TV and frowned. "And now you've made me miss Cole Early on the news again." He sighed dramatically. "It's not fair. You'll get to go home and sleep in your bed after he's slept in it, and park your little tushie in the same chair he parked his in, and shower in the same bathtub he used . . ." He shivered deliciously for effect. "And I can't even watch him on TV."

A blast of heat exploded in Lulu's midsection at Eddie's words. She narrowed her eyes at him. "What do you mean I'll go home and sleep in my bed and sit in my chairs and shower in my tub after he's done all those things?"

Eddie's eyes widened in panic. "I didn't say that out loud. Did I say that out loud?"

"Yes," she told him, straightening on the sofa. "You did. What did you mean?"

"Nothing," he quickly countered. A little too quickly, ac-tually. "I didn't mean anything. I didn't even say that. You never heard it."

"I heard it, too," Bree said, moving to the sofa to sit on the other side of Eddie.

As if of one mind, she and Lulu both moved in closer,

squeezing him to the spot between them. When he tried to stand, they each clamped a hand over his forearms and pulled him back down.

"Eddie, what did you do?" Bree asked.

He closed his mouth tightly, folding his lips inward and said nothing. Nor did he look at either woman. He simply fixed his gaze straight ahead.

"Eddie . . ." Lulu said more adamantly.

He lifted a hand to his mouth, mimicked the zipping of his lip, and dropped it again.

Lulu wasn't about to let it go that easily. "Are you telling me you rented my house to Cole Early?"

This time when Eddie lifted a hand, it was to pretend he was locking the zipper in place. Then, for added emphasis, he tossed the imaginary key over his shoulder.

Bree got up from the sofa, went behind it to pick up the invisible key, then returned to both unlock and unzip Eddie's lip. Then she smacked him upside the head with her—very real—hand. "Come on, Eddie," she cajoled. "We know you rented a house to him, because Lulu saw him in your office."

"And he showed up right when I was dropping off the key," Lulu remembered, "and you told me my timing was perfect. I thought you were renting it to the guy in front of me. But it was Cole Early, wasn't it?"

"You know I can't divulge that information," he said. "Some of my clients are celebrities and major players in the industry. If it gets out that I'm telling people where they're staying, that'll be the end of the Derby rental arm of Hot Properties. And a huge chunk of my annual income, too," he added.

"Oh, come on, Eddie," Bree said. "You're among friends here."

"It doesn't matter," he said. "I'm not telling you anything about any of my clients. Especially who's renting Lulu's house. If I reveal that information, the next thing I know, there's an angry, torch-bearing mob of time-share Realtors on my front porch demanding my head."

"Yeah," Bree agreed derisively. "And God knows there's nothing scarier than an angry, torch-bearing mob of people in ugly blazers hounding you."

"But, Eddie," Lulu said, the heat in her belly swelling to panic when she thought about Cole living in her house and cavalierly using her things. "Cole Early is a party animal. He's probably completely trashed my place by now. He's probably having wild parties every night. Drinking and smoking and carousing. He might even be doing drugs. You know how those people from southern California are."

"Hey, my aunt Mimi lives in Encino, and the only drug she ever does is Dulcolax," Eddie objected. "Besides, Cole Early can't be having wild parties at your house," he added dismissively. "You've seen him on the news every night. He's always at someone else's party. I mean . . ." He quickly backpedaled. "*If* it's Cole Early staying at your house— which I'm *not* saying it is—then he isn't having parties there every night."

"Then he's probably taking home all those sleazy women he's with at those other parties and . . . and . . . and . . . *doing* things with them in my house. In my bed. Things that are probably illegal in Kentucky. This is still the Bible Belt, you know."

Eddie arched his brows indignantly at that.

"If there's illegal stuff going on at my house," Lulu said, "I need to know about it."

Eddie thrust his hand into the pocket of his blue jeans and pulled out his keys, then dangled them in front of Lulu. "Darling, if there's illegal stuff like *that* going on at your house, you need to rush home and be a part of it. Take my car. It's faster than that little bug thing you drive."

Lulu stuck her tongue out at him.

"That's a good start," he said with a laugh. "But there's so much more you need to learn. And I can't think of a better teacher than Cole Early."

"Aha!" Bree cried. "Then you admit he's the one staying in Lulu's house."

Eddie expelled a long sigh of resignation. But he only said, "I'm not saying he is, and I'm not saying he isn't."

It was the equivalent of saying yes as far as Lulu was concerned. Because if it wasn't Cole Early staying at her house, Eddie would have said so. Not that she needed even that much verification at this point.

"Eddie!" she exclaimed. "How could you *do* that? How could you rent *my* house . . . my house that I've worked *so hard* on refurbishing . . . with my *bare hands* . . . for more than a *year* . . . How could you let someone like Cole Early go in and turn the place into party central?"

"Lulu, I'm sure it's fine," Eddie said in a placating voice. "The guy's too busy being out and about to do any harm to your place."

"How do you know?"

Eddie said nothing.

"Guys like that have no respect for other people's property," Lulu said. "Guys like that never think about anyone but themselves. Guys like that don't care who they run roughshod over."

Eddie met her gaze levelly. "How do *you* know?" he asked, turning her words back on her. "He might just be one of the nicest guys in the world."

Lulu shook her head. "Nice guys finish last, Eddie. Everyone knows that. No way is this guy going to settle for last place. He intends to be number one. And he doesn't care who gets in his way."

Lulu looked at Bree. Bree looked at Lulu.

"There's just one thing to do," Bree said.

Lulu nodded. "I'm going to have to go break into my house."

"No, *we're* going to have to break into your house," Bree corrected.

Oh, right. Bree would want to be along for this, wouldn't she? Lulu thought. And why did the realization of that make her feel worse, not better? She would have thought having

Bree along for the ride would reassure her. Instead, it kind of hacked her off.

"No, *you're* going to stay here with me and watch *Kingdom of Heaven*," Eddie said, curling his fingers over Bree's arm. "You know I can't handle those Crusade scenes by myself. I always cry."

Bree opened her mouth to object, but Eddie reminded her of Orlando looking all scruffy and defeated in his suit of armor, and in dire need of loving care, and she relented. "You better do it now, though, Lulu," she said. "While Cole Early is still on the news. He was at the Peterson-Parson party. That thing'll run 'til dawn. It always does."

"What if he leaves early?" Lulu asked, her determination suddenly wavering at the thought of actually running into someone at her house—especially Cole Early.

"Oh, please," Bree said. "Early to Cole Early is A.M., not P.M. It'll be hours before he heads home. Go, Lulu," she told her. "Go find out who's been sleeping in your bed. 'Cause I'm betting it's the Big Bad Wolf himself. And I'm betting Goldilocks has been sleeping there with him."

TWENTY MINUTES AFTER PULLING TO A STOP AT THE end of her block, Lulu was still sitting in her car, trying to work up the nerve to approach her own house. She felt ridiculous in the extreme. There was obviously no one home, and even if there was, it was *her* home. She had a key and everything. Which she would use. So it wouldn't be breaking in. It wouldn't even be illegal entry, since she was the owner of the house. All it would be was a violation of the contract she signed for Eddie. That was only unethical. And Lulu had been unethical lots of times.

Well, okay, maybe she'd only been unethical once or twice. And maybe it had never been on purpose. That would be good when she appeared before the judge, right?

Stop it, she told herself. She wasn't going to get arrested for this. She would just pop in to *her own home* and see if everything was okay. Make sure Cole Early hadn't, at best, broken anything or, at worst, trashed the place. Make sure he hadn't been doing anything he shouldn't. Make sure there weren't any, oh, say . . . drunken debutantes passed out on the sofa. Or any, oh, say . . . empty liquor bottles strewn about the floors. Or any, oh, say . . . illegal drug paraphernalia clogging the pipes. Or any, oh, say . . . appalling—if somewhat interesting—sex toys stuffed under the bed.

Enough, Lulu, she told herself. *Let's just get this over with.*

As quietly as she could, she opened her car door and exited, making her way down the uneven sidewalk the way she had a million times before when finishing up her evening walk. Automatically, she sidestepped the gaping crack in front of Mrs. Krautheim's house and the spot where the root of Mr. Leonard's sycamore had buckled the concrete. She slowed her pace as she approached her little bungalow, having never really paid attention to it from outside in the dark before.

Cole Early had left on the same light in the living room she generally switched on at night herself, and something about that heartened Lulu. As she drew nearer, she saw that he'd left on a light in the kitchen, too, the one over the stove that she left on when she knew she would be out after dark. From where she stood, all was calm and bright, the house glowing cozily in the pitch-black night.

She told herself she should be satisfied with that, that Cole Early didn't appear to have done anything *too* horrible to her house . . . yet. But even though she could see a bit of the living room through the windows, and it appeared to be as tidy as she left it, she couldn't quite bring herself to leave without going inside.

She'd just take a little peek, she told herself. Just buzz through the house to make a quick survey and reassure herself that all was well. It would only be a few minutes. And Cole Early would never know. Her desire to go into the house had *nothing* to do with her curiosity about him that had been growing ever since she met him.

She made her way stealthily up the driveway to the back door and inserted her key into the lock, turning it swiftly and pushing the door open wide. She left it ajar behind her as she strode into the kitchen, noticing right away that her guest had made himself at home. The wine rack on the counter that normally held only one or two bottles of wine now housed four. There was a short stack of periodicals about the Thoroughbred industry sitting on the counter near them. An empty glass was sitting in the sink. Through one of her glass-doored cupboards, she saw both a bottle of what looked like *very* expensive cognac, and another of what looked like *very* expensive Scotch. A man's jacket was slung over the back of one of her chairs. Striding toward it, Lulu ran an idle finger over the fabric, noting not just its fineness, but the faint aroma of something spicy and masculine that was stirred by her fingers.

So he smelled good, she thought. So what? Lots of men smelled good. He probably didn't fit any of her other criteria for what made a man attractive. To prove that to herself, she moved to the refrigerator and opened it, then pulled out the drawer of the meat keeper, which usually held only cheese. Yep. There was a package of roast beef from Kroger *and* a package of bacon, though that latter had yet to be opened. He clearly was *not* a vegetarian. And—just a shot in the dark—she bet he didn't bake bread, either.

She noticed a few other additions to her refrigerator that weren't normally there—a six-pack of imported beer, eggs, doughnuts—but nothing that would endanger anything more than someone's weight or cholesterol level.

Little by little, Lulu made her way through her house, double-checking to be certain Cole Early hadn't used any-thing he wasn't supposed to, and making note of any miss-ing possessions. She only noticed one, however—a glass vase on the marble-top table by the front door that had been one of her first completed pieces, and she hadn't been all that crazy about it anyway. She'd only had it on display to remind herself of how far she'd come as an artist. Still, she was curious to know what had happened to it. Then she saw a ding in the plaster on the wall beside the front door that was about knob size, and she made an educated guess. Door opened too hard, slammed with enough vigor to shake the vase free. Still, as damage went, it would be easy enough to fix. Certainly easier than sobering up drunken debutantes or disposing of drug paraphernalia and appalling—if somewhat interesting—sex toys.

The rest of the house, she noted as she passed through it, looked just the way she'd left it . . . until she climbed the stairs to her bedroom and switched on the light. Here, Cole Early had clearly made himself at home. The bed was barely made; he'd done nothing more than toss the sheets and spread up over the pillows. Clothes were draped over it and the chair, and her computer had been pushed to the far side of the desk to make room for his briefcase. She checked to be sure the note was still attached and the computer was still off—yes to both—then wondered why she bothered. Even her untrained eye could see that the guy's laptop on a nearby chair was state-of-the-art and couldn't possibly lack anything her desktop might have on it. There was a scattering of papers on the desk, too, topped by that day's racing form, and some phone numbers scribbled onto a scratch pad she recognized as her own.

Okay, so the guy wasn't the tidiest person in the world, and he didn't think twice about appropriating someone's scratch pads. He hadn't done anything to her house that wouldn't be fixed by his vacating it. There was no reason for her to hang around.

Except that, for some reason, she wanted to hang around.

Her hand hovered over the papers by his briefcase, and she had to halt herself from sorting through them. Snooping like that would be tantamount to his having turned on her computer and rifled through her files, and no way would she tolerate an invasion of privacy like that. So she turned and started to make her way out of the bedroom and back down-stairs. From the corner of her eye, however, she saw some-thing else that was different from the way she'd left it, something that halted her in her tracks. The photograph of herself and Bree and three of their friends from high school who lived elsewhere now, but with whom they vacationed every summer, had been moved from her dresser to the nightstand.

Huh. That was odd. Why would he move a photograph? Then she gave herself a mental smack. Because it was a photo of five women in bathing suits, that was why. Well, four women in bathing suits and Lulu in one of the oversized T-shirts and ball caps she always wore to the beach to keep herself and her fair complexion from spontaneously com-busting. She waited for the disdain she told herself she should feel at his having appropriated her memories for his own salacious enjoyment. Instead, what she felt was a tiny thrill of something that felt suspiciously like pleasure.

You're nuts, Lulu. Absolutely nuts.

She stood there looking at the photo for as long as it took to work up the righteous indignation she knew she must be feeling. But that, unfortunately, took way more time than she would have liked, so she finally gave up on feeling it. Not certain why she did it, she moved the photograph back to her dresser. There. Let him make of that whatever he wanted. It was time for her to go. Past time, really.

Oh, hell. She never should have come here at all. Because instead of reassuring herself that Cole Early wasn't turning her little bungalow into a brothel, all she'd done was mag-nify her curiosity about Cole Early even more than before. And the guy was already using up way too much of her men-tal energy, popping into her head at inopportune times, even invading her dreams from time to time at night. She barely knew the guy, but there had been times when he commanded more of her attention than she gave even to her work.

She really was nuts.

She turned to look at the stack of papers sitting next to his briefcase again. They *were* right out there in the open, she rationalized. So it wouldn't really be snooping. Never mind the fact that they'd been left in the open because Cole Early hadn't thought anyone would be breaking into his house.

But it wasn't breaking in, she reminded herself. And it wasn't his house. And it would only be a few minutes. And he'd never know.

Rationalization—however lame—completed, Lulu made her way back across the room to her desk.

·Twelve·

IT WASN'T UNTIL COLE WAS ALMOST AT THE FRONT door of his rented house that he realized something was wrong. He hesitated before inserting the key in the lock, trying to figure out what had set off his always reliable internal alarm system. The street behind him was silent, and the front door was locked. But something niggled at the back of his head, just out of reach . . .

The bedroom light, he realized. It had been on when he pulled in the driveway. But he distinctly remembered turning it off before he left. Living in California—or, more accurately, paying electric bills in California—a person got used to never leaving things on frivolously. Habits weren't broken just because one was out of town, so he was no different with a house he was renting than he was with his own. Just as he did at home, he always left on a living room light and a kitchen light when he went out, because he was never sure which door he'd come in when he returned.

Just to make sure he hadn't been seeing things, Cole silently descended the porch steps and looked up at the bedroom window from the front walk. Yep, the light was on. Not only that, a shadow moved in front of the closed curtain as he was looking at it, telling him someone was up there poking around.

He started to reach for his cell phone to call the police, but the light in the bedroom went off, indicating whoever was up there might be on their way out. Instinctively, he made his way around to the back of the house and saw a finger of timid light filtering through a crack in the back door, an indication that it was ajar. Whoever was inside had entered through there, so it was a good bet that was where the intruder would be exiting, too. Quickly, Cole darted into the kitchen and pushed the door back the way he'd found it. Then he moved to the stove and switched off the light there and pressed himself into a dark corner, just in time to hear footfalls coming down the stairs that lay behind the door opposite him.

His heart rate doubled when that door swung open and a shadowy figure emerged, hesitating before moving forward, clearly uncertain what had happened to the light. Cole didn't waste any time. Lunging forward, he tackled the shape and knocked it to the floor in the hallway. In the handful of seconds it took to complete the action, he registered a surprising number of things.

First, that the figure was a lot smaller than he'd initially thought. Second, that because of that first thing, both he and the figure landed on the hallway runner a lot harder than he'd planned. Third, that because of that second thing, he discovered the figure was a lot less masculine than he'd realized. And fourth, that because of that third thing, he would be going straight to hell, since, in an effort to subdue the previously-thought-to-be-masculine figure, he accidentally cupped the man's, uh, woman's, breast and was, for the briefest of moments—but still a hell-worthy amount of time—just the tiniest bit grateful and just the tiniest bit aroused.

He had just enough time after marveling at the fact that

he had been turned on by a common criminal trying to steal his stuff—and after making a mental note to go out and get himself laid as soon as he got back to California— to form the words *What the hell?* Unfortunately, the words never quite made it out of his mouth, because they were cut off by the way the figure freed an arm and belted Cole in the mouth—hard. It surprised more than hurt him, but it made him reel backward just enough to give the figure leverage that allowed her to pull herself up and shove him backward—hard.

Then she was on all fours, scrambling to get up and run, something she was almost able to do. But Cole regrouped quickly enough to grab her around the waist and pull her backward and upward, off the floor and against his body.

Man, for someone who didn't weigh anything and fought like a girl, she was one tough, tenacious dame.

He dodged her fists as well as he could as he felt along the wall for the light switch, but he still got socked a few times. She kicked, too, landing her heels again and again in his shins, his calves, and his knees. It was because of that last that, just as he found the light switch and flicked it on, his legs buckled beneath him, then both he and his captive went tumbling onto the hallway runner again. He caught himself on his forearms before he would have squashed her, but pressed his body hard on top of her to keep her from wriggling free again.

The sudden eruption of bright light into the hall blinded him momentarily, but it also halted her fists—momentarily. Nevertheless, it was long enough for him to grab both her wrists in his hands and push them high above her head, pinning them to the floor as effectively as her body was pinned beneath his. She began to jerk wildly when she realized how thoroughly he'd incapacitated her, but her slight build was no match for his. In the chaos, he couldn't get a bead on her features, but her scent he recognized immediately. And that faint hint of patchouli brought his gaze to her face pronto. When he saw that that face was obscured by a riot of auburn

curls, he knew without question that he was indeed the luckiest son of a bitch on the planet.

Good things came in threes. Three times lucky. Third
time's a charm.

On three occasions now he had encountered her, through
nothing but sheer dumb luck. That had to mean something,
he told himself. If he could just figure out what . . .

"Hortense?" he said softly in disbelief. What was she doing breaking into houses? Or, more specifically, this house?
How had she found him? More to the point, why had she
gone to the trouble to try? And, most important of all, why
had he not noticed before what great breasts she had?

At the sound of her name, she immediately stopped struggling and shook her hair out of her eyes as best she could to
see who had said it. "Cole?" she asked in the same incredulous tone.

"What are you doing here?"

She slumped back against the floor, all signs of struggle
gone. For some reason, though, he wasn't quite ready to lift
himself off of her. Not until he had answers to some of his
questions. Especially that last one.

She blew out a long, weary breath. Then, very softly, she
said, "I live here."

It took a moment for that to register. And even when it
did, because it was just too weird a development, he said,
"I'm renting *your* house?"

She nodded.

Definitely weird. Maybe a little too weird?

In fact, the whole scenario bothered him on a number of
levels. It was, after all, a pretty major coincidence that he was
renting the house of a woman he'd decided only the day before he wanted to employ as a buffer against overenthusiastic
groupies. But what if Hortense was one of those very overenthusiastic groupies he was trying to avoid? She'd been at
the realty office when he arrived—had she known in advance
he was coming? That he was the one who'd be renting her
place? She'd turned up in not one, but two, bars where he'd

gone for a drink, too. Had she been following him? Maybe since his arrival? Cole wasn't so self-centered that he thought someone would go to so much trouble to make his acquaintance, but it wasn't unheard of for whack-job fans to follow—and even stalk—the objects of their affections.

And what if this *wasn't* her house? What if she'd just broken in knowing this was where he was staying—on account of she was stalking him—to steal a souvenir of some kind while he wasn't here? Or, worse, to try to get to him while he *was* here?

"Prove it," he said.

She lifted her head from the floor and narrowed her eyes at him in confusion. "What?"

"Prove this is your house," he told her.

"How am I supposed to do that?"

"You must have some paperwork somewhere with your name on it. Bills, checks, library card, something that says Hortense Waddy."

She slumped against the floor again. "No, I don't," she said.

"Why not?"

"Because my name isn't really Hortense Waddy."

He had a mixed reaction to the news. On one hand, he was relieved that she hadn't been saddled with such an unsuitable name. On the other hand, it wasn't looking good for the stalker thing.

"Look, I can explain everything," she said. "Let me up."

"Nuh-uh," he said.

She snapped her head up again, and this time her eyes flashed with annoyance. "Let. Me. Up," she repeated with significantly more nerve.

"No," he said just as adamantly. "Not until you tell me what the hell is going on and who the hell you are."

"My name is Lulu Flannery," she said. "Eddie Mahoney, the guy you rented the house from, is a good friend of mine. He convinced me to rent out my house for Derby weekend, then, when a request came through from someone who needed a place for two weeks, he called in a few favors." With clear reluctance, she added, "And he reminded me how much my Home Depot bill is."

Cole eyed her warily. "Home Depot?" he repeated.

She nodded. "I've spent way more on the house than I planned since I moved in."

"You've been fixing this place up yourself?"

Another nod.

Well, that explained the cracks in the walkway and the crumbling stairs. Obviously, she was working from the inside out.

"Okay, so let's say you're telling the truth," he said, "and that this is, in fact, your house."

"It *is* my house," she insisted.

He continued as if she hadn't spoken. "How do you explain the fact that, virtually every time I turn around, I see you standing somewhere in my immediate vicinity?"

"Oh, please," she muttered indignantly. "What? You think I'm your number one fan girl or something?"

He shook his head. "Actually, I'm beginning to think you're my number one stalker girl or something."

She gaped at that. "Stalker? Are you serious?"

"Hey, you're the one who keeps showing up everywhere that I am."

"Or maybe you're the one who keeps showing up everywhere that *I* am," she countered. "Who says *you're* not *my* stalker?"

He gazed at her in amusement. "Because your reputation didn't precede you, sweetheart. When I left California, I had no way of even knowing who the hell you are. You, however, were inundated with information about me from your local press."

"*I* wasn't inundated," she said snottily. "And I wasn't impressed, either. And besides," she hurried on before he had a chance to say something snotty back, "I myself have a *very* popular website in the art glass community."

This time, Cole gazed at her in indulgence. "Do you now?"

She lifted her chin defiantly. "Yes. I do. It's very inter-active. I get e-mail every day from someone telling me how great it is and how much they enjoyed visiting it."

"Every day?" he asked with clearly feigned admiration.

"Well, almost every day," she qualified with clear reluc-tance. Then, when Cole only continued to study her with skepticism, she amended, "Okay, twice I got that kind of e-mail. My point is, you're not the only one who's stalkable in this town, pal."

In response, Cole only continued to study her in silence.

Her response to his response was the expulsion of an irri-table sigh. Then she said, "The first time we ran into each other, it was scheduled."

Really not looking good for the stalker thing, Cole thought. "Come again?" he said.

"Eddie told me to drop off my keys at five o'clock Friday because that's when you would be arriving to pick them up."

"And he told you who I was?"

"No," she replied in a way that told him she thought he was nuts for thinking that. "Eddie's client list is confidential. In fact, I thought the other guy who was there when you and I were there was the one renting my house. It was why I wasn't worried about renting out my house. He seemed like a nice man."

"Oh, and I didn't?"

"Of course not."

His eyebrows shot up in surprise at that. "Excuse me?"

"You knocked me down," she reminded him. "And you kept calling me sweetheart."

He had? He couldn't remember that.

"I hate guys who do that," she added.

She did? He'd try to remember that. But all he said was, "What about that time at the Ambassador Bar? Was that scheduled, too?"

"Hey, Einstein, I was there *before* you that night," she told him.

That was right, he recalled now. She had been seated at the far side of the bar when he came in.

"I'm there a lot, waiting for Bree to finish her shift. So that was *your* fault we ran into each other that night. You were invading *my* turf."

Oh.

"Just like you're invading my turf now," she added.

"Oh, no," he immediately objected. "This is *my* turf until next Sunday. It's bought and paid for. I don't care if this is *your* house. You're the invader here, not me. So tell me, Ms. . . . Flannery, was it?"

She nodded but said nothing.

"Tell me then, Ms. Flannery. Why did you break into your house-slash-my turf?"

She sighed with much annoyance, though whether it was for him or for herself, Cole couldn't have said. "Because when I found out it was you staying here, I wanted to make sure you hadn't trashed the place."

Cole told himself he should be most concerned about the fact that, in spite of her friend's keeping his client list confidential, she'd still found out he was staying here. If she could find that out, what was to keep any number of other women—women he'd just as soon *not* see—from finding out, too? But really, what concerned him most was the fact that she thought he had it in him to trash a place like this. Any place, really. But especially a place like hers that was warm and welcoming and offered solace and serenity to a man who had a lifestyle like his, a lifestyle that contained neither of those things. He knew King Cole's reputation wasn't sterling, but neither had he thought it was tarnished to the point where people could think him so crass and careless.

"I'm no neat freak," he agreed, "but I'm not a slob, either. And I sure as hell wouldn't trash a place. Especially one as nice as yours."

That seemed to mollify her some. "You think it's nice?"

"I think it's great," he said sincerely. "I like how you use color."

"Thanks."

"It's a very inviting space."

"That's nice of you to say that."

It occurred to him that they had just slipped from stalker/stalkee accusations into an interview from HGTV rather effortlessly, but decided not to dwell on why. It was enough that the pinched, uneasy look had been erased from her face, and that she was talking to him now the way people did who were making each other's acquaintance for the first time. And he decided not to dwell, too, on why that made him feel better.

"And you have great taste in art, too," he told her, because . . . Well, just because, that was why. And it was a damned good reason.

She actually blushed at that. "Some of it's mine."

"The glass, right?" he said, already having figured that out.

She nodded. "And some of the paintings, as well."

"No kidding?" he asked, genuinely impressed.

"Glass is definitely my first love," she said, "but oil on canvas is my second favorite medium. And I love sketching, too."

"Really. You know, I don't know anything about art, but I know what I like, and—"

She laughed at that, halting his words. Not that she sounded scornful or anything. She just had a really nice laugh.

"What?" he asked.

"That's such a cliché, you know." She deepened her voice in a fair mimic of his as she continued, " 'I don't know anything about art, but I know what I like.' " She went back to her regular voice as she added, "That's what people say when they're trying to impress someone but don't have a clue what the art means."

And her point was? He shook the thought off. "Anyway, I like your house and I wouldn't wreck it."

"Thank you."

"You're welcome."

"Cole?"

"Yeah?"

"Would you let me up now?"

Only then did he realize he was still sitting astride her in her hallway, holding her arms over her head. Strangely, though, instead of immediately releasing her, which was what any decent guy would do, he discovered he kind of wanted to keep her there for a while longer.

He was *so* going to hell.

His hesitation must have made her think he still didn't believe her, because she added, "Look, if you let me up, I'll prove to you that I'm Lulu Flannery and that this is my house."

Although he was still reluctant to let go of her—and that reluctance, he had to admit, had nothing to do with any potential mistrust of her intentions—he released her wrists and levered himself off of her. She immediately wrapped her left hand around her right wrist and rubbed it gently, then mimicked the gesture with the opposite hand. Something chilly and unpleasant nicked his insides at seeing it.

"I'm sorry if I hurt you," he said.

Her reply was what seemed like an unconcerned shake of her head, but whether that meant she was saying that it was okay, it was nothing, or that he hadn't hurt her, or that she was blowing off his apology altogether, he wasn't sure.

"I left my purse out in the car," she said as she scrambled up from the floor, "so I don't have my driver's license on me."

He started to tell her that it was okay, that he believed her, but she hurried on before he had a chance, chattering as she pushed past him and she made her way toward the door at the end of the hall.

"But I have some things upstairs in my bedroom that will prove I'm telling the truth."

She was halfway up the stairs and rounding the landing before she finished talking, so Cole gave up and followed her. She strode easily into the room, which made him forget, again, that he needed to duck or else he'd bump his head on the ceiling, again, which he did, again. When he muttered a ripe oath at having done so, again, she spun around to look at him. When she saw him rubbing his forehead, she must have realized what had happened, again, and she bit back a smile.

"Guess it's not exactly built to your specifications, is it?" she asked.

"Usually I remember to duck," he lied.

"Mm," she said, the sound telling him nothing of what she might be thinking.

He was about to say something else, but she chose that moment to drop to her knees by the side of the bed and pull up the spread, then lean forward even more to look for something underneath it. Cole's mouth went dry at the sight, because her T-shirt rode up and her already low-riding jeans rode lower, giving him an incredible glimpse of twin dimples at the base of her spine and the top of her rump. He'd noticed that first day what a nice ass she had. Seeing her in this position . . .

Well, it wasn't just the reaffirmation of what a nice ass she had going through his head just then. Her position just brought forth all kinds of intriguing possibilities. Starting with how much he wanted to flick the tip of his tongue against each of those dimples, then trace the line of her spine upward, pushing her shirt higher as he went, until he could—

"Here it is," she said, scattering what had promised to be a really nice little fantasy. Too nice, he thought, when he realized his brain wasn't the only organ her position had stimulated.

He gave his head a good shake, as if that might physically dislodge the errant—and none too appropriate—thoughts from his mind, and tried to focus on what Lulu was doing instead. She withdrew a flat metal box with a combination lock on it that she proceeded to twist first right, then left, then right again. With a final click of the dial, she folded the lid back to reveal a stack of manila folders inside. She dug down to the bottom of them and pulled out a passport, which she then handed to Cole.

"Proof of my identity," she said.

He opened it to find the requisite lousy photograph, but it was good enough that it resembled her perfectly. He flipped a page to read her personal information and found that her name was indeed Lulu Flannery and that she did indeed live at this address. Then he flipped some more pages and noticed a few other things.

"It's expired," he said.

"It still proves I'm who I say I am."

"There are no stamps in it," he pointed out.

In response to that, she covered the short distance between them on her knees and snatched it out of his hand. "I just never got around to using it, that's all," she said. Then she kneed her way back to the metal box and dropped it inside, slamming the lid shut and giving the combination a good spin.

"Don't get any ideas," she told him. "Everything in here is just personal fluff. There's nothing valuable or anything."

"I wouldn't dream of intruding," he replied. Since, hey, he'd found way more interesting stuff on her computer than he'd ever find in that box.

Then another thought hit him. The journal. It was *Lulu's* journal he'd been reading all this time? All that passionate rambling and all those erotic fantasies . . . They'd been *Lulu's*? The woman he'd once dubbed Craggedy Ann was the same woman who'd written about making love on the Tilt-a-Whirl at the Kentucky State Fair? The woman who'd blushed at the merest contact of her body with his was the same woman who'd written about petting herself to multiple orgasms while listening to Barry White's "Love's Theme"? Parts one *and* two? The woman who wore Birkenstocks and blue jeans was the same woman whose lingerie drawer was filled with lacy confections in dreamy colors, some of them seeming too small to even cover what they were supposed to cover? That was Lulu? Lulu?

Lulu?

Holy cow.

He watched as she bent over again to push the box back under the bed, trying to jibe the flesh-and-blood Lulu with his fantasy Delilah. There was no way. There was just no way the two women could be the same person. He'd never seen Lulu in anything but jeans, T-shirts, and ugly shoes. No way was she the owner of the rich colors and textures hanging in the closet, and no way was there pale lace or dark silk under such practical, no-frills clothes. She'd been uptight about something every time he encountered her. No way could she write about sensual and sexual pleasures with such a massive lack of inhibition.

Everything in this house pointed to someone who was vivacious, effervescent, and unreserved. Someone who enjoyed every moment of life and never sweated the small stuff. Someone who raced headlong into whatever came her way and relished it. Not . . .

Not Lulu.

"Look, I'm sorry I bothered you," she said as she pushed herself up from the floor and rose to standing.

Cole studied her for a long time in silence, taking in her face, her clothes, her posture, herself, looking for something—*anything*—that might hint at the fun-loving, self-indulgent hedonist who called this house home. But all he saw was a wholesome, responsible, serious-minded woman. A woman who could never in a million years be his Delilah.

The realization of that hit him harder than he would have thought it would. It was almost as if something inside of him that had been full and content a moment ago was suddenly empty and alone. As if someone who'd become very special to him was now lost to him forever. As if he'd finally met a woman who could distract him in a way that he liked, a woman with whom he could share a part of himself he'd never shared, a woman with whom he might possibly even fall in lo . . .

Well. It just felt like he'd lost something wonderful, that was all.

He was struggling to find something to say that would ease the awkward moment that had risen between them when Lulu lifted her hand to the back of her head and ruffled her hair, a gesture clearly born of nervousness from his silent study of her. And that was when Cole saw it. Riding just above the waistband of her low-slung jeans, to the left of the button—her left, not his—where her shirt rode up when she lifted her hand.

A tattoo.

Small, but still noticeable. A Chinese character he recognized from a framed ink sketch that was hanging in her kitchen. The symbol for chaos. The caption under the print had been something from the *I Ching*. Something about chaos being where dreams are born. And how before there could be something brilliant, there must first be chaos.

Lulu Flannery, wholesome, responsible, serious woman had a tattoo on her torso of chaos. And from that chaos, Cole realized, something brilliant and dreamy truly was born. A woman who decorated her body with something more permanent than a Sharpie must be capable of decorating its trappings and its environment in excessive ways, too. This was Lulu's home. It was her bedroom. Her dresser drawer. Her lingerie. And it was her computer and her journal he had been reading, too. Delilah was in there. She must be buried deeply for Lulu to be able to hide her so well, but Delilah *was* inside her. Somewhere.

All Cole had to do was figure out how to set her free.

"Ummm," Lulu began again when he said nothing in response to her statement.

But what was he supposed to say? Other than, *Would you mind lifting your shirt again so I could see your tattoo?*

"I guess I should get going," she added uncomfortably.

She took a few cautious steps forward, then one to the side, then a few more that carried her past him in as wide an arc as she could manage in the small room. And with every step she took, Cole told himself to say something that would keep her from leaving. But his brain was too full of questions and riddles and puzzle pieces to be able to get any of them out of his mouth. He watched in strange detachment as Lulu lifted a hand in farewell, registered, somehow, the distant sound of her voice as she bid him good-bye, saw her retreating shape disappear through the bedroom door. Then he heard the scuff of her shoes as she went down the stairs, and then the creaking of the floor as she strode through the kitchen, and finally the latch of the back door as it closed behind her.

That last sound finally snapped him out of the stupor into which he had fallen. He raced down the stairs and into the kitchen, yanked open the back door, and nearly stumbled down the back steps in his effort to reach the street. But the street was empty when he got to it. He looked left, then right. Stepped left, then right. Stopped and listened for the sound of a car motor. But where he'd been able to register every tiny sound a few moments ago, suddenly Cole could hear nothing. Nothing but a voice at the very back of his brain telling him he might have just blown the best chance he ever had.

No, he immediately told himself. He really did know her name now. And he knew how to find her again. Even better, he knew what kind of woman she really was, even if she didn't know that herself. Best of all, he had a plan for helping her find that woman. All he had to do was locate Lulu Flannery. And then, when he found Lulu, he could start looking for Delilah, too.

·Thirteen·

THE NURSING HOME BREE'S MOTHER HAD CHOSEN for herself when she still had the presence of mind to do so was the best Rosie Calhoun had been able to afford. It was pretty no-frills, but it was clean, and the nursing staff were as attentive and caring as they could be for people who were underpaid and overworked. One of the nurse's aides had gone to high school with Bree, and she relied on her former classmate to report anything that might cause concern. After nine months in the place, though, Rosie Calhoun was reasonably happy.

Of course, after nine months in the place, Rosie Calhoun's already meager savings were about half what they used to be. At this rate, in less than a year, Bree was going to have to find another home for her mother. One that cost a lot less and was a lot more no-frills. One that had a staff even more overworked and underpaid. One where Bree didn't know a soul who could keep an eye on her mom when she couldn't be here. And at that point, her mom was going to need even more care and attention than she required now.

Bree waved to a handful of patients and staff she recognized as she strode down the no-frills corridor toward her mother's no-frills room. Sundays were actually pretty lively at the home, but most visitors came during the day, not just past dinnertime, like Bree, since she'd worked the day shift at the bar. Whoever had decorated the place had strived for a spa atmosphere with the pale green walls and faux marble flooring, but Bree wasn't fooled. She doubted the inmates were, either. At least until they hit stage four or five. When she walked under an air vent, she was grateful for the denim jacket she'd pulled on over her jeans and purple T-shirt. Old, infirm people must stay unusually warm for the place to keep the AC turned down so low. Or maybe it was the overworked, underpaid staff who preferred the thermostat set at subarctic.

Her mother was sitting in a chair by the window when Bree entered her room. Although the sun wouldn't set for a couple of hours, it was cloudy outside, so not much light was filtering in. Even without it, though, Bree could see that her mother's skin looked even more delicate and thin than usual, that her eyes were a little more vacant than the last time she'd seen her, and that her hair, which she'd once taken such pains to keep tidy, was even messier than it had been before. She was dressed, though, which was reassuring. Even if her sleeveless, lightweight dress *was* a bit inappropriate for the coolness of the facility, and even if her shoes didn't match. The pale blue color of the garment complemented Rosie's eyes and gave them a little more life.

Bree scooped up a hairbrush from the dresser as she passed it, took a moment to put her happy, carefree face in place, then greeted her mother with a breezy hello and bent to kiss her cheek.

Rosie Calhoun smiled when she saw her, but it wasn't a smile of recognition. Some days, her mother recognized her just fine and the two of them could carry on conversations about things that stretched back to before Bree was born. But other days, like today, she had no clue who the woman was she'd raised for more than a quarter of a century. Sometimes, she thought Bree was one of the nurses. On especially bad days, when she didn't even recognize her surroundings, she thought Bree was a waitress. Or a hairstylist. Or a bus driver. Or any number of other people she'd encountered in her life.

"How are you feeling today, Mom?" she asked in an effort to jog what she could of her mother's memory.

Her mother frowned at the question, obviously confused about the Mom part. But she said nothing to reveal her confusion, still in that stage of Alzheimer's where she often recognized that something was wrong, but was too embarrassed to let anyone think she didn't know what was going on.

Bree attended occasional meetings of a support group for the families of Alzheimer's victims. The woman running it had told them that the best way to describe Alzheimer's to someone who didn't have it was to think about what it was like to start a new job without the benefit of orientation. You went into a place you'd never seen before, knowing you had something to do. But no one had told you what your job involved, and they hadn't told you where to find the tools you needed to perform that job, and they hadn't told you any of your coworkers' names or titles or how you were supposed to interact with them.

It was like one of those anxiety dreams Bree had from time to time where she was thrust into a situation for which she was completely unprepared and panicked when she didn't know what to do. But where she eventually woke up from her nightmare and was relieved to realize it was all a dream, Rosie Calhoun lived it every single day. And every day, her plight got just a little worse.

"I'm fine," she said now. "Never better."

Although Bree knew that wasn't true, she was glad to see that her mother was at least in a place today where she could have a conversation. Some of the other patients here never left their beds. Others sat in near catatonia in front of the TV in the common room or gazing out the window. Still others wandered up and down the hallways looking for a way to get out. Bree honestly wasn't sure which state was worst. And knowing she would have to sit by helpless and watch her mother go through all of them was almost more than she could bear. Especially since most victims of Alzheimer's didn't suffer its onset until much later in life than Rosie Calhoun's fifty-five. Physically, her mother was one of the healthiest people Bree knew. She could potentially linger with the disease for decades. And once her mother's money ran out . . .

But that was still a ways off, Bree told herself as she always did when her thoughts began to venture down that path. She still had plenty of time to find herself a rich benefactor to take care of her and her mother. With any luck at all, she might even be able to give her mother in-home care and get her out of her bleak little room here. Bree had kept a few of her mother's favorite things after Rosie sold off everything else to help pay for the nursing home. And she'd put those few favorite things in her mother's room here, in the hope that it would make the tiny space a little more familiar, and a little more comfortable. But there was only so much comfort one could get from a flowered chair and hand-crocheted throw and milk-glass floor lamp. *Bleak* was a hard thing to disguise.

"Hey, how about we go for a walk?" Bree said brightly. "It's cloudy, but it's not raining. There's a nice breeze. You want to go out to the courtyard for some fresh air?"

The courtyard was actually more of a patio on one side of the facility that abutted the parking lot, and not the most scenic place in the world. But there were two broad maples that canopied it, and someone had planted a few flowers in terracotta pots along one side. There were a couple of wooden park benches to sit on, birds to listen to, and clouds and some lingering spastic sunlight to enjoy. It would be better than sitting in here.

"That would be nice, dear," her mother said, standing.

Bree went to the closet for a sweater and arranged it over her mother's shoulders and, together, the Calhoun women strode down the hall to the courtyard at the end. They sat on one of the benches, and Bree did what she could to elicit memories from her mother's murky thoughts. Mostly, they talked about what Rosie had had for lunch, and about the nice woman who had brought her a book to read, and who Rosie liked better in the upcoming presidential election, Reagan or Mondale. Bree sighed and said she was thinking about voting for the Independent candidate herself.

RUFUS LEANED AGAINST THE SIDE OF THE CRESTVIEW Nursing Home that faced the parking lot, and watched the two women sitting on the bench with their backs to him. He was close enough to hear their murmuring speech, but not so close that he could make out what they were saying. He knew one was Bree, and that the woman with her bore enough of a physical resemblance that she was almost certainly a relative. He hadn't meant to intrude on something private, something that Bree didn't want to share with anyone. The only reason he'd followed her home after her shift was to make sure she made it home. He'd been worried that her car might break down again somewhere along the way and leave her stranded. He'd been puzzled when she didn't follow her usual route and confused when she'd pulled in here. Initially, he'd kept on driving and told himself to keep going, that Bree's car seemed to be running just fine. But something had made him turn around and come back. Visits to nursing homes were al- most never fun. And he'd thought maybe . . .

Well. He'd just felt like maybe he should be sure Bree was okay.

The woman she was talking to didn't look old enough— or sick enough—to be in a nursing home. From where he stood, she looked to be maybe fifty or sixty, and she chat- tered with animation and smiled often. Bree, on the other hand, didn't look nearly as happy. She smiled, too, but it wasn't her usual smile, and there was a strain around her eyes that Rufus had never seen before. Whoever the woman was, Bree was worried about her.

He told himself to go, that he'd invaded Bree's privacy long enough, that he never should have followed her, that do- ing something like this was skirting stalker territory, and

God knew he wasn't one of those. He loved Bree Calhoun, sure. But he didn't want to be in her life where he didn't belong. Certainly not where he hadn't been invited.

When he pushed himself away from the wall and began to turn toward the parking lot, the motion, however small, must have been just enough to catch Bree's eye. Before he was fully around, she was staring right at him, her mouth partially opened in surprise, her brows arrowed downward in what was obvious distress.

"Rufus?" she called out. And there was more than a hint of accusation in the word.

Lamely, he lifted a hand in greeting. "Hey, Bree." Immediately, he launched into an apology. "I'm sorry. I didn't mean to intrude. I was afraid you wouldn't make it home with your car being in the shape it is, so I followed you. I'm sorry," he said again. "I didn't have any right. I'm a jerk. I know you can take care of yourself. I was just worried about you. I'm really, really sorry."

She'd lifted a hand at the second apology, but he hadn't been able to stop himself. He really did feel like a jerk.

"It's okay," she said, sounding very, very tired.

"I'm sorry," he said again as he took a few tentative steps forward.

"Who's this, dear? A friend of yours?"

It was the woman with her who'd spoken, and Bree's shoulders slumped in defeat at hearing it. "This is Rufus, Mom."

Mom? But Bree had told him her mother lived in Florida.

"He and I work together," she added.

"Oh, at the copy shop?"

Bree shook her head. "No, Mom, I haven't worked at the copy shop for almost ten years. I tend bar now."

The woman, Bree's mother, threw Rufus a rueful glance and blushed. "Of course," she said a little unsteadily. "I knew that. You've been doing that since . . . Well, for some time now." Then, very uncertainly, she looked at her daughter and said, "Right?"

And in that moment, Rufus knew the woman, Bree's mother, had no idea who her daughter was. The bottom fell out of his stomach at the realization. Bree had never really talked much about her family in the past, even when Rufus had tried to pass slow shifts at the bar with her by asking the kind of bland getting-to-know-you questions people asked when they were trying to do things like pass slow shifts at the bar. She'd said something about being an only child and her mother living in Florida, and the way she'd said it, he'd gotten the impression the two of them didn't get along. Nothing wrong with that. A lot of people didn't get along with their folks. But he'd made a mental note to never ask her about it again.

"Rufus, this is my mom," she said now. "Rosie Calhoun. Mom, this is Rufus Detweiler."

"It's lovely to meet you, dear," Ms. Calhoun said.

A million thoughts were zinging around in Rufus's brain, but he managed to cover the few steps left between them, take her hand, and shake it gently. She laughed at the gesture, clearly thinking it funny, and he supposed women of that generation probably hadn't done a lot of handshaking in their time.

"He's charming . . ." she started to say to Bree. Then she must have realized she couldn't remember the name of the woman to whom she was speaking, and both her smile and her hand fell. She regrouped quickly, but the sparkle was gone from her expression. "I'm sorry, dear," she said to Bree, "but I'm terribly tired. Would you mind walking me back to my room? I think I need to rest."

She turned to say good-bye to Rufus, but something in her eyes told him she'd already forgotten who he was. He smiled and told her it had been nice to meet her, then turned to Bree to give her a reassuring look. But Bree wouldn't meet his eyes, and instead focused all her attention on her mother. He watched the two women go back into the building, then watched through the panorama window as they walked down the hall not saying a word to each other. Then he strode slowly back to where he'd parked the Wagoneer next to Bree's Honda.

And he debated whether or not to drive away.

Bree hadn't seemed to want to say anything more to him. On the other hand, she hadn't told him to take a hike. Going with his gut, he decided to wait for her. After about twenty minutes, she emerged from the main entrance of the nursing home, her head down as she looked for something in her purse.

She looked up again as she fished out her keys, and when she saw Rufus leaning against his truck, she halted in her tracks. For a moment, she only looked at him, then she began to make her way slowly forward again. He said nothing as she drew nearer, waited to see if she would get in her car and drive away, or if she would say something. For a minute, he thought it would be that first. She unlocked the driver's side door of her car and stepped behind it, never saying a word.

Then she looked at him from over the car's roof and said, "She was diagnosed with early onset Alzheimer's a little over two years ago. She was okay living by herself until about nine months ago. That was when she started showing bad judgment in things—let some guy in the house for a"— she made quotation marks with her fingers—"carpet cleaning estimate, and he stole her wallet and checkbook while he was there. Then, in one day, she bought about two grand worth of jewelry she couldn't afford from one of the shopping channels. Then she ran a red light and got broadsided by another car. Everyone was okay," she hastened to add, "but it was strike three. I had to find a place where someone could watch her, because I can't be there for her all the time."

"Bree, you don't have to explain any of this to me."

He might as well have not spoken, because she didn't seem to hear him. She just kept looking at him and kept talking. "You know, when you get past the tragedy of Alzheimer's, it's actually a fascinating disease. It attacks the most recently matured part of the brain first and then moves backward, so the sufferer kind of begins to age in reverse. They pretty much go from being a mature, responsible adult, to a less mature, less responsible young adult, to an immature, irresponsible adolescent, to a child you have to watch every minute, then to an infant where they can't take care of themselves at all. Right now, my mom's moving from stage four to stage five. She has the maturity and judgment of about a twelve-year-old. And her memories are disappearing pretty quickly."

Rufus had no idea what to say. So he only said, "I'm sorry, Bree. I know it must be hard to see someone you love go through this kind of thing."

Again, though, it was as if she didn't hear him. "She goes in and out of recognizing people and things, too. The last time I was here, I had dinner with her, and she put salad dressing on her spaghetti and parmesan cheese in her iced tea." Now she did focus on Rufus, meeting his gaze steadily. "The woman who runs the support group said you have to have a sense of humor about Alzheimer's. You have to laugh when stuff like that happens, otherwise you'll never get through it. But you know what, Rufus? That's bullshit. You can't laugh about this stuff."

Her chin crumpled just a little, and her eyes grew damp, and she looked away when she spoke again. "Today wasn't a good day," she said, her voice coming out a little rougher now. "Some days, she does remember who I am. Some days she remembers all the way back to the day I was born. Some days, it's almost like having my mom back the way she used to be. But those days are coming fewer and farther between."

She swallowed hard and shook her head, a smile coming from out of nowhere. "I wish you could have met her before this. She was always so vivacious and funny. I mean, she had this crappy life full of hard work and she was saddled with a kid she had to raise herself, but she was never bitter or angry. She never raised a fist to curse fate. She always made do with what she had, and she squeezed as much out of life as she could."

"She sounds a lot like her daughter," Rufus said softly.

Bree shook her head. "No. No way. Mom was a way better person than me. *Is* a way better person than me," she hastily corrected herself, a look of vague horror crossing her face when she realized she was speaking about her mother in the past tense. "She's braver than me. And smarter than me. And more content than me." She met his gaze again. "It's not fair. It's not fair that she had such a hard, crappy life, and now she has to spend what's left of it like this. It's going to get bad, Rufus. Really bad. And her money is going to be gone in less than a year. And then I'll have to put her in a place where they don't give a damn about what happens to her."

He understood so much about Bree in that moment, realized so many things he should have realized way before now. "She's the reason you want to find a guy with money," he said. "You don't want to tie yourself to some rich guy because you want an easy life and want to be taken care of. It's because you want someone to take care of your mom."

She folded her arms on the roof of the car and rested her forehead on them. "Don't make me sound so noble," she said. "Ask anyone. I've been saying since I was a little kid that I was going to grow up and marry a rich husband and do nothing but play tennis and eat bonbons and drape myself in jewelry."

"Yeah, well, a lot of kids say they're going to grow up to be something frivolous, Bree. I used to tell everybody I was going to play for the Celtics when I grew up. I'd make millions of dollars a year playing ball, make even more millions hawking aftershave and foot powder, drive a big Cadillac, and date a different Hollywood starlet every month."

She lifted her head to look at him, then smiled. A real smile, too, not one of those brave ones she'd given to her mom. "So what happened?" she asked. "How come you're not living the high life in Boston and sporting Lindsay Lohan on one arm?"

He smiled back. "Well, I'd like to say it was because I grew into a mature adult who realized he could contribute so much more to the world doing medical research or social work or volunteerism." He shrugged. "Fact is, I blew an ACL my junior year in high school—for the second time—and that shot any chance I had for a scholarship, never mind the NBA."

She studied him intently in silence for a moment, as if she were analyzing him from the outside in. But all she said was, "Bummer."

He nodded. "Yeah. But you know what, Bree? I've done okay with what I have. I've managed. I'm happy. Maybe it's a different kind of happy than Lindsay Lohan–happy, but I don't feel like I've missed out on anything." He toggled his head a little. "Well, maybe one thing. But I'm workin' on that. And even if she doesn't come around, it still feels good to be around her."

She sighed at that, but said nothing for a moment. When she finally did speak again, it was to tell him, "You really are a good guy, Rufus."

For some reason, it didn't bother him to hear her say that as much as it used to. "Thanks, Bree." He hesitated for a moment, then said, "So how about you come over to my place one night this week, and I cook you dinner?"

She started shaking her head before he even finished asking the question. "Rufus, I—"

"It's just dinner, Bree," he said. "Dinner between two friends. You look like you could use a night off."

He thought she was going to decline, and if she did, he wouldn't push it. He prepared himself to hear no, and he told himself he was okay with it. And he was. He loved Bree Calhoun. He would always love Bree Calhoun. And even if she never felt the same way toward him, loving her the way he did was enough to keep him happy.

"Okay," she said, surprising him. "Dinner between two friends. I'll bring dessert."

He hoped his grin didn't make him look as goofy as he felt. "That's a deal."

· Fourteen ·

LULU OVERSLEPT MONDAY MORNING, SOMETHING that made her have to scramble to get to work on time. Not that she had to punch a time clock—it was one of the perks of a job where one was self-employed—but she had a lot to do that day, and she'd wanted to get to her studio by eight at the latest to ensure she had time to complete it all. The Mellwood Arts and Entertainment Center, where she sold her glass in one of the shops, was taking advantage of all the tourism the week before Derby and hosting a huge art exhibit and sale that was opening Wednesday. Lulu wanted to have as many pieces to show as she could, and a couple weren't finished yet. And since Bree was still blissfully asleep and doubtless would be 'til noon—one of the perks of *her* job—Lulu had to scramble in silence so as not to wake her friend up.

As a result, she was a bit frazzled when she dashed down the stairs juggling a travel mug of coffee in one hand and her oversize, overfull backpack in the other. That frazzlement only compounded when she blasted out of the side of the big

brick building and into the morning sunlight and saw Cole
Early leaning against a car parked at the curb.

At first, she thought maybe she was dreaming, that the
whole running-late-for-work thing was just an annoying
by-product of her restless sleep—the band at Deke's last
night had been an electronic funk ensemble called Venus
Rising that had made her dream she signed up for a computer dating service, not realizing that it specialized in men
who needed redheads to sustain intelligent life on the
planet X12. She'd hoped maybe Cole's appearance was an
extension of that—not that she necessarily thought he was
from the planet X12 or anything—and that the alarm
would go off any minute at the time it was *supposed* to
have gone off, and she'd have plenty of time to get ready
for work.

Then she realized that no, she was indeed wide awake and
running late, and that was indeed Cole Early, and he did indeed look much fresher and more dapper in his slate blue
suit and slater blue shirt and slatest blue necktie than she did
in her usual work clothes of white tank top and denim overalls and heavy work boots—glassmaking was a hot, messy
activity—her hair caught loosely atop her head to keep it out
of her way while she toiled in her hot, messy studio.

"Good morning," he said, frazzling her thoughts even
more thanks to the way he said it, all familiar and friendly
and soft and sexy. No way did aliens from the planet X12
have voices like that.

"Hey," she replied absently, hoping she didn't sound as
confused as she felt. How had he known where she was staying? More to the point, why had he cared where she was
staying? What was he doing here anyway? Considering the
way they'd parted Friday night—with him looking at her as
if she were a complete moron who'd broken into her own
home, which, okay, maybe only a moron would do—she
would have thought the last thing he wanted was to run into
her again. Especially on purpose.

Just as he had before, he seemed to hear her mental questions as if she'd spoken them aloud. "I needed to see you," he told her. Then, as if he'd said something he shouldn't, he rushed on, "I mean, I need to talk to you about something."

"How did you know where to find me?" she asked.

He kind of made a face in response to that, one that indicated he wasn't all that happy to have to respond. "I figured if I was renting your house, you had to be staying with someone. Since you and Bree seem joined at the hip, I took a chance it was her."

"Bree's not listed in the phone book," she pointed out.

His gaze glanced off of hers. "No, but she's in *your* phone book."

It took a moment for that to register. She hadn't exactly gone out of her way to hide her address book, but neither had it been lying out in the open. It was in her office closet, on the top shelf, in a basket she used for a catchall. She hadn't used her address book for some time, either. Meaning it was probably close to the bottom of that basket.

"You went through my office closet?" she asked.

"Look, I'm sorry," he said. "It was an emergency."

"Jeez, what else have you gone through while you were there?"

"Oh, come on," he said. "What kind of a guy do you think I am?"

He sounded genuinely stung when he replied. And really, she supposed the question had been unfair. Even a guy like Cole Early wouldn't rifle through a woman's personal things. If nothing else, he didn't have the time. And anyway, there were women lining up in every bar in Louisville just begging to show him their personal things. What would he need with hers?

And, hey, hadn't *she* gone through some of *his* personal things at her house Friday night? Granted, the stack of papers on her desk had mostly been e-mail and records related to a horse farm he evidently owned and operated in California and had ended up being not personal at all. But she hadn't known that when she started glancing at—okay, voraciously reading—them. They *could* have included all kinds of personal stuff about him. They just hadn't. Dammit.

"I didn't want to wake anyone ringing the bell," he continued. "So I figured I'd just wait until you came out."

"Okay, so here I am. And now if you'll excuse me, I have to go."

"I'll walk you to your car," he offered.

"I take the bus to work," she said.

His smile fell. "You don't own a car?"

By his tone of voice, he might as well have just asked, *You have a body buried in your backyard?*

"I own a car," she told him. "But I don't use it unless I have to. My work is right on the bus line, and taking the bus is better for the environment."

She could almost see the mental roll of his eyes. Fine, she thought. He could just be that way. It was no skin off her nose if he wanted to be environmentally irresponsible. Just see how he liked it when the only glacier left in the world was the limp ice cube melting in the virus-ridden water that accompanied his bland, genetically engineered burger he enjoyed al fresco in one-hundred-and-twenty degree temperature while his melanoma slowly killed him.

Not that Lulu wanted to paint a bleak picture of the future or anything. But such thoughts did inspire her to take the bus to work.

"Then let me give you a lift," he said.

"Thanks, but I can't accept," she told him. "I do a lot of my work on the bus, and today's one of those days where I really need the extra time." Which was true. She was still making sketches for one of the pieces she was working on.

"I promise not to say a word in the car once I tell you why I need to see you."

"I can't, Cole, I'm sorry. Thank you anyway." Hoping to appease him long enough to make her escape, she added, "Maybe another time."

She lifted a hand in farewell and started toward the bus

stop, three blocks away. She'd missed the 8:05, but if she hurried, she might make the one at 8:20.

"Then meet me after work somewhere," he called after her, his voice close enough that she knew he was following her.

She turned, but kept walking backward, casting a glance over her shoulder every few seconds to make sure she wasn't going to run into anyone on the busy sidewalk. She was tired of wondering what the hell was going on, so she asked him flat out, "Why? Why were you waiting for me this morning? What could you possibly have to tell me?"

He hesitated for a second, then doubled his pace to catch up with her. When he did, she turned to walk forward again, increasing her own speed.

"I just need to talk to you," he said. Then he hesitated, as if he were reluctant to say more.

"About what?"

Instead of answering, he expelled an exasperated breath and said, "Just meet me someplace where we can talk. Please, Lulu? Please?"

There was something in the way he voiced that last word that made her go all hot fudge sundae inside, so warm, gooey, and sweet did she suddenly feel. She sensed *please* wasn't a word he used often, but he'd used it twice for her, and somehow, it sounded heartfelt. The fact that a man she'd thought so arrogant and ostentatious before could be so solicitous and diffident now made her do something she told herself she really should know better than to do.

She stopped walking and turned to look at him fully, having to crane her neck back to meet his gaze. Man, he was tall. His green eyes reminded her of the deepest part of the ocean, where it was dark, mysterious, and intense, and her heart hammered hard in her chest the same way it would had she just fallen overboard into them and was drowning in their depths.

She inhaled a deep breath, hoping the extra oxygen might slow her heart rate. Instead, it only filled her nose and lungs with the scent of him, that work-play, inside-outside, business-pleasure smell that made her heart beat faster still. "There's a Heine Brothers Coffee shop a couple of blocks down Bardstown Road in the opposite direction we're walking in now," she said, blaming her breathlessness on the fast pace she'd been trying to keep as she walked. "I should be done at work by around seven. Meet me there at eight. We can talk then."

"Eight o'clock," he echoed. He jutted a thumb over his shoulder. "Coffee shop back that way. I'll see you then."

Yeah, he would, Lulu thought as she started walking forward again—alone this time. More to the point, though, she would see him. Looking gorgeous, sexy, and tempting. And way, *way* out of her league.

COLE TAPPED HIS FINGERS RESTLESSLY ON THE SIDE of his cardboard coffee cup and glanced at his watch again. Two minutes 'til eight. She wasn't late, he told himself. So why was he so anxious?

He blamed it on the day he'd had. After he'd made the date with Lulu—ah, agreed to meet Lulu, he hastily corrected himself—this morning, he'd had to meet Susannah and a handful of local Thoroughbred owners and trainers for breakfast. Then he and Susannah had attended a meeting with some of the Kentucky Derby Festival officials to see about their participation in—or, at the very least, presence at—some of the local events. He'd spent the rest of the day at Churchill Downs working with Silk, Esteban, and Jason. He'd barely had time to wolf down bad fast food from a drive-thru before heading back to his rented neighborhood—whose traffic at rush hour, he'd discovered, was brutal—to shower and change into a fresh suit, this one as coordinated in shades of tobacco as the other had been blue.

In spite of all that, he'd arrived at the coffee shop ten minutes early and had immediately begun checking his watch. Like he did just now. Again. And this last time—like all the other times he'd checked his watch in the past nine and a quarter minutes—wasn't because of the day he'd had, either, he made himself admit. It was because he was afraid Lulu wasn't going to show.

Unbelievable, he thought. He was never afraid of something like that. People always wanted to see him. No one ever tried to avoid him. But Lulu Flannery had been uncomfortable around him since day one. Uncomfortable enough that she might very well stand him up. And then where would he be?

He still hadn't reconciled the fact that she was the woman he'd come to think of as Delilah over the last week, still couldn't imagine her doing or saying any of those things she'd said or written about doing in her journal. He still couldn't imagine her wearing the brightly colored clothes or the glittery cosmetics. Hell, he couldn't even imagine her executing any of the artwork he'd seen in the house. The more he'd thought about her, the more intrigued he'd become. And the more determined he'd been to prick the surface of Lulu and release her inner Delilah. He just wished he knew *how* to do that.

Before he had time to ponder that further, she was coming through the coffee shop entrance, the last of the evening sun streaming in behind her like some cosmic goddess whose celestial aura traveled perpetually in her wake. Cole smiled at the uncharacteristically whimsical thought. Or maybe it was just seeing Lulu again that made him do that.

She scanned the crowded room and found him quickly, then held up a finger in one of those I'll-be-right-there gestures, and went to the counter to order something to drink. By the time she picked up her cup, a table by the window had opened up, so Cole grabbed it. When she joined him, she was blowing on her beverage, some kind of tea that was the color of weak beer. She was still dressed in her attire of that morning, something he'd thought reminiscent of a construction worker. But she'd added an accessory to the mix, a faded blue bandanna that was tied over her head, pirate style, something that only enhanced the deep blue of her eyes. The previously tidy overalls and tank top were grimy and stained, and her face was pink with the remnants of hot labor. Even that, though, couldn't detract from her beauty.

Prettiness, he corrected himself. She was too wholesome and girl-next-door for beauty. Still, the look suited her somehow. Another puzzle, he thought, because it wouldn't suit Delilah at all.

"Hey," she said as she took her seat across from him. She sounded a little winded, though, as if she'd run from the bus stop. She took in his fresh suit and necktie and ran a hand self-consciously over an especially nasty streak of dirt on the bib of her overalls. Apologetically, she added, "I didn't have time to stop by Bree's and clean up. I'm sorry."

She concluded the statement by lifting her hand to a stray curl that had escaped onto her forehead and tucking it back beneath the bandanna. It was a gesture that was totally unnecessary, because she'd looked great with the errant corkscrew falling over one eye.

He smiled. "No apology necessary. You look terrific."

Funny, but he wasn't lying when he said it. She *should* have looked terrible. Any other woman wearing grimy overalls and work boots who'd been sweating all day would have. But she really looked good enough to—

Well, she looked terrific.

She laughed at the compliment, clearly convinced he was lying, still sounding self-conscious. But she stopped fiddling with her appearance and curled both hands around her tea, lifting the cup to her mouth to blow on it some more. Somehow, though, he suspected it was less because the beverage was so hot and more because she wanted to avoid his gaze.

In spite of that, she said, "So you need to talk to me about something." Into her tea.

All day he'd rehearsed different ways to say, "I need a buffer and you're it," but he still hadn't come up with anything that didn't make it sound, at best, like he was desperate for a date with anything that breathed and, at worst, like he was looking to hire the services of a—*wink, wink, nudge, nudge*—escort. So he said, flat out, "I'd like to hire you to go out with me for the rest of the week."

Oh, great job, he congratulated himself after hearing what he'd just said. That had made it sound like he was desperate for a date with anything that breathed *and* looking to hire the services of a—*wink, wink, nudge, nudge*—escort.

Lulu seemed to think so, too, because her eyebrows shot up and her mouth dropped open, and she started making a noise that reminded Cole of the sound of his clutch going bad on the old Ford Fairlane he drove as a teenager.

Then she said, "I . . . I . . . I . . . *What?*"

He sighed heavily and tried again. "I need an escort . . . but not that kind of escort," he hastened to add when her eyebrows shot even higher. "I need, like . . . like a *real* escort. A woman to go out with me for the rest of the time that I'm in town. To restaurants, to parties, to different race-related functions that are going to require my presence. Hell, to the Derby, for that matter." When she narrowed her eyes and continued to stare at him in openmouthed silence, he continued, "You're the only person I know in town, and from what I gather, you're not dating anyone, so—"

She flushed at that. "How do you know I'm not dating anyone?" she asked.

Oh, crap. He knew that from reading her journal. But the passage that had indicated that was two months old. What if Lulu had a boyfriend? A steady boyfriend? A fiancé, even? And why did the prospect of something like that bother him even more than the prospect of her not showing up tonight? In a way that had nothing to do with having to find someone else to be his date/escort/damn-he-wished-there-was-a-better-word-for-what-he-needed.

"Uh . . ." he began, scrambling for a good answer to her very good question. "I just always see you with Bree, that's all. *Are* you dating someone?"

With clear reluctance, she told him, "No. Not at the moment."

The relief that washed through him on hearing that was way stronger than it should have been. He shrugged the feeling off.

"Look," he tried again, "here's the thing. I don't know if you noticed the other night, but I have a little trouble when I'm out in public with people wanting to talk to me."

Lulu was still sitting rigidly in her chair, but she closed her mouth and met his gaze, however warily. "I did notice that, yes."

"Usually," he continued, "I don't mind so much when that happens."

She muttered something under her breath that sounded like, "I bet."

He pretended not to notice. "But in a matter of days, I have a horse running in the most important race of my career, so I'm feeling a little more stressed out than I normally do, and I'm not my usual magnanimous, gregarious self."

This time what she muttered sounded like, "Oh, please."

Again, Cole ignored the remark. Not that that kept it from wedging under his skin anyway. He folded his elbows onto the table and leaned forward, lowering his voice a little. "Look, it's just that I'm a little tense this week, and I can't be Mr. Easygoing. I can't handle all the demands put on me by the race fans and the groupies. I need to focus on Saturday, and I can't do that if every time I go out anywhere, I have to be . . . *on* all the time. Does that make sense?"

Slowly, she nodded. But she didn't say anything in reply.

"The other night, when you and Bree and I were out, people didn't bother me the way they do when I'm alone. And the only reason I can figure why they left me alone when I was with you and Bree was because I was with you and Bree. You two were a nice"—there was no way around the word, so Cole just spit it out—"*buffer* for me." He paused to see what her reaction would be. Mostly, he noted, it was just a slight squinting of her eyes that could have meant anything.

"So that's what I'd like to hire you to be for the rest of the time that I'm in town," he concluded. "A buffer. Any chance you'd be interested?"

LULU WAS HAVING TROUBLE HEARING IN THE LOUD, crowded coffee shop. Because first, she could have sworn Cole Early said he wanted to pay her to go out with him for a week. Then she thought she heard him say he wanted her to be a buffer for him.

Just to be sure, she repeated, "A buffer?"

Instead of laughing and saying, Oh, God, no, of course he hadn't asked her to be that, that wouldn't exactly be flattering, would it? No, what he wanted was for her to go golfing with him and be a duffer. Or maybe he wanted her to play charades with him and be a bluffer. Perhaps he needed a pillow fluffer. Or a turkey stuffer. Or maybe he wanted her to be gruffer, or rougher, or tougher.

Because what woman would want to be told she'd make a great *buffer* keeping sexy, beautiful women away from a guy, something that suggested—no, designated—that the guy didn't think she was particularly sexy or beautiful herself? Especially if the guy telling a woman that was Cole? The only thing worse would be if he offered to pay her money to be a buffer.

Just to reassure herself that that *wasn't* what he was asking, she hurried on before he could reply, "You want to pay me money to be a *buffer?*"

He nodded. "Yeah, that's pretty much what I want."

Ah. Well, then. Good that they had that cleared up.

She lifted a hand to her forehead to rub away a headache that suddenly appeared out of nowhere. "Okay, I think I'm having a little trouble here grasping certain, ah . . . nuances of what you're saying."

He looked nonplussed. "Which nuances?"

"The nuance about you wanting to pay me money to be a buffer."

He looked even more nonplussed at that. "I'm not sure I follow you."

Lulu wasn't surprised. It was hard to follow someone who had no idea where this was going. She tried again. "Although I get the part about wanting a buffer—"

"*Needing* a buffer," he interjected.

"Needing a buffer," she conceded, "I don't understand why you feel like you have to *pay* someone to go out with you. Unless you're expecting way more than someone to just, you know, go out with you."

"See, I knew you were going to think that," he said.

Oh, good, she thought. Because it would make things so much easier if he was trying to solicit sex from her. She could just throw her scalding tea in his face, stomp on his foot with her steel-toed work boot, call him something that wasn't fit to print and be on her merry way.

"There are actually several reasons for why I need to pay someone for that," he told her.

Hey, Lulu wasn't greedy. She'd settle for one.

"First," he began, "because I don't know anyone in town except you. And Bree. But I feel like I know you better, since I met you first."

For now, though, she only said, "I understand. But considering the way women flock to you when you're out, I can't see that being a situation that will last very long."

"And that's reason number two," he said. "Those women who come up to me when I'm out are the reason I need someone else. Those are the women I need to keep away. Because they're all . . ." He blew out a restless breath. "Well, they're all . . . gorgeous. And built. And hot. And way, way too distracting."

"And that's not what you want," Lulu said.

"Right."

"So you're asking *me* to go out with you, because I'm *not* gorgeous, built, hot, or distracting."

"Right," he said. Then, "No!" He quickly backpedaled when he realized what he'd just implied. Implied hell, Lulu thought. He'd flat out told her she was unattractive and off-putting. Then she reminded herself that she *was* sitting in front of him wearing filthy overalls and a worn-out bandanna, and that she was probably, ah, redolent of her day's work. That was beside the point. The point was she *wasn't* gorgeous, built, hot, or distracting even when she was at her best. And that wasn't something a woman liked to be reminded of. Especially by a guy who was gorgeous, built, hot, and distracting.

"That's not what I meant at all," Cole assured her. And although Lulu told herself it wasn't possible, two faint spots of pink appeared on his cheeks. He was embarrassed, she marveled. Or maybe it was just the heat from his coffee. Yeah, that had to be it. "You're . . . you're lovely," he added.

Uh-huh.

"Really."

Yeah.

"You're just not . . ."

Go on.

No way was Lulu going to help him out of the hole he'd dug for himself. She leaned back in her chair, crossed her arms over her midsection, and raised one eyebrow in silent inquiry.

He expelled another frustrated sound. "You're just not the type of woman I usually go out with," he finally said. "And I'm not your type, either," he hastily added. "You've made that clear."

She had?

"That's why I think this could be a perfect situation," he told her. "You and I can go out and enjoy ourselves, and neither of us will risk being distracted by the other. Naturally, though, what I'm asking you to do will take up a lot of your time. So it makes sense that I would compensate you for it."

Well, when he put it that way . . .

He *wasn't* her type, Lulu told herself. That didn't mean he wasn't gorgeous and built and hot. It just meant he wasn't the type of guy *she* went for. So there was no reason she should feel insulted by anything he'd just said. If she were looking to ward off an unwanted romantic entanglement—or, as was Cole's case, a *sexual* entanglement, because she couldn't imagine a guy like him even being capable of romance—what he was proposing would be what she would do, too, she told herself. She'd avoid the kind of guys she usually went for—bookish, gentle, quiet, safe—and find a guy who was arrogant, mouthy, brash, and dangerous. Just like Cole Early.

So why was she thinking it would be a bad idea to go out with Cole Early for money she could put to good use on her house or business when he was perfectly right—there would be no chance of anything happening between them? More to the point, why was she thinking she'd do it, even if he didn't offer to pay her?

"How much?" she heard herself ask, surprising herself. She honestly hadn't even meant to consider it. Even if she was no longer insulted by Cole's offer—well, not much—there was no reason for her to accept it. She had a busy week coming up, too. And she wasn't the partying, socializing type. On the contrary, she was the sort of person who always showed up late for functions, stayed only as long as it took to say hello to everyone so they would remember she'd been there when the host or hostess asked where she was, then left early to go home. She wasn't comfortable in crowds.

Then again, if he paid her enough, she wouldn't have to worry about finishing her last few pieces on time for the show . . .

She told herself if he offered her as much as it would cost to put a new roof on her house, she'd take him up on it. The reason she'd agreed to Eddie's request to rent her house out for Derby in the first place was because she'd sunk so much more into refurbishing the place than she'd originally planned, and she'd needed to recoup some of it. The money she would make from the rental was going to pretty much do that, but she still needed a new roof, and that was going to run her another three thousand dollars. She couldn't believe

Cole Early would pay that much for someone to go out with him a few times, even if he could afford it—and then some. But she couldn't deny that she was curious about what he might potentially offer.

He looked as surprised at hearing the question as she'd been to voice it. "Are you serious?" he asked, sounding almost hopeful.

She hesitated. Weird, but she actually was. "Maybe. Depends on how much you're willing to pay."

He hesitated, too, and she could tell he was going to low-ball her. "A hundred dollars."

She laughed out loud. "Don't you think you've insulted me enough for one night?"

He had the decency to look contrite. "Okay. A hundred dollars per function."

"How many functions?"

"I have something going on almost every night this week. And then there's the Derby itself."

She shook her head. "Not worth it."

"Oh, come on," he said. "There are a lot of women who would jump at the chance to go to some of the things I'm going to need a date for."

This time Lulu nodded. "Yes, there are. But they're the ones you're trying to avoid, remember? Gorgeous, built, hot women are a dime a dozen. If you want plain, graceless, and ordinary, it's gonna cost you."

She thought he was going to argue with her over the price, but what he said, very softly, was, "You're not plain, graceless, *or* ordinary, Lulu." And then, before she could respond, he said, "Name your price."

Her heart was hammering hard in her chest, but she told herself it was because she was about to get a new roof for her house, not because of the way he'd told her she wasn't any of the things she'd always felt like she was. "Three thousand dollars," she told him.

He hesitated not at all this time. "Done."

· Fifteen ·

LULU REALIZED THERE WAS A SLIGHT PROBLEM with agreeing to Cole's offer of employment less than twenty-four hours after conceding to it. In fact, she'd realized there was a problem within minutes of agreeing to it, but it was only now, as she stood in Bree's bedroom looking at the clothes she'd brought with her from home, that it wasn't actually a *slight* problem. It was, in fact, a great, hulking, gargantuan problem that was roughly the size of Canada. He'd told her as they'd parted ways last night that most of the events for which he'd need her to join him this week would require the sort of attire Lulu hadn't brought with her. More to the point, it was the sort of attire she didn't even own. Which meant one thing.

She was going to have to borrow something to wear from Bree.

Hence the great, hulking, gargantuan problem—even though the two of them wore the same size, and even though Bree had a number of cocktail dresses she'd collected over the years, due in large part to her frequenting events where she trawled for rich men. But because she was always trawling for rich men, Bree's dresses were all brief, snug, and low-cut, in colors bright enough to blind, and a lot of them had sequins, beads, and God knew what else sewn on them to make them sparkle even more.

And, okay, so Lulu liked bright colors and sparkly things. She used lots of both when she made her glass—then mixed them together to make even more colors and sparkles—and she gravitated toward them whenever she shopped for clothes. And on those occasions when Bree dragged her into Sephora or Ulta, Lulu couldn't help admiring the pots, compacts, and cylinders filled with glittery shadows, powders, and glosses, and she could never quite resist buying a couple for herself. Of course, then she got the clothes and cosmetics home and realized she'd never be able to muster the nerve to wear them for fear that they might draw attention to her. So all of them hung or sat neglected in her closets while she donned her trusty jeans and T-shirt and went out barefaced to greet the world, never drawing a single eye.

That was beside the point.

The point was she needed something to wear to the Trainers' Reception tonight. And since Cole had said the invitation read *Formal,* which she was reasonably certain translated into *Not the Ratty Stuff Lulu Flannery Usually Wears that She Bought on Sale at Value City Like Ten Years Ago,* she didn't think her Levi's and Timberlands were going to cut it, even if they were—sort of—designer names.

"This one will look fab on you," Bree was saying as she pulled a fourth dress out of her closet after Lulu nixed the first three.

"Redheads aren't supposed to wear red," Lulu said. Which was actually her very diplomatic way of saying, *But, Bree, you always look like a 'ho in that dress.*

"Oh, please," Bree retorted. "That just goes to show how little you know about fashion."

Lulu nodded. "And your point is?"

Bree made a face at her. "That rule is so five years ago.

Redheads look great in red. I'm telling you, Lulu, *this*"—she shook the brief, beaded little number at her—"is your style. Not . . ." She waved a dismissive hand at Lulu's jeans and black T-shirt. "*That*."

"No, Bree, I really think this"—she struck a pose like a *Price Is Right* model—"is the real me."

Bree shook her head at her friend. "I don't know what Cole Early was thinking to hire you for this when I'm clearly a better qualified applicant."

There was nothing malicious or demeaning in Bree's tone—or even her statement. It was simply a statement of fact, one that had crossed Lulu's mind more than once since yesterday. Cole had met both her and Bree, had spent time with both her and Bree. Bree had been far more interesting a conversationalist and far more dazzling a woman than Lulu. Bree had made clear her interest in getting to know him better.

Which, okay, was probably why Cole had offered the position to Lulu instead of Bree. Because Bree was the sort of woman he was trying to avoid—gorgeous, built, hot, and distracting.

Lulu pushed the thought away. She also pushed the dress away. "Not that one," she told Bree. "I just wouldn't be comfortable in it."

Bree blew out an exasperated sound. "Lulu, the only way you're going to be comfortable tonight is to wait out in the car."

She had a point.

"So as long as you're going to be uncomfortable," her friend continued, "you might as well look smokin' hot, babe. And this dress"—she shook the garment at Lulu again—"will do exactly that."

Of the four Bree had pulled out of the closet, the red one was, without question, the last one Lulu wanted to wear. She looked at the other three that her friend had tossed onto the bed. The first was a hot pink strapless number with a wide skirt that reminded Lulu of a tutu. Lulu in a tutu was *not* going to happen. The second was a sapphire blue sequined thing that might be comfortable because it was stretchy, if it weren't for the fact that it was stretchy because it was the size of an electron. The third was an emerald green, off-the-shoulder creation made of a matte-finish satin that was actually very pretty, but its wraparound cut promised to fit pretty snugly.

Nevertheless, it was that dress that Lulu picked up. "This one," she said. "I'll wear this one."

Bree smiled. "Excellent choice. I have some great shoes and jewelry to go with that you will absolutely love." She tilted her head at Lulu and narrowed her eyes in a way that Lulu had seen some of her artist friends do when they were studying an especially problematic piece they were working on.

"What?" Lulu said. She lifted her hands to her face. "Do I have a big zit?"

"Worse," Bree told her.

Lulu's eyes went wide. "Poison ivy?"

"Worse."

She ran her hands over her face, but her skin felt as smooth and unblemished as ever. Her hair then. Well, hell, that was always a problem. So what was Bree so worried about?

"What, Bree?" she asked.

Bree sighed and tossed the red dress onto the bed with the others, then took Lulu by the hand and led her to the cheval mirror in the corner of the room. She turned her so she was facing it, then went back for the green dress, which she held up in front of Lulu on the return trip. Lulu saw the problem immediately. The dress was gorgeous. So gorgeous, that Lulu was nearly invisible standing behind it. The addition of great shoes and jewelry would doubtless make her disappearance complete.

"It's okay," Bree said. "I have hair product and lip gloss, and I'm not afraid to use it. Even on you. When I get through with you, Lulu, the dress is going to be incidental."

Lulu doubted that. Still, she had just enough pride to not want to be shown up by a bit of fabric—even if it was pretty incredible fabric. She squared her shoulders as she turned to look at Bree. And her voice only trembled a little when she said, "Do your worst."

COLE SLUNG HIS EMERALD SILK TIE THROUGH A second loop to finish the perfect double-Windsor, a knot he'd completed so often, and did so well, that he didn't even have to look in a mirror anymore to complete it. As he leaned over the bed in Lulu's tiny bedroom, reading the *Daily Race Form* he'd opened on it, he absently—and perfectly—adjusted the collar of his black dress shirt until it completely covered the tie. The jockey silks of Susannah's stables were emerald and black, and Cole wanted to be sure he dressed in those colors tonight, for the Trainers' Reception. And he breathed a mental sigh of relief that Susannah Pennington, although a girly girl in many ways, was a woman of bold fashion taste. Although he was a man who liked color in his clothing, Cole didn't think he could have done Pennington Stables justice if he'd had to go out in Barbie pink and My Pretty Pony lavender. Bad enough he even knew what Barbie and My Pretty Pony were—though that was thanks to Susannah's niece Madison, who was an even bigger girly girl than Susannah was.

He finished reading the latest odds for all the Derby entries and reached for the black suit jacket he'd tossed over the desk chair, shrugging it on and arranging the emerald silk handkerchief in the breast pocket just so. When he turned to head out, his eye fell on the photograph of the five women he'd moved from the dresser to the nightstand. He now recognized not only Lulu among the women, but Bree as well. The white string bikini was still a mystery—he made a mental note to ask Lulu about her at some point, simply to assuage his curiosity—but his gaze no longer strayed to the blonde. As always since discovering Lulu was the owner of the house, Cole's gaze always fixed immediately on her. The one in the long T-shirt and hat. Squinting into the sun. Looking like she wasn't having a good time.

Just who was the real Lulu Flannery? he wondered, not for the first time. Was she the one in the flesh, all buttoned up and battened down? Or was she the one underneath, off-center and on fire? His money was on the latter—hell, the woman wielded a blowtorch for a living; the heat had to come from somewhere—but for the life of him, he had no idea how to draw her out. Hiring her to be his buffer brought her closer—at least physically—but how could he coax her inner Delilah to the surface?

He set the photo back on the nightstand, but his gaze remained on Lulu as he wrapped a gold watch around his wrist and fastened it. He tried to picture her in the white string bikini. Didn't happen. He tried to imagine her in the pale lace lavender. Couldn't do it. He tried to visualize her in the gypsy apparel of the closet. Never came close.

The problem, he realized when he knocked at Bree's front door a half hour later, was that he just hadn't pictured Lulu in the right thing. When she opened the door and offered him a less-than-breezy, "Hey," he realized he should have instead wrapped her in some shimmery, jewel-toned fabric that hugged her body like a lover's embrace. Although Cole had noticed before that Lulu had some decent curves, what her dress did to them now made them positively *in*decent, which any man would tell you was really the way to go.

The garment had slipped off her shoulders—though he was pretty sure it was supposed to do that—showing off the elegant lines of her collarbones and riding just low enough to reveal the top swells of her breasts. When he skimmed his gaze lower, he saw that the hemline stopped well above her knees, offering him a view of extremely nice legs. He'd never really thought of himself as a leg man—he was infinitely more interested in what a woman carried on top—but Lulu Flannery's legs certainly gave a man pause. He dropped his gaze lower still to see that she'd slipped her feet into gold high-heeled shoes that were more high heel than they were shoe, and then, *then,* his heart nearly stopped.

There, on Lulu's toes, was glittery nail polish the color of a summer sunset. It was replicated on her short fingernails, he noted as he drew his gaze upward once more, and again on her mouth. And suddenly, all Cole could think about was what he'd have to do to get some of that glitter on his mouth, too. And then on other body parts that probably shouldn't be wearing glitter, either, if they were male, but if the glitter got on there the way he was thinking it would get on there, no man in his right mind would refuse.

"Wow," he said before he could stop himself. "You look . . . *wow.*"

She'd rendered him speechless, Cole thought. It took a lot to do that. But then, she looked . . . *wow.* So that explained it.

"*Wow* yourself," she said with a smile. But it was a shaky smile. A none-too-confident smile. A smile that said she was in no way comfortable with the way she was dressed. Cole wasn't comfortable with it, either. But he was pretty sure his discomfort was way different from hers.

But that was okay. He had all evening to get them on the same page. And then, if he was lucky, he'd have all night to keep them there.

He'd worried a little since hiring Lulu to do what he'd hired her to do, about the wisdom of having done it. Not just because any other man would have killed to have Cole's problem—too many beautiful women coming on to him—but because the press might get wind of the arrangement somehow. He'd hoped like hell he didn't wake up the morning after the Derby to find his face splashed on the cover of *People* and *Us Weekly* with a headline that screamed, "*King Cole Didn't Call for His Pipe or Bowl! He Called for a Girl! And Bought One!*"

He wasn't worried anymore. There was no way anyone would look at Lulu and think anything other than that she was a dazzling woman he'd met while in town and fallen for. Because that was exactly what Lulu was.

"Hello," he finally managed to greet her.

Then, impulsively, he leaned forward and kissed her on

the cheek. When he pulled back, he could tell she was surprised by the gesture. But she couldn't have been more
surprised than he was. He didn't think he'd kissed a woman
on the cheek since he was ten years old. And then, it had
been his great-aunt Rhea, not a woman like Lulu who should
inspire way more than a kiss on the cheek.

"You look beautiful," he told her.

The look she gave him in response told him she didn't believe him, but she smiled a little more and said, "Thanks."

A moment followed where neither of them seemed to
know what to say, then Lulu mumbled something about getting her purse. She blew an air kiss to Bree, who, Cole noted,
was giving him a funny kind of assessing look, and told her
friend she wouldn't be out late. *Hah*. Then she made her way
back to Cole with surprising grace for a woman he was reasonably certain usually sported shoes with heels no higher
than a compact disc.

"I'll get the door," Bree said as she followed Lulu. Before
she closed it behind them, though, she had a word of advice
for Cole. Literally *a* word. As in *one*. "Behave," she told
him. Then she gave him a curiously intent look and pushed
the door shut.

Behave, he echoed to himself. Hell, that could mean anything. Behave well. Behave badly. Behave like a brother. Behave like a lover. Just what was Bree trying to tell him,
anyway?

When they reached the foot of the steps, he glanced back
over his shoulder, as if Bree might be standing up there giving him a clue. But the door was still closed. The landing
was empty. The building was silent. No answer was forth-
coming. So he would have to interpret the admonition himself and behave like a . . .

Something. Well, he'd figure it out. Eventually.

It finally came to him as he and Lulu were crossing the
lobby of the Brown Hotel and, without even thinking about
it, Cole took her hand in his and tucked it into the crook of
his arm. *Gentleman,* that was the word he'd been looking

for. Okay, actually, it wasn't, because his feelings for Lulu tonight were anything but gentlemanly. But that was the word that came to him as they neared the reception. That was what Bree had been telling him to behave like. Probably because she'd known what he was thinking about. The way Cole had looked at Lulu was doubtless a look Bree had fielded herself on more than one occasion. Of course, it was a look Bree courted and counted on, one she knew exactly how to react to. It was a look to which Lulu would be oblivious and one she would have no idea how to handle.

That was hammered home harder when she stiffened beside him as he tried to curve her hand over his arm, her fingers flattening out like they were all fused together.

He leaned in close to her ear and whispered, "I don't bite, Lulu. You're safe with me."

She said nothing for a moment, but relaxed her hand until her fingers *almost* curled over his arm. Then, very softly, she asked, "Am I?"

The reply puzzled him. Mostly because she seemed to be talking more to herself than to him. At least, she wasn't looking at him when she replied. She was looking past him, at three couples around Cole's age, all about as dressed up for a function as people could be. The men were attired in dark suits, dress shirts, and ties, but the women absolutely dazzled. Slender and tanned, coiffed and manicured, they all wore beaded, sequined gowns and were dripping in gems that caught the light overhead and threw it back in a spectacular display of light and color. Somehow, Cole knew it was the female members of the party Lulu was watching, in spite of her being every bit as spectacular as they were—hell, even more so.

He understood, though. He knew what it felt like to be on the outside looking in, even when you *looked* like you fit in. It hadn't been that long ago that he was standing where Lulu was, thinking exactly what he knew she was thinking just then. That she wasn't like them. That she didn't belong here. That she was the common clay people trod upon every day, and they were a higher breed, wrought from fine marble by an artisan's hand.

In some ways, she was right. The rich were different from the poor and middle class. But life and fate had a way of equalizing things, and it was true that money couldn't buy happiness. Not for everyone. Lulu had gifts the other women would envy, and she mattered in ways they didn't. Yeah, even if money couldn't buy happiness, it could buy comfort and security. But money wasn't the only thing that provided those things. And the comfort and security that *wasn't* paid for was way more scarce, way more important, way more valuable.

He started to tell Lulu all that, started to say something about how he understood what she was feeling and that she shouldn't worry about the evening ahead. He started to tell her that she was every bit as entitled to be here as they were, that she was no different from them. But he stopped himself. Not just because it would have sounded patronizing to say such things, but because he knew they weren't true. Lulu wasn't like them. When it came to the big karmic escalator, she was actually several steps higher than they were. He knew that because standing here next to her made him feel exhilarated, exultant, extraordinary. If he were standing next to the partygoers over there, all he'd feel was bored.

So he only covered her hand with his and told her, "Yes, Lulu. You are. Safe with me, I mean."

She tugged her gaze away from the trio of couples and looked at Cole again. Although he could tell she still felt uncomfortable, she smiled. It wasn't a big smile, but it wasn't bad. It was something they could work on tonight.

"Come on," he told her, tilting his head toward the ballroom's entrance. "We don't want to miss the party."

LULU SIPPED HER CHAMPAGNE CAREFULLY AND TRIED not to feel nervous, doing her best to focus on the conversation going on around her. She'd never attended an event like this, and she told herself she should absorb as much of the experience as she could while she could, because God knew when—if—she'd ever have an opportunity like this again. There were hundreds of people here, all crushed together in the Crystal Ballroom like sardines. Extremely well-dressed sardines, but sardines nonetheless. She and Cole had been at the party for more than an hour, and she was no more re-laxed now than she'd been when he took her arm and walked her in.

And what had that been about, anyway? she wondered. That and the kiss on the cheek at Bree's. She knew she was supposed to look like a romantic interest of his, but there hadn't been anyone watching them at Bree's. And here at the hotel, where there were spectators to see whether or not she was a *real* romantic interest of his, she would have thought he would do a lot more than take her hand. Like walk up to her, bend her back over his arm, and lay a Hollywood kiss on her that lasted a solid minute.

Not that she'd *wanted* him to do something like that. Of course not. But the kiss on the cheek and the hand in the crook of the elbow seemed so out of character for a man like him. It seemed so . . . sweet. So gentlemanly. Probably, he'd only done it because she must have looked as nervous as she felt, and he'd thought it would put her at ease. But instead of calming her nerves, the innocent gestures had ratcheted them up even higher. And then, when they'd entered the room and she'd seen all these people . . .

Inevitably, her gaze was drawn to the ocean of partygoers again. The seemingly limitless sea of people. The Crystal Ballroom hadn't been named that for nothing, and a dozen massive chandeliers cast sumptuous light down upon the crowd. Buffet tables draped in white linen and bedecked with silver serving pieces only made the scene that much more shimmery—and that much more intimidating. As Lulu looked at the crowd, it seemed to swell in size. The conver-sation seemed to move faster and the laughter seemed to be louder, and suddenly, it felt like everyone was looking at—and talking at and laughing at—her.

Oh, God. It was even worse than being on the news. She'd only had to talk to one person then, and there had been only one bright light—the one on the mobile camera. Even at that, she'd completely choked. Then she'd panicked. Then she'd become Pufferfish Girl.

How on earth could she have thought she could pull this off? Cole Early lived in the limelight. But when Lulu was pushed into the limelight, she spontaneously combusted.

"And this is my, ah . . ." She heard Cole's verbal stumble from her right and turned to try and smile at whoever he was introducing her to. She was grateful for the distraction and used it to remind herself that she needed to pay closer attention to what was going on in her immediate vicinity and not get so overwhelmed by the crowd. The large crowd. The immense crowd. The crowd that seemed to go on forever. The crowd that, at times, she felt closing in on her like a massive, writhing tentacle attached to an enormous, bloodsucking, brain-eating, liver-loving—

"I'm Lulu," she said to the silver-haired man on Cole's other side, pushing thoughts of neurosis-induced killer octopi to the very back of her brain. When the man, his apparent wife, and Cole all looked back at her with expressions of concern, she realized her voice had succumbed to the jumble of nerves tumbling through her stomach by replicating the sound of a cat hacking up a hairball. Delicately, she cleared her throat, closed her eyes so she wouldn't see the crowd, and tried again. "I'm Lulu," she repeated with a bit more control this time. "Lulu Flannery." She opened her eyes and held up her champagne glass, then touched her free hand to her throat in the hope that the other couple would form some nebulous idea that the champagne had gone down wrong or didn't agree with her. "Nice to meet you," she added, even though she hadn't heard a word of Cole's introduction so, technically, she had never met these people in her life.

When she looked at Cole, he seemed to be silently asking for her help in identifying exactly what she was to him, since she hadn't exactly finished his unfinished statement for him. So she added carefully, "I'm Cole's . . . ah . . . best friend here in Louisville."

She could tell by his expression that that hadn't been the relationship he was looking for, but it seemed to satisfy the other couple just fine.

"So you're from around here?" the woman asked.

"Born and bred," Lulu told her.

"It's so unusual to meet natives at these gatherings," her husband remarked. "Except for the Festival officials and some local politicians, I don't think I've met anyone tonight who was actually born in Louisville."

"Where are you all from?" Lulu asked.

"New York."

"Ah."

"It's our first time in town," the woman added. "Our first Derby."

Lulu nodded. She couldn't imagine anyone being around Derby for the first time. It was a part of her heritage, a fact of her life. Every spring, her hometown went a little wacky for Thoroughbred racing. People who didn't give a thought to horses the rest of the year suddenly bought racing forms, chose favorites, and could quote statistics and identify trainers and owners. The whole city changed in the two weeks leading up to Derby. It was more festive, more playful, more energetic. Boutiques filled with flirty, track-appropriate dresses and department stores filled with exuberant hats. White stretch limousines suddenly appeared on winding, tree-lined country roads where there would normally be tractors or pickup trucks. Lamborghinis and Ferraris belonging to wealthy out-of-towners suddenly appeared on the highways with all the mom-driven minivans and teenagers in Toyotas. Standiford Airport became a parking lot for private jets. Restaurants and bars were more crowded, downtown streets swelled with people, the nightly news carried images of parties and celebrities instead of fires and crime, and the newspaper was filled with stories about pulled-up-by-their-bootstraps, rags-to-riches, larger-than-life personalities.

Every April, Lulu saw her hometown come to life for two weeks in a way it didn't the rest of the year, almost as if it were throwing open its doors for a big, brassy party and wanted to be at its best. Which, she supposed, was exactly what was going on. As much as she loved being able to say she was a native Louisvillian, she liked it even better this time of year. It was like being part of something special that no one outside the community could call their own. The Derby belonged to everyone, for sure, but people who'd grown up here could embrace it in a way that was theirs alone.

But since Lulu couldn't think of any way to tell that to the couple with Cole, she only said, "I hope you have a good time while you're here."

Cole chatted with them for a few minutes more in a way that let her know he'd met them somewhere before tonight, and she wondered if there would be anyone here tonight that *she* knew. Doubtful, she thought as she scanned the room. Louisvillians might be able to embrace Derby in a way that was theirs alone, but affairs like this one were more for Derby insiders—or people who could buy their way into the Derby insider crowd. When all was said and done, much of what went on for Derby was a rich man's—and rich woman's—game. Commoners like Lulu rarely saw this side of the event. If she did see someone she knew at the Brown tonight, chances were good that person would be working the event, not attending as a guest.

"Looking for someone?" Cole asked when he saw her gaze traveling around the room.

She shook her head. "Just thinking that you probably know more people here than I do, and I live here."

He smiled. "Thoroughbred racing is an international sport. And the Kentucky Derby is the most famous Thoroughbred race. Naturally it's going to bring people in from everywhere."

"I know." She smiled. "But even though it's international, Kentucky horses are the best."

He opened his mouth to argue, obviously realized it was pointless, so only said, "There's a lot to be said for California horses, you know. Some people are rather partial to them." He smiled, too. "And one's going to win the Derby this year, so you better get used to that right now."

Oh, no, Lulu thought. She'd forgotten Cole's horse would be an out-of-towner when she told him she'd bet on it. She always bet on Kentucky horses. Once, you know, she picked one whose silks and name she liked.

"I'll still bet on your horse," she told him. "But I'm going to bet on one from Kentucky, too."

His smile broadened. "You don't even know who's running yet, do you?"

She deflected her gaze to a point over his left shoulder, saw the crowd coming at her again, and met his gaze once more. "No," she admitted. "But I will by gate time."

He laughed, a soft, relaxed laugh that crinkled the corners of his eyes and turned his mouth up higher on one side than the other. Something inside Lulu shifted a little at seeing it. It was as if, one minute, she was unsteady from all the people and buzz around her, and the next, she was standing on solid rock, her equilibrium restored. Which was weird, because usually when Cole smiled, it made her think of that panties and silver platters thing. This smile was different from the other ones, though. The other ones had been bold, brash, and arrogant. This one was soft, slow, and intimate. Instead of knocking her down this time, Cole shored her up.

"Come on, I'll get you another glass of champagne."

She shook her head. "Oh, no. I've already had—"

"One," he interjected. "You've been nursing that same glass ever since we got here. It's got to be warm by now. I've never seen anyone nurse champagne. Especially champagne as good as this."

As if to illustrate that, he downed what little was left in

his glass, pried hers from her numb fingers, and set both carefully on the tray of a passing waiter. Just as deftly, he swept up two freshly filled ones from another server passing by, as if he'd called ahead to orchestrate the whole thing.

Amazing, she thought. Where she seemed to have absolutely no control over what happened in her life—case in point, here she was, drinking champagne in a room full of millionaires where, scarcely a week ago, she'd been wrestling with the bartender at Deke's for control of the TV remote— Cole Early seemed to make things happen just by willing them to. She'd never met anyone who was so sure of himself. She wouldn't be surprised if his horse did win the Derby. He could probably make it happen just by being somewhere in the solar system when the race took place.

"Here you go," he said as he handed one of the frosty flutes to her. "Really, it's okay to drink the whole thing. They always have plenty of champagne at these things."

Lulu gazed at the tiny golden bubbles effervescing in the tall, graceful glass. "I know, but . . ."

"But what?"

She looked at Cole again. "I'm just not much of a champagne person, that's all."

He looked like he was going to say something, but hesitated. He took her glass from her, said, "Don't move from this spot," and then turned and took a few steps before dissolving into the swarm of people behind him.

The moment the crowd swallowed him up, Lulu felt her heart rate quicken. The only thing worse than being in a crowd like this was being in a crowd like this alone. She did her best to smile at people and greet them pleasantly, but she felt so conspicuous that she just wanted to disappear the same way Cole had. Except that would mean getting swept up by a massive, writhing tentacle attached to an enormous, bloodsucking, brain-eating, liver-loving—

"This should do the trick."

At the sound of Cole's voice behind her, Lulu spun quickly around. He was holding two champagne flutes filled with what looked very much like beer, and he was smiling. At least, he was smiling until he got a good look at her face. Then the smile fell and was replaced by a look of concern.

"What's wrong, Lulu? Are you okay?"

She nodded quickly, took one of the glasses, and enjoyed a healthy taste. It was indeed beer. And never had she been happier to see one.

"Thank you," she told him when she swallowed.

"Hey, is everything all right? You don't look so good."

Before she realized what he intended, he took a step forward and cupped his hand over her forehead, then her cheek. Then he surprised her by tucking his hand under her hair and curling it over the nape of her neck.

"You feel warm," he said.

Well, *duh*, she thought. That was because he'd cupped his hand over her forehead, then her cheek. And because he'd then surprised her by tucking his hand under her hair and curling it over the nape of her neck. Of *course* she was warm after that.

"I'm fine," she said. But her voice was shallow, even to her own ears, and even she didn't think she sounded okay.

"Let's walk," he told her, slipping an arm around her waist.

"It's okay, I'm—"

"It's crowded in here," he interrupted her. "We could both use some fresh air."

Without awaiting an answer, he wove the fingers of his free hand with hers and tugged her gently through the crowd, until they were back in the hotel lobby. There were considerably fewer people here, and that coupled with the sumptuous decor of gilded baroque ceilings, dark walnut paneling, and jewel-toned Oriental rugs made Lulu feel a little calmer. The quieter atmosphere also went a long way toward soothing her, since the music drifting in from the ballroom was just loud enough for her to hear. Cole guided her to a grouping of sofas and chairs obscured by some potted palms and sat her on a loveseat, then folded himself down alongside her.

When he started to extend a hand toward her forehead again, Lulu dropped her gaze to prevent him from making contact. His hand hung in midair for a few seconds, then slowly fell to his lap. "Sorry," he muttered. "But you still look a little flushed."

"I'm fine," she told him. "Just not a big fan of crowds is all."

He nodded as if in sympathy, but it was more likely because he just wanted to make her feel better. A guy like him thrived in crowds. Cole Early was just one of those people who was born to the spotlight. He'd probably emerged from the womb squalling, "Hey, everybody! Look at me! I'm gonna be a force to be reckoned with!" Every time she'd seen him on TV, he'd been completely confident, utterly comfortable, thoroughly in his element. As she'd watched him interact with other people tonight, many of them complete strangers, he'd acted as if he'd known them all forever and was delighted to see them again.

Lulu couldn't imagine being able to do that. Even when she was in her element—which was considerably more elemental than Cole's—she had trouble with the whole extrovert thing. It was doubtless something that had contributed to her pursuit of art. Certainly she loved what she did for a living and had known since she was an adolescent what career she wanted to pursue. But had she been forced to go out into the world and interact with others on a daily basis to complete her artwork, she wouldn't be nearly as good at it. She might not have even sought to make a living at it and would have instead made it her avocation. She would have chosen a career doing something that enabled her to remain anonymous and in the background.

Cole dipped his head toward her beer. "Have another sip. It'll calm your nerves."

She did as he instructed, not because she thought it would make her feel any less anxious, but because she didn't want to just sit there looking like an idiot while she collected her wits. Then she realized she'd already collected her wits.

Thanks to being away from the crowd—and thanks to Cole sitting next to her and being nice to her—she felt better than she had since her arrival at the gala.

He grinned suddenly, the off-kilter one that knocked Lulu so off-kilter. "C'mon, let's get out of here."

The remark surprised her. "But you said it was important that you made an appearance at this thing."

"And I've made an appearance at this thing," he told her. "Now I can go."

"But—"

His grin softened, but somehow the smaller one made her feel even more off-kilter than the off-kilter one did. "It's okay, Lulu. Really. You're not comfortable here, and I've made all the requisite small talk I need to make. There were only a couple of people here I really needed to talk to, and I found them both right away. C'mon. Let's go do something fun."

Although she had no idea why she was balking at his offer of escape, she heard herself say, "You're not paying me to have fun."

He laughed at that. "Then consider yourself off the clock."

· Sixteen ·

BREE LEANED BACK AGAINST HER FRONT DOOR AF-
ter Lulu and Cole left, staring at her empty apartment and
thinking it somehow seemed even emptier than usual. But
even more than that, she was thinking that Cole Early was
Lulu's for the taking, if she wanted him. But Bree could
tell her friend didn't even realize she had him eating out of
the palm of her hand. God knew how that had happened, but
Bree had seen that look on a man's face often enough to
know what it meant. It was, after all, exactly the sort of look
she'd always wanted to win for herself. A look that went beyond the superficial recognition of physical beauty to the
realization that there was something massively special underneath it.

Of course, Bree already knew there was something massively special under Lulu's physical beauty. She'd known
that since they were kids, and she knew it better than Lulu,
who, for some reason, had never recognized her own potential for anything other than her art. But how Cole Early had
discovered it after spending just one evening with her was

pretty amazing, considering how Lulu took such pains to make sure no one ever got too close.

Ah, well. That just showed what a smart, observant guy he was, for one thing. And what good taste he had, for another.

Cole Early was going to fall in love with Lulu, Bree marveled. Hell, the way he'd looked tonight, she would have said he was already in love with her. But that was impossible. The guy barely knew her. Then again, Bree would bet good money that was going to change tonight.

She sighed. Lulu, who had never gone looking for a man in her life, was about to win the golden ring—in more ways than one, Bree was thinking. She'd reeled in the great white whale, the pirate's treasure, the lost city of Atlantis, and every other prize of mythic proportions the sea of men had to offer. And Bree, who had made it her life's work to land a guy like that, was going to wind up with . . .

Well. She had dinner with Rufus tonight, she reminded herself. That was something.

It was actually a lot more than something, she thought as she pushed herself away from the door. But she wasn't allowed to think about how much more. Instead, she made her way to the bedroom to clean up the remnants of Lulu's extemporaneous makeover. For what it had been worth. It really hadn't taken much to bring out her features. A swipe of shadow on the eyes, a little mascara, a little bronzer, a little lip gloss. Even her hair had behaved once Bree moussed it. Lulu had so much more natural beauty than Bree did. Bree had always had to work a lot harder to look good.

She didn't feel it necessary to do so tonight, however. Not because she didn't think Rufus was worth the effort—*au contraire*—but because Rufus seemed to like the way she looked no matter what.

He really was a good guy.

She did change out of her jeans and T-shirt, though, and into a red and black print skirt and black tank edged with lace along the top. And, okay, she swiped a bit of shadow,

mascara, bronzer, and lip gloss across her own features. And
she wound her long black hair into a makeshift French twist
and held it there with two cloisonné chopsticks. And she
stepped into some strappy little black shoes that showed off
her calves. It was just because the weather had gotten
warmer, that was all. It had nothing to do with wanting to
look nice for Rufus.

When she pulled to a stop at the curb in front of the address he had given her, she had to double-check to make sure
it was the right one. Then she had to triple-check. Then she
had to replay the conversation in her head again to be sure
she'd written down correctly the address he'd told her to
write down. The house that belonged to the address on the
piece of paper just didn't look like the kind of place Rufus
would call home. She'd expected him to live in one of the
older, more tired-looking apartment complexes in Crescent
Hill. Or else actually live in Clifton, which abutted Crescent
Hill and was just as charming but much more affordable. At
best, she'd figured he would rent a nondescript duplex. But
this? This was none of those things.

It wasn't a huge house, but it was certainly more than one
person needed—a two-story frame Dutch colonial whose
façade was painted barn red. Half of the front yard was
shaded by a massive sugar maple, and the curved walk was
lined by freshly planted red and white begonias. The driveway spilled into a garage behind the house that looked to be
the same age, one with doors that folded open vertically instead of horizontally. Sure enough, she saw Rufus's old,
beat-up Wagoneer parked in front of them. This was indeed
his place. But it didn't look like him at all.

Or did it? she asked herself as she strode up the walk to
the front door. What did she know about Rufus, really?
She'd never tried to get to know him beyond coworker status, had never exchanged any information with him other
than the most cursory pleasantries. She'd always told herself
it was because she didn't care enough about him to want
more than the most cursory pleasantries. After that kiss the

other night, though, she'd forced herself to admit she cared about Rufus a lot more than she should. The reason she'd never asked him more about himself, she realized now, was because she hadn't wanted to start caring for him even more than that.

Now, as she made her way to the front door, she noticed other things she wouldn't have thought seemed very Rufus, but told her a lot about him. A white wicker swing swayed at one end of the broad front porch, a porch that also hosted a profusion of potted peace lilies and ferns. When she went to push the doorbell, she noted it was shaped like a small bronze lizard. There was even a welcome mat beneath her feet that read, WELCOME.

Maybe he inherited the place, she thought. From a fussy maiden aunt or something. Recently enough that he hadn't had time to let the place get into disarray. Guys like Rufus too often lived like frat boys, the victims of extended adolescence. Their homes had the barest minimum of boring furniture, were overloaded with electronic and gaming equipment, had pantries empty of anything except chips and Twinkies, and fridges boasting nothing but beer.

But a look through the screen door told her that wasn't the case here. The inside of Rufus's house looked to be as charming as the outside. The furniture wasn't Early American Maiden Aunt, though. It was boxy, masculine, and tailored. She hesitated before pushing the doorbell, giving herself a chance to take it all in. There was a leather sofa the color of good red wine pushed against one sage green wall, worn and buffed from years of enjoyment. Instead of looking ratty, though, it looked comfortable and appreciated. There was a big club chair in the corner to match it, and an overstuffed chair near the fireplace upholstered in a complementary stripe of burgundy, blue, and green. The rug spanning the hardwood floor was what looked like a hand-knotted Persian, and the lamps were low-key bronze. The mantelpiece over the fireplace was cluttered with guy stuff: a model of a tall ship, a bulky antique clock, a half-dozen old books, and a cluster of framed photographs.

The overall mood was comfortable metrosexual. Never in a million years would Bree have guessed this was the environment Rufus came home to at night.

As if the revelation had conjured him from her dreams—or, rather thoughts, she corrected herself, since she didn't dream about Rufus—he suddenly appeared in the hallway on the other side of the living room, carrying a basket of laundry. He was wearing jeans, but no shoes or shirt, and when he turned to do what looked like closing a door behind himself, his bare back was to Bree. She was about to call out a greeting to let him know she was there, but her mouth went dry at the sight of that expanse of naked flesh. Never had she beheld a more beautiful vista than Rufus Detweiler's back. Long and lean, taut and tanned, it was a masterpiece of muscle and sinew, bunching, relaxing, flexing . . . sculpting, molding, carving. There was no two ways about it—Rufus's back belonged in the Louvre.

He turned toward the front door, and when he saw Bree standing there, he started badly enough that he dropped the basket of clothes. "Jeez, you scared the hell outta me," he gasped, lifting one hand to the middle of his chest as if to ward off a heart attack, bracing the other against the doorjamb. The action clenched the muscles of his upper arm even more artistically than the muscles of his back, and Bree's dry mouth was suddenly awash with enough moisture that she feared she would start drooling if she wasn't careful.

"I, uh, I was just getting ready to ring the bell," she said lamely.

He nodded, inhaled a deep breath, then bent to pick up the scattered laundry. Bree pulled open the screen door and let herself in, going straight to where he was stooped down, kneeling beside him to help.

"I'm really sorry," she said as she reached for a stray sock. "I didn't mean to scare you."

"It's okay," he said. "You just surprised me. I wasn't expecting you for another fifteen minutes. I'm not even dressed yet."

So she'd noticed. She started to tell him not to bother on her account, but checked herself. "I thought traffic would be worse this time of day," she told him. "But I lucked out and got all the green lights."

"Well, I hope you brought an appetite with you."

She smiled. "Always."

They finished gathering his things—including an intriguing pair of silk boxer shorts that Bree just *knew* a woman had given to him because men never bought silk boxer shorts for themselves. Especially ones that were decorated with lipstick kisses. What intrigued her more was that they were in his laundry, meaning he had actually worn them, and still did, even after he and the woman had clearly broken up. Did that mean he still cared about his ex? And why did Bree care if he did?

"They were a gift from my sister Camille," he said.

At first Bree thought he'd read her mind. Again. Then she realized she was holding the silk boxers in a way that indicated she wasn't planning to let go of them anytime soon.

"Oh," she said quietly as Rufus plucked them from her hand.

"Camille's always trying to fix me up," he said. "She thought racy underwear would help nudge me in that direction."

"And did it?"

He didn't look at her as he began to fold them. "You know me, Bree. I'm saving myself for Ms. Right. My underwear hasn't seen a lot of action for the last two years."

She started to make some flip comment about how you could lose things if you didn't use them, then the gist of what he'd said hit her. Like blunt force trauma to the back of the head. Was he saying he was saving himself for *her*? That he hadn't had sex with anyone since meeting *her*? Oh, surely not.

"I'm sorry?" she said, certain she must have misunderstood.

Instead of replying, he only finished folding the boxers and carefully set them atop the rest of the laundry.

Bree, however, wasn't willing to let it go that easily. "You're not serious," she said. "About the two years, I mean. That was just a joke, right?"

Rufus remained silent.

Unsure why she wanted to belabor the subject, she insisted, "You're not telling me you haven't had sex with anyone since you met me." When he still said nothing, she added, halfheartedly, "Are you?"

He did finally look at her after that, but only for a second. Then he bent and picked up the laundry basket and started carrying it toward the stairs on the side of the living room that had been blocked from her view before. Bree followed him as far as the bottom step, then halted. Rufus continued blithely up to the top, but still didn't say a word.

Two thoughts occurred to her at once, and she didn't know which was more troubling. First, that by not answering in the negative, he'd pretty much indicated he was saying yes, he hadn't had sex with anyone since meeting her. And second, he was going to be putting on a shirt.

Damn. And double damn.

Unable to help herself, Bree started up the stairs, too, pulling herself along the handrail until she hit the top, because her legs, for some weird reason, suddenly felt like Jell-O.

"Two years?" she called incredulously when she reached the top, uncertain which room he'd disappeared into. "You've gone two years without . . . you know?"

There was no answer from any of the three bedrooms off the hallway before her. Or from what looked like a bathroom, either.

"Rufus?" she called out.

"What?" his voice came from the farthest room.

"Can I come back there?"

"Sure."

She started walking slowly down the hall, then hesitated again. "I mean, you're decent, right?"

"Of course I'm decent," he called back.

She took a few more slow steps, then halted at his bedroom door. He was standing with his back to her looking at two shirts lying flat on the bed, as if he were trying to decide which one to put on. Evidently he hadn't decided on pants yet, either, because he was standing there in the lipstick-kissed silk boxer shorts and nothing else.

"You said you were decent," she said lamely to his back.

"I am decent," he told her without turning around. "I'm also in my underwear."

She gripped the doorjamb and bit her lower lip hard, mostly to prevent herself from crossing the room, because what Bree wanted most in that moment was to stand behind Rufus and . . . lick him. "Next time," she said shallowly, "I'll try to be more specific with my questions."

"You do that."

He finally made a decision and scooped up a well-worn polo the color of a pine forest after a hard rain. Then he dragged on a less disreputable-looking pair of blue jeans than the ones he'd had on, stuck his bare feet into a pair of extremely well-worn Top-Siders, and turned to face her.

She remembered then that there was one question she had been specific about that he hadn't answered. So she asked it again. "Have you really not had sex with anyone since you met me?"

He dropped one hand to his hip and, with the other, reached back to rub his neck in that way men do when they know they have to say something they really don't want to say. "Yeah," he admitted. "I really haven't had sex with anyone since I met you."

"Why not?"

He dropped both hands to his sides, expelled a restless sound, and looked at her as if she should know the answer to that better than he did. "Because I haven't wanted to have sex with anyone since I met you, Bree. No one except you."

She thought about all the times she'd worked with him when she'd been going out with other guys. All the times she'd talked to one of the other female bartenders—while Rufus was within earshot—about a date she'd had the night before with some wealthy guy she'd managed to snag. She thought of the times she'd come into the bar with a date when he was working. And she thought about how he must have felt on those occasions. She'd always known Rufus had a thing for her. But she'd never realized it went as far as this.

She told herself she should apologize. But that might just sound patronizing. So all she said was, "I didn't know it was like that."

He shrugged. "Now you do."

Something about the way he said that made it seem like he was tacking on an unvoiced, *So what are you going to do about it?* But really, what he was probably thinking was, *So what am I going to do about it?*

They stood there in silence for a moment, each clearly having no idea what to say. There was something heavy and uncomfortable hanging between them that was thick enough to hack with a meat cleaver, but damned if Bree could identify exactly what it was. Tension, maybe. Embarrassment. Confusion. All of the above.

"Maybe I should go," she finally said. She even went so far as to take a small step backward, into the hall.

"No," Rufus said quickly, completing three giant steps to catch up to her. "No, you shouldn't. I promised you dinner. And I always deliver."

She took another step backward into the hallway, a larger one than was probably necessary to let him pass. If he noticed, he didn't say anything. And if he seemed to take a larger step than necessary to get around her, well . . . Bree pretended not to see it.

She followed him to the kitchen, which, like the rest of the house, was cozy and well appointed with everything anyone could need to feel comfortable. The furniture here was older and well used, too, but sturdy and nice. He had all the essential appliances like a coffeemaker, toaster oven, and microwave, and a few that surprised her—espresso maker, bread machine, food processor.

"I didn't know you liked to cook," she said, remarking on those last two.

He shrugged. "It's not a passion," he said. "I just like to be self-sufficient."

"Next you'll be telling me you grow your own food in the backyard."

He colored a little at that.

She laughed. "No way."

"Just tomatoes and peppers. Those *are* passions. And maybe a few herbs, too."

"Do you have a microbrewery in the basement?"

Now he laughed, too. "No. But there's some Red Stripe in the fridge."

Her favorite brand. What a shocker.

He went to the fridge and pulled out two of those, along with a ceramic bowl in which, she discovered, he was marinating a couple of steaks. After opening the beers, he pushed a button on the portable CD player on the counter, and the room was filled with mellow guitar.

He tilted his head toward the back door. "Keep me company while I light the grill. It's such a nice evening, I thought we could eat out. Literally."

The hours that followed were some of the most pleasant Bree had spent in a long time. She didn't do enough of this, she thought as Rufus brought a couple of after-dinner coffees out to the deck for them to enjoy. By now, the sun had dipped behind the trees, and the sky was stained with the last orange and gold remnants of daylight. The mellow guitar music had segued to sexy saxophone, and when she sipped her coffee, she realized Rufus had laced it with Frangelico—another favorite. As she leaned against the deck railing beside him, she could feel what little tension was left in her body gradually easing away. Even more important, the anxiety that normally gnawed at her brain began to evaporate, too.

"You have a really nice place here, Rufus," she said softly as she watched a rabbit in the far corner of the yard nibble at a patch of clover.

"You sound surprised," he replied just as softly.

She set her coffee mug on the deck railing and turned to face him. "I guess I kind of am."

He turned to face her, too, but still cupped both hands around his own mug. "Why?"

"I don't know," she said. "I guess you just never struck me as the home and hearth type."

He hesitated only a moment before saying, "Maybe that's because you never tried to find out what type I am."

"True enough," she admitted.

He dropped his gaze down to his mug. "And now that you know what type I am?" he asked.

Oh, that was a question Bree really couldn't let herself answer. So she lifted her mug again, drank deeply of the rich brew, and said, "How do you manage it? Owning a home like this doing the kind of work you do? I barely manage to make ends meet by month's end. But you have this great place, and all these creature comforts, even though you always seemed like the kind of guy who didn't need much to be happy."

As she spoke, he continued to study his coffee, never once looking up at her. When he finally did lift his gaze to hers again, he seemed more tired than he had before. He seemed distant. He seemed disappointed. Nevertheless, he played along.

"I am a guy who doesn't need a lot to be happy," he told her. "A roof over my head that doesn't leak, a steady income that allows me to live above the poverty level, the love of a special woman I know will be by my side forever. That would do it for me." He lifted a shoulder and let it drop. "Two out of three ain't bad, I guess. Unfortunately, it's that third one I don't have that I consider most important."

"Rufus . . ."

"Look, Bree, I'm not trying to put you on the spot. But the

same way you've always been honest with me about what you want, I want to be honest with you about what I want. It's only fair."

To both of them, she supposed. It couldn't have been easy for Rufus the last two years, caring for her the way he did and she not reciprocating. Why should he make it easy on her? Especially since, thanks to that little interlude in her kitchen last week, she'd given him some small hope that she returned his feelings. Of course, she did return his feelings. That was the problem. She just couldn't afford to, that was all.

Instead of pressing the subject, which a lesser man might do, Rufus went back to the original topic. "I've worked at one job or another since I was thirteen," he told her. "First cutting people's lawns and washing their cars and babysitting. Then, when I turned sixteen, I started working real jobs. Sometimes two if I could swing it. Where my friends in high school graduated and went to college, I went to work."

"Why didn't you go to college?" she asked.

"Didn't want to," he said matter-of-factly. "I never liked school, except for playing basketball. I knew I'd hate college, too, unless I could go on a basketball scholarship, and that didn't happen. Work I didn't mind so much, so I went for that. I'd been saving my money since I was a kid, so I kept on. Like you said, it doesn't take a lot to make me happy. I didn't spend that much. Eventually, I had enough to put down on a house with a mortgage that doesn't run me much more than paying rent would." He looked back at the house. "It wasn't this nice when I bought it. I've put a lot of work into it." He smiled when he realized he'd used the word *work* again. "Different kind of work," he said, "but still enjoyable."

"But you could have made a lot more money if you went to college," she said. "You could've gotten a better job with better prospects."

"Oh, like you?" he asked. But there was nothing bitter or sarcastic in his voice. It was just a very good point.

"Yeah, okay, but still," she said. "You could've majored in something besides English."

He shrugged again. "I didn't want to, Bree. People who go to college get all bogged down in getting ahead, and getting promoted, and getting the company car, and getting the corner office . . . getting, getting, getting. I didn't want to fall into that lifestyle. I just wanted to be able to work at a job I enjoy, then come home at the end of the day to a house I can call my own and to the woman I love. Maybe add a golden retriever to the mix at some point. And maybe, someday, if the planets are aligned correctly, a coupla kids, too." He met her gaze levelly. "What more is there than that?"

He already knew the answer to that, but she repeated it, anyway. "There's taking care of your mom," she said quietly. "There's needing to know she won't wind up in some craphole where they don't give a damn about her. There's knowing that after she took care of you for twenty-five years, you have an obligation to take care of her."

"It doesn't take a million bucks to do that, Bree."

"Do some reading on the health care industry, Rufus. It takes even more."

She couldn't do this, Bree thought. She couldn't stand out here on this gorgeous, gentle night with this gorgeous, gentle guy and try to justify not being with him. Because there was no justification for that, not really. And if she gave in to what she wanted to do at the moment, it would just make things harder tomorrow—for both of them.

"Look, thanks for dinner," she said quickly. "But I have to go."

"Bree, no."

"This has been a really nice night, and you're a good guy—no, a great guy—but I have to go, Rufus."

He opened his mouth to object again, so she gave in to a

lesser impulse. Pushing herself up on tiptoe, she covered his mouth with hers—briefly, intensely, hotly. She skimmed the tip of her tongue along his bottom lip, stole a quick taste of the corner of his mouth, then pulled away.

"Thanks again," she said breathlessly. "For everything."

Then she turned and hurried through the back door, through the comfy kitchen and relaxing living room, across the cozy front porch and down the flower-lined walk, ignoring Rufus's petitions for her to come back. She braved a look at the house and saw him standing on the front porch watching her, one arm braced against a column, still holding his coffee in the other hand. The lights inside the house fairly glowed behind him, bathing him in an otherworldly amber light. Any sane, smart woman would be on that porch with him, looping one arm through his, curling the other around his waist, pulling him close in a way that told him she never planned to let him go.

Bree turned the key in the ignition. She threw the car into gear. And then, with only one quick look back, she sped away.

· Seventeen ·

WHEN COLE TOLD LULU HE WANTED TO GO DO something fun, this wasn't exactly what he had in mind. Not that he hadn't been to artsy functions before, but this one was a little weird, even by southern California standards.

He looked at the four . . . Well, he supposed *artists* would be the right word, since they were four people and Lulu had told Cole this was an art gallery. But at the moment, he was hard-pressed to be able to actually identify them as people. Certainly, he wasn't able to tell what any of their genders were, even though they were all stark naked. In fact, the only way he knew there were four people on the platform in a corner of the tiny darkened gallery was because each was painted a different color. A different Day-Glo color. None of which complemented the others. One was sort of pink. One was kind of orange. The third was in the green family—barely. And although Cole had never actually seen the color puce before, he was pretty sure that was what the last color was. Up 'til now, though, he'd always thought the existence of puce was one of those urban legends whose validity nobody could prove.

Their bodies, however, complemented each other very well. In fact, they complemented each other so well that Cole was keeping one eye on the door at all times, just in case the vice squad raided the place.

Well, okay, maybe it wasn't so weird by southern California standards—he was pretty sure he'd seen something almost just like this on Venice Beach once where all the bodybuilders worked out—but it was still definitely weird.

"It's performance art," Lulu said softly beside him, evidently sensing his, ah . . . bewilderment? Yeah, that was it. Bewilderment was a much better word for what he was actually feeling. "The human body and its natural movements as an art form," she continued.

Okay, *that* he could see. Not in this particular performance piece, since what they were doing wasn't what he would call natural, on account of it had to be painful to keep your legs in that position for any length of time, but he could see it elsewhere. In fact, he'd been seeing Lulu's body and its natural movements as an art form ever since she'd opened the door at Bree's apartment. The way she looked tonight . . .

Well. Let him just say that, had Michelangelo been around today, the ceiling of the Sistine Chapel would be all Lulu, all the time. As would be the walls of the Sistine Chapel. And the floors of the Sistine Chapel. And the nave, apse, and transept, too. Never let it be said that Cole Early hadn't paid attention in his Art History 101 class. And had the Sistine Chapel been painted to look like Lulu, he would have changed his major pronto.

She just looked so beautiful. He'd thought she was pretty the first time he saw her. And all the other times, too. But with the addition of a little color and a little sparkle, Lulu Flannery came alive. Tonight, she looked as colorful and vivacious as the house she called home. And since leaving the party, she'd begun to act more colorful and vivacious, too.

The moment he'd suggested they leave the reception, the color had come back to her features, and her smile had become less strained. As they'd driven to the art exhibit she'd told him she wanted to see, she'd gradually warmed up even more. But it was only once they entered the funky little gallery housed in what she'd told him was an old fire station on Main Street, that Lulu had really come alive.

Surrounded by the art and artists that made up her world, Lulu was clearly in her element. He'd actually felt her physically relax as they entered the darkened room, and she seemed to genuinely breathe more easily in this rarefied air. It was funny, because the atmosphere had had the opposite effect on Cole. While he considered himself a chameleon in many ways and could make himself at least look at home in just about any environment, this one eluded him.

It wasn't that Lulu's friends and colleagues were unwelcoming. On the contrary, whenever she'd introduced him to someone, they'd been warm, friendly, and open. None had pestered him about his trainer status, either, even though many knew who he was. He ought to feel more comfortable here than he had in any number of other situations this week. But the whole creative vibe was one that made him a little nervous. That artistic types could create something that was often transcendently beautiful out of virtually nothing was just getting too close to the whole Meeting His Maker thing.

Funny, though, how he didn't feel that way when he was around Lulu. Maybe because she was a maker he'd gotten to know beforehand. And maybe because she was a maker he wanted to get to know better.

"You don't like it, do you?" she asked now, her disappointment in his pedestrianism clear.

"I'm sorry," he told her. "I'm sure it's brilliant. It's just not my thing."

She made an *Oh, well* gesture with her shoulders. "That's okay. Art is subjective. But if you hate my stuff, will you promise to pretend you like it?"

"I *love* your stuff," he said. "I already told you that."

"I know, but I thought you were just pretending to like it."

"No," he assured her. "Like I said, I'm not the foremost authority on art, but it doesn't take a genius to see how gifted you are."

She smiled shyly at the praise. "Thanks."

"In fact, I'd like to see more of it. Do you have a studio somewhere? I mean, I didn't see anyplace at your house that looks like you work there."

"No, I don't work at home. I do actually have a studio. It's not far from here."

"When can I come by?"

Her smile fell. "Gee, I don't know, Cole. I get kind of wiggy about having people in my studio. There's a lot of work in progress there, and I don't like sharing it with anyone until it's done."

"But seeing work in progress is so fascinating," he objected. "Work in progress is so much more spontaneous and genuine than the finished product. It's so much purer. In a lot of ways, the work in progress is more honest than the finished product."

She arched her brows in surprise. "Wow. That's really pithy. You sound like a real connoisseur."

He laughed. "Actually, I was thinking about horses. About the whole process of going from foal to yearling to race status. That's a different kind of work in progress, but you ask me, it's still art."

"I totally agree," she said, brightening. "It's performance art. Only in that case, it's the horse's body and its natural movements as an art form."

He looked at the, ah, piece on the platform again. The four bodies were in a different position than they had been in before, but Cole had missed the actual motion. Did that mean he'd missed the art? Dang. Too bad.

"So can I come to your studio sometime?" he asked again.

She didn't answer at first, but dropped her gaze to the

glass of wine she'd been nursing since their arrival. Which, he supposed, was an answer itself.

So he added, "It's just that you can learn a lot more about people when you see them in the environment they love most. The environment they're most comfortable in."

Finally, but still without looking up, she told him, "But that's just the point, Cole. It's not an easy thing you're asking. Almost no one has ever visited my studio. I'm very protective of it. And of my art. They're both like extensions of myself, you know? My art and my studio and my creative process . . . All of them are a big part of me, and I don't share them that easily."

"But you make your living selling your art, don't you? You have to share it eventually."

She nodded. "Yeah, but the only pieces that go out in the world are the ones I choose to put there. And only when I'm ready to share them with others. The only pieces I sell are the ones I know are perfect. Or as close to perfect as I can make them. It's the flawed ones that I don't want anyone to ever see. And my studio, Cole . . ." She rolled her eyes and shuddered for effect, an action he supposed was meant to be comical, but instead looked more fearful than she probably knew. "My studio is full of flawed pieces. My process is a messy process." She dropped her gaze again as she continued, "A lot of times, I have no idea what I'm doing. A lot of times, I make huge mistakes."

Cole curled a finger under her chin and gently nudged her head up so that she was looking at him. "But it's the flaws, Lulu, that are the most interesting. And sometimes it's the biggest mistakes that lead to the greatest discoveries."

She said nothing in response to that, only met his gaze in silence. But her lips parted fractionally, as if she wanted to say something but was afraid to put voice to it. Thanks to the darkness of the gallery—and the even darker corner into which they had wandered—her pupils were wide and dark, yet somehow her eyes seemed brighter, too. Two faint spots of color bloomed on her cheeks as he studied her, and her breathing suddenly seemed to quicken, her breasts rising and falling noticeably above the scooped neck of her dress. Her spicy scent teased his senses, taunting him, tempting him, making him want things he really shouldn't be wanting in a public place, even if it was a corner of that place that was dark. And secluded. And quiet.

He started to say something else, something about perfection being overrated, because once you achieved it, what was the point of going on? Instead, before he even realized what he intended, he was dipping his head to brush his lips over Lulu's, once, twice, three times, four. Then he was cupping her face in both hands and slanting his mouth over hers to kiss her more deeply. She covered his hands with hers and kissed him back, firing a shot of something hot and needy right to his core.

It was damned near close to perfect. But not quite. So what else could he do but go on?

The second kiss was even better than the first, maybe because this time they each took a step closer and their bodies touched as well as their hands. Or maybe this time it was because they were both a little more confident. A little more daring. A little more passionate. This time, Cole dropped a hand to her bare shoulder, skimming his thumb along her collarbone . . . back and forth and back again . . . softly, leisurely, methodically. He dragged his fingertips to the base of her throat, then brushed his bent knuckles up over her tender flesh until he could curl his hand over her nape and kiss her more deeply.

She was so soft, so warm, so responsive. He gently nipped her lower lip, making her gasp, rolling his tongue into her mouth when she did. She accepted him enthusiastically, opening her mouth wider, inviting him deeper still. As he intensified the kiss, he dropped his other hand, too, moving it down over her other shoulder, flattening his palm on the warm skin above the neck of her dress. Then he nudged it even lower, splaying his fingers wide over her breast.

For a long moment, they seemed suspended that way, his

tongue in her mouth, her breast in his hand, the fire in his belly raging out of control. Then she was pulling away, tugging away the hand on her breast and ducking her head in a way that left his mouth at her temple. So he kissed her there instead. He understood. They were in a public place, even if it was a darkened corner, and there were people here she knew well, among whom she didn't want to generate chatter. But that one embrace had only enflamed Cole with the desire for more, and there was no way he was going to spend the rest of the evening A) pretending it didn't happen or B) pretending it wasn't going to happen again.

So he lowered his mouth to her ear and said, "Let's get out of here."

He was prepared for her to say no, that they couldn't leave yet. And he told himself if she did, he'd stay. For five more minutes, and then they were outta there. Instead, she nodded silently and laced the fingers of their clasped hands together. She said nothing to him as they threaded their way back through the gallery toward the exit, only smiled at the handful of people she knew and lightly bid them good night, sounding no more flustered by what had happened than she would be by reading the program they'd been handed at the door upon arrival.

They made the short walk to Cole's car in silence, too. He watched her closely as he unlocked her door and handed her in, but she never once made eye contact with him. He watched her through the windshield as he rounded the front of the car to the driver's side, but she kept her gaze firmly focused on her lap. Once he was seated inside, she lifted her gaze to look straight ahead. But still she said not a word.

So after starting the car, he turned to look at her and asked, "Where to?"

Still gazing straight ahead, she said, "Home. Take me home."

Excellent, Cole thought. He couldn't imagine a more perfect place to make love to her the first time—or the second or third—than the bedroom in her house that was both hers and his.

She turned to look at him then. "Bree's apartment, I mean."

Wait a minute. That wasn't home. "Bree's?" he said.

She nodded. "It's been a long night. It's time to go home."

"Yeah, but your house is—"

"My house is being rented right now," she told him. "For now, my home is at Bree's." His confusion—hell, his disappointment—must have shown on his face, because she added, "We can't do what you're thinking you want to do."

The hell they couldn't. Had it not been for the fact that they'd been standing in a public place, they'd be doing it right now. Aloud, however, he said, "I'm not *thinking* I want to make love to you, Lulu. I *do* want to make love to you." She closed her eyes when he said it so baldly. In spite of that—or maybe because of it—he added, "And the way you responded to me back there, I think you're more than thinking about it, too."

"All I did was kiss you," she said softly. "That doesn't mean I want to fall into bed with you."

"Fair enough," he said. "But you didn't want to stop what was happening any more than I did."

"No," she admitted.

"Then kiss me again."

She closed her eyes at that, too. But she only said, "We're in the middle of a parking lot, just as exposed as we were inside."

Oh, the ideas that popped into his head when she said that. Instead of putting voice to them, though—instead of putting voice to anything—Cole threw the car into gear.

He'd become fairly familiar with the area around Lulu's house by now, and found his way back to the neighborhood with little problem. It helped that Bardstown Road stretched virtually from one end of the city to the other, and that the street the gallery was on was only a few blocks away from it, though quite a few miles from where Lulu lived. It wasn't a problem, though, because it wasn't to Lulu's house Cole was headed. However, neither was it to Bree's apartment. Instead, once he got his bearings and began to recognize his surroundings, he turned several blocks before arriving at Bree's place—and he turned east instead of west.

Lulu, who had said not a word since leaving the parking lot, snapped out of her silence when he did. "You took a wrong turn back there."

Cole feigned confusion. "Did I?"

"Yeah, you should have turned right, not left. And you turned too soon."

He shook his head. "Sorry. Out-of-towner. I'll try to find a place to turn around."

He did find a place to turn around. Then he found a few more places to turn around. Lulu kept trying to give him directions, but he played the man card and insisted he didn't need directions, that this was a shortcut he'd discovered and that he knew perfectly well where he was going. Until finally, they arrived exactly where he wanted to be.

"Well, would you look at that," he said as he braked to a stop in a wide paved area to the side of the road. "Somehow we got lost in the park."

"We're not lost," Lulu said wearily. "I know Cherokee Park like the back of my hand. I can get you out."

Yeah, he'd figured that. So he looked down at the dashboard and said, "Uh-oh. I think we're out of gas."

"What?"

He pointed at the gas gauge. "See for yourself."

She scooted across the seat and leaned across Cole to look at the gauge on the other side of the steering wheel and saw what he himself already knew. That the red needle was firmly planted at three-quarters of a tank. When she turned to look at him, her mouth open to, presumably, demand to know what he was talking about, he met her gaze levelly and threaded the fingers of one hand through her hair. The silky curls wound around them in invitation, and he couldn't help thinking it was a gesture he hoped the rest of her felt like offering, too.

Very softly, very tentatively, very hopefully, he said, "Kiss me again, Lulu. There's no one looking now."

LULU'S MOUTH WENT DRY AT COLE'S QUIET REQUEST. There was no demand in his voice, no insistence, no expectation. There was only petition, solicitude, and longing. It should have been easy to tell him no. He'd contrived this whole episode. He'd never been lost, and they had enough gas to drive to Cincinnati and back. She shouldn't have any trouble returning to the other side of the big car's long front seat—much bigger and longer than other cars and seats Lulu had found herself in and on as a teenager steaming up the windows in this very park. She wasn't a kid anymore, she reminded herself, and she didn't have to resort to parking at Chauffeur's Rest to deal with adolescent hormones. She was a grown woman with her own home, and her hormones were totally under control. Or at least, they had been. Until Cole had told her to kiss him.

Damn her hormones anyway.

Because they were the reason she didn't say no. They were the reason she didn't move back to her side of the car. They were the reason she tilted her head toward his. And they were the reason she kissed him. It was all her hormones' fault that she did that. It had nothing to do with how much *she* wanted to kiss Cole, too.

But kiss him she did, turning her body more fully toward him, lifting her hand to cup his rough jaw as her mouth covered his. He responded immediately, as she'd known he would, roping an arm around her waist and pulling her into his lap. He buried his other hand in her hair and tilted her head backward, filling her mouth with his tongue and her belly with heat.

She lost herself after that. Utterly and completely. One

minute, she was Lulu Flannery, paid buffer, and the next, she was that nameless, faceless creature who lived inside herself. The one who shaped glass into sensuous colors and shapes. The one who arranged words into erotic prose and fantasy. The one who felt things Lulu couldn't let herself feel when she wasn't creating, for fear that they would overwhelm her.

And overwhelm her they did.

When she felt Cole's fingers strum over her rib cage and his palm curving under her breast, it was like a great wave of fire crashed over her. She uttered a low sound that was needy and demanding as she arched against him, and he responded with a feral growl of his own as he moved his hand higher, covering her completely. She didn't object when he began to tug at her dress, pushing the off-the-shoulder garment lower, down her arm and over her breast, until she felt the warm rush of his breath against her naked flesh. Then she felt his mouth replace his hand on her breast, his tongue flattening over her nipple as he held her more firmly in his hand. Again and again, he dragged his tongue over her, then he opened his mouth wide and pulled as much of her tender flesh inside as he could. The damp pressure was almost more than she could bear, and when she tightened her fingers convulsively in his hair, she didn't know if it was to push him away or pull him closer.

Then he moved his hand lower again, over her hips and her thighs, finally finding the hem of her dress and immediately tugging it upward. Higher and higher she felt the garment rising, until she was shifting on his lap so that he could bunch it around her waist. He opened his hand over the curve of her fanny, rubbing his palm over the lace of her panties in wide circles, as if he were trying to imprint the pattern on his skin. When she instinctively pushed her body backward to greet his touch, he dipped his fingers beneath the lace, curving his palm this time over her naked flesh, and pressing his long middle finger into the delicate cleft of her behind. She gasped at the intrusion, but when he began to draw his hand away, she pushed her fanny back against his fingers harder, in the hope that he would do it again.

Where had this come from? she wondered wildly as he pushed his hand lower again. She had only intended to kiss him, not succumb to a passion completely beyond her control, a passion unlike anything she had felt for a man before. But when his petition and solicitude had turned to confidence and expertise, she hadn't been able to help herself. She'd never been with a man who was more certain of his actions. What was truly her undoing, though, was that he seemed to be even more certain of hers.

As if proving that, he folded his fingers deeper into the cleft of her fanny again, scooting them lower this time. After pushing one long finger into the delicate opening he found there, only briefly enough to make her deliciously shocked and enticingly curious, he drove his fingers lower, between her legs, where she had grown damp and hot with wanting him. For long moments, he only fondled her wet, swollen flesh, something that made her rise from his lap to give him better access. Her new position put her breast at the level of his mouth, and as he licked and tugged at her nipple, he guided his finger into her slick canal. Lulu closed her eyes and bit her lip, waiting for him to repeat the action. When he did, she moaned in pleasure and tilted her head back. He moved the finger again, this time sucking her flesh deep, *deep* into his mouth. Lulu felt an almost forgotten heat building in her midsection, spiraling tighter with every passing moment.

So long. It had been so long since she'd felt this way . . .

Just as she was about to give herself over to the tight little circles in her belly, Cole withdrew his hand and moved it forward, this time dipping it between her legs in front. Instinctively, Lulu opened them as wide as she could in the cramped confines of the car, but it was enough to allow him ample exploration. He slipped his fingers under the fabric of her panties and into her damp flesh, stroking her, flicking her, entering her again. She covered his hand with her own and guided his movements, broadening and increasing his strokes, pushing his finger deeper and faster inside her. As he penetrated her, she dragged her own fingers over herself, increasing her pleasure, and together, they brought her to a shattering climax. Lulu cried out in her completion, her entire body convulsing in the aftermath, then collapsed against Cole's shoulder.

For a long moment, neither of them spoke. Cole removed his hand from her panties but left it between her legs, brushing his fingers gently and slowly along the insides of her thighs. It was a tender gesture, one meant to bring her down more gradually, something a lot of men—even those with whom she'd had what she considered fairly serious relationships—had never bothered to do. For a long moment, she only let herself feel him surrounding her, stroking her thighs, brushing his mouth along her neck. Eventually, though, she had to come back to herself. And when she did, she immediately wished she hadn't. Hadn't come back. Hadn't left in the first place. Hadn't allowed to happen what had happened.

Oh, God, what had she done? She'd just shared something with Cole—had experienced something with Cole— that she hadn't with men she'd been much more serious about. This wasn't like her. Lulu Flannery was cautious to a fault. She didn't have orgasms on the front seat of rented cars while parked with a guy she'd barely known a week. Cole brought out that thing in her she'd thought she could keep leashed, and all he'd had to do was kiss her. She didn't want that thing driving her, didn't want it roaming free when she couldn't contain it. Because it might lead to things like . . .

Well. Like having orgasms on the front seat of rented cars while parked with a guy she'd barely known a week.

As delicately as she could, Lulu crawled off his lap and to the other side of the car. Then she pushed her dress back down over her legs and pulled the top back up over her breast. She pushed her hair out of her eyes, straightened her posture, pressed the back of her hand to her mouth. And never once did she look at Cole. She couldn't imagine what he was thinking. Unless maybe it was that he'd just gotten a lot more for his money than he'd anticipated.

For a moment, neither of them said a word. Then Cole draped an arm across the back of the seat and scooted across to her side, too. So Lulu looked out the window and pretended she was somewhere else.

Not one to run from the facts, however, Cole leaned in close and said, very softly, "Are you okay?"

She managed to nod, but said nothing.

"'Cause you suddenly don't seem okay."

"I'm fine," she said. But the words came out rough and hoarse.

He said nothing for a moment, then, even more quietly than before, he said, "There's nothing wrong with what just happened, you know." When she said nothing in response, he added, "I mean, it was a lot more than a kiss, but . . ."

Still, she remained silent, looking out the window. So he reached across her and pressed his hand to her cheek, gently turning her head to look at him.

"If it's any consolation, nothing like this has ever happened to me, either." He lifted a shoulder and let it drop, then offered a small smile. "Well, not since I was seventeen, anyway."

"It's not that, Cole," she said softly.

"Then what?"

"That . . . what just happened . . . that's not me."

"News flash, Lulu," he said just as softly. "That *was* you."

She shook her head. "No, I mean, I don't *do* things like . . . like that. Ever."

He gave that small smile again. "If you're trying to flatter me, it's working."

She wanted to laugh at the comment. Really, she did. But she couldn't. She wished she could shrug off what had happened the way he had. Wished she could make light of it, the way he was. But what had happened went way too deep for her to be able to do that. She felt too many things right now, and she felt them deeply, and she couldn't make sense of any of them.

"Will you take me home now?" she said instead. "Please? Bree's home. For real this time."

He opened his mouth to say something, seemed to think twice about whatever it was, and closed it again. He only nodded silently, moved back over to his side of the car, and turned the key in the ignition.

They said not a word on the drive to Bree's apartment, and when Cole told Lulu he would walk her up, she didn't argue. After she unlocked the door, she turned to tell him good night, and he pulled her into his arms. He kissed her gently, tenderly, affectionately. A warm glow ignited deep in Lulu's belly at the embrace, but she kept it banked low until he pulled back again.

However, he didn't go far.

He dipped his head to press his forehead against hers and cupped his hands over her bare shoulders. She absorbed his warmth, inhaled his scent, savored his taste on her tongue. And when he said softly that he wanted to see her tomorrow, she told herself to tell him no. She needed some time. Needed to figure out what was going on. Needed to get a handle on herself and her feelings. Then she remembered she didn't have time. In a matter of days, he would be gone. And she might never see him again.

She told herself that would be a good thing. A small, quiet life like hers didn't have room in it for a man like Cole. He was too big, too brash, too confident. He made her forget things she needed to remember. Things like . . .

Oh, damn. She'd forgotten them already.

"Come to my studio tomorrow," she heard herself tell him. "If you come around four, I'll be ready for you."

·Eighteen·

BREE MADE IT ALL THE WAY HOME BEFORE CALLING herself an idiot. But that was only because she'd spent the rest of her driving time calling herself a fool, moron, dummy, imbecile, ignoramus, simpleton, dunce, dolt, jerk, dumbass, bonehead, blockhead, dimwit, half-wit, nitwit . . .

Well, suffice it to say she talked to herself *a lot* on that particular drive home.

And when she turned onto the side street by her apartment building and saw Cole Early's Town Car parked at the curb, she halted her own car, folded her arms over the steering wheel, rested her forehead against them, and did her best not to cry.

She just wanted to go home. She'd held herself together all the way back to her apartment, and now she wanted to lock herself in her bedroom and fall apart. She wanted to put on her pajamas, get the gallon of Neapolitan ice cream out of the freezer and the lasagna spoon out of the drawer, and she wanted to eat and cry until she was sick. She wanted to remember what it had been like to kiss Rufus once, and she wanted to dream about what it would be like to kiss him again. She wanted to pretend everything in her life was fine and ordinary, that she didn't have to worry about the future, that when she woke up tomorrow morning, bloated and sticky, it would be to a day filled with glorious mundanity.

She couldn't do any of that if Lulu was upstairs with Cole. Not that she thought they were making use of her bedroom—she knew Lulu well enough to know that—but if Bree had to look at the two of them falling in love, which was what they were doing, whether they realized it or not, and know she would never have that herself, then she would do more than make herself sick on ice cream.

So without thinking about what she was doing, she turned down the alley behind her building and up the street on the opposite side until she was heading back in the direction from which she'd come. She'd just drive around for a little while, she told herself. Until Cole was gone and Lulu was in bed and she could sneak in and feel miserable without anyone knowing. She popped a CD into the player without even looking to see what it was, then smiled when the car was filled with the mellow crooning of Bobby Darin, one of her mother's favorites. Bree started to sing along, to avoid talking to herself, not really paying attention as one song bled into another. Until Bobby started singing to her that all he could give her was country walks and a hand to hold and a love to warm the winter night. And then Bree was singing back to him that that was all she could give him, too. And all he wanted from her in return—and all she wanted from him—was to know they would adore each other for now and evermore. That was all.

That was all.

She wasn't much surprised when she found herself pulling into Rufus's driveway a little while later. Nor was she surprised that his lights were still on. She was even less surprised to see his silhouette appear behind the screen door when he must have heard her car.

He looked surprised, though, when he pushed the screen door open at her approach. Confused and puzzled, too. When he said, "Bree? Is everything okay?" she put her fingers gently against his mouth and shook her head. Then she moved her hand and pushed herself up on tiptoe, curled her fingers over his jaw, and put her mouth on his.

He didn't question what she did. Maybe he was afraid she would stop. Maybe she was afraid of that, too. Maybe that was why neither of them said a word as Rufus took a few steps backward, into the house, and closed the door behind them. Maybe that was why neither of them stopped kissing the other, either.

Rufus buried his hands in her hair and slanted his mouth over hers, first one way, then the other, again and again and again. Somehow, Bree registered the fact that they were moving. Across the living room, up the stairs, down the hallway, into his bedroom. She felt him tugging her shirt tail free of her skirt, found herself fumbling with the button of his jeans. It was dark in the bedroom, the only illumination coming from a tumble of moonlight outside the open window. She registered the chirp of crickets, the rustle of leaves, the disinterested bark of a neighbor's dog. Then all she could hear was the rasp of Rufus's ragged breath against her neck and the hammering of her own heart.

The bed sheet was cool against her back when she fell against it, but his body was warm atop her. He hooked her thigh in one hand and wrapped her leg around his waist as he entered her, deep and hard and strong. She lifted her hips to meet him, matching his rhythm and gradually escalating it. And then he was coming inside her, and she was crying his name, and he was saying, "I love you, Bree," and she was saying, "I love you, too." Then he was lying in bed beside her, one arm curved protectively around her shoulders, the other hand tangled in her hair, and she was curling her entire body into his.

And never in her life had Bree felt safer or more secure.

RUFUS LAY IN HIS BED BESIDE BREE, ELBOW BENT ON the mattress, chin resting in hand, watching her sleep. He'd woken at five, nearly an hour ago, feeling sated and rested and content, in spite of having enjoyed what couldn't have been more than a few hours of sleep. Now, the sun was just starting to come up, a slender ribbon of pale yellow light slipping through the curtains and slanting across the bed, leaving a stripe of illumination across Bree's naked back. She lay on her stomach beside him, the sheet draped low enough to reveal the slope of her delectable derriere. Her black hair was a pile of tumbled silk on the pillow behind her, and one hand was curled loosely on this side of the pillow in front of her face.

He had always thought her the most beautiful woman he'd ever laid eyes on. But in this moment, totally relaxed in the aftermath of a night of spectacular loving, she took his breath away.

How could she think she could share moments like this with someone who didn't deserve them? Who didn't deserve her? Rufus had done everything he could last night to show her how good life could be with the most basic necessities. How could she want more than what the two of them had shared in this house? What more *was* there than what the two of them had shared in this house? She had everything she needed right here.

Of course, that wasn't the problem, he knew. It wasn't her own needs Bree was worried about. It was her mother's.

He didn't know why she had come back last night after leaving. At the moment, he didn't care. All that mattered was that she *had* come back. That she had told him—and shown him—she loved him as much as he loved her. And that she was still here when he woke up this morning. Now all he had to do was show her there was no reason for her to ever leave again.

As if cued by the thought, she began to stir, inhaling deeply and releasing the breath slowly, in a way he could only describe as contented. It was a good sign. Her eyes fluttered open, then closed again, then opened once more. It took her a moment to focus, to remember where she was, and he waited for signs of panic or embarrassment or regret. When her gaze finally found his, though, she smiled. Then she pushed her hand across the mattress and curled her fingers affectionately around his arm.

"Good morning," he said quietly as he covered her hand with his.

In response, she only murmured a soft, satisfied sound and closed her eyes again.

"You'll have to forgive me," he told her, "but I wasn't expecting anyone for breakfast, so the pickings there are pretty slim."

Her eyes still closed, she said, "I find that hard to believe."

"What? That I forgot to stock up on Wheaties?"

She smiled. "No. That you weren't expecting anyone for breakfast."

He smiled, too. "Let's just say last night was a *very* pleasant surprise."

She opened her eyes again. "It was, wasn't it?"

Telling himself not to do it, because he didn't want to risk ruining the moment, he said anyway, "Do you remember saying what you did?"

She studied him in silence for a moment, and he waited to see if she would use the question as an out. Either say no, she didn't remember saying anything, or claim that what she'd said was the sort of thing everyone said in the heat of a moment like that.

Instead, she said, "I remember telling you that I love you."

His gaze fixed on hers, but he said nothing.

"And I do love you, Rufus."

He would have been relieved if it hadn't been for the fact that she delivered the news in a tone of voice that was generally postscripted with a *but*.

"But," she said, and his gut clenched tight again, "it isn't that simple."

Oh, well, if that was the only objection she had, then there was no problem. Because that was the beautiful thing about love. It was the easiest, most uncomplicated thing in the world.

He kissed her on the crown of her head, then levered himself off the bed. He looked around for his clothes of the night before, but could only find his blue jeans. So he pulled those on commando style, loving the way her eyes darkened as she watched him do it.

"C'mon," he said as he zipped the fly and extended a hand to her. "I want to show you something."

She didn't move, only narrowed her eyes at him. "What?"

But all he said was, "It's something I wanted to show you last night. C'mon."

She started to glance around for her clothes, too, reaching for a pair of panties that were puddled on the floor where they'd fallen. Before she could snag them, Rufus tossed her a T-shirt from the laundry basket sitting on the floor at the foot of the bed. "That'll cover as much as you need covered," he told her with a smile. "And it'll be easier to get off again later."

"Rufus . . ." she said. But her voice held none of the mild irritation she used to use when she uttered his name after he made a vaguely suggestive comment. Instead, she kind of purred his name this time.

It boded well for the future, he thought. Which was good. Because the future was what he wanted to talk to her about.

She pulled the T-shirt over her head, and when she climbed out of bed, it fell to midthigh. Perfect. He didn't bother with a shirt, since they weren't going far. And he did have plans later that would make clothing unnecessary. No reason to overdo it.

"What is it?" she asked as she padded along after him through the bedroom door.

"You'll see."

She followed him down the stairs and through the kitchen, hesitating at the back door when he passed through it and into the backyard.

"It's okay," he told her. "Privacy fence."

She still seemed hesitant, but she tiptoed carefully out. It was too early for his neighbor on the left to be up, anyway. The guy worked nights at the Ford plant. And his neighbor on the right, a landscaper, got up before dawn and was long gone by now.

"Okay, I'm out here," she said as she came to a halt beside him, tugging the T-shirt lower, even though it was perfectly acceptable the way it was. He never figured Bree for the modest type. For some reason, he liked it that she was.

"The way I see it," he said, pointing toward the northeast corner of the house, "there's enough space over on this side of the yard that we could build a good-sized extension onto the house. Big enough for your mom to have a bedroom and private bath, and a little alcove for a sitting area, too. That side of the house gets the evening sun, so maybe the whole sundowning thing with Alzheimer's wouldn't be as bad."

Bree studied him for a long time in silence, her dark brows knitting downward. "Sundowning," she finally said. "You know about sundowning?"

"I've been doing some reading," he told her. "I still have a lot to learn about your mom's illness, but yeah. I know about sundowning. About how some Alzheimer's patients get more restless when the sun goes down. How that's when a lot of them start to wander."

She nodded, but said nothing.

"If that happens with your mom," he said, "you won't have to worry about her getting out of the house. All the doors have keyed dead bolts. And I can put keyed bolts on all the windows, too. She won't be able to leave the house without someone unlocking something for her, and you can be in charge of the keys."

Now Bree nodded. "That's reassuring. And I appreciate it. But wandering's not the worst of it, Rufus."

He met her gaze levelly. "Yeah, I know. But between the two of us, and with a little help from our friends, I think we could take care of her. As long as we have each other, we can handle whatever comes."

She hesitated a telling moment, then said, with much less conviction than before, "It's not your responsibility."

"No, it's not," he agreed. "It's *our* responsibility."

She shook her head slowly. "How can you say that?" she asked softly. "You didn't ask for it."

"Neither did you."

"Even so, I can't ask you to take on something like that."

"You didn't ask. I offered."

"But why?"

"Because, Bree, that's what people who are in love do. They take care of each other. And they take care of what's important to each other. They accept each other's responsibilities. They take what life gives them *together*, and they face it *together*, and they deal with it *together*." He smiled. "That's just one of many perks the job has." He covered the few steps that stood between them and cupped his hand over her cheek. "Anything that affects you, Bree, anything that worries you, or scares you, or hurts you, I want to be the one who makes you feel better. I can't cure your mom. And I can't take away your fear for her. But I can offer you a safe place for her. And I can be here for you whenever you need someone to remind you that you're not in this alone. 'Cause, Bree, you're not in this alone anymore. Not if you don't want to be."

He could see the fight leaving her by the way she tilted her head into his hand and by the way her entire body seemed to bow as the tension left her. Even so, she said, "It could take more than we can manage. I've done a lot more reading than you, and I've talked to other people in the support group. Alzheimer's is—"

"Alzheimer's is horrible," he finished for her. "And it's something that affects a lot of families, Bree. Rich, poor, it doesn't matter. And they all manage somehow."

"Not all of them," she said.

"Yeah, they do," he said firmly. "They learn to manage. Because they know they have to." The way she looked at him then, he thought maybe he was getting through to her. So he hurried on, "You have a lot of friends, Bree. I do, too. They'll help us out if we ask them. Give us breaks when we need them. Do whatever they can to make it a little easier for us. I'm not saying it's going to be smooth sailing. There will be some rough times ahead. But you don't have to go through them alone."

Her eyes filled with tears at that, and her legs almost buckled beneath her. Rufus swept her into his arms, and she clung to him, crying silently at first, then letting go with great, gulping sobs. He let her go as long as she needed to. He couldn't imagine what it must have been like for her, carrying around the fear, the worry, and the sadness she must have been carrying around for some time. And not just carrying, but hiding it, too. She hadn't wanted to share the responsibility of her mother's illness with her friends, even though that was the very thing friends would want her to do.

For a long time, he held her, rubbing her back lightly and brushing back her hair, until her sobs lessened to sniffles and she was able to mumble something about needing a tissue. Rufus smiled and guided her back into the kitchen, pulling a paper napkin from a holder on the countertop, and pretending not to notice when she blew her nose indelicately into it.

"You really do have everything a woman could ask for," she told him with a shaky smile as she brushed the napkin under her nose a final time.

He grinned back. "I'm glad you finally noticed."

She winced a little at the remark, even though he hadn't meant anything by it. He really was glad she'd finally noticed. "Will you ever forgive me for being a jerk?" she asked.

"No forgiveness necessary," he said gently. "You were never a jerk."

She made a face that told him she knew better, but he wasn't going to argue about it. Whatever was in the past was in the past. He wanted to focus on the future now. Especially since it looked like he'd be spending it with the only woman he'd ever loved. Handy, that. Having Bree in his life was, really, all he would ever need.

She tossed the napkin into the trash and turned to lean back against the counter, crossing her arms in a way that wasn't so much defensive as it was protective. "I was wrong about a lot of things, Rufus," she said softly. "But mostly about one thing. You're not a good guy."

He arched his eyebrows in surprise. How many times had he hated hearing her say that? And now that she was taking it back, why did it bother him so much?

She grinned. "You're the *best* guy." She strode across the kitchen and circled her arms around his waist. "Better than that," she said as she leaned her head against his chest. "You're *my* guy. And I love you. And no matter what happens between now and forever, that will keep me going."

Rufus wrapped his arms around her shoulders and rested his head atop hers. "That's all I want and can ask for, Bree," he told her. "That's all."

·Nineteen·

IT TOOK COLE A FEW DRIVE-BYS BEFORE HE FINALLY saw the numbers of the address Lulu had given him as her studio's, stenciled above the door of a narrow limestone-fronted building on Main Street. She'd told him if he came at four, she'd be ready for him, which was why he had arrived at quarter to three. He didn't want Lulu to be ready for him. Lulu was much more herself when she was unprepared.

He had replayed the episode in the car the night before a dozen times after he'd gotten home, and he still wasn't able to figure out exactly what had happened. He really hadn't intended for things to go as far as they had—at least not in the park. He'd thought they could neck like teenagers for a while, and then, if things went well enough, they could go back to Lulu's house and spend the night together. If things didn't go well enough, then at least they could have enjoyed some great necking.

But almost immediately into that first kiss, something had taken hold of both of them. Kissing Lulu wasn't like kissing other women. He didn't know why that was, only that it was true. It took awhile for him to warm up with other women. Not that he didn't enjoy physical closeness with the opposite sex, but at any given moment, he generally had a lot on his mind, and it took him awhile to be able to focus, even on something like physical closeness with the opposite sex.

That wasn't the case with Lulu. The minute he'd laid eyes on her at Bree's apartment, he'd stopped thinking about everything except her. And being physically close to her. The closer, the better. Hell, the more physical, the better. And the minute their mouths touched, everything else in the world ceased to exist. There had just been sensation, desire, and passion. There had been Lulu. And getting closer to Lulu. And touching Lulu. And once he'd started touching Lulu . . .

He nearly tripped over his own feet at the memory and had to grab the bannister of the cramped stairwell as he made his way to the fourth, and uppermost, floor. Never had he been with such a spontaneous, uninhibited woman. He didn't know why he'd been so surprised by the quickness and intensity of her response to him. After some of the things she'd written in her journal, he knew she was a deeply passionate, profoundly sensuous woman. But she didn't come across that way in person. At least, she hadn't until last night. What had happened in the car had been completely unplanned and totally unexpected.

Which was why he had come to her studio before she planned for or expected him to be there.

When he finally crested the top stair, two doors greeted him, each identified by a different letter. B, he knew, was Lulu's studio, but there were no windows for him to look through, and nothing that indicated the space belonged to her. Pressing his ear to the door, he heard the downbeat and backbeat of hard rock, but not much else. With music that loud, there was no way she would hear him knocking. So he tried the knob and, finding it unlocked, turned it and pushed the door open.

The music was overwhelmingly loud now, so he ducked inside and closed the door behind himself before it escaped to

space A across the way, potentially invading someone else's
studio and harassing someone else's muse. Or whatever the
hell those things were that artsy people were allegedly inspired
by. The studio itself was small, no more than fifteen feet by
fifteen, and there were no windows to speak of, save a row of
long skinny ones near where the wall joined the ceiling on the
far side of the room all propped wide open. In spite of that, the
space was crowded with more color and light than Cole had
ever seen in one place before.

Lulu had more than made up for the lack of sunlight by
hanging dozens of halogen lamps overhead that rained down
enough white-bright light to illuminate the studio to its farthest corners. Adding to the brilliance was a freestanding
blowtorch in the middle of the room that erupted in even
more light, though this was a glowing mix of yellow and
blue amid the white crystal clarity of the other.

And the glass. Good God, it was everywhere, what
seemed like dozens of pieces in even more colors, sitting on
shelves, scattered about the floor, leaning against the walls,
hanging from a grid work of stainless steel overhead. Most
of it was unstructured and fluid, frozen rivers of mottled
hues that flowed into one another so seamlessly, it was hard
for Cole to tell where some of the pieces ended and others
began.

Lulu hadn't heard him come in thanks to the heavy hiss
of the blowtorch doing battle with the music that blasted at
about a billion decibels, some guy roaring about bleeding it
out, digging in deeper, and then throwing it away. She sat on
a low stool in profile to the left of the blowtorch, her eyes
covered by old-fashioned riveter's goggles made of heavy
canvas and dark green glass to protect her eyes from the
fire's light. She was dressed in her construction worker-type
garb again of white tank top and overalls, one denim strap
having come undone to let the bib fall diagonally across her
breasts. Her hair was bound haphazardly atop her head, but a
few errant, sweat-dampened curls corkscrewed around her
face and over her equally damp neck. Perspiration streaked

what he could see of her face and throat, and as he began to circle slowly around toward her front, he saw that one very enticing rivulet was streaming down between her breasts.

Even when he stood within a few feet of her at an angle of only forty-five or so degrees, she didn't see him, so focused was she on her work. In one leather workgloved hand, she gripped a long stick that held a blob of orange-hot glass being made oranger and hotter by the fire, and with the other hand, she adjusted the flame on the torch. The loud hiss grew louder still, louder, even, than the music, and Cole had to battle the urge not to cover his ears with his hands. Clearly the noise didn't bother Lulu, so he wasn't going to let it bother him, either.

In fact, the noise seemed to energize her, because as the flame grew higher, she drew nearer to it, picking up a small metal tool and touching it to the molten glass. Cole watched in fascination as the formless blob took shape, though, he had to admit, it was a shape he couldn't quite identify. It seemed to please Lulu, though, because she withdrew it from the flame and held it up toward one of the halogen lights, turning it one way, then another before pulling it back toward herself and making a few adjustments with the tool.

As she moved her arms, Cole noticed muscles at work he hadn't noticed on her before, the elegant bow of her biceps, the delicate curve of her forearm, the graceful camber of her shoulder. When she turned her body away from him, the cutout sleeves of her shirt revealed muscles in her back, too, that had developed through her art. Where he would have thought such muscles on a woman would be mannish and unattractive, he instead found them incredibly sexy. That Lulu had such strength and power in those arms meant she was in no way fragile or passive. On the contrary, her strength and power was something he liked.

Something he liked a lot.

When she turned her body back toward him again, he noted how the sheen of perspiration refracted and shone on her face the same way the glass did with the light shining through it. As she worked, Lulu became one with the glass that surrounded her, as vibrant, delicate, and clear as the art itself. It had never occurred to Cole that the act of creation could be so unbelievably sensuous. But Lulu made it inexorably so.

For several more minutes he watched in silence as she worked, noticing more things about her he hadn't noticed before. The way her hair wasn't just one color—it was dozens of shades of auburn and amber and gold. The way she bit her lower lip when she was concentrating on an especially precise task. How she wiped away the sweat the same way a man would, with a complete lack of decorum. How no matter how hard she was concentrating, or how carefully she was forming the glass, her left foot still tapped perfectly in time with the blaring music.

Then, without warning, she looked up from her work and saw him. Immediately, she pushed the goggles up onto her forehead so she could meet his gaze. And then . . . *zing.* Just as it had that night in the bar, time for Cole came to a stop, and everything in the room went out of focus. Everything except Lulu, who became clearer to him than ever.

"Hello," he heard himself say as if from a million miles away. Even though he'd had to raise his voice for the greeting, he scarcely discerned the word.

She studied him without moving for another moment, then squeezed her eyes shut tight and shook her head once, as if she, too, had lapsed into a sort of otherworldly existence.

"Hey," she shouted back when she opened her eyes again. She lowered the flame on the blowtorch until it was barely a flicker emitting little more than a low-grade whisper of sound. She rose from her stool, moved to a bucket of water and lowered the hot glass into it, then covered the few feet to the boom box—stepping over and around a half-dozen pieces of glass as she did—and lowered the volume on the music.

"Sorry," she said as she shed her gloves and scooped up a

rag to wipe off her sweaty hands. "The piece dictates the music, and today I'm working on one that's a bit in-your-face. Linkin Park is perfect for that."

He smiled as he drove his gaze over the richly variegated items littering the studio. "What? No glass unicorns?"

She smiled back as she whipped off her goggles and swiped her forehead with the rag. But instead of cleaning herself up as she intended, the action left behind a smudge of dirt that Cole found, for some reason, incredibly erotic. "Not since sixth grade, no," she told him. "But I did recently complete a commissioned piece called 'Leda and the Swan.' Does that count?"

He shoved his hands into his trouser pockets and took a few steps toward her. "I don't know. Did it have a unicorn in it?"

She chuckled. "No," she said with mock impatience. "My studio is a unicorn-free environment. Please extinguish your horn before entering."

He could have said something then about how he hadn't had a horn until he entered, but refrained. Instead, he lifted a hand to her forehead and touched his thumb to the smudge. But he didn't wipe it off. He just followed the ragged line of it lightly, threading his fingers into the damp hair at her temple when he reached it.

Her eyes widened at the gesture, her pupils expanding until only a thin circle of blue surrounded them. But she neither did nor said anything to halt him. This close, Cole could smell her, the combining odors and aromas of physical labor, unbridled heat, and the inescapable patchouli that mixed and mingled into something almost narcotic.

"I told you I wouldn't be ready for you until four," she said.

"That's why I'm here now," he replied.

And before she had a chance to respond to that, he leaned forward and covered her mouth with his. She started to pull back, but he followed her, covering her shoulders with his hands as he deepened the kiss. Her skin was slick and hot from her perspiration, and the knowledge that she was already smoldering and damp—and that he had some catching up to do—increased his sense of urgency. She must have sensed it, because instead of pulling away this time, she kissed him back, her hands moving to the knot of his necktie and working feverishly to loosen it.

Cole's last coherent thought was that it was just like last night, the velocity and totality with which he lost himself to her. The moment their bodies made contact, everything else ceased to exist. There was just heat and need and hunger and desire, all of which demanded satisfaction.

As Lulu pulled his tie from his collar and went to work on his shirt buttons, she took a few awkward steps forward, pushing Cole back. "The lights," she mumbled against his mouth as she reached past him. "Too bright."

She flicked a quartet of switches on the wall, something that took care of that problem, and they were thrown into semi-darkness lit only by the flickering flame of the blow-torch and the long afternoon sun that seeped through the windows overhead. It was enough for him to see what he wanted to see—Lulu's face as he unhooked the other strap of her overalls, pushed the garment down over her hips, tugged her shirt over her head, and covered her naked breasts with both hands. Her fingers fumbled on his buttons as he gently kneaded both tender globes, her sweat-dampened skin making his hands slip easily over her flesh. He released her long enough for her to push his shirt off his shoulders and over his arms, then captured her again when she moved her hands to his belt.

The next thing he knew, she was on her knees before him, one hand curving over his taut, naked buttocks, the other moving on his hard cock. She palmed the head gently, then circled her thumb and index finger around his shaft, and slowly slid both down to its base. Then she pulled her hand back up again, and pushed it slowly downward once more. For a long moment, she teased him that way, then she curled her entire hand around his hard length. Instead of stroking him, though, she guided him to her mouth and pulled him deep inside.

Oh, Lulu . . . oh, man . . .

He tangled his fingers in her hair as she went down on him, laving him with her tongue, loving him with her lips, increasing the pressure of her mouth with every slow pull. He watched her head move backward and forward, got harder whenever he saw his cock disappear into her mouth and reappear again. She must have felt his knees giving way at the same time he did, because she pulled back and released him and rose, taking his hand in hers and leading him to the corner of the studio, where there lay a pile of discarded tarps.

When they'd both shed what was left of their clothing, instead of lying beside him, she straddled him with her back to him. Before he realized what she had planned, she was bending forward, lowering her head to take him in her mouth again, clearly wanting to finish what she had started.

Cole reached for her hips and silently urged her to lift them, pulling her back until her knees were on each side of his chest and her sex was open above him. As she sucked him deeper into her mouth, he lifted his head and pressed his own mouth to her damp flesh, kissing her, tonguing her, tasting her as deeply as he could. She halted her ministrations on him for a moment to let herself enjoy the sensations rocketing through her, and when she took him again, her tongue worked even more feverishly. That, in turn, doubled his attentions to her, and their passion ignited as they fed off each other.

When he felt himself nearing his breaking point, he tasted her deeply one final time, then cupped her waist with both hands and pulled her delectable ass back toward him, a silent indication for her to climb off him. She turned to face him and started to lie beside him, but he shook his head and smiled.

"On your knees," he murmured, remembering an especially erotic passage from her journal. He spoke the same instructions to her that her imaginary lover had whispered to her on those pages. "I want you on your knees, babe, shoulders down, cheek pressed to the floor, legs spread wide."

Her eyes widened when he said it, her cheeks flushing even darker than they already were. Without a word, she turned her back to him and bent forward on all fours. Then she lowered her shoulders and face to the floor, spread her legs wide. Cole very nearly came right there. Instead, he gripped her hips in his hands and knelt behind her. There was something so erotic about a woman's naked back and ass, something so arousing about such an uninhibited position.

Before entering her, he opened his palms on her back and skimmed them upward, then back again, his cock moving between her legs and against her sex with each forward and backward motion. The next time, he leaned forward even more, catching her breasts in his hands and holding them for a moment, rubbing the pads of his thumbs over her stiff nipples, generating a long groan from somewhere deep inside her. When he pulled himself backward this time, he settled one hand on each hip and thrust forward, pushing himself into her waiting heat.

Her groan of anticipation became a moan of satisfaction as he took his time to fill her, and he muttered something hot and profane under his breath, another quote from the lover in her journal, about making her take all of him, even if he split her in two. And as she took him, he told her other things, too, in his own words now, all the things he would do to her before the day—and the night—were finished. His promises seemed to enflame her even more, because every time he thrust his body forward, she cried out louder, uttering steamy words about how good it felt to be so full, and murmuring a few explicit plans she had for him, too.

Cole had never known a woman to speak so frankly during sex, to be so open during sex, to respond with such a lack of inhibition during sex. Lulu opened herself to him in ways no other woman had before—physically and otherwise. She rode astride him, lay beneath him, took him kneeling, sitting, and standing. It was in that last position they finally surrendered to the climax they'd just barely been keeping at bay. Lulu's back was pressed against the wall, one leg wrapped around Cole's waist as he pummeled her. They came at the same time, crying out together, their bodies going rigid as they rode out the waves of their orgasms. Then her arms tightened around his neck as the rest of her went limp, and they both eased back down to the floor together.

For a long moment, they lay entwined on the tarps where they had begun, neither saying a word. Lulu opened her hand over the center of Cole's chest, noting how the rapid-fire beating of his heart mirrored her own. Gradually, it slowed along with hers, too, until both of them were thumping along in happy, contented rhythm.

Only then did Lulu say, "You read my journal, you bastard."

She waited for him to deny it, to say that was ridiculous, that he'd obeyed all her notes and had never gone near anything he wasn't supposed to. To do the typical guy thing of sweeping it under the rug and pretending it never happened before changing the subject to something more important, like baseball statistics or the latest thing in socket wrenches.

Instead, Cole told her, "I went through your underwear drawer, too."

She closed her eyes and wondered why that surprised her. Hadn't she known from the beginning what kind of man he was? The kind who did what he wanted, took what he wanted, got what he wanted. Case in point, Lulu Flannery.

Not that she hadn't gone along perfectly willingly, even after realizing he'd read her journal. That was exactly the point. Even knowing he'd violated a trust like that, she'd given herself to him completely. Because she couldn't resist him. The more time she spent with him, the more of herself she would lose to him. Until there would be nothing of her left that he wanted.

"Double bastard," she said in response to his underwear confession.

"I ate some of your M&M's, too," he said. "And I didn't replace them."

"Don't make light of this, Cole."

He sighed heavily in the dim light. "I'm not making light of anything, Lulu. On the contrary, I want to be honest with you. I need to be honest with you if this thing between us has any hope of working."

She battened down the swell of hope that rose inside her at his words. "There is no thing between us," she told him.

He turned onto his side, pushed himself up on one elbow, and gazed down at her. Even in the sparse light of the torch, she could see his expression was incredulous. "You're joking, right?"

Now Lulu was the one to be incredulous. "Hey, you hired me to be your *buffer*, remember?" She had hoped she wouldn't sound hurt when she said it, but no such luck. "I wouldn't call that a *thing*."

His expression softened at her words. "The only reason I hired you to go out with me was because I knew you wouldn't if I just asked."

She wasn't sure whether to believe him or not. Until she realized the truth in his words. Despite that, she asked, "Really?"

He lifted his hand to her hair and coiled a damp curl around his finger. "What happened here, Lulu . . . What happened in the car last night . . . That's something, all right. Something major. Something massive. Something neither one of us seems to be able to control."

"Which is why we can't pursue it," she said.

"What?" he asked. "Lulu, what's happening between us is huge. How can we not pursue it?"

"Cole, it would never work. We're too different from each other."

"Too different?" he echoed. "Lulu, you and I are more alike than you realize. Or at least more than you'll allow yourself to admit."

"That's nuts," she said, suddenly feeling defensive for no

reason. "We are nothing alike. You're so . . . out there. You're so bold and brash and larger than life. I'm timid and deliberate and smaller than life. You go out and meet the world head-on. I hide from it. You'll challenge anything or anybody. I don't want to make waves."

"You are so wrong." He shook his head. "Not just about yourself, but about me, too. Look at this studio," he said. "Talk about bold and brash and larger than life. This place is incredible."

"That's my art, Cole, not me."

"You said your art is an extension of you."

"That's not what I meant when I said that."

"Wasn't it?"

"No." He started to object again, so she hurried on. "Cole, I've seen you in action the past two weeks. You're a showman. You're always on. You never take a break for a minute. You're type A all the way."

He nodded. "Yeah, I've had to be for the past two weeks. It's what people expect of me at times like this. But my life isn't just two weeks a year. It's not just the Kentucky Derby."

"No, it's the Santa Anita Derby, too," she said. "And the Preakness. And the Belmont Stakes. And a host of other races." He opened his mouth to say something more, but she continued, "You love the world you live in. You thrive in it. The brighter the spotlight and the more intense the scrutiny, the more you shine. Admit it. You love being King Cole. And you've been King Cole so long, you can't be anyone else."

She could see he wanted to deny it. But that he knew there was truth to what she said. "I love racing Thoroughbreds," he said. "I love the people who populate that world. I love the character, the color, the excitement, the risk, the energy, the potential, the life." He lifted a hand to her hair and brushed a damp curl away from her forehead. "But, Lulu," he added, "those are the things I . . . like . . . about you, too."

This time Cole was the one to hurry on before she had a chance to respond. "I'm not the only one who does his work under a spotlight," he said. He pointed at the halogens overhead that were dark now. "Your light is even brighter than mine when it's on. And there's more to Thoroughbred racing than what you've witnessed this week," he added. "There's another side to my world. Another side to me. And it's a side I love just as much as the other one, a side I thrive in even more. Remember how I said at the gallery last night that you can't really know a person until you've seen them working in the world they love most and where they feel most comfortable?"

Lulu nodded cautiously. "Yeah."

He smiled down at her, but there was something kind of sad mixed with the contentment she saw there. "I really didn't come here with the intention of making love to you this afternoon," he said. "But watching you here in your world, surrounded by your art, creating your art . . . I couldn't resist you. Because you're yourself here, Lulu. Your most genuine, honest self. You're not the cautious woman who wears the blue jeans and the bland T-shirts. You're the woman who has a million colors and textures in her closet. You're the one who writes with such passion in her journal." He looked at the glass surrounding them, tempered by the darkness, but still vivid and glittery in the waning light. "You're the woman who creates this incredible beauty. Because you have so much color and texture and passion and beauty inside."

Lulu didn't know what to say to that. She told herself he was wrong. That as much as she knew her art was a part of her, it was different from who she really was. But if that was true, then couldn't what Cole did for a living be different from who he was, too?

He covered her shoulders with his hands and dipped his head until his forehead pressed lightly against hers. "Do me a favor," he said.

"What?" she asked softly.

"Come out to the farm in Shelbyville. I want you to meet someone."

The request puzzled her. "Why? Silk Purse is at the Downs by now, isn't she? The race is only a few days away."

"Yeah, she is," he said. "But she's not who I want you to meet. I mean, I do want you to meet her. Eventually. But this is someone way more important."

"Cole, I don't think—"

"Please, Lulu."

"But—"

"Just have dinner with me the night before the Derby. For luck."

She expelled a sound of derision. But, as in everything else, she simply couldn't resist him. "Okay," she said. "For luck. But not for any reason other than that."

• Twenty •

LULU FOUND THE FARM JUST OUTSIDE SHELBYVILLE with no trouble at all. Nothing in Shelby County was very far from anything else, and virtually everything was off Highway 60, which ran right through the middle. Mayhew Farms was only a few miles past Claudia Sanders Dinner House, a local landmark for decades and host to one of the most exuberant wedding receptions Lulu had ever attended. The narrow asphalt lane down which she turned wound first one way, then another, then seemed to double back on itself before straightening out again. The landscape around her was rolling green hills broken up by ponds and copses of poplar and redbud, the bright blue bowl of the sky arcing cloudless and perfect over all of it.

She slowed when she saw a groundhog up ahead poking his nose from some brush at the side of the road, then stopped completely when he took his time waddling across. As she waited, she listened to a swaggering blue jay argue with a more pragmatic cardinal, inhaled a great gulp of honeysuckle flourishing fat and fragrant on a wire fence, and loved the way the soft spring breeze wandered through the open windows and danced with her hair.

When the groundhog disappeared into the brush on the other side of the road, Lulu put her car in gear again and inched forward, keeping an eye on the odometer to compute the passing miles between Highway 60 and the Mayhews. She stopped when she began to see horses in the fields to her right, big glossy-coated animals of black and brown, cinnamon and chestnut, cantering and cavorting behind white wooden fences. The late afternoon sun spilled long trails of amber and orange over the countryside, the colors shimmying in the coats of the horses and turning them to gold.

They really were gorgeous creatures, she thought as she slowed the car again to watch them. Such power and beauty, such strength and grace, all of it moving with incredible speed and elegance. No wonder Cole was drawn to Thoroughbreds. He had a lot in common with them.

A sign appeared a little farther down the road, letting her know she'd arrived at her destination. *MAYHEW FARMS*, it read. *EST. 1921. CHAMPION THOROUGHBREDS BRED, RAISED, STABLED, AND TRAINED.*

Cole had told her to continue all the way up the winding driveway until she saw the main house, which, he'd told Lulu, she would know when she saw it. She passed barns and outbuildings, a silo and alfalfa field before it came into view, a massive Federal-style house with a broad, wraparound veranda and what looked like floor-to-ceiling windows across the front.

This must be the place.

She rolled to a stop beside the rented Town Car she recognized as Cole's, then took a few seconds to steady her breathing, collect her thoughts, and shore up her nerve. But before she was anywhere close to doing any of that, Cole was coming down the front steps of the house toward her, looking nothing like the Cole she knew, making it even more impossible for her to get a grip on what she was thinking or feeling.

Gone was the high-powered, flashy business suit in which she'd become so accustomed to seeing him. Gone was the splashy-colored shirt and silk necktie. Gone was the expensive Italian footwear. For Derby Eve, a night when virtually everyone in his line of work and social stratum was dressing in their finest duds to make the rounds of dozens of parties and events, Cole had opted for a denim work shirt, blue jeans, and hiking boots. And instead of going out to party, he'd elected to stay in tonight. With Lulu.

She opened the car door and climbed out, smoothing a hand over the yellow and orange batik sundress that fell to mid-thigh. She'd paired it with beaded sandals and chunky beaded bracelet and earrings, letting her hair bounce free around her shoulders. It was an outfit she'd bought two years ago and never worn. Wearing it now, she felt . . .

That was strange. She would have thought she'd feel overdressed and uncomfortable. Instead, she felt kind of good. The sun on her bare shoulders was warm and welcoming, the balmy breeze caressed her arms, and the long grass by the drive tickled her calves as she began to walk toward him. Instead of making her feel like the center of attention, the bright colors and bold pattern made her feel like . . . herself. She loved color. She loved bold patterns. Her work and home were decorated by both. So why shouldn't she be?

Oh, right. Because bold colors and patterns brought unwanted attention. At least, it had been unwanted before. And because indulging her desire for those meant opening the door to indulging other things, too, things she didn't want to indulge outside her art. At least, she hadn't before. Before she met Cole. Before he gave her a reason—besides her work—to let herself be herself. Before he entered her life and filled it with colors she'd never even known existed. The colors of passion. The colors of happiness. Maybe even the colors of love. Not that she hadn't had those things in her life before he came along, but they hadn't been like this. Never, ever, like this.

"Hey," he said as he drew near her.

She arched her eyebrows at the greeting. "Hey?" she echoed. "What happened to *Hello*?"

He grinned. "Guess I've fallen under the spell of you Kentuckians. I actually used *y'all* this morning, too."

She grinned back. "But did you use it correctly, that's the question."

"What do you mean?"

"Were you talking to more than one person when you said *y'all*?"

He shook his head. "No."

She uttered a soft *tsk* and said, "You non-Southerners. *Y'all* is plural, not singular."

"Then I used it correctly," he told her.

"But you said—"

"I was talking to a barn full of horses at the time."

"Ah. Is that part of the Kentucky spell, too?" she asked. "Talking to horses? 'Cause I have to tell you, Cole, not all of us are that comfortable around them. Case in point, me."

His mouth dropped open in surprise. "You're afraid of horses?"

"Only up close," she said.

He looked thoughtful for a moment. "Well, this is a bit unexpected. But we can work around it." Before she could ask him what he meant, he hurried on, "I've talked to horses all my life." Then he smiled again. "And I grew up in Virginia," he added.

That surprised her. "No way. You're from the South?"

He nodded. "When I left Virginia, I stopped saying *y'all*. I thought it made me sound like a hick. But coming back here and hearing everyone use it so matter-of-factly, I realized saying *y'all* doesn't make you sound like a hick. It makes you sound like . . ."

"What?"

"Charming," he told her. "At least it is when you say it."

He took the two steps necessary to close the space between them, tucked his hand under her hair and curled it around her nape in the way she loved so much. Then he dipped his head to kiss her, also in the way she loved so much. Not too hard, not too soft. Not too passionate, not too chaste. Just right. The way she felt whenever she was with him. The way she was going to miss feeling after he was gone.

He pulled away, but didn't let go of her, his gaze fixing on hers. "But then, I think everything you do is charming," he said softly. And before she had a chance to respond, he tilted his head back toward the house and added, "Come on. I'll show you around."

The hand cupping her neck slid over her shoulder, dawdling long enough on the spaghetti strap of her dress for him to murmur, "Pretty," before skimming down her arm to tangle his fingers with hers. The cicadas kicked up a fuss as they walked, their chatter swelling to a loud crescendo before falling back to a manageable volume. The breeze ruffled the leaves of a huge maple tree in the front yard, and somewhere in the distance, a tiresome woodpecker *tap-tap-tapped* for his dinner. Something warm and contented settled around her heart, and she closed her eyes for a second, inhaling a deep breath and holding it inside, thinking maybe by doing so she'd keep a little bit of the moment inside her forever, too.

Then she opened her eyes again to see Cole looking at her, a soft smile playing about his mouth. "It's nice, isn't it?" he murmured.

She nodded, but said nothing.

"It reminds me a lot of the farm where I worked when I was a teenager."

"In Virginia?" she asked.

"Yeah."

"I never would have guessed that's where you're from."

He stopped walking, even though they hadn't yet reached the walkway leading up to the house. "There's a lot you don't know about me, Lulu. Which was why I wanted you to come here tonight. So you could see the real Cole Early."

"I've spent the last week with Cole Early," she said softly, sobering a little. "I think I've seen the real him by now."

He started to shake his head, then hesitated. "Once," he told her. "You saw the real me once. When I made love to you."

She felt her face flame at the reminder. "Cole . . ."

"You saw more of the real me that day than I show anyone," he interrupted. "But you haven't been spending your time with Cole Early for the past week, Lulu. You've been spending it with . . ." He blew out an exasperated breath. "With King Cole. The guy that the fans and the press like to see. Tonight, that won't be the case. Tonight, you'll be seeing the real me again."

She straightened. "Don't you think you're presuming a lot here? I mean, just because of what happened in my studio . . ."

He grinned. "I'm certainly not ruling that out, but that's not what I meant. I meant that this"—he swept his arms wide and did a slow three-sixty, encompassing the entire farm as he went—"is a lot like the place I call home in California. Yeah, the flora, fauna, and landscape are different, and we don't have these damned cicadas—" As if insulted by his words, the cicadas' prattle swelled loudly for a moment, then receded, making him smile. "But for the most part," he continued, "Mayhew Farms of Shelby County is like Early Farms in Temecula." He dropped his hands to his sides. "This is much more my life than what you've seen this week." He tilted his head toward a long stable a few hundred feet to the left of the house. "Let me introduce you to the boys and girls, and then we can work our way gradually back to the house."

The boys and girls turned out to be horses, of course, but no Mr. Eds were these. Some of them, Cole told her, had been insured for millions of dollars. That was because some of them had already earned millions of dollars and still had quite a bit of racing time left. Lulu had never been a big fan of horses, though she did always catch her breath whenever she was driving somewhere near a farm and saw some of the majestic beasts running over hill and dale. Up close like this, she realized they were even bigger than she'd thought. They were enormous, powerful animals, all muscle, muzzle, and shimmering coat . . . with lovely brown eyes and long, long lashes that tempered her fear a little. Cole was completely relaxed with them, rubbing their noses and talking to them in gentle tones, chuckling when one of those big muzzles nudged his hand, and laughing outright when their heads bumped his.

Lulu could never be that comfortable with them, but neither was she quite as intimidated seeing how affectionate they were with him.

"Ready to saddle up?" he asked when he saw her watching one of the larger creatures.

She wondered if the blood actually drained from her face as quickly as it felt like it was fleeing. "What?"

He laughed even harder at her expression. "Don't worry, Lulu, I won't make you ride if you don't want to. Besides, I sure as hell wouldn't start you on one of these guys."

"I don't want to start on any of your guys," she told him. "They're beautiful, but I'm not a horse person."

"Fair enough," he said. "I'm not an art person."

Well, she didn't know about that. She'd been thinking he was a work of art since the moment she met him.

He buried his hand in the big animal's mane, and it turned its head toward him in a way that was clearly playful. "Maybe someday you'll want to learn to ride," he said a little absently.

Maybe. But she doubted it. "Maybe someday I'll try my hand at equestrian art," she said instead. "Or maybe someday you will."

He smiled at that. "Maybe I will."

From the stable, he took her on a quick tour of the grounds closest to the house, explaining how a working horse farm operated, starting with the predawn waking to early morning exercising to feeding, grooming, breeding, boarding, and every other thing that happened on a place like this. Lulu learned everything a person could learn about Cole's line of work in a couple of hours' time, and it was enough to make her head spin. It was demanding, time-consuming work. But he obviously loved it, and it was obviously what he was meant to do. Like her art was to her, raising and training Thoroughbreds was a part of him. Without her art, she wouldn't be Lulu Flannery. And without his horses, he wouldn't be Cole Early.

He was right, though, that the man she was with tonight was different from the man she'd accompanied to the Brown Hotel, the man she'd had drinks with at Felt, the man she'd run into at Eddie's office two weeks ago. As they sat down to dinner on the veranda—a meal he told her the Mayhews' cook had prepared earlier, but which Cole put the finishing touches on now, since everyone else was off and gone for Derby Eve events—he was more relaxed than she'd ever seen him. Even though he had the biggest race of his career the next day, he wasn't edgy or anxious or tense. Instead, he seemed . . . happy. Untroubled. Content.

By the time they carried their dishes back into the house, the sun had set completely. Cole poured them each another glass of wine and led her back out to the veranda, and, as if by mutual agreement, they took their seats in a white wicker swing at one end. The crickets had taken up the chorus from the cicadas, accompanied by the occasional croak of a frog and the leathery flutter of bat wings. The moon crept over a trio of oak trees in the distance, and one by one, stars winked on overhead, until the black velvet sky was lit by diamonds. Cole toed the swing into slow motion, its leisurely creaking and the occasional jangle of its chain backing up the crickets nicely. When he stretched an arm along the back and dropped it over her shoulder, what else could Lulu do but lean into him, tucking her head into the curve of his neck

and shoulder, and feel like she was right where she was supposed to be?

All over Louisville, to celebrate Derby Eve, his colleagues were carousing like Vikings and running amok at
any number of nightspots and parties. But Cole Early,
splashily dressed, larger-than-life media darling, the man
everyone was probably looking to interview at those parties
and nightspots, was tucked away on a quiet farm in Shelby
County with Lulu. Didn't that tell her everything she needed
to know? If he really was brassy, brash, arrogant King Cole,
he'd be out running amok himself right now. Or, if he were
stuck here with her, he'd be anxious and nervous because
he'd feel so out of place, and he'd want to be out carousing
like a Viking and running amok.

Beneath his surface, he wasn't arrogant, brassy, or brash.
Beneath his surface, he was actually a very sweet guy. But
then, on some level, Lulu had already known that about him.
Otherwise, she wouldn't be here with him right now. In fact,
she never would have been anywhere with him. Because she
never would have had anything to do with a brassy, brash,
arrogant guy in the first place.

At some point after meeting him—maybe even the
minute she did meet him—she'd seen beneath his surface to
the sweet guy underneath. The same way he, at some
point—maybe even before he started reading her journal—
had seen beneath hers. And when people were able to do that
with each other, when they were able to see beyond the outer
trappings and fall for what was underneath, it wasn't something to be taken lightly. Rather, it was something to celebrate. Something to pull close. Something to hold on to.
Maybe forever.

"So do you like Mayhew Farms?" Cole asked beside her.

She listened to the crickets, looked up at the night sky,
and snuggled a little bit closer. Then she nodded. "It's beautiful, Cole."

His body went lax beside her when she said it, and he exhaled a long sigh of what sounded very much like relief.

"Good," he said softly. "Because I bought the place this afternoon."

She tilted her head back to look at him, certain she must have misheard, certain she must have only imagined what he said, because it was something she would have loved so much to hear. "You did what?" she asked, just to be sure.

"The place was going to go on the market next month. So I made an offer to the Mayhews this afternoon, and they accepted it."

Her lips parted in surprise. "Just like that?"

He looked down at her and smiled. "Just like that."

"Why?"

He gave a little shrug, but there was nothing casual in the gesture. "I'm branching out my business," he told her. "Bringing some of it East. Like you said, Kentucky horses are some of the best."

"I said they're *the* best," she corrected him.

"Right. Some of the best," he repeated, grinning. "I've been thinking for a while now that it might be nice to have a second location for Early Farms."

"How long have you been thinking about that?" she asked.

"Oh, man, for a while. At least two days."

She laughed at that.

"Anyway, the Mayhews mentioned over dinner last week that they were going to retire and put the place up for sale next month, because both their kids pursued careers outside the Thoroughbred business. That got some wheels turning in my head. Expanding my business here makes sense. This farm has been producing champions for almost a century. The Thoroughbred heritage here in Kentucky is incomparable. The state is gorgeous."

"Commonwealth," she corrected him.

"What?"

"Kentucky isn't actually a state. It's a commonwealth."

"Now, see, that's the kind of thing I need to know if I'm going to be living here six months out of the year."

Something that had been squeezed tight in Lulu's chest for much of the evening eased up at hearing that. Too fearful to even hope, she asked softly, "You're moving here?"

"Part-time," he told her. "I don't think I could handle your winters after being in southern California for so long, but I figure April through October has got to be pretty pleasant—"

"Well, we do have pretty humid summers," she felt obligated to tell him. "And the temperatures can hit the nineties fairly regularly."

"Which is why the HVAC gods created central air-conditioning." He grinned. "And an April arrival will ensure that I'm here for all those wacky Derby events," he added.

"You really want to relocate here?" she asked, still afraid to believe it was true. Seeing him six months out of the year was better than no months out of the year. "Even part-time?"

He nodded without hesitation. "Yeah," he said. "I really do. I like Kentucky. I don't think I could leave it behind if I tried. Louisville and Lexington are two of the nicest cities I've ever visited. And the people here . . ." He covered his heart with his free hand and splayed his fingers wide. "Lulu, I just love the people here."

The pressure around her heart eased some more. "Do you?"

He nodded. "I do."

She scooted a little closer to him on the swing. "Well, you know, I think a lot of the people here have grown pretty fond of you, too."

He scooted a little closer to her, too. "Actually, there's one person here whose feelings I'm more interested in than others."

Still looking up at him, her head settled against his shoulder, she asked, "Anybody I know?"

"You know her now," he said, moving his hand to her face, cupping her jaw in his palm. "And she . . . you . . ." He smiled. "You're the reason I want to spend half the year here." He hesitated a telling moment before adding, "And maybe, someday, you might want to spend the other half of the year in Temecula with me."

By now, the pressure in Lulu's chest had evaporated, letting her heart race free. And race it did at the thought of maybe—probably . . . definitely?—spending every day of every year with Cole. It was a huge, unspoken commitment he had just made, buying a farm here. He had pretty much just said he wanted to begin work on a future that included both of them, a future that was far-reaching and potentially permanent. He was telling her she was massively important to him. The way he had become massively important to her. It didn't matter where they were—Kentucky, California, or Timbuktu. As long as she was with Cole, Lulu was where she wanted, needed, to be. Of course, it helped that she could take her art with her wherever she went. It was, after all, a part of her. The same way Cole had become a part of her, too.

He must have thought her silence was the result of indecision, because before she had a chance to tell him she rather liked his idea, he hurried on. "I know it's a lot to presume," he said, "but at least think about it. I have a small barn on my property that you could turn into a studio. And the arts scene in southern California, Lulu, is huge. *Huge.* And I'm not far from the ocean. Lots of artistic inspiration there. I mean, how many poets have compared the ocean to glass? Or vice versa? And I'm close to the mountains, too. And Mexico's not that far away. There's inspiration everywhere. And if you don't like the ocean, or the mountains, or Mexico, we can spend our weekends in Santa Fe sometimes. Now *there's* a place that's just—"

She halted him by placing her fingers lightly over his mouth. And she smiled as she told him, "You had me at 'Sorry about that, sweetheart.'"

He looked confused for a minute, then he smiled, too. "And you had me at 'Don't forget your sunscreen and Mardi Gras beads.'" He hesitated another moment, and when he spoke again, his fear was almost palpable. "So does this mean you're interested?"

She nodded. "Anywhere you are, Cole, that's all the inspiration I need."

His body went even more relaxed beside her, as if hearing her agreement finally chased away whatever was left of his fear. "It'll mean shouldering the mantle of Queen Cole from time to time," he cautioned.

She shook her head. "No, it won't. I'll be shouldering the mantle of Queen Lulu."

He smiled. "And that'll be okay?"

She nodded. "Now that you've put me in touch with my inner hedonist, not only do I know just what to do, but I think I'll probably have fun doing it. As long as we have nights like this, too."

He curled his arm more securely around her. "Oh, I promise you, Lulu, there will be many, *many* nights like this in our future."

And that, Lulu thought, was about as good as a life could get.

Epilogue

HAD COLE PUT IN A SPECIFIC ORDER FOR DERBY DAY weather, he didn't think the meteorologists could have filled it more perfectly. Lulu had told him she recalled Derby Days that had anything from ninety-plus humidity-dripping degrees to near-freezing sleet. Springtime in Kentucky, she told him, was always an adventure. Today, however, the sky was a crisp, perfect blue with just enough gauzy wisps of cloud stretched here and there to break the glorious monotony. The temperature hovered at around seventy-two degrees, and the humidity had taken a vacation. As he stood in the clubhouse of Churchill Downs staring down at the crowd below, he almost felt like he was home in California.

He smiled as the thought unrolled in his head. He was home. Just not the one in California at the moment.

But that had nothing to do with where he happened to be standing and everything to do with the woman standing beside him. For Derby Day this year, Lulu had gone all out. Her dress was a blue and yellow print that hugged her curves, showcased her legs, and doubtless would have brought out her eyes beautifully if it weren't for the big yellow sunglasses she was wearing. She'd bought her hat from Louisville's premier milliner, Audrey Fine, who ran her shop on the first floor of an old brick Victorian on Third Street that was reputed to be haunted. Audrey and her shop, Finery, had both lived up to their names. Within minutes of walking through the door, the milliner had had Lulu, ah, milled in a hat whose colors were identical to her dress, with a broad blue straw brim and a crown covered with yellow silk roses.

It was actually a conservative hat compared to the hot pink, chartreuse, and orange number her friend Bree was wearing on the other side of Lulu. The brim on hers was so wide, it covered half of her back, and there were enough feathers atop the damned thing that she was going to take flight if the breeze picked up even the slightest bit. Still, it suited Bree and her hot pink minidress perfectly. Her husband, Rufus, seemed to think so, too, because the guy hadn't taken his eyes off her since Cole and Lulu picked them up at their house that morning in the stretch limo they'd rented for the day.

Cole wasn't the only guy who'd gotten lucky in Kentucky last year. Even when Silk Purse missed winning the first jewel in the Triple Crown, it hadn't diminished Cole's certainty that he was the luckiest SOB on earth. Besides, his and Susannah's entry this year, Shimmering Pearl, *would* go all the way.

A voice over the loudspeaker announced that the horses for the Derby would be making their way around the track to the gates, bringing him back to the matter at hand. Susannah Pennington was on his other side, smiling in a way that let Cole know Esteban, *her* new husband and Pearl's jockey, was in a *very* good mood today. She looked over at Cole and winked at him, letting him know that was indeed the case.

"So are you feeling lucky?" she asked Cole.

He nodded enthusiastically. "Oh, yeah." Of course, he was thinking about how lucky he was in another area of his life, but he was sure that would wash over into the race, too.

The race fans and bookies had caught on to Pearl's potential right off the bat, her odds making her this year's favorite. In a few more minutes, she was going to be the toast of the town, the way Silk had almost been last year. Along with Cole, Susannah, and Esteban. And, of course, Lulu.

Just as she had been last year, she would be with him to help field the crowd, but not because he wanted a buffer. No, what Cole wanted now was, well, everything. And what he'd gotten in Lulu was exactly that.

She slipped her arm through his and pulled him close. "This is always so exciting," she said as she watched the horses canter and prance on the dirt track below. "There's so much energy here. So much vibrancy. It's like the air itself is alive."

"There's not another feeling like it in the world," he assured her. "The minutes before a race are always magic."

And they felt even more magical now that she was here with him to enjoy them.

The announcer asked everyone to rise for the singing of "My Old Kentucky Home," something that was unnecessary, as far as Cole was concerned, because who could be seated at a time like this? Nevertheless, he once again had to consult his program to find the lyrics, even though Lulu, Bree, and Rufus sang them by heart. As the song drew to a close, he noticed a tear slip from beneath Lulu's sunglasses, which she hastily swiped away at the same time Bree performed the same function. The two women laughed as they did so, as they had last year, confirming it was something they did every year.

As he watched the last of the horses entering the gate on the other side of the track, that old feeling seeped into him again. A barely restrained force of power that put his entire body on alert. The crowd went curiously silent as the final gate was closed and stayed that way in the few interminable seconds before the announcement of—

"They're off!"

And then Cole was in the zone he entered the moment

one of his horses hit the track. It was as if a bubble descended to surround him, blocking out everything except the horses pounding the dirt below and throwing them into crystal clarity. But now, Lulu was in the bubble with him. Now, he had her fingers woven with his, her cries of "*Go, baby, go!*" chorusing with his own, her exhilaration, her vitality, and her passion mingling with his and doubling its power. And when Shimmering Pearl rounded the final curve, when she began to pull away from the rest of the horses, when she began to *run*, Lulu grabbed both of his hands in hers, and it was like a jolt of something white-hot and frenetic shot through them both.

By the time Pearl crossed the finish line, she was three lengths ahead of the placing horse. But when Cole swept Lulu into his arms and kissed her and kissed her and kissed her, it wasn't the joy of having his horse win that filled him with such euphoria. It was the joy of having Lulu beside him to share it. And it was the joy of knowing she would be there forever.

· Author's Note ·

I grew up in Louisville, still live just outside of town, and absolutely love writing about it. I know the city and its environs intimately, having lived and worked in many of those environs. However, I have taken some literary license with my hometown. The Ambassador Hotel is fictional, modeled after Louisville landmark the Seelbach Hotel, because I know the venerable and elegant Seelbach would never tolerate some of Bree's hijinks or the trawling of call girls in its bar. Deke's, likewise, doesn't exist, and is an amalgam of Highlands nightclubs, some of which, alas, are no longer in business.

I've also played fast and loose (if you'll pardon the pun) with Louisville's seasons, something one wouldn't think it possible to do considering the fact that Louisville's seasons are so unpredictable. But the locals will recognize areas where I've done that and can feel smug thinking, "That's so wrong," while others will find in reading those passages the enjoyment of, I hope, some evocative and lovely prose.

And although there are scores of real Derby Festival events I could have had Lulu and Cole attending, I invented a few for my own selfish purposes. This is the first of a three-book series, and I need to save some of the good stuff for later novels. I have done my best to include some local color, and if I've made mistakes with any of it, it's due to the fact that, since I started writing full time, I don't get out much anymore. So I apologize if there are any errors within. (Please address all angry e-mails to elibev@gimmeabreakwillya.com.)

And, finally, if you're interested in renting a house for Derby sometime, you can find more info at www.rentmyhouse4derby .com. (Really.)

Turn the page for a sneak peek at

The Ghost and Mrs. Magill

by Elizabeth Bevarly

Coming soon from Berkley Sensation!

NATHANIEL SUMMERFIELD WAS ALREADY HAVING A rough day when his assistant Irene announced that he had a visitor who hadn't made an appointment. Normally, he would have told Irene to tell the person to come back when they did, even if it *wasn't* a day when his phone was ringing off the hook and he was fielding all kinds of obstacles to his about-to-be-signed contract with Edward Dryden. Man, everyone from the Fair Housing Commission to the Small Business Owners Association was breathing down his neck over this thing. Edward would be at Nathaniel's office in less than three hours, and he still had to review part of the contract before the man's arrival.

But it was just past noon when Irene informed him of Audrey Magill's need to speak to him, and anyone Nathaniel might need to call or do business with would probably be breaking for lunch, anyway. Plus, Irene said Ms. Magill promised she would only take a few minutes of his time. Then he caught a glimpse of Audrey Magill standing just beyond the door, and Nathaniel decided he could spare more than a few minutes for the woman because she was stunning.

So stunning that he was momentarily taken aback when she strode into his office. The reaction surprised him, since she wasn't what he would have really called beautiful. She was too wholesome-looking for that, with her fresh-scrubbed face and hair pulled into a simple ponytail and attire that was better suited to a Sunday brunch than any kind of corporate affair, something that indicated she wasn't here on business. Which was just fine with Nathaniel, since a woman who looked like Audrey Magill didn't exactly inspire businesslike responses in a man.

Even though she wasn't conventionally beautiful, she was stunning. Had he mentioned that? The ponytail might have been simple, but it was nearly as thick as her wrist, holding razor straight, ink black hair that spilled nearly to her waist. The kind of hair a man's fingers itched to tangle themselves in. And her eyes. My God. They were huge and abundantly lashed, as blue and serene as a Caribbean bay. She was slim but curvy, her generous hips and breasts only enhanced by the straight khaki skirt and black T-shirt she was wearing. Her only jewelry was a gold chain that disappeared beneath the scooped neck of her shirt and gold hoops in her ears.

Not only was she unconventionally beautiful, but she wasn't the sort of woman that normally attracted Nathaniel, either. He preferred women who went out of their way to play up their attributes, the kind who took hours to put on their makeup and fix their hair and choose their outfit for a date—provided they were ready when he got there and didn't make him wait. Women who wore lots of jewelry that swayed and glittered, and who chose outrageously feminine clothing meant to exaggerate their, ah, assets.

Audrey Magill, however, didn't seem like the type to exaggerate anything. Which meant that whatever she was packing, it was entirely, genuinely, hers.

Hell, yes, he could spare a few minutes for her. He even straightened his sapphire necktie and smoothed a few nonexistent wrinkles out of his charcoal suit as he covered the few steps necessary to greet her.

"I might as well get right to my point, Mr. Summerfield," she said after shaking his hand. "I know you must be very busy."

Her handshake surprised him, too, as it was solid and masculine, the sort of handshake he didn't normally receive from a woman, even those who worked at the same corporate level he did. She took the seat he indicated on the other side of his desk, seeming in no way intimidated by his office environment, which he'd deliberately decorated in Early American Despot specifically to intimidate people. She just sat up straighter in the leather wing chair and met his gaze evenly over his expansive mahogany desk.

Then she had to go and ruin everything by asking him, "Do you believe in ghosts, Mr. Summerfield?"

Nathaniel hoped his feelings didn't show on his face. Because at that moment, what he was feeling like was picking up the phone and calling Dial-a-Shrink.

Hopefully that didn't show in his voice, either, when he replied, "Ghosts, Ms. Magill?"

She nodded. And said, "It's *Mrs.* Magill, actually."

Married *and* a nut job, he thought. Two major strikes right there. Good thing she had the stunning, curvy thing going, otherwise, she'd be out the door right quick. "*Mrs.* Magill," he corrected himself obediently. But he couldn't quite stop his fingers from inching toward the phone as he replied, "Ah, no. I don't believe in ghosts."

She nodded. "I don't either, actually," she said.

The hand that had begun to creep toward the phone stilled. Score one for the former nut job.

"But I had the strangest dream last night," she continued. "Your great-great . . . several greats grandfather was in it and told me you were—"

Nathaniel's hand started to inch forward again, and he feared the reason she'd stopped talking was because she noticed that. Then she smiled in a way that made him think she realized how questionably sane—or sober—she sounded.

"Can I start over?" she asked. "I sound like a raging nut job."

Which may or may not be indicative of actual nut jobbiness, he thought. Willing to give her the benefit of the doubt, however, he said, "Of course." But he left his hand near the phone. He wasn't going to give her *that* much benefit.

She took a deep breath and tried again. "I recently bought a house in Old Louisville that, it turns out, belonged to one of your ancestors."

"Really . . ." Nathaniel said, not sure how this was relevant to, oh . . . anything.

"Then yesterday afternoon, I went into an antique shop on Third Street and discovered a portrait of that ancestor—Captain Silas Summerfield—for sale. I thought that was an interesting coincidence."

Nathaniel would have thought it interesting, too. Had he, you know, been interested.

"Naturally, I bought it," she said.

Naturally, Nathaniel looked at his watch.

"And then last night," she continued, "I had a very strange dream, and I woke up to an even stranger reality."

She launched into an account that promised to take considerably more than the few minutes she'd already used up, something about his great-great-blah-blah-blah grandfather showing up in her dream and telling her that Nathaniel was in danger of losing his soul, followed by something about a break-in at her house that turned out to not be a break-in after all, but some kind of possibly-perhaps-sort-of ghostly mischief, and then . . .

Well, Nathaniel stopped listening about then, so he really wasn't sure what she said after that. All he knew was that she was about to use up his entire lunch hour—which, okay, granted, he never used to actually eat lunch anyway—with some cockamamie story about an ominous warning from beyond the veil.

Stunning and curvy thing notwithstanding, Nathaniel didn't have all day, and he *did* have a sound mind. So the next time she paused for a breath, he said, "Ms. Magill, I appreciate your concern, but you'll understand, I'm sure, when I tell you I don't share it."

She studied him in clear confusion. "It's *Mrs.* And why would I understand that? I mean, I know this sounds—"

"Ludicrous?" he finished for her. "Because it doesn't just sound that. It *is* that."

Now she studied him in clear offense. "Look, I realize what happened to me last night and this morning might seem a little out of the ordinary."

Nathaniel shook his head. She really didn't get it. "It doesn't seem a little out of the ordinary," he told her. "It *is* complete hooey."

"And believe me," she lurched onward as if he hadn't spoken, "I weighed my decision carefully before coming here, for the very reason that I was afraid you'd think I'm nuts."

She paused, evidently awaiting a response to that. So he said, "And?"

Evidently that wasn't the response she had been expecting, because she narrowed her eyes at him. "And I don't expect everyone to believe in the possibility of an afterlife or any sort of conduit between that and the here and now. I'm as skeptical as the next person about that kind of thing. But I'm not completely closed-minded about it, either. And I thought you might at least be like me in finding the whole concept as . . . as . . ."

"As ridiculous?" he supplied helpfully. Well, okay, maybe it was less helpful than it was antagonistic. At least he'd offered her something.

"As interesting," she finished tersely.

"Ms. Magill—"

"*Mrs.*"

"*Mrs.* Magill," he corrected himself again, wondering why he had trouble remembering she was married, "you can't think I would put stock in a dream you had—a dream *anybody* had—even if it did feature one of my ancestors. Dreams are just images that unroll in a person's brain while they're unconscious. All the more reason to *not* put any stock in them. My advice to you would be to lay off the Hostess Ho Hos before you go to bed at night."

She narrowed her eyes at him. "It was Chunky Monkey ice cream, and I know perfectly well this sounds like nonsense. But don't you find it strange that I would have a dream like that?"

What Nathaniel found strange, she didn't want to know.

"And then wake up this morning to see an article about you in the paper?" she added. "One that your great-great-etcetera grandfather said I would see in the paper?"

"Ms. Magill—"

"*Mrs.*," she corrected him yet again, more vehemently this time.

"*Mrs.* Magill," he corrected himself yet again, less graciously this time. "There have been articles in the paper about me and Edward Dryden almost every day for two weeks. The development deal he and I are putting together is going to be one of the biggest ones this city has seen for more than a decade. For all I know, that was what caused you to have your dream, not some portrait of my great-great . . . whatever . . . grandfather. And certainly not any danger my soul might be in."

She opened her mouth to say something, apparently reconsidered whatever she was going to say, and closed it again. But she kept her gaze homed in on his as she stood and tugged her handbag over her shoulder. She started to turn toward the door, then looked back at Nathaniel. "I'm sorry if you think I've wasted your time, Mr. Summerfield. But as Shakespeare himself said—"

"Is this going to be the quote about there being more things in heaven and earth, Horatio?" Nathaniel interjected before she could finish. "Because quite frankly, *Mrs.* Magill, I can dream of *a lot* in my philosophy. And none of it has to do with ghosts or souls."

She nodded once, curtly. "Oh, believe me, Mr. Summerfield, I can see you don't spend much time worrying about your soul. What I'm trying to figure out now is why Captain Summerfield was so worried about it. Since it's abundantly clear that any soul you might have ever had is already long gone."

And with that, she turned around and headed for the door. Nathaniel told himself he was grateful, even as he watched with something akin to wistfulness the way that long pony-tail swayed even more seductively than her hips. The last thing he needed in his life these days was a raging nut job, even if she was stunning. This deal with Edward was going to command more of his time than any other project he'd ever been involved in. Hell, if it caused him to lose his soul, that was just one less thing Nathaniel would have to feel responsible for. He was reviewing his contract with Edward before the door behind Mrs. Magill was even closed.

"THIS IS THE START OF SOMETHING GREAT, Nathaniel."

Three hours after Audrey Magill left his office, Nathaniel welcomed Edward Dryden into it. They'd gone over every clause in their contract together, had discussed the development in detail, had reviewed and approved all the arrangements left to make. All that was left was to sign on the dotted line—in triplicate—and the deal would be done. Edward signed where indicated with a narrow, crowded signature, then handed the pen to Nathaniel. He bent over the desk and placed the pen to paper and was about to scrawl the first of three signatures when his hand stilled. Because something Audrey Magill had said during her long spiel suddenly erupted in his brain.

If you sign this contract with Edward Dryden, you're going to lose your soul forever.

That was supposedly the gist of what his great-great-blah-blah-blah grandfather had told her. That was what Captain Silas Summerfield had allegedly come from the grave to say. That if Nathaniel went through with what would undoubtedly be the most financially rewarding deal of his career, he would be soulless.

Nathaniel didn't even know if he had an ancestor named Silas Summerfield. He knew little about his family, other than that his own father had died when he was too young to remember him, and his mother had struggled to provide for the two of them the whole time Nathaniel was growing up. He wasn't big on heredity and family trees, having never had much of a family to rely on. He knew there were other Summerfields out there—there must be, somewhere—but he'd never given any of them much thought. Present *or* past. And now suddenly, some strange woman—in more ways than one—intrudes into his life to mess it up because of some dream she had about a long-dead relative.

She was crazy, he told himself. One of those weird people who weren't content to go through life believing in things they had no business believing in to begin with, but who then had to foist off their bizarre beliefs onto others. They were people whose lives were so empty, and who needed attention so badly, that they had to harass other people to get it. True, Audrey Magill hadn't looked like that kind of person. She'd seemed normal enough. But sometimes it was the most normal-seeming ones who were actually the biggest nut jobs.

This contract with Edward was the start of great things. The sort of deal that only came along once in a man's career. So what if the land he was developing was originally targeted for quality, low-income housing that would have enabled struggling families—like, oh, say, Nathaniel's had been as a child—to live better lives? So what if, instead of safe homes for underprivileged kids, Edward was going to build overpriced lofts and boutiques for people who had more dollars than sense? That wasn't Nathaniel's problem. He wasn't the world's moral compass. He was just a guy trying to make a buck.

And this deal would make him a mountain of those.

"Having second thoughts, Nathaniel?"

He glanced up at the question to see Edward smiling at him, but there was something in the smile that wasn't quite genuine. As if the man honestly feared Nathaniel was about to change his mind. As if, should Nathaniel do just that, there might be consequences. Consequences beyond the financial ones outlined in the contract.

Nathaniel shook the feeling off. Edward Dryden just wasn't much of a smiler, that was all.

"Of course not," he said as he dragged the pen across the line, leaving his signature in its wake. He repeated the action two more times, on two more copies of the contract. Then he tossed the pen onto his desk and turned to shake Edward's hand.

"No going back now," the other man said with a laugh.

"No way I'd want to," Nathaniel assured him. "It's a done deal."

As those last words left his mouth, Nathaniel felt a strange twinge in his chest, right in the area of his heart. Nothing scary, nothing that made him think he needed to head to the nearest ER, just . . . weird. Something weird. He felt as if something in his chest, something surrounding his heart, just . . . evaporated. He couldn't think of any other way to describe it. As if a part of him just suddenly disappeared.

Unconsciously, he lifted a hand to his chest and pushed against his breastbone, where he'd felt the sensation, as if that might allay the uneasiness that was slowly creeping over him.

"You okay, Nathaniel?" Edward asked. "You look a little pale."

Nathaniel shook his head. "I'm fine," he assured the other man. "It's nothing. Probably just something I ate."

Because in spite of what Audrey Magill had tried to tell him, it couldn't be something he'd just lost.

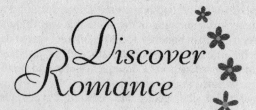